Oracle of the Thousand Hands

In My Parents' Bedroom

by Barry N. Malzberg

Stark House Press • Eureka California

ORACLE OF THE THOUSAND HANDS /
IN MY PARENTS' BEDROOM

Published by Stark House Press
1315 H Street
Eureka, CA 95501, USA
griffinskye3@sbcglobal.net
www.starkhousepress.com

ISBN-13: 978-1-951473-25-9

Book design by Mark Shepard, shepgraphics.com
Proofreading by Bill Kelly

First Stark House Press Edition: January 2021

ORACLE OF THE THOUSAND HANDS

The biography of D'Arcy's life isn't meant to be definitive, but D'Arcy's biographer is being as diligent in his efforts as he can. Scant attention will be paid to his childhood. D'Arcy's story will start with his formative years, detailing his discovery of The Magazine and the curious pleasures D'Arcy experiences within, setting him on his path of sexual discovery. The biographer promises that he will present "a shattering picture of our protagonist, revealing wonders and implications hitherto never before revealed." Unfortunately, the biographer himself is operating under a certain degree of restraint, confined as he is to an institute that he is not free to leave. Fortunately, he has the biography of D'Arcy to distract him.

IN MY PARENTS' BEDROOM

Michael and his companion are taking the Westfield Tour, a fascinating look into the lives of the Westfield family. Michael has a rather special insight into the family, for Michael is the youngest son of the Westfields, forbidden by the terms of the grant to set foot in the family home—but compelled to do so. He and his companion—girlfriend? he thinks so, though he can't quite remember her name—join a small group and their tour guide through the various rooms in the house. Each room prods at Michael's memories. While the group and the tour guide argue over the fine points of the Westfield's predications and proclivities, Michael journeys into his own past. And as each revelation brings Michael new insight, it also leads to the final mystery.

Oracle of the Thousand Hands

by Barry N. Malzberg

To my wife, Joyce

"I'm never sad; I'm always kind of glad, when
chickens come home to roost ..."

MALCOLM

ONE

D'ARCY'S GENITALIA: They were of unusual size; even in a state of purest flaccidity they measured several centimeters in the usual three directions. Under engorgement, the subject himself as well as several partners measured them as well over a foot in length. It is further attested that the unusual "slickness" and "warmth" of the organ made penetration unusually easy, even with "slightly built" companions.

D'ARCY'S SEXUAL PREDILECTIONS: They were, as we all know, completely heterosexual; any rumors to the contrary have been created by jealous and envious homosexuals whom D'Arcy again and again spurned to seek female companionship. He preferred normal intercourse in the seventh and eighth positions of Lilly, with certain pre-coital variations mostly involved with the buttocks and thighs of partners. Breast (buccal) tendencies were negligible, D'Arcy having been known to state often that he felt himself too well-endowed for "that preliminary nonsense."

D'ARCY'S SEXUAL PERFORMANCE: It was, as all sources have testified, facile and almost incredibly accomplished, leading partners again and again to the "sublime" peak and letting them down always at their own pace and without embarrassment. Ejaculation was plentiful, fluid was copious, sufficient to "open-up" partners so inclined. Pre- and post-coital maneuvers were swift, gracious and wholly respectful of companion and circumstances. It can be said, then, that the subject's sexual performance was excellent.

D'ARCY'S SOCIAL IMPORTANCE AS SEEN IN HISTORICAL PERSPECTIVE: It cannot be minimized. Dealing with the "quintessence of heterosexuality" (his phrase) raised to the 'nth degree of pleasure" (words of Mademoiselle M, a lady of his acquaintance), it came along just at the right time to reverse the slow trend of the Age toward narcissism, masturbation and latent homosexuality. D'Arcy's contribution, infusing as it did, all of his sexual "mainstream" with "new blood," was nothing less than the reversal of history, the setting aright of the microcosm he knew.

WHY THIS STUDY IS WRITTEN: I must admit that there are some questions about that to be squarely faced.

This study will deal with the "lover" D'Arcy from the inception of that self-imposed role in December of 196- to its tragic—and unpremeditated conclusion—in October of 196-. It will in no fashion attempt definitive biography nor does it presume to be more than a documentary of the public years of D'Arcy's existence. The early years, the growing years, the dwindling years, even the brief but poignant dying day ... little of this will be touched upon within the confines of these pages. The historian must delimit to better define the quintessence of his insight. So few of our contemporary "biographers" admit this simple fact. As we diffuse, so must we move ever further from that basic kernel of insight which may, for all we know, be the metaphor for the folly of life itself. Aha!

So delimited, this work will address itself to such primary questions as these: did the subject feel love? Did D'Arcy, in the last smoke and plumes of love's consummation, know emotional release beyond his gigantic physical bursts? Was he ever, during the public years, frustrated in his pursuit of sexual conjoinment? What did some of his partners think of him? What conclusions can be drawn? Exactly what was the breadth and length of a typical D'Arcy orgasm?

We will answer those questions all in due time. On hand we have documents and testimonies of many of the subject's partners, none of them ever before revealed, confidentially given to the one who transcribes this memoir. In tandem they will piece together, we promise, into a shattering picture of our protagonist, revealing wonders and implications hitherto never before revealed.

THE QUESTION OF QUALIFICATION: It is always asked of the historian: who are you? What is your particular credential? Why do you presume to give the sense of this material to a gullible and easily misled audience? This is a painful century; the question of credibility perhaps its nexus.

Let me state modestly, therefore, that I knew D'Arcy well; far better than any other during the public years and during many of those years I stood by his side. Friend, confidant, partner, assistant, I lived in the closest conjoinment with the subject. The public prints do not indicate this, of course.

The reason for that is that I always demanded anonymity. "Not for me notoriety or exploitation, D'Arcy," I said to my friend once while we were drinking wine together during one of his periods of "convalescence." "I would be less a friend and more an agent of the opposition were I to attempt to benefit in any way from the fortunate fact of our interrelationship. I prize your friendship above all others, I will not have myself known. But, in my quiet way, I will stand by you always."

And my dear, dear friend said to me, sipping his wine slowly, stirring the sediment with his finger in that characteristic gesture, "Truly, you are a friend. But I cannot ask this of you. If there is profit to be made from our friendship without discredit or interference to me, then take it, I say. Give an interview. Let your face be known. Tell them what I say about women, when I am in a kindly mood, of course. Advise them of my culinary idiosyncrasies. This will keep my name as always before them and you will derive a small income from your ramblings. I give you permission to do all of this as long as you understand from whom the permission comes and from what high motives; that is all I ask." And lifted his glass in the sun so that the purple glittered as stone, mixing toward the purest refraction of his driven, absent face.

And once again I said, raising my own glass, my blunt features dwindling to infinitesimal condition as the sun darted behind a cloud, "never, my friend; this will never be. As long as I have health and strength to continue on our mutual travels I will never lend you the betrayal of publicity."

Even so, it is with a heavy heart that I begin this journal. Well-qualified as I am, there are certainly others who would be equally so: having never, for instance, truly "known" the hot embrace of D'Arcy in bed nor felt the pressure of his massive, earnest thighs against mine, I am obviously less qualified than many to talk of some of the more explicit aspects of D'Arcy's performance. But who else—I say again, who else?—could possibly take up the wearisome pen, shuffle the papers and commence?

Most of those juxtaposed to D'Arcy in the way I mention can neither read nor write, some cannot spell, the majority cannot perform the simplest mathematical examples. Too, a large percentage of these people are missing, which is to say that they are beyond the efforts of local authorities and institutions to find them.

It is peculiar but it is so: a high percentage of D'Arcy's companions are so far on the margin of our society as to be beyond its devices. *Nothing*, an acquaintance of mine once said, *nothing is as unlocatable as a common tart; even in the bedroom it is often impossible to find one.* D'Arcy's career, then, like a rocket in full, booming flight, discharged a trail of gas and combustible matter which negated its origins to the exact degree that the major ascent opened up new territory. I have often found that this is a general rule; being, of course, a strong adherent of the great man theory of history.

Only I, then, an Ishmael of the post-coital ecstasy, remain to tell the tale. My whereabouts fixed firmly by due process of law and institutionalization, my literacy shaped by 18 years of tutors smuggled from the public schools, my credentials beyond dispute, my humility attested to by my years of close friendship with the subject, I would not think that a further apologia is necessary. Awash, then, in the sea of possibilities, tossed by the whale of retrospection, I cling to the flotsam and jetsam of total recall, trying to spare immersion to the thousands who wait cheerlessly on the sands.

Of course, I remain attuned to the possibility that I may be prohibited from the removal of these notes from my present confines. There is a rich precedent for this: so many of my companions and enemies within these gates are similarly "writers;" were all the tracts, correspondence, romanticized history and pseudo-legal writs composed daily in this place to be piled in one stack, it would probably reach to half the height of the senior attendant who demands that all our written material be placed in his hands for censorship and approval. Since this senior attendant, a bulky man with large ears, can neither read nor write, it is suspected by many of my companions here that their writings are being instantly tossed to perdition, most likely after "taps," when scufflings and rustlings and billowings in the hall might suggest the lively flush of toilets sending handwriting on its way. Nevertheless, I discount the possibility. The press visits me now and then and also some acquaintances; surely I could place my jottings in their hands were I to feel an imminence of capture. The important thing, as has been truly said, is to do one's work; a good conscience is its own best reward.

THE CIRCUMSTANCES UNDER WHICH THE STUDY IS BEING WRITTEN: Art and craft, being inextricably linked to environment, it would be fair, perhaps, to describe what it's like here. It is not the most felicitous of ambiances.

For one thing it is wretchedly cold in these rooms and for another, it is almost unspeakably foul much of the time. My collaborants in this large institution are, to an incalculable extent, unbearably dull—their efforts at the written word to the contrary—and entrapped by their small, circular obsessions. They are incapable, in short, of the mildest form of self-amusement, let alone the divertissement of one as complex and sophisticated as I. (It might be said, then, that I have taken to these notes out of boredom but this is not half the fact of the case; the act of writing can be as offensive as that of self-abuse and far less interesting.) The two young men, for instance, who share these rooms with me, seem to have reached an accord of many years' standing—they preceded me here by a long time—not to address one another unless under the governor of extrinsic need, and then in some kind of bizarre code which appears to be the least inventive amalgamation of French, English and the arcane mumblings of the retarded. I find this a great burden upon an active sensibility, but I am completely unable to alter this.

Not that I have not tried. There was a time when I hammered upon the dense barrier of their sullen alliance repeatedly: did it with small jokes, quips, reminiscences and even—for their sake—the admission that I was a companion of D'Arcy's throughout his notable career. I had thought that this final revelation would, when all else had failed, break us through to a small network of feeling or (at least) remonstrance but, shockingly, neither of them had ever *heard* of D'Arcy, much less possessing the slightest knowledge of his travels. It was when they made offensive comments to me about this acquaintanceship and my dear friend himself that I gave up on further attempts to establish a normal relationship in these rooms.

I exemplify: the other evening I was on the way to the "dayroom" here, prepared for yet another desultory game of chess with the bearded fossil who sits silently in front of the board all day, so immobile that it is necessary for his partners to contribute both sets of moves and announce imminent captures, when the elder of my roommates, a fierce man with wild eyes and blond hair so sheer that it might have blazed, said to the other, *Monsieur ici est entrappe.*

Non, non, chattered the other who was under the best of circumstances, rather elfin, *il est disappointe.*

Entrappe and disappointe together. Un jolie homme despite tout, however, est that non vraiment?

"Listen," I said, "there's no need to discuss a man to his face, it isn't polite and it shows a lack of intelligence in the bargain. I'll be wandering down the hall just a bit and you can say all you choose but for the moment call it off, yes?"

Est uproarious, said the first, taking a comb from somewhere around the perimeter of his waist and running it through his hair, squeezing the dandruff pods as they sifted downward. This never failed to excite the elf who stood, then, to the limit of his short frame and, running his own hands through a rather ferocious beard, gestured at me.

Felon, he said.

At that moment, my aged, bottled temper, stirred to the sediment, burbled forth. "Look, gentlemen," I said, "I do not need such talk from you. The same institutions which committed me here have placed you as well and for a much longer period, I might observe. I tell you frankly that unless this behavior stops, I will be compelled to seek new quarters and whoever succeeds me will be far less tolerant of your display of manners. Does that seem clear?"

They laughed at that.

"Now look," I said, "if I must start at the beginning, I will. I am a close friend, perhaps the closest, of the late, honored Justin D'Arcy and in that regard—"

I could not finish. I heard, interchangeably from them, an explosion of guttural monosyllables which sounded vaguely like curses. *Ha, ha!*, they added, *ha, ha!*

"Ha yourself," I said then, and for the first time told them my secret. I had to, to quiet them.

They stopped laughing. The elf seized an ashtray instead and made with it a complex, obscene gesture involving three parts of his anatomy. The gyrations were quite intricate. Then he ceased and both stared, apparently assessing my countermove.

"Makes no difference," I said, grandly, and with enormous dignity folding me like a shroud—that dignity I can conjure up under almost any circumstances—I quit the room and their presence.

THE PHILOSOPHICAL AND PSYCHOLOGICAL BIAS OF THE STUDY: There is no point in concealing this final notation: this study will be, inevitably, composed of a set of digressions from D'Arcy and deal on the personal level. My condition, of course, is so inseparable from his that our circumstances—until his unfortunate disappearance, that is to say—conjoined completely; our obsessions were so linked that it would be presumptuous to even assume that I could part from him. No, I am no cool, detached biographer although, to be sure, I am a faintly bewhiskered one. But D'Arcy's *ficelle*; I see that now, despite my own considerable, prolonged and irreversible detumescence.

But, by all means, let me proceed, wander into the sunset of recollection, the old, hollow features tilted wistfully to the horizon, the faithful old frame complying, possibly for the last time, to the Master's demands.

TWO

D'Arcy first connected with a female under a large, dishevelled tree in the province of R—, a delightful, slightly archaic area which lies in the circumference of the quaint city of Q—. It was only in the aftermath of the experience that his attitude toward masturbation underwent severe changes; all extant documents show that while in the actual act of conjoinment, D'Arcy was under the impression that his partner was teaching him a new way in which to flagellate himself, lending her body's assistance, and that her function—that is to say, her relation—was entirely neutral. Ah Youth, youth, youth! How swift its passing, how unmourned its memories, until the frame itself begins to disintegrate; by which time memory can be trusted least of all....

D'Arcy recollected his experiences to me in his comfortable rooms on an August evening a long time ago. This particular reminiscence came in the first blush, so to speak, of our acquaintanceship; at this time we had not known each other long, and it was with considerable shyness that D'Arcy broached to me the possibility of an oral sexual autobiography. When I assented to this with vigorous nods, heavy twitching of my beard and a certain clouting gesture of my eyes which indicates the most forceful compliance, he leaned toward me, balancing his wine glass between his thumbs and said:

"Well, then, I must tell you of the first time I ever had sex with a female; this was at the age of 17 many years ago in a delightful local province and do you know that it took me several weeks to realize exactly what had happened to me that goldish afternoon in the orchard?"

"You are implying to me, are you, that you did not even realize at the time that you were having sex?" I responded, gripping my own glass and leaning forward with my jaws clamped firmly shut, an attitude which has always imparted great masculinity to my appearance. I was anxious, then, to gain D'Arcy's good opinion and, although almost frantic with eagerness to hear what he would reveal, I did not betray myself with a flicker of anticipation; our friendship already well-launched by a profound mutuality of outlook and insight—but not of experience; an emotional *castrato*, I had never had carnal knowledge of either sex and had confessed this at the outset of our relationship to save future embarrassments—

worked sheerly in terms of its masculine restraint and decorum, and would not have been well served by tempestuousness. "Well," I added, "this is most entirely interesting, you must tell me about that, in full."

"I am 35 years old," D'Arcy said, "and have, perhaps, experienced the ravages of orgasm in one fashion or the other some 20,000 times or more; these explosions, for all their momentary exhilaration, moving retrospectively to the dull level of gloom always verified by the aftersex, but this, I must admit, was something unusual. Would you like to hear it, my friend? I seem to be constituted for rhetoric this afternoon."

"Oh, yes!" I cried, "I surely would." Then more circumspectly (even cunningly) I added, "Of course, it isn't that important, you know. Only talk about it if you want to."

"I do want to talk about it, I believe. I am weary, weary; I am 35 years old. Yes, I believe I have told you that, no?" he said with a delightful toss of his well-rounded head, "And having moved well past the half-life of carnality and finding so little to show for the experience, I have been longing, with increasing poignancy, for someone with whom I can really talk; an auditor—if you will—who will share my recollections with me and by his quiet assimilation of those memories, help me to achieve a final kind of sense. For I am truly past accomplishment now; you understand that, don't you? There is very little left within the realm of sexual knowledge or activity which is worth doing."

I had found his rhetoric rather tortuous and I told him so. I added that what he was saying was, for me, however, a thrust of the first magnitude and that I could only seek to honor it. "I too have been looking for someone I can trust," I said quietly. "Someone for whom I could be, so to speak, a witness, a friend, a kind of auditor."

"Then you wish to hear the story of my first entrance at the age of 17 in an orchard full of apples and diverse fruits and the sounds which were made under me as slowly I felt myself drawn past the folds of earth's tent into the carnival itself?"

"Exactly," I said.

"Permit me," said D'Arcy.

I was (D'Arcy said, then) a normal product of adolescence in the country of my origins. My awareness of sex, nil until the age of 12, exploded at pubescence much like a complex mold kept in dark places under the right conditions will evince no life at all for a long time and will suddenly teem with it: wild, aimless, disoriented. Such was I. One evening I was a schoolboy immersed in a schoolboy's concerns and obsessions, cajoled by the media, cajoled by my own restlessness; but in the morning—alas!—I was something else entirely. It was as if an unearthly secret which had been kept from me all of my life was suddenly sprung without preparation of any sort. I was not ready for it.

Let me explain. The *emissio nocturnis*, relegated to the status of a footnote in most journals of sexual behavior, discarded by even the fatal Kinsey as the least prevalent and significant of all initiations into sex, was the trigger which launched me past apprehension into the ecstasy and danger of the pit itself. In my sleep that night I dreamed that there was pressure; an even, slow, sinuous pressure up and down my body as, fishlike, I poked at sonorous depths; as fishlike, I ducked small obstacles to find a kind of homing. Happy little ontologist recapitulating all phylogeny I swam and swam in the bowl of self, feeling the fluid pour into my open gills with increasing facility, feeling my gills beating back at the waters, feeling the rising all within and without and then, with a series of dull, tearing explosions, my fishlike form had surrendered its integrity, scales and substance, and had imploded in several small, rapid jerks over the bottom of the aquaria, disintegrating as it did so, becoming fragments of purple, iris and aquamarine which went at cross-purposes, finally drifting to the ceiling of the aquaria and for all I know, into the piscatorian equivalent of Gehenna. This remained spread out through the water in wavelets which ever lightened and finally blurred into the background of indistinguishability. I awoke out of this to find that it was full dawn, that my undergarments clung to me with uncustomary enthusiasm, and that my limbs were possessed of a fainting weakness which could only be equated with energy.

I do not mind saying that the day that passed held little interest for me. All that mattered—and how easily I admitted it, even at the beginning!—was to get back to the bed, hopefully as early as possible, and give the horror a chance to repeat itself. It was exactly as if something which had happened completely on its own terms had reduced me to the status of audience; never before and since have I confronted my body: my pale, familiar body, with the admixture of woe and poignancy with which I examined it that evening. Everything seemed the same but was ineffably changed. With several encouraging pats administered to myself hither and yon, I placed myself between the sheets and willed myself to sleep.

It would be pleasant to say that the experience not only repeated itself that night, but awakened me as it did so, allowing me to make certain necessary connections between sensation and phenomenon, and inciting me to take matters further into my own hands ... But such was not to be; it was almost three full weeks until the sensations repeated themselves, and then I was not a fish but a bird: a gigantic eagle, to be precise, suspended at a condor's height above a distant city, and as I leaned down toward it, my claws seemed to fold in upon one another and the already familiar wrenching, the tearing, began at the very center of my feathers, spreading outward until my beak itself seemed to be caught in the rapid convulsion and then I, a male giant eagle, found himself laying eggs one by one in the air, centered in flight, calmly swooping as the circles of life came pouring from that center of congestion, uttering mingled cries of woe and delight as my spawn fell heedless on the reaches of the continent below. The question of fertilization never occurred to me. I imagine that they must have made a pretty smash in the cities; but my recollection, instead, was of their landing in some haystack in the countryside, a haystack patrolled by louts and hired hands who would look at these droppings from the sky in gentle amazement and then, fingering their ears, step forward to examine them more closely.

As you can see, my earliest intimations of sexuality were tied into a rather natural or rural imagery; happy enough, no doubt, and doubtless recapitulatory of that fashion in which our ancestors themselves had enacted their troubles and joys but I regret to say that not then, and not for a good quantity of time, did I link my dreams with that peculiar source nor did I, in any way, link the source with the idea of mingling with members of the opposite sex. I have read studies and texts, sooner and later, which include the case histories of farm boys and urban inhabitants alike, male and female, who come to sex as merely the most exquisite of all the refined sensations available to them but who, until further notice, seemed unable to accept the orgasm as anything more than an independent phenomenon visited upon the flesh by sheets, tree bark or vigorously wandering hands, having absolutely nothing to do with population, or some of the more flamboyant romantic abstractions of our time. Indeed, and much later, I met a seventeen-year-old beauty, well-cleaved from head to toe, with a ripeness of her core of such viscosity as to surpass even my most aimless fantasies, who seemed utterly unable to understand—until with fingers and the lower cunning I brought it to her attention—that those sensations she had been inducing in herself for half a decade had anything whatsoever to do with what she had, presumably, been reading about or seeing in the television for at least that much time. My own case, then, without interference, might have proceeded very much in that direction; the occasional covert spasms in my thighs under cover of quasi-delirium merely a welcome relief from the schoolboy tensions of existence; it might have gone on and on that way until, at the age of 25 or 36, say, a chance nightly spasm undergone while coincidentally juxtaposed to a female (just a house guest or someone I had taken to my bed to comfort), would have brought knowledge to me with an explosion of embarrassment so wrenching in its dire implications as to abate the emotional losses of all these years; it might have happened in exactly this fashion or in some other more dreadful (perhaps I would have taken a male friend to my rooms for some respite with the same results), but I was saved from all of this. I want to say that I was saved. I came across The Magazine.

Now, The Magazine that I found (actually, it was no chance encounter, I came upon it most deliberately and paid for it with my schoolboy's lunch money) was no stranger to me; its cover with its pale backgrounds and restlessly juxtaposed foregrounds was at least as familiar to most of my contemporaries and myself during those years as other elements of the Shared Unconsciousness; I have yet to meet a male over the age of 12 and under that of 45 in this country who is not as familiar with The Magazine as he is attuned to his own muddled interior, somewhere at that shared level of recollection where dreams, loss, scatology and hope all mingle to produce what we call our "memory of youth." The Magazine is embedded as firmly as first loss, first desire, first rage and defeat. While the circumstances of my juxtaposition with it were unusual, in short, its effect upon me and its presence were not.

The Magazine at issue—that is to say, the issue of The Magazine which launched me upon a different and better career far removed from the night-animals—was held loosely between the thumb and index finger of a small, almost miniscule man whose rump adjoined my own in the subway on that April morning when, late as always, I had piled my schoolbooks against my pubis and run wildly for the last express. Finding a seat as usual, I opened a physics primer to an innocuous page and began to confront myself with images of ball bearings, balanced weights and the extrapolations of energy in the universe, when from somewhere in the vicinity of my left eye, a picture of a naked female came slowly into view, passing over my scientific ruminations much as the eagles and denizens of the deep had infiltrated the quiet tenor of my dreams.

The female I saw was bare from nipple to nipple, with a series of garments which had apparently covered them originally now located somewhere in the vicinity of her waist, much as if they had been urgently torn by someone in search of two stray aureolae without the patience to be reasonable. As the page swam further into my view I became aware of the fact that this female was as fully clothed below the waist as she was unclothed above; she wore heavy leather boots which came to the center of the shiny black trousers, and a small whip—or perhaps it was merely a riding-crop—jutted from her left pocket.

I was astounded. I admit that freely. This was not the first picture of a naked woman I had ever seen nor the tenth for that matter, but a certain quality of juxtaposition—having to do with the proximity of the picture, its relations to the physics textbook, and the relation of that textbook to my genitals, leaning on them with some weight—produced a set of responses as mysterious as they were urgent.

What I did was begin to rub my textbook gently over the area of my genitals, the better, no doubt, to concentrate upon its essentials because I bent upon it a gaze of such fixated intensity that one would have thought that I was trying to apprehend the root nature, so to speak, of the study, all this time my left eye sliding gracelessly up and down the contours of the photograph while my elbows flopped and banged and the neighbor to my left—the possessor of that magazine—seemingly oblivious, flipped a page or two with the near thumb and then turned one over, concealing the picture from my view. I found this removal infuriating, almost a cheat and made frantic efforts at retrieval, giving anxious glances, that is to say, out of the corner of a clouded eye while I switched my books to even greater proximity on my lap and then, finally, closing my eyes entirely, began to work into a highly internalized state of visualization, picturing before me what I was able to remember of the departed picture while I breathed deeply of the odors of my own sweat. A rustle of pages on my left, becoming progressively insistent, forced me to open my eyes again and as I did so I found myself confronting the picture once again, my neighbor virtually proffering it toward me with shaking hands while his own gaze seemed turned somewhere distantly toward a window. He was doing me a favor but he was not going to make an exhibition of it. This sense of participation—kinship, really, and the slow apprehension of need—so touched me in the area of the groin that I found myself beginning to enter upon the first twitches and gloom of the sensations I had had during my night-journeys and then, with a gasp, I found myself plummeted toward the first and truest, the most valuable and meaningful, orgasm of my life.

"It must have been most intense," I remarked to D'Arcy at this point in the recollection. "What with all the frustration and tension you'd built up and then not even knowing what was happening to you. It must have been a truly shattering experience."

It was not an intensity in the groin (he told me, lighting up another cigarette and leaning back in his chair, his toes pointed skyward, his hands dropped across the famous lap itself now quiescent, unstirred by memory) so much as one of the sensibility; I found myself being actually *wrenched*, eyeballs first, toward the source of my pleasure which I interpreted oddly enough as the picture rather than the conjoinment I had prepared on my lap and as, half-turning to confront it wholly, a small groan purred from my lips against the screech of the brakes, I realized that the train had jolted into a subway stop and that, laws of physics asserting themselves in and out of the textbook, intense inertia had catapulted me half out of my seat. The momentum, in fact, had placed me in almost instant juxtaposition with a large clump of passengers of both sexes who now eyed me incuriously, as with a series of slow, spasmodic gyrations I tried frantically to work my way to the door —for I could not afford to be late for class—at the same time desperately trying to maintain that fragile contact between textbook and genitalia which had already made my morning so spirited. As I did so—as I reached, that is to say, the door itself—I felt a wrenching and tumbling coming to force in the area of my groin and then, as I stood stricken before the slowly closing doors themselves, I entered upon the first true orgasm of my life, a feeling of spinning and convulsions, still trying through all of this to arc myself onto the platform and then, as the doors closed, the train started with a hiss and there I was, physics text still against my genitalia, squeezing out the last drops of moisture, while one passenger told me that I "ought to make up my mind what to do before giving everybody fits."

I realized almost immediately what had happened to me. This knowledge was, to no small degree, abetted by my seatmate who rose and came to stand against me as the train continued its rocketing passage. The magazine, now jauntily seen to be emerging from a jacket-pocket, was still folded to the picture which had precipitated my fall from grace and as I stood now, quite drained, almost at ease, and wanting nothing but to be by myself and think about what had happened to me, he favored me with a small, slow wink and whispered into my ear:

"It's better not to do it on trains; you can't concentrate too good. If you don't want to do it at home do it in the movies, that's my advice."

Fortunately, this rather horrid confidence was for my ear alone and did not transmit itself to other passengers. I was still trying to think of an appropriate reply—one which would show him that I had taken offense without in any way conceding the truth of his evaluation of what had happened—. When the train once again came to a stop and its unrolled doors permitted me to stagger onto the platform and into a small enclosure behind a gum-dispensing machine where I was able to stand limply until the station cleared. My partner in knowledge, now cheerfully slapping the unrolled magazine against his palm, was one of the passengers who exited as well but he had nothing further to say to me nor I to him—what, after all, could I have replied?—and after a while, in the almost-empty station, I arranged my books and other holdings into a fairly respectable package and went to the street. My groin felt limp, uncoiled; a new collaborant now with a certain chuckling knowledge, it seemed to be whispering: *I'm through for the moment, but I'll be coming back. We'll be seeing a lot of each other now; you take good care of me and I'll take the best care of you.* Feeling like someone who had tried, almost successfully, to assassinate himself, I went into the street and on an extremely thoughtful journey to class. I still thought that it might have been some kind of an accident.

That afternoon, through careful trial and error, I was able to locate and purchase a copy of the magazine which had made my morning so lively. What I wish to point out is that this was the first copy of the magazine I had actually bought; although it had been passed around from hand to hand in school and although I had often looked at it covetously on newsstands, the actual act of purchase was one which had seemed far beyond me: the magazine seemed as inaccessible for private use as the other side of the moon. But since the question of use had never been previously defined—since I had not realized until that morning that the magazine had a function as precise and self-limiting as any other piece of schoolboy goods—it had been abstract; now it was a reality. I bought one copy of the magazine and one copy of a rival, either for purposes of comparison, or more extended study; I was not sure.

It would be easy to say that I proceeded from these purchases (they were made in a store some 18 blocks from the school and at least twice that distance from home and the proprietor, horrifyingly, had tried to strike up a relationship with me based upon the venality of his magazine distributor who, he said, insisted that he sell so many copies of these magazines per month or lose his business) immediately to my rooms and to an orgy of masturbation but this would overestimate my intelligence and its ability to make sense of what had happened to me that morning. Actually, I was not sure that the magazines would "work," nor was I even sure that I wished to repeat the experience of the morning. All that I was doing at that time was recapitulating my history, an important gesture toward self-understanding. What I did was to put the magazine carefully away in my briefcase and I did not go into them until much later that evening, long after I had completed my studies, finished my necessary activities in the bathroom—with a plentiful washing of the hands—and wedged a chair under the knob of my door so that, for all intents and purposes, I felt impenetrable. Then, with hands that shook, perhaps, a bit more than I would have expected, I withdrew the magazines and, placing the rival under my bed, took The Magazine itself, opened it to the picture which I had glimpsed that morning, and looked for my physics textbook.

Finding it—I had placed it under a pile of other texts and was almost frantic with relief when it finally emerged—I pressed it to my lap in a repetition of the morning's position and then repeated the gestures and gyrations I had made, at the same time casting my eyes leftward toward the magazine which I had propped next to me on the bed at eye-height, on a music stand.

For a long time, nothing happened. My groin remained static, the wild elf who had tenanted it this morning seemingly out on probation or perhaps asleep. I tried to imagine screeching and huddling to further recapitulate the morning's sensations, even toyed with my visions of night-metamorphoses, but since I was confusing results with causation, I was on the verge of total failure. At last, however, I hit upon the key. I cannot sufficiently impress upon you the importance of this insight. I began to imagine to myself that I was being discovered.

I conjured images of parents and relatives, grown to enormous size, bursting into the bedroom to confront me poised at the moment of entrance into the rolled-up magazine: conceived to myself the possibility of a gigantic renunciation scene parting me forever from my history as, helpless to detach myself from my aching organ, my strokes formed rhythmic counterpoint to monomaniacal insistences; I imagined this and much more, images of the sea and flying creatures somewhere toward the rear of my skull, and as I put all of this together—as all of it began to coalesce my aching, frenzied skull, the rapidly beating butterfly of a hand which was only an extension of my skull, I felt it truly beginning to work.

How can I describe to you what happened to me then? Men have, for centuries, annotated the raptures of first love, first entrance, first connection, but I think that all of them are liars, what they are really talking about is first masturbation upon which they have superimposed the heterosexual or homosexual connections for politeness' sake, but what they are really recollecting are the earliest, almost archetypal memories of orgasm which begin in the winging joint, the open, gasping, sobbing mouth. *There is nothing in this world but masturbation, everything comes out of it; that is all I have to tell you.* The rest is fakery, trumped up around the core. I was trying to say that I felt myself storming from the very center of my being.

No sea-creature now, no bird either, no animal of play or relative ontologist but only a desperate adolescent concentrating on first fruition, I frantically manipulated myself the more, the magazine now ignored other than to perform its secondary function of becoming a rolled-up tube near the offending organ. Strange groans and cries came from my throat: they were replies to the accuser that stood just beyond my door, the huge, overbearing accuser that could, at any moment, burst through and catch me in that microcosm of destiny: I raved and screamed, fomented and justified, moving closer and closer all the time and then finally, past ecstasy, past movement, past even necessity's quiver I felt the rotten fruit of me being split open, lush with corruption and I came forth.

I came forth.

I came, squealing into the bedjoints, whimpering a whimper somewhere between pain and joy, as suspended between those absolutes as my dangling, pulsing prick was suspended by text on the one side and a distended, distorted aspect of female flesh on the other, came until I thought indeed that I had been experimenting not with the prick but with the aorta or some ominous, lurking cells of the intestine, came until my release had edged down into a kind of panic and finally I stopped and it was all out of me, all the fluid that is to say, none of the memory and there was no one standing beside the door and there was no one examining me in the room, and there were no oceans or aviaries beside my bed but only my tired, dying genitals clamped stickily in dripping newsprint and with a sigh, I withdrew myself—that is to say, more properly, that I withdrew the enclosure from *them*—and collapsed panting on the bed. I had not had a single thought of a woman.

I lay there for a long time. Tinkling at the edge of my consciousness, almost a bell or summons, was an intimation: an intimation or insight so enormous that my juvenescent mind could not possibly have grasped it, did not see it for many years: all that it could do in its wandering was to make a metaphor and the metaphor became a feeling and that feeling was of irreplacable woe under which lay a layer of whimsy—for it had been so ridiculous what had happened to me—and underneath all of that a feeling of being cheated so profound that my young, healthy, inexhaustible limbs began to quiver froglike in the silence and stayed so for a long, long time.

"So that," I said, "was your first direct sexual experience, the first one which was self-induced. How well you tell it! What rhetoric, what insight, what imagery! D'Arcy, my dear and becoming-dearer friend, you should have become a writer."

"I doubt it very much," he said, removing a sock and examining, with a rather crestfallen expression, a severely indented toe (we were in his rooms at that time, sipping our inevitable port and now fully relaxed, in a highly unbuttoned state, the end of the evening have coalesced with the beginning of dawn, leaving us in a unique and rather wistful state of suspension), "I have no ability for structure, no long-range novelist's gift for molding, I can see only in fits and starts rather than through to the end of a highly transmuted vision."

"But we are not talking about novels," I reminded him. "Autobiography or the personal essay would suit just as well. Or you could write a series of reminiscences. There is no need for fictionalization."

"Yes there is," he said, shaking his head sadly. "It could only survive as fiction. One must lie, you see, to tell a certain kind of truth. But the novel will never be written."

"Well, then!" I said in a burst of enthusiasm, "let me be your scribe. *I* will write the story, the fiction-that-is-more-than-fact. All you will have to do is relate to me, as you are now, all of your experiences, and I will order them and put them in print."

An expression of ineffable sadness crossed that dear, crushed face. "No," he said, "that could not possibly work. I have not the patience to relate to you all my experiences nor you the temper to absorb them; then too there is more to writing than simple chronology as you would find out if you applied yourself. Everything becomes turned inside-out, convoluted and involuted like life itself; old wrenches, old dreams, doomed perceptions, flashes of possibility, coming together in such a way as to negate the possibility of a present. I tell you, I have thought all this over and it is true."

"No, no!" I cried, clutching his wrist, not to disagree with him in emphasis so much as to comfort him, try to bring him back from that mood of tragic withdrawal which characterized so many of our conversations, so much of our relationship as it passed into the darkness. "Life is real and earnest and proceeds carefully in its honest, plodding way toward a just and total destiny. To know what happened before and after is to apprehend the fullest sense of it. I really can't bear to see you in such a mood."

D'Arcy shakily passed a hand across his forehead and then cupped his eyes with it; the eyes disappearing one by one as if two soft, distant lights had winked out and then, fishlike, they emerged one by one and stared at me again. "You are a good friend," he said, "although, alas, a blockhead. But that is possibly for the best; I could not, at this difficult and final stage of my ascension, stand to deal with anyone who was not imperceptive. Shall I continue my narrative?"

"Of course," I said, pouring us two more glasses of wine and passing one on to him. "I want to hear everything you have to say. I think that what you are saying is truly important."

"Do you really? Do you really, my friend? I feel so old, so tired, so wretched and useless. Is anything I say important?"

"Very much so," I said, "more than you could possibly grasp, being as sensitive as you are. I don't know how the world could pass on without knowing more and that is why I want to hear."

"I began by discussing my first sexual contact with a girl, did I not?" D'Arcy asked, balancing the wine glass prettily on his knee (a characteristic trick, accomplished with much subtlety but without that excessive grace which would have created embarrassment), "and then, somehow, I wandered off into this question of masturbation. I wonder how it could have happened."

I passed on, then (he said after a moment's pause during which he rapidly finished his wine) into a period of my life which was so circumscribed by masturbation as, perhaps, to preclude questions of logic. Having settled for the first time on that historic afternoon my ability to induce the sensations and culminations within myself, I think that I must have arrived at a qualified definition of manhood: that is, my goals were within the realization of my methods. Little concerned me but the act itself and all of life—non-masturbatory life, I mean to say—that stretched out dismally both fore and aft was merely a means of passing time, meaningless events to be worked through before it could all begin again. It was biologically impossible for me to induce orgasm more than three to four times a day and, in addition, there were any number of routine tasks which had to be performed to keep up the appearances of life during which masturbation would have obviously been impossible or highly embarrassing.

There was schoolwork to attend to and relationships to build upon; there were parental admonitions (they called it "being close") to satisfy and there were the needs of my own self, those of replenishment. Nevertheless, I was able to work things down to a schedule and it was a schedule, I must admit, which I adhered to for better part of two years. It involved spending as much time as possible in my own bed or in locked cubicles in public places. It circumscribed everything.

I masturbated in sheets, in toilet paper, in the rolled-up wads of magazines; I did it with my own trembling fingers. I scurried from one useless, meaningless task to the next, counting out the pulses of my body and urging restocking. I found small sophistries, both physical and mental, which could affect the sensations qualitatively although never quantitatively; that is, I could relate in different ways to the moment of ecstasy, being either under or over it, as I chose. I became, in short, a sophisticate. A few examples will, I trust, suffice: there is no way in which I can sufficiently overstate the apocalyptic dreariness of this period of time nor, in certain fashion, its total irrelevance: I will thus be forgiven, I trust, for a certain compression of the narrative; as I have already said, I severely dispute chronology in relation to life, and although there is a need, perhaps, to adhere to its detail, there is no reason to be overwhelmed by it. The only true chronology is the inner clock which twitches back and forth, all directions in one, guiding us toward the true and naked perceptions of our destiny. I do not mean to wander.

Some examples:

1) I was able, in the public toilet at a large railroad terminal, to wedge my briefcase solidly against the otherwise resistant door and, by careful attention to the luck of process, bring upon myself within 30 seconds a peculiarly intense climax redolent of ancient odors and connections, vaulting me into some cell of gloom, some hitherto undiscovered part of myself which, torn free by the exercise of joints, sobbed and bucked its juices away as I sat in silent wonder and let the odor: foul, fecal, faintly perfumed, smoke and loss, drain over and through me, secure in the after-knowledge that I had found the most important because the least known part of myself. Until the porter opened the door to find me still confronting my prick and balls in that frieze of woe, eyes turned loosely, slackly up, the hint of stain still dribbling from the center. He looked at me for a very long time while I reached futilely for my briefcase, trying to drag it atop my lap, but found in the afterglow that my strength was gone so that I could do nothing, nothing at all but try feebly to close the door which he pushed against my hand with his strong knuckles. He was carrying a heavy mop.

"Hey," he said, "what in the hell are you doing? This is a public place, man."

"I'm doing some reading," I said, I was at a thorough loss.

"Doesn't look to me like you're reading, son. It looks to me like there's been some very active joint-work in these premises."

"No," I said in confusion, not even sure what the term he had used meant other than that it was more than faintly obscene. "Nothing like that at all. I promise."

"Personally," he said—he was a squat, broad man with an aimless smile and small darting eyes, the very picture of accusation and discovery which I had conjured up so very long ago—"I don't care what you're doing here. This is a civil service post. But it makes very bad for the other customers. You'd better pull your pants up. What magazine is that you've been using?"

"It's a textbook," I said wildly, "my physics textbook. I was just studying it and you have no right to come in on me like this. I could get you in trouble."

His smile gleamed most purple against the dark bulbs on the ceiling. "A physics textbook," he said with high amusement, "well, I've seen 'em do this and I've seen 'em do that but a *physics textbook*— That's a mighty queer kick you got there, it could damage you in your later life." And he began to laugh without concealment then, the sound of his high squeals bringing aimless rustles up and down the row of cubicles, a feeling of weary observation emerging toward me from all angles of the room.

I was frantic, of course. You must understand that this was not only—preposterous luck!—my first adventure in discovery but that it was also my first excursion into terminology; I had had no idea until then what the outside world actually thought of what I was doing to myself. I had seen it as a rite, a private, mystic ritual of purification, utterly self-absorbed if not self-discovered, and now it was coming upon me, most rapidly, that in the eyes of that world all of it was sheer scatology and laughable to boot; not at all spiritual but a belch from the devil. How could this be? How could anything which did this to me be at the level of laughter? But so it appeared to be. I pulled my pants around me in an explosion of energy.

Meanwhile, the attendant was already closing the door. "That's all right," he whispered amidst his giggles, "you go right ahead and do whatever you want to do; ain't gonna be nobody here to bother you. I'm just sorry you ain't got a home to do it in; the least that a man should have is a private place." I heard a dull banging, a clanging of the mop's metal against the surface. Then he had gone away.

I was shattered. But in the midst of all this there was that high, tight, refined series of perceptions which always seems to have assaulted me at periods of crisis; which has been my salvation again and again. It was a feeling of disconnection, of utter severance of causes and outcome, much like the sensations of orgasm themselves, but different because there was no passion in it. As I felt this feeling come over me I knew exactly what I had to do: I adjusted my clothing neatly and removed the contents of the bowl by flushing; I picked up the scattered tissues from the floor and restored my text to briefcase; only then, and with a glance in the mirror to make sure my tie was adjusted and my fingernails clean, did I move slowly, even grandly, from that wretched terminal, stopping by the door to drop in the palm of the attendant's hand all the change which was in my possession. It came out to be thirty-three cents in silver and copper and the sound of his wheezing, groaning inhalation as he seized them from me, the utter obverse and cancellation of his laughter, was enough to fill me with a wild exaltation as I moved from him, through the swinging doors, and into the larger spaces of the terminal itself, my briefcase banging wildly against my calves, my breath harsh in my throat as I fled from what, in retrospect, was my first connection with the possibility of options.

2) An old family friend, Bernice, had a daughter approximately my age and during Bernice's occasional visits—she drove through three states to visit my family; there was apparently some kind of relationship underlying this persistence which was not to be divulged to a person as junior as myself—it was left to me to entertain this daughter, a dull, round girl named Rona who liked nothing at all that I was doing. The visits lasted all afternoon and far into the evening, encompassing drinks at both ends and a minuscule dinner in between, and since my family and Bernice would only concede to me that they were discussing "old times," Rona and I were in a state of exile during all of this; funds were provided me early in the day to take her "to the movies" or the like. All of these difficulties, of course, might have been avoided if Rona had had a male parent, someone sturdy and dependable whose idea of "old times" was not a fundamental excision of all who, perhaps, represented "new times," but there was something sinister about Rona's parentage; my parents would only tell me that her father had "left a long time ago" and when pressed further had said that it was possible he had never come in the first place. What I am trying to say is that Bernice was unmarried fore and aft and Rona very possibly a bastard; this would have been a difficult intuition, arrived at only in retrospect through the most careful and insidious kind of reflection, were it not for the fact that this dear girl made absolutely no secret of her ancestry, invited speculation, as a matter of fact, by saying that to the best of her knowledge her father had been a wandering gigolo whom her enlarged mother had enticed into her desserts through careful planning and the offering of a premium rate. This fact, announced almost at the time of our first meeting at the beginning of our mutual adolescence—Bernice and daughter had lived on the "coast" for the decade before that so the renewal of acquaintanceship was thus delayed—was reiterated three times yearly at our reunions and more richly embroidered every time; Rona's bastardy was, perhaps, the key to her identity.

One would have hoped so … assuming, of course, that the possession of identity is the most crucial need of the mid-century adolescent … for outside this, Rona was of little interest; she was overweight, overbearing and afflicted by that sullenness which, perhaps, can only be found in adolescent girls who are a good deal less attractive than they feel they should be and who know the reason why. We never got along particularly well together, but our self- and reciprocal loathing was of such proportions that we did not find it necessary to "go to the movies" together during these visits, finding enough interest in trading our points of view and experiences which always seemed to be antithetical. I hasten to note that there was at no time even the intimation of sexual attraction between us: in the first place, I was then and for some time to come in a literally pre-sexual stage, and in the second place, the only men Rona said she would "let touch" her were certain movie and political personalities who were at least as alien to me as my magazines would have been to her. It was my mention of the magazines, as a matter of fact, which precipitated all of the trouble between us.

We were, at that time, sitting on the convertible couch in my bedroom which nightly and in the early mornings still remained the battlefield of horror; sitting at a median distance from one another while from below came the exhausted drone of voices which, although already at the lowest levels, would not fully run down for several more hours. We had passed through the most minute stages of boredom: had plumbed each other's feeble mutual recollections and experiences, had engaged in mild antagonisms for the sake of repudiation and were now at the point where, literally, we had nothing to say or even to mumble to one another. Yet the evening dragged on: we were forbidden to enter the living room while the "visit" was in progress and although the movies were a possibility, the sheer terror, for me, of walking through the streets with Rona held me back from even that proposal. I had the idea that everybody who passed would think she was my "date," and although I had little knowledge of precisely what "dates" were for, I knew that I did not want it thought that I was seeking it, whatever it was, from Rona. So we sat, in a numbness so deep as to be beneath the reaches of the spirit itself and looked at the walls; the worst visit yet, the worst in history, and finally, out of desperation—for my hatred of this girl was so palpable that I could imagine myself doing something violent to her—I wondered if she might be interested in looking over some of my literature. Just so that she could see the kind of things they were publishing these days; I had no idea if girls were ever interested in this kind of thing but felt they should be because, after all, they were half, if the less interesting part, of the human race. All right, it was an insane impulse. I do not deny this. The normal adolescent hides his materials, snuggles them to the core of his person, would equate discovery with obliteration. But I was not a normal adolescent, you see. These materials had only the most peripheral relation to my activities; I considered them a fillip; a freak, fortuitous addition which related to the actual sensations induced only through idiosyncrasy. It was inconceivable that, for many, the magazines could be the prime means when for me they were only a kind of satellite.

Her dull eyes twitched somewhat, at any rate. "Magazines?" she said. "What kind of magazines?" "Oh, you find them on newsstands all over the place if you only look for them," I said. "It all depends; like I said, if you didn't look for them you wouldn't even know they exist." I reached into the space between mattress and frame bed and, with some difficulty, brought out two of them, stiff and luminescent. "Like these," I said, and passed them over to her.

She took them and placed them carefully on the portion of rumpled skirt which composed her lap, began to go through them slowly, wetting her finger as she turned each page, pausing at certain pictures which had, indeed, won my own approval. These were not The Magazine but some of its inferior competitors and the poorer quality of photographic and page stock made it difficult, from my angle of vision, to see exactly at what she was looking, but most of them absorbed her for quite a time. Her face flushed dimly, her shoulders twitched and finally she turned the last page over and looked up at me. She regarded me as if she had never seen me before; I could see the recognition staggering at the corners of her eyes and finally moving into the center. She put the magazines to one side.

"Do you have any more?" she said.

Yes, I had more. I took out another sampling—it was necessary for me to urge both of us off the bed in order to get the next batch from that interior—and gave them to her diffidently, observing, without interest, that the magazines seemed to have brought out more response from her than I had seen in some half a decade of desultory visits. Of course this was of no interest to me whatsoever—the idea of response of any sort being too dreadful for even the aberrant adolescent mind to contemplate in relation to a girl like this—but I did feel the dim satisfaction of knowing that, for Rona at least, this would not be the least memorable of her visits. And it passed the time.

"Must you stay here?" she said in a high whine, raising her head and staring at me. "Couldn't you go to the bathroom or go out for a walk or something?"

"I can't go out for a walk. We're supposed to be together, you remember? I'm supposed to entertain you."

"So go to the bathroom, then. You're entertaining me enough."

"I don't want to go to the bathroom."

She took one of the magazines she had finished and handed it to me with a thrusting gesture, rolled it into my open palm. "Here," she said. "That should make the difference. Now do you want to go to the bathroom?"

"No," I said in mystification, "I don't."

"You mean you're all cleaned out already?"

"What?" I asked. "What's that? I don't understand what you're talking about."

She stood with a vaulting, almost prideful gesture and placed two of the magazines in the coil of her armpit. "Well, if you don't understand," she said, "I guess that I'll just have to go to the bathroom myself. I haven't been there for a long time and I'll not be out for a while."

She was not out for a while. She remained in the bathroom for the better part of an hour while I gloomily inspected my fingernails, read through some of the text of the magazines—the photographs had no appeal for me other than at times of self-abuse, and since I had flagellated myself twice that morning before arising they fell upon blank eyes—and wondered if I was finding out something about girls that I hadn't known previously. I hoped dimly, somehow, that I wasn't: it would be a terrible thing to believe that they all behaved in a manner like this. After a long time, Rona came through the hall, making flat, thumping noises, and into the door, tossing the magazines onto the bed. She picked up her large, brown handbag which had been lying in a corner, fumbled with its latch until it opened, and ran a comb listlessly through her hair.

"Filth," she said.

"What? What's that? What are you talking about, anyway?"

"The whole lot of you are poisoned, diseased filth. I'm going to go downstairs and get my mother and make her go home. I don't want to ever see you again."

Oh, the flame that burst within me as I heard this! But confusion was there as well. Always this duality of emotion. It is historic. "Why?" I said. "I don't understand."

She motioned toward the magazines. "If after looking those things over, if after you having them in your room in your bed and showing them to a houseguest, if after all of this you don't know why I want to go home ... well, I just can't talk to you. I can't."

"They're just magazines. What about them?"

"The women. The positions. Is that all you men really think about? Is that all you have on your minds? I feel sorry for all of you. I didn't even know this kind of thing existed."

"It isn't that it exists," I said. "They just show them that way. I don't know whether it exists or not. What are you so excited about? What does it matter? They're not asking you to pose for those pictures, are they? I didn't force you to look at those magazines, did I? I wasn't the one locked up in the bathroom with them for such a long time, was I? Listen, Rona, where are you going? Now, don't be like that. What are you taking those with you for? Come back, Rona, stop that. Come back, now!"

But she had already left the room, two of the magazines clutched under her arm, handbag aswing. I swear to you, I had no idea what she had in mind. It occurred to me that she was going back to the bathroom again or had decided, in an explosion of sanitary impulse, to toss the magazines into the incinerator instead, but it was only as the mumble of voices, rising and rising, cut dully through the tapestry of my room and into my horrified ears that I realized what she had had in mind; she had gone downstairs, into the nest of adults, magazines in hand, and had betrayed me. She was showing the magazines to all of them. She was showing the magazines, most specifically, to Bernice.

Betrayal, was, of course, the least thing in my mind. One can only be betrayed in possession of guilt and as I have already pointed out, the magazines had no significance to me whatsoever; they were the private adjunct of an obsessive act and no more; thoroughly arcane I believed. But as the voices rose and rose, as I heard heavy sounds on the stairs, as I heard shaking, shaking moving through the eaves, the walls, the corridors of being, the first perception came upon me then, the first suggestion of ominousness. Rona had been far more concerned with the magazines than ever I had been. I was still at the skulking, animaline level in my sexual experimentation. But the girl, the girl; the girl as I was trying to say, the girl—

The door opened. Standing in classic position, caught by the dusklight, almost transfigured in that picturization, Bernice stood before me raising the largest, loosest, grandest admonitory finger that I had ever seen.

We were lying at our ease draped on our separate couches then,

D'Arcy and I, wineglasses forgotten and casually empty by our sides, only the uneven ticking of the many clocks in his apartment——D'Arcy was a modest collector of antique timepieces—breaking the dark silence that followed. For a while, at that point in his recollections, I thought that D'Arcy had fallen asleep but as I turned slowly to verify this it became apparent that he hadn't; his eyes on me huge and stricken, his mouth trembling slightly, he had instead reached a point of absolute block. Tentatively I reached out a forefinger and touched him on the wrist. He trembled.

"That must have been terrible," I said. "The traumatic effect and so on." Someone plugged in an electric drill several floors below us and a whining, shrieking knife of sound moved slowly up toward us, passing on its way to the heavens, filtered by the beating of the clocks. "Was this the same girl—this Rona—that you said you copulated with under the disheveled tree in the province of—"

He shook his head restlessly, energetically. "No," he said. "Not at all. That only happened much later. That was a long time after. No, I never saw her again. After that night. It was the province of Q— where the tree was, a delightful place." His head drooped. "No, this all happened in the city. I never had much luck in the city."

"Do you want to continue?" I said. "The hour is late; I can tell that on your clocks, valuable and rare timepieces all. We can take this up another time. The truest instinct of the biographer is his patience, his talent for propitiousness."

"Oh, I guess so," he said, "but it means that I haven't gotten to the point of all this, the initial point I made at the beginning. It speaks very little for my sense of organization, of compaction."

"But my dear friend," I reminded him, "it was you who said just a few moments ago that chronology was a function of meaning not the other way around. So you can stop wherever you want and begin afresh the next time."

"That is true," he said with a sigh, "that is absolutely true. In fact, now as you look at it that way—" and I waited for him to say more but after a long pause it became evident that he had nothing left to say, that the pounding of his breath had become regularized, that D'Arcy, in fact was asleep. His marvelous powers had so dwindled, his attunement had become so blunted that there was, for him, literally no longer a barrier between consciousness and annihilation. So I left him that way, stealing deeper into the caverns of my own recollection, moving more warmly toward the core of my own mystery as all around me the sound of D'Arcy's muffled gasps and cries filled the room, and so the first of our nights, the most meaningful of our nights, the night of our joining was over. In the forest of dreams that I entered I too saw Bernice and she was even more horrifying than D'Arcy had said, one blunt finger shaken to the heavens in a gesture vigorous enough to displace the bowels of sensibility and I understood everything, I understood almost everything; I felt the room close around me tighter and it must have been for a long, long time, then, that I too slept.

THREE

More remains to be said about the circumstances under which this memoir is written before I can proceed.

I resent the attitudes of the staff in this institution more than I can possibly communicate. Their manner is not only insulting, it is heinous; so self-delimiting as to raise the most serious questions of free choice. The regularization of existence can in itself be tolerated; I am a man who, having existed within the framework of one institution or another through the while of my life finds, perhaps, his only freedom *within* the routinization and bureaucratization which the institution imposes by necessity. But there is a line to be drawn between regularization and abuse and I believe that they have passed it here, moved into another territory altogether. This makes my work infinitely more difficult, of course. Creative expression under the best of circumstances is an agony; under the series of humiliations with which I have been recently forced to deal it is almost impossible.

Yesterday evening, my two roommates having left the premises to engage in some woodburning on the rear lawn—they permit this under strict supervision and every night half of the recreation area is set cheerfully ablaze to be resuscitated the next morning with new devices—I was sitting alone in these rooms, fingering my beard idly and wondering if I should continue another chapter of these revelations or retire early to be the more refreshed on the following day. (The following day would be today, just to keep my records straight.) The question of chess was out of the question, inasmuch as my partner had suffered a nervous relapse and had been placed in custodial care for an indefinite period and, the chess board possibly being haunted, no one had chosen to supplant him. The library was a gesture on the rim of possibility but it is small, oppressive, ill-stocked and presided over by one of the queen-bitches of recent history, a large, sweating lady who is interested only in enlisting those few devils who drift in upon a private and rather horrid formation of impulse. So I was on the verge of retiring for the night—having resolved to double my output on the succeeding day as penance—when one of the attendants here, a squat, menacing nameless man who wears dark glasses even under the thinnest moon entered without knocking and stood before me, his arms folded, a hypodermic needle (I could tell) cunningly concealed in a cavernous palm. He beamed at me ingratiatingly.

"How are you doing?" he asked with a shrug which he thought would conceal all purpose, a heavy deference assumed with cunning. But I could see the left palm slowly travelling toward me, describing a small, malicious arc. Nevertheless I did not cringe; it is not within me to display emotion. This is the secret of living whether within or without institutions.

"Perfectly well, my good man," I said, crossing one knee casually over the other and contriving to retreat a few subtle inches from him, the meantime putting a hand behind me to grasp a book I could throw at him *in extremis*. "I am at the moment, however, thinking of going to bed."

"Why is that?"

"Because I am very tired. The slow pace of the days here commands their own enervation; in the midst of inactivity comes that perception of doom which guides us to the womb of sleep." I was deliberately oversimplifying so that there was no way in which he could miss my message, its substance being an urgent desire for his speedy removal.

"Perhaps a little shot would help," he said with a horrid grin. "A relaxant. I brought something in for you right here."

"I am in no need of palliatives. I feel perfectly well and can move into sleep without assistance of any sort."

"Well then," he said, sitting on the bed next to me and putting the offending hand out of sight, gesturing vigorously with the other, "failing that, some conversation. Would you care to talk a little about it before you go to bed?"

"Talk about what?"

"The way you're feeling, the way things seem to be treating you, your objects, goals and ambitions. That kind of thing." The needle twinkled from his reappearing palm. "Of course you don't have to do it if you don't want to. There's no compulsion here."

I could see the consequences of a swift jab dealt by that shy hand, the shocking vault into unconsciousness, the slow murmuring and passage of forms above me just as had happened—well, when had it happened? Anything was preferable to this, at the same time I did not honestly want to converse. "Well," I said, "perhaps we could talk a little if you wish. Not that I have too much to say and I am *extremement fatigue*."

"You find your life here oppressive?"

"Not particularly. There is a sufficient internal freedom to countermand external restraints. Of course my roommates are something else again. Yes, they are a problem."

"You dislike your roommates?"

He was a short, squat man—this entire institution seems to be populated by short squat men; I am one of the few lean, towering persons in the place—and as he made this last statement, framed almost as a proposal, as an item brought up for reconsideration, he leaned close toward me in a horrid assumption of familiarity, the needle still gleaming wisely in his palm. His gaze turned toward one of the blank windows, pursuing the form of a large, brown, sullen tree almost out of sight and my own gaze swung along with his, caught in the topmost branch where a single trapped bird sat heavily on a limb and dropped pellets to the ground below. As I was considering all of this—the bird was no stranger, he appeared to be part of the package which included the tree—I felt the grim, inevitable prick of the needle, as well-known and assumed as the moment of entrance itself; that cold slam dragging me back to the oldest intimation of all and I must have toppled, in my abandonment, from the bed to the floor where I sat cross-legged on my haunches confronting the assassin for several moments. He put the needle back into his pocket with an expression close to pleasure and looked at me reasonably.

"You might as well stand," he said. "It doesn't work *that* fast. Believe me, I know these chemical compounds."

Oddly enough, the betrayal had not foamed me into rage; if anything, this confirmation of worst possibilities had left me almost completely at ease: the institution can only become oppressive through resistance and it was resistance which I was not bound to feel. I wanted to touch the attendant in the face, then, croon simple songs to him, whisper old messages and pledges; assure him that I bore him no grudge at all for what he had done to me; that there was rich, rich precedent for all of this. But this kind of demonstration has always been repugnant to me, even at moments of necessity. I stumbled to my feet and went near the window, snatched at it and tried to haul it up to take large gasps of air.

"They're locked," the attendant said. He now seemed perfectly at ease, immersed in a resignation which only a few moments ago had been my own. How little it takes to accomplish this shift of roles; only a little authority and there you are. The fallacy is to see roles, functions, relationships as lasting when they are merely the casual outcome of certain organic twitches. Ha, ha, ha!

"I know it," I said. "You had no reason to do that to me."

"I wanted to help you relax. Relaxation is very important in a personality of your type; you are an extremely tense man. We were talking about your roommates, weren't we?"

"We were until this happened."

"You said you disliked them. Why is this so? We always try to keep our people happy."

I wanted to tell him that they were pigs, useless, Southern pigs possessed of that whimsy and arrogance which only the perpetually confused could know, but even as I opened my mouth then to tell him the truth, the final truth, I felt the drug he had injected into me take over with such stunning force that my jaw was virtually wrenched amidships, my legs buckling all the while so that I could barely make it to the bed. I felt dimly the pressure of his assistance, then the sheets themselves, and fell into them limp, like rubber, my eyelids beating furiously. His face like a balloon over me, inflated to enormous proportions, the eyes sunken within, the grey, sweating panels of his eager cheeks limp and hanging, and, as he moved toward me then, he whispered words: words which I could not possibly distinguish, words which seemed to have no meaning. Yet in some anterior part of the consciousness I must have recognized all of them because I passed then into true, deep slumber and that was the termination of the evening.

That is what I mean about this place.

They simply won't let you function.

It is impossible to compose a meaningful retrospection confronted by such factors.

FOUR

"I never did get to the dishevelled tree in that province," D'Arcy said cheerfully, the large mirror in his apartment casting back ruddy tones, tones of comfort, as he raised the sparkling glass delicately to his lips, "so I thought that this evening perhaps I would pick up the string of my narrative and get there."

"Whatever you say, my friend," I said, my own wine glass once again snug in my hand; everything as it had been, everything changeless from the past; that fine feeling of stolidity and permanence which I always derived from D'Arcy's presence at its ripest flush, then. "I consider myself honored alone in that you pick me as your auditor; granted that you can tell me whatever you wish to say; I will listen."

"Flattery, flattery," D'Arcy said, a tone of harshness creeping into that complex voice. "How many times have I already told you that it is not necessary; that we must function—as I tell my reminiscences to you—on the closest of terms, not two persons but one, not distant souls but conjoined. Does a single person feel the constant need for self-praise and reassurance?"

"Sometimes," I said.

"Well, by the same token, there should be no need for that between us." D'Arcy seemed stricken with a meditative mood, his body a solemn frieze before the mirror, his hands clasped rubbing on the glass; then he emerged and beamed at me with a renewal of that flickering, wandering gaze which was the most salient feature of the beloved personality. "Let me tell you what happened to me then."

I took out my pad and pencil and, draining the glass, placed it with a crash on the floor.

My experience with Bernice (D'Arcy said) was, of course, consequential. Not so much in its declamatory aspects—Bernice had come to do little more than express her own curiosity about the magazines and to ask me mildly enough if I really thought them fit for her daughter; what I had interpreted as the finger of crucifixion was little more than the fingertip of interrogation. No, it was the question of implication so richly aroused by this incident which can be said to have truly put me on my path. It became apparent to me that the magazines were important—in fact, central—to the performance of the masturbatory act.

I was not aware of this, as I have made clear to you. They were merely an adjunct. But the unusual significance ascribed to them by both Bernice and Rona; the sullen lecture which my father felt constrained to deliver to me that very evening, terminating with the public disposal of the magazines down the garbage chute, my own feeling of dim excitation as I realized as the sum of the wasted months that the magazines were *crucial,* all of these contributed to the development of what can be called my new philosophy. I purchased a royal sampling of replenishments on the succeeding day but I found a much more secure latch for them than the underside of the bed ... and the experimental period, then, truly began in earnest.

It was clear to me that the orgiastic act was related to women in some way; that, in fact, it represented some kind of tribute to them. Self-stimulation was a means toward that pouring of seed which was the only stock for women's vanity and, perhaps, women stimulated themselves as well, reciprocally, with men in view. At the moment of *extremis*, therefore, one's organ should be always pointed toward the woman if not, in fact, lodged somewhere upon her. I bent to this with a will. It was not my desire to obstruct or conflict with social mores in any fashion; I was a true adolescent. I wanted to make people happy.

A question might arise at this time: granted my naiveté—and there is no other word for it, unfortunately, one cannot call it social deprivation or lack of opportunity which caused my misreading of the sexual act—how could it possibly be maintained against the constant flow of schoolboy reminiscence, speculation and comparison which is the archetypal possession of everybody's midcentury adolescence? Didn't someone try, wittingly or unwittingly, pleasantly or cruelly, to straighten me out? *How could such misapprehensions flow in the midst of the peer-group?* A child-psychologist in the audience wishes to know.

I plead *nolo contendere.* In order to apprehend the peculiar facts of my development—a development to bear such fruit, of course, as to be entirely self-justifying and therefore beyond such questioning— one must apprehend the nature of the boys with whom I went to school. This is not easy. There was never such a group before or since in the whole history of the world. Or does every exceptional man say this, casting back to the retrospective glow of his accomplishments, causing his history to seemingly transcend itself? I leave the metaphysics to less practical men.

All of us in this school at that time—and I only made my acquaintances through the school, Rona having hardly counted as a "legitimate social contact"—were in a "special" category and the school itself was "special." By "special" I do not mean the pejorative sense at all; we were not the insulated spawn of privileged fathers, but rather a different category altogether, boys whose development and tendencies had manifested themselves so early as being noteworthy that it was decided that we deserved to be placed only with one another. In this school there was a large staff—one for every other pupil, it seemed—who met our needs graciously and sympathetically, even to arranging that we be conveyed between home and school daily without the necessity of sullying ourselves with ordinary human contact. (This is why I got into so much trouble initially on the subway; if I had arranged for discreet pickup as usual nothing at all would have happened but I was late that day and from that single act of tardiness all kinds of enormous consequences flowed.) Pupils themselves were encouraged to find fulfillment in various means of their own selection and because the "special" nature of our category and facilities was impressed upon us from the first, relationships tended to be sullen and cautious. There was simply no saying what a "special" student or peer might do to one, one was already too familiar with what one could do to oneself. So we existed in a state of rather contrived fellowship, trading confidences very carefully and only one for one, and sexual matters were not within the realm of barter. One's sexual experiences or lack of them were too provocative to be released to anyone. There were some hideous examples to point them out.

There was, for instance, the fat boy who it was rumored some years ago had confided to a schoolmate that he had cohabited with a pet sheep given him by his father to educate him in farming. Before the sense of this, seemingly, had even sunk into the school at large, the fat boy disappeared into the office of one of the principals for several hours, emerging shaken and uncommunicative. Wild rumors spread that he had been compelled to act out his sexual performances with the sheep—which had been sped by covered truck to the school—to an audience of faculty, and equally hideous tales asserted that the faculty had settled for long, picaresque descriptions. At any rate, this boy was never heard from again—not by the students, in any event—nor was the one who, it was similarly rumored, had pulled a dazzling supply of pornographic playing cards from his briefcase to display to others during a lunch break. The tales in this case indicated that he had been compelled to give a command showing of his entire stock to the faculty which was assembled in a dismal, small alcove known as the "teachers' lunchroom." At any rate, such tales breed a kind of caution, as you are doubtless aware.

So, I was on my own. In the truest sense of the term, of course, I have always been on my own; most important men, I find, have been, as well as the largest proportion, of course, of insignificant people. What I had to do, of course, was to reconstruct the entire nature and history of human sexual functioning upon the basis of a few magazines, one raised forefinger and one reaction from a contemporaneous female, along with the performance of my healthy, juvenescent self. This was not easy.

I found that preliminary masturbation was still best accomplished in a state of entire mindlessness, a deliberate revocation of consciousness, but as the crucial twinges and twitches made their reappearance, I would attempt frantically to relate them to the pictures of females which I held plastered by sweat against my throbbing organ. *Oh, oh, oh*, my vocal cords would mutter as I would attempt to direct the stream directly against a nipple or a slab of white skin below the buttocks and after I finished these excursions it was never without a sense of complete dismay; the other way had been so much better, a coincidental occlusion of semen and graphics adding up to a representation of completion. The other way, painfully developed, had been the direct outcome of my needs and intimations imposed upon my physical self; to negate it was to negate a year of assiduous research. Consider a chemist or a medical doctor placed in such a position! Nevertheless, I persisted. I wanted to be normal. I wanted to be doing whatever everybody else was doing, whatever the hell it was, of course.

This led me into difficulties.

In the first place, I was functioning entirely within the private realm at a time when most men began cautiously, for the first time, to enter into the public. And in the second place, my masturbatory ritual was now so unbearably prolonged by necessity that the danger of interruption was compounded enormously; nor more could I risk doing it in public or semi-public places (such as the men's room in the terminal) and even in private it was taking so hideously long to traduce the first limpid drops of completion from my tumescent self as to multiply the chances of discovery. Yet there was no other way. I was stubborn.

Consequently, of course, I was found out. I was caught by my father in the very act of ejaculation one dreary Saturday afternoon when the choice had been between the movies, study or masturbation, and replenishment from the previous evening had been sufficient to justify the latter choice. My father found me *in extremis* itself, poised like a hound-bitch over a litter of magazines, my body half-twisted toward the grey overcast of the windows, my mouth uttering its customary *uh, uh*, as I strained to direct the stream toward its proper place, the jets soaking my fingers, the bed, as well as its presumed place of completion. He had come up, it appeared, to see if I needed help on my mathematics. My father fancied himself to be of an analytical turn of mind although he was actually a dismally failed poet who in his later years, on the brink of senility, took to belaboring his fellow-accountants with excerpts from what he called his "great unwritten ode."

I am told that discovery-by-the-father is the prime Oedipal nightmare and I do not doubt the truth of this, at least in the case of youths who are directed toward normal completion. My father's entrance in this case, however, was only slightly more embarrassing than it would have been if I had been interrupted in the simple act of defecation. I was only trying to be reasonable and normal, this was my feeling: what father could possibly take offense at a son who was only trying to fulfill by release his manly functions? So although I turned to confront him with mild trepidation there was more than a small underlay of pride ... at least he could not say that I wasn't trying to be reasonable about the whole process. The presence of the dripping magazines scattered on the bed would add further confirmation, if such confirmation was at all necessary.

But there were intricacies to my father, of course, which were beyond my anticipation; this is, perhaps, the fundamental tragedy of human relations. He came into the room using a series of bounds which escalated his movement very much as if he were a rabbit and, terrible in his grandeur, in the verification of his worst anticipations, seized the magazines from the bed and hurled them to the floor.

"Look at the mess you've made of everything," is what he said. "Is that the best thing you can find to do with yourself? Haven't you got other things on your mind? What if your mother had seen this?"

"She's not here," I said. "She's gone for the afternoon. There's no chance that she could have seen me."

He slammed me brutally on the back of the neck, midway between the ear and the *medulla oblongata*. "I'm perfectly aware of where your mother has gone and why she isn't home. Now, I want an explanation of this. Do you know what you're doing?"

"Yes, of course."

"Do you?" There was another slam, somewhat softer this time since his physical energy, at best, was limited, and had to be hoarded for special occasions like this. "Give me the word for it."

"The word? I don't understand."

"Damn you," he said, leaning toward me, his eyes wide and intolerant in his damp face, the eyes caught against their will by the scatter of magazines on the floor, "*Tell me what you're doing.*"

"You were downstairs. You were supposed to be reading or something. I didn't know you were coming up here." I found a shred of reasonableness, even of counter. "I'm entitled to some privacy."

"Tell me what you were doing," he said again. There was a slow insistence to his voice, a dreadful unaccustomed drawl; it was evident that he wanted to know the word for it at least as much as he would have wanted to know, on judgment day, his eventual outcome. "If you don't tell me I'll hit you again where it hurts."

"I was masturbating," I said.

"So that's it? You were masturbating?" I had mispronounced the word, slightly placing the accent on the *tur*—and as he repeated it as I had said it, he seemed vaulted to a new level of fury. "Is that the word for it? Do you want to say it again?"

I said it again. "You know what it is," I added, almost petulant now because he had gone beyond the rights, it seemed, of discovery.

"No you don't," he said, leaning toward me even closer, his teeth gleaming dully out of his stretched face, an aspect of frantic gloom seeming to shape him into caricature. "That wasn't it. What you are doing has another name. That name is *self-abuse*. Do you know what self-abuse is?"

"They have it in the books," I said, eager to cooperate, and to bring the scene to some kind of conclusion. My organ was stinging wet, my pants still around my ankles and I wanted little more now than the usual oblivious aftermath of the act at whatever cost. "It means the same thing."

"Yes," he said, "it means the same thing. And do you know what that same thing is?"

"It is the same thing," I said meaninglessly. "I read it. They call it one or the other. What is it?"

But he was off in another direction. "Now I know why Bernice's girl was so upset," he said. "*Did you do this in front of her?*"

I was infuriated. How dared he intimate that my night and day flights were for any witnesses? "No, I didn't," I said. "But she took all the magazines into the bathroom by herself. *Maybe she was doing it.*"

I received a smashing slap on my left cheek, half-kneeling me into the bed, doing this with such force as to leave a small indentation in the mattress which was to plague me for several months thereafter when I tried to masturbate on my side. "Don't you ever say that again," he screamed with such force that those bellows could hardly have come from such a small man. "If you say it again, I'll kill you."

"Such hostility!" I remarked to D'Arcy at that point. "He could not have been more upset if you had discovered *him*."

"Which in certain senses, perhaps, I had," he agreed. "You always find the apt summation. But that is not the crux of the interview, not at all. You should not interrupt me when I am proceeding so nicely. There are so few crucial, chronologically-ordered events in my history that when I truly find one I should be permitted to proceed without interruption. This is the key to being a sound biographer, my friend."

"I am sorry," I said, chagrined. "It was just that the incident, even as you describe it so far, seems so relevant, so crucial, so interlocked with your magnificent career."

"Hear me out," D'Arcy said. "What was I saying?"

Oh, yes (he said, after a pause), I was talking of the small indentation on the mattress which now absorbed me like a cove. As it did so, I heard my father's voice ranting, bellowing, pleading; he was indulging me, now, in a precise description of what self-abuse was; its meaning, its implications, its consequences. The lecture was spiced with detail and example; a never-mentioned uncle, my father said, had abused himself casually for a period of time and had died of congenital insanity. Also he had on evidence the fact that a very good friend of his who had never abused himself—*never, not once*—was led to the practice by evil and simple-minded companions; the first time he had ever indulged in it he had gone completely insane—it was a variety of paranoia; he believed that everybody was trying to abuse him—and had been institutionalized ever since. Did I think, he asked me, did I ever think for a moment that a man such as my father would engage in the practice?

"No," I pleaded, "that had nothing to do with it. I wasn't even thinking of it that way at all. I only wanted to—" I must admit that I was in a state of severe shock.

He grasped me unresistingly by a shoulder and dragged me off the bed, brought me staggering out of the room, down into the hall and through the door of his own room, showed me the huge double bed which he and my mother had purchased at great expense some months ago and which my mother referred to often as her "only true luxury."

"Do you see that?" he said, pointing at the bed, kicking at the iron framework for emphasis. "Do you see that bed?"

"Yes."

"That's the marriage bed. It embraces everything that is holy and meaningful in life. Under contract a man and woman can come to that bed to know and pleasure one another as they choose under the cover of night. They can find fulfilment and joy in one another."

I had never thought of my parents in that context. I was certainly not interested in seeing them that way now. I was not even sure that I knew what my father was talking about. With a desperate bound, I managed to tear loose his embrace but stumbled and collapsed against a wall, landing on my haunches with bruises, facing the bed. He stabbed a forefinger at me.

"That," he screamed, pointing, "that is the only place where such acts must go on. To perform them in any other place, to perform them in any other fashion, is to sin between God and man. Do you understand that?"

"Yes," I mumbled, "yes, yes."

"How much of this can I take, do you think?" he bellowed. "Don't you think that many times, more than you could ever know, I would have liked to submerge myself in your filth and abuse myself? Don't you think a man has thoughts, a man has desires, a man has possibilities? But I keep myself clean for your mother. Clean for her, do you understand me! I preserve the temple of my body, the temple of my holy spirit so that it may be purified for the rite with your mother!"

"Yes," I said, "Oh, yes. Oh, yes. I have to go to the bathroom now. Do you think I can—"

"How much can I put up with? But I protect myself, I hold on to myself and it has its own rewards! I tell you, the goddamned thing has its rewards and plenty of them; I could tell you stories, you rotten little snip, if you wouldn't trundle right back to your room and start jerking off to them! But I have control, I have the ability to structure my passion. I am a *man*, goddamn you. Where did you get all those magazines from?"

"Bathroom," I gasped, "bathroom—"

"I bet you pick that filth right up from the newsstands, take it right into your briefcase, smuggle it home so that it can desecrate your house, four or five feet away from your mother! Oh, I bet you laugh as you strew your seed, I bet that every twinge and jerk is a joy to you, a *double* joy, I should say, because it not only defiles you but your mother. Oh, I see it now: I understand everything. *Don't you think I'd like to do it? Don't you think every man would like to do it?* But you have discipline, you have control, you see it as a sharing rather than a wandering, you save your seed for where it means best, which is deep in the body of a woman; deep in the temple, the temples meeting, the places meeting, the bodies joining and then—"

But I was far gone, past warning. My poor bowels had opened and the flood had come in earnest, an odor so communicable as to even override my father's last admonition. I squatted desperately, trying to hold back what remained, but knew with hopelessness that the devil inside was going to clean me out. Small squeals and gasps added to the sense of utter disgrace until finally, utterly spent, I knelt before my father, the consequences of my explosion clear to the two of us. He said nothing, his face slowly slackening back into its accustomed puzzlement and I was able to make my escape.

I stayed in the bathroom for a very long time, cleaning myself out and making further adjustments. When I came out, I found that my room had been cleaned and placed in an almost ceremonial order, the magazines themselves stacked carefully beside the bed, wiped dry, obviously by careful hands. I hadn't the slightest idea what to do. The impulse to masturbate came upon me maniacally, but I repressed it. I suppose the point is that I was stunned.

After some time, there was a knock on the door and my father came in. He seemed to have shrunk subtly within his clothing, almost as if he had been engaged in some vigorous exercises of his own. He nodded to me and started to say something, shook his head and turned around, then turned back toward me violently and raised his hand.

"Nothing of this," he said. "Nothing of this to your mother at all. Do you understand me?"

"Of course."

"I could kill you for what you've done but I'll allow you to forget it.

This will be between the two of us only. I don't want any more discussions of this unless you start them."

"All right," I said.

"I could have you institutionalized. I could have you committed for what you've done. But I'm willing to let it go."

"Okay. We'll let it go."

"Only because you're my son. If it was someone else carrying on the way you have, there would be terrible trouble here."

"Yes," I said. "Yes." The capacity for speech seemed to have left me. I had nothing to say. There was absolutely nothing to say.

"But I'm your father. I have a duty to protect you. I realize that now." He ran a hand through his sparse hair and looked at me. "I couldn't possibly forget that."

"Yes," I said, "yes."

"But you are never to do that again. Never, do you understand me? My outburst may have been a little violent; I admit that now. But that doesn't change the seriousness of your activity. You must promise me that you will stop."

"I will," I said. Why not? My bowels were clean, my testes were clean; I had been purged of all normal and abnormal desires and terrified as well. It was the slightest of concessions.

"Until you're married."

"When I'm married I can do it?"

"When you're married you won't *have* to do it." He walked toward the door, opened it, turned back on me. "You don't think that that has any place in the marriage bed, do you?"

"Oh, no," I said. "Oh no."

"Well, then—"

He closed the door.

I contemplated myself for a long, long time as night came fully through the windows and into the eaves of being; after a while I heard the slamming of doors and shrill laughter which meant my mother had returned. I found myself, against the background of the voices, wondering for the first time what my parents were really doing with one another. It didn't seem to make that much difference. I took the magazines carefully, cautiously one by one and put them back in their hiding place, then went down to greet my parents. My father's face must have looked as purged as my own. Mother said that we both looked dreadful.

"Shocking," I said, nodding vigorously, running both hands through my beard and going in search of the wine decanter which, when last seen, had been near the rear of D'Arcy's small, sparse bar. "Indeed, the implications of this must have been vast."

"Not necessarily," he said, his own two hands reaching to move restlessly through his thin, slightly decaying hair. "As a matter of fact, although I once thought this incident to be of the highest significance, being absolutely central to most things which I did subsequently, I now regard it as mildly laughable; provocative, certainly, but in ways more relevant to my father than to myself. You must understand that he was a man of exceedingly weak temperament, and that the discovery must have been even more disconcerting to him than it was to me. Otherwise, his reaction must be inexplicable."

"Perhaps," I said, and then overwhelmed with a burst of admiration (as I found the decanter and cracked it open heartily to pour three dashing inches into my glass), added, "but surely, no little credit can accrue to you as a result of this. For an ignorant adolescent to be so accosted and abused by a father at the most delicate stage in his formative years ... why, it might have turned a lesser man, a less exceptional man I was trying to say, into a thorough-going homosexual! But you, D'Arcy, my dear, great, discovered friend ... you went in the other direction entirely!"

"That is only if you link causes and effects in the normal, routinized fashion," D'Arcy said quietly. "But as I have pointed out, there is very little in my life, exploits or functioning which is so easily explicable. Do you really think I would have become homosexual?"

The query was delivered so insidiously and with such emotion underlying its bland exterior that I realized that I had, very possibly, hurt D'Arcy to the bone and this afflicted me with terrible dismay; I had only been making conversation, a kind of transition! "Oh, no, no, no," I cried, "that would be impossible for any man such as you and doubly so in your case, granted your sensibility, your compassion, your warmth! I did not mean in the least to imply this kind of aberration in your development, but only to indicate that for a far lesser man this possibility existed. It never occurred to me, not for a moment."

"I have never understood homosexuality," D'Arcy said after a pause, his voice rich and meditative as he fondled his glass. "The dreariness, the overwhelming reiteration of it. I have always thought of sex, even in my greenest years, that folly I am now recounting to you, as, perhaps, the last true available means of self-liberation, of the release of the doomed self. But this homosexuality, the entwining of forms upon the same forms, passions upon their mirror, has always stricken me numb; it is such an eternal reaffirmation of the very dwelling which the orgasm has been created for us to escape. Instead of a renewal it is a rediscovery of everything contemptible because already known. Surely, my friend, only a man not aware of himself, only a man who had not yet found his own identity could possibly be a homosexual as he tries to trace out the form and shaft of his being on another. Having once known oneself, one could not possibly be a homosexual. Would you not think that true?"

"Of course," I said. "The majority of homosexuals whom I have known strike me as the dreariest kind of types, really; people who indeed, as you so aptly say, lack identity. Only the proud, functioning, historic heterosexual—such as you, D'Arcy—can be truly known as the liberated man because his functioning has torn him free from his history, blown him loose from entrapment. Yes, of course, you are perfectly correct."

But D'Arcy, seemingly unmoved by this sincere burst, remained in a pensive attitude, his hands damp on the glass, his brow drawn tight with thought. "The breasts," he was saying, "the thighs, the buttocks, the true, warm flesh of these women who are both our partners and the eternal strangers ... *this* is the key to the unlocking of the door that is the doomed, departed self: in those surfaces is the beginning of our voyage. I simply cannot understand this fellatio, this anal entrance, this series of metallic contacts which appears to circumscribe the life and times of the homosexual. No, this means nothing to me, it is not even metaphor, for if the life of this country can truly be interpreted as the flight from self, the search for identity through the superimposition of diversion—and please understand me, I do not approve of any of this in the slightest—then surely the homosexual is a functional anachronism. You are quite right, my friend: I do concede the point after all; if there were ever a time when the possibility of homosexuality flaunted her equivocal head, it was after this interview with my father. Yet it could never be. Never. I assure you of that. Of such contacts, I have never had the slightest knowledge. You do believe me?"

"Of course," I said, sipping the wine gratefully and realizing for the first time that D'Arcy's apartment was slightly oppressive, cluttered with far too many furnishings for its limited spaces and stuffy in the bargain; repressing with anger a sudden compulsion to go around flinging up windows and singing heartily to myself to be reminded of the existence of air. "What do you think brings me to your rooms? Why do you think we have embarked upon this study? Surely not the laughable prospect of homosexuality!"

"Tell me," D'Arcy said shyly, his eyes full and round, now. "Tell me why you are here. Tell me the true reasons for this study as you call it, my reminiscences, your attention."

"Do you really need to know?"

"Of course I do. Otherwise, why would I ask?"

"Why," I said, "your heterosexuality, of course. Your monstrous, overbearing heterosexuality which cut a swathe through three nations, several subdivisions and literally hundreds of women; that consuming, tormenting, transcendent heterosexuality which has made you, D'Arcy, virtually a legend before your senescence; that is the whole of it and the reason for it. Of course! Do you really need reassurances at this date?"

His eyes held infinite knowledge, infinite sadness. "Yes," he said, "sometimes I do. Sometimes everyone does. You have no idea of the burden, the obligation, the responsibility—"

"Of course," I said.

"I guess I should go on. There is so much that is crucial for me to explain to you and so little time. Life is a feather; it can be wafted away at any instant. And I have barely started."

"We have time," I said comfortingly, "We have time." And indeed, between the wine, the clamor of D'Arcy's conversation and the constriction of his room I felt a dismal lightheadedness, an apprehension of consequence in that I suspected, with enormous gloom and for the first time, that I would pay; that I would pay in some obscure and costly way for being D'Arcy's biographer; that nothing was without recompense and that my recompense might take a particularly ghastly form. But there was nothing to say, not when his limpid dark eyes were holding me so closely. So I merely leaned back, clutching the glass in my fingers and feeling the volatility of the liquid driving up against my palm and said, "Yes, yes, by all means go right ahead, don't feel that I'm limiting you at all. Please go on and tell me what happened next. I simply can't wait to find out and I want to get all of it down into your memoirs."

Did I grasp the institution then, this end, these forms, this penance? Did a breath of still air move back from this time to that, enveloping me in its vapid chill? Or was I merely distressed by the power of D'Arcy's recollections, his rhetorical ability to transmit his own oppression?

"Go on," I said, rather restlessly.

The interview with my father (D'Arcy went on) forced certain alterations upon my life just as the interview with Rona had, although they took a different outlet. No man is immutable. In my case, they tended to once again force me to examine my considerations of sex, my interpretation of the role of orgasm. I did not stop masturbating of course, not even for the length of a day. There were two reasons for this.

The first reason is that I could, under no circumstances, have stopped for any reason at all; I was then entering my sixteenth year, and ripeness being all, demanded an outlet of some kind under any circumstances. It was no more possible for me to stop masturbating than it would have been for my parents to have withdrawn me from the "special" school which yielded, upon entrance, a contract committing the student for several terms of study through graduation, to be revoked only in the event of death or insanity. The second reason was only slightly more complex: I suspected that if caught again my father's reaction would not be worse and might be considerably better. There was no possibility that he would turn me in, so to speak, to the proper authorities. Rather, we were collaborators toward a solemn destiny which was being worked out through the thumpings and thuddings of that agent, my prick. Although I was never found out again it was not for lack of opportunity on my father's part because, on almost all the occasions that we were left at home together, I would withdraw from his presence to either "nap" or "do some studying," leaving no doubt in his mind as to my true intentions. I suppose the fact of the matter was that I wanted to be discovered again. My father had never been so interesting before or since. On the other hand, he evidently decided that it would not be in his best interests to reiterate the scene. I can respect this.

I had to, as I say, reevaluate the sexual act. My father's talk of the "marriage bed," to say nothing of the "temple of the holy spirit," had convinced me that there was more to the spurtings of orgasm than simple mechanization, more to its involvement with women than coincidence. It was possible—this was a new thought!—that women were participants in the orgasm themselves, that the actual ejaculation spurred them into a responding, if minuscule parody of what occurred within my own body. Perhaps—this was an interesting possibility—the "temple of the holy spirit" was the body of the woman itself and the spurtings of orgasm a kind of ritual offering. This would have been easier to work out had I come from a religious background.

There were at this time, doubtless, all kinds of texts available to me which could have solved the mystery in a trice. But, considering it somewhat more profoundly, I doubt if they would have after all. The sheer, medical facts of copulation I knew—insertion, excitation, further excitation, orgasm—what I did not comprehend was the actual relationship of the bodies. My original assumption had been, of course, that the male masturbated directly into the vagina rather than with the use of his hands, a minor inconvenience which was imposed by what were known as the "marital responsibilities" the counselors were always talking about, but it did not go into the quality of that masturbation itself. Rona's reaction to the magazines had been my first real clue, my father's lecture had been the second. But there were still loose ends. How did they—females, that is— derive their own satisfaction? What did they think about when it was being done to them? Wouldn't it be easier if they offered their hands instead of their orifices? And so on.

I put these questions, incidentally, to a prostitute in T— many years later and I am sorry to say that she did not produce answers any more satisfactory than my frenzied imagination did at that time. She was a charming and responsive girl, well-built, with that kind of easy languor which moves into the most rigid and desperate kind of pumping; but her intellectual processes, at least in relation to my queries, were almost nil, although she approached them with a good deal of sophistication. "What do we think about, darling?" she asked me as we lay exhausted from the afterplay, our cigarettes joined to one another as our slimy organs had been only a few moments ago, "Well, that all depends. I mean it's hard to tell you. Sometimes we think about one thing and sometimes we think about the other. And sometimes we don't think at all. It has a lot to do with the mood you're in and with the man you're with, if you know what I mean." And gave me a rattling good wink and a thumb in the ribs. "What else can I tell you?"

But I persisted, trying to ascertain what her responses were, the quality of feeling, the very quality of *ambition* that underlay the conjoining of the female in bed, that fine, desperate, oily winding in the limbs. "What do you make of it?" I asked her, reasonably enough, I thought. "What makes you do it, anyway?"

"Well," she said, "sometimes it's money and sometimes it's love and sometimes it's both but more often than not it's simply something to do." And gave me the wink again and a lingering caress moving from shoulder to balls in a swoop, fingering them to the suspicion of pain and then releasing to plumb the depths of my buttocks. "We have our thoughts," she said demurely, and put the leftward of her two enormous breasts in my mouth. "Suck away now, darling D'Arcy and don't ask so many questions."

So I sucked away, a willing nursling for her better pride, subsiding in the numb awareness that I would never know; that 31 as 16, the true quality of their marvels would never be known to me, the thrust of their obsession, the purposes of their drifting. And she made the proper whore's noises, groaning away properly under me while I gave her what I thought she wanted and as I did this I realized for the first time the truth of it: if I had known it many years ago it would have saved me all kinds of trouble, but knowing it even then as I did, it could have been the beginning of salvation because a man's sexual powers do not dwindle and vanish at 31 but, in certain subtle ways, are only undergoing their truest metamorphosis: there could be many a decade of merry fucking if I could only grasp this insight and hold it close and the insight, then, was this: there was nothing inside them at all. They had nothing to say, there was no interior; it was boredom and the genes and certain slow convulsions of the juices which brought them into the bed, and for the remainder there was nothing at all, absolutely nothing that could be touched.

And, oh yes, the whole legend that they had built up of feminine demureness, feminine mystery, feminine coyness, was only to cover up all of this: the suggestion being made that what they felt was beyond the reward of words, but the fact of the case being—deponent maketh a proper case—that inarticulacy was the best defense against discovery. And as her huge nipples, one by one, exploded slowly and ripely in my mouth, her peculiar moans—twenty dollar moans, to be sure, perhaps thirty dollar moans and mine for the all-night rate of twenty-five and a half—carried me back past the web and network of the years toward the oldest necessity, the truest necessity, the original necessity of all, and a massive glowing eagle with wings of fire, I carried her on my back in slow circles, wrenching her into position as I moved skyward, free at last from the sea and caving waters, moving in my element at last past the broken and crumbling land.

I digress. The questions I wished to have answered I could, I suppose, have verified through experience; I was at an age where "dating" began and even for tenants of the all-male "special" school there were sufficient opportunities afforded by dreary dances provided by the school management once a month at which the tenants of a girl's "special" school were the constant and sole invitees. Girl "special" students were unlike the boy specialists I had known; both more boisterous and adventurous, there were whispers, even in our sullen corridors, of quick rewards asked and given during and after these dances in secret places. But I was not interested in these girls. They had no allure for me whatsoever. They struck me as barely female. What I was truly after were the girls whose pictures lay in the magazines. *They* were the ones to take up the issue with; hadn't I, in one fashion or another, been dealing with them in huge fidelity for years?

But the girls in the magazines were almost wholly inaccessible. I am finally at the point now where I want to tell you what went on in that blasted and deserted province during the summer to which I referred. We were some time getting there, that is perfectly true. But by the same token, we will be some time in getting out. There is no way to sufficiently overstate the importance of the events which occurred to me. Or do you misunderstand me, my friend? Do you like the rest of them now find D'Arcy contemptible, weary, effete, something of a bore? Do you repudiate him as so many of them have been prone to do? Or do you truly understand him? Can you understand the connections, the fine, limpid connections which so key in to his mystery? I hope you are attending well, my friend. I hope you are manifesting the proper emotional concern toward me; that this is not all an elaborate joke—this biography, this attentiveness, this constant, flattering auditor—prepared by my enemies for my greater humiliation.

At this point, D'Arcy's handsome head lolled upon his shoulders, drifted toward his chest and receded, passing out of the reciprocal gaze of the mirror. Immersed as I was in my notations, the necessity to catch everything he was saying without a single lapse, it was some time before I realized that he had fallen asleep.

And so, then, on the second of our nights, on the second night of our reconciliation, I sat quietly in the ticking and beating spaces of D'Arcy's lodgings, tapping one hand upon a knee and listening to his breathing while I waited for the dawn and wine to come again so that D'Arcy could speak to me of the provinces, of the wild lost provinces, of the bare, deserted provinces where the horses themselves came out in the dusk and cast their screams at one another while the diseased sun sent shafts of misery catching them timeless in a stricken frieze, a frieze much as my poor friend's head might have formed, suspended as it was between cabinet and mirror, between ceiling and floor, between history and judgment.

FIVE

I had a conversation with the taller of my two roommates today while the other was in one of the recreational areas and he, on a mild dispensation due to a virus, was being permitted to stay in his bed all day. My dispensation was of a clearer order; the injection I had received the previous night was of stunning and pervasive force and left me quite limp, entirely unable to confront the possibility of any activity at all, let alone the particularly horrid and "cheery" tasks of the recreational staff of this institution. I began by telling him of what had happened to me the previous evening.

He jerked his head as a full lever of dismissal and turned it to the wall, indicating, perhaps, that he did not seek conversation with me. I persisted, however, describing the reaction of the attendant, his gestures with the needle and the eventual stultifying outcome and at last it became apparent to him that I really meant to talk, that there was no way out of it. He turned wearily to face me, his face now cast open by the illness seeming surprisingly more youthful, and it occurred to me to wonder for the first time what he was doing in a place like this. I am a much older man, of course.

"That is impossible," he said. "Attendants are not licensed to dispense drugs. Only the doctors are. And there are no doctors patrolling this place after working hours, you can count on that. *Impossible!*" he repeated, this time with a French accent, apparently about to lapse into his execrable, arcane phraseology again.

"But I tell you, he did it. He gave me an injection right here." I showed him the spot on my arm. "And then I became unconscious."

"Nonsense. You stabbed yourself with a pin or crushed it with a fingernail. I am really not interested in your imagined slights and brutalities. I am ill—I mean, that is *mal*—and I wish to go to sleep."

"But they are committing atrocities here! Isn't anybody aware of the fact that people are being maltreated?"

"You do not seem maltreated to me. You seem to be in entirely good spirits, offensive and boorish as usual, full of quips and slights." He groaned faintly. "I must get some rest now. Further interruptions will force me to call one of the attendants."

"How about your companion?" I said archly. "Why don't you call him? He will take care of you."

Instantly he was out of bed—not that *mal* after all, it seemed—and standing huge before me, his face palpitating oddly. "I wish to know exactly what you mean by that remark."

"I mean to get your attention. They are filling us full of injections here. They are making us stuporous and undoubtedly picking our brains. They are all out to get us. Don't you think you could transcend your silly virus enough to be sensible and listen to me? I'm telling you that there are enormous things going on here. For all you know your own virus may have been caused by their drugs. Think about it."

"The next slur you make upon my roommate will meet with instant retaliation. *La Guerre*. I will strike you violently."

"Oh, go to hell," I said, quite disgusted, quite hopeless and, for the moment, sharing my roommate's disinterest in all aspects of the institution. "Get back to bed and cover yourself up."

He did so, heavily, making snorting noises with his back turned toward me, apparently intimating gross and terrible vengeance, and went unhappily between the bedsheets. I sat up shakily and fumbled for my bedroom slippers, found them at last and moved around the room slowly, testing my limbs, examining them for defects. When my roommate's breathing had subsided to the even tempo of sleep I stole upon him and carefully looked at his left wrist, the wrist which he had thrown casually around the pillow, embracing it as if it were an impossibly distended breast.

It was just as I had suspected, of course. The institutional stamp was on the wrist, over the pulse itself and as his blood throbbed evenly in his healthy veins, it dilated and expanded slowly, regularly. I looked at the mark for some time and then at the face of my roommate, expected to see that face rise to greet me with a cackle but the eyes were shuttered in sleep, the face a cold mask and it was quite obvious that he was not feigning, that he was actually unconscious, that he had dared to go to sleep in the same room as one confined in the institution … an institution which was his employer.

That confirmed everything I needed to know.

Truly, truly, all of them are out to get me. This intimation, first known many years ago, but stated in its final, most succinct form, only to D'Arcy himself, and then at the conclusion of our relationship, has pursued me all of my life, has shaped so many of my responses; has, in a sense, conditioned and structured the very quality of my inner life and yet there is nothing, nothing after all, that I can do. It explains everything: the abominable French, the sneers and sly winks exchanged behind my back, the high, cold arrogance which these two roommates have always sustained toward me, the strange solicitousness of the outer "staff," the actions of the attendant himself.

But, in addition, it is completely irrelevant. I have my work, after all; I have my work to do and as long as I can function I intend to do it. It has fallen to me to write the last, the true, the encapsulatory memoirs of the wonderful career of D'Arcy and while capacity yet remains with me I will do this because this task is vital, because his voyage was vital, because I was his only true confidant. So I will continue then, weary as I am I will continue; there is no one who can stop me, there is no one who has the ability to stop me; I will persist. Before it breaks apart I will have told it all.

There are other factors at work too. I could kill either of my roommates in a twinkling if I desired. There is no way they could anticipate this or head me off. I have the weapons, you see; the means. I have the final insight. They are as grass before me.

The needle that glints in the palm that strikes in the frame that buckles has a different voyage. Aha, aha, aha!

I was trying to talk of D'Arcy before I was so crudely interrupted by these irrelevancies.

SIX

"The province," I said to my dear friend, once again lifting the glass to my lips; it was a stein this time since we had switched to foaming, Alpine beer in order to "beat the weather," as D'Arcy put it, and to regularize our discussions which had begun, in their later nightly stages, to take on more the aspects of the drunken preamble than the sensitive, polished, transmuted retrospective. "You were going to tell me about the province."

He shook his head and took an uncapped bottle from the table, drank beer that way and finally replaced it with a grimace. "I will get to that in due time," he said. "I was still talking, as I believe, about the inaccessibility of conventional sexual objects."

"But the last thing you said to me was that you were just about ready to tell me of the province, of the dishevelled tree, of what happened to you on that afternoon so long ago."

"And who are you to say that?" he asked rather belligerently, brandishing the bottle at me and then taking another swallow. "You're only the biographer. What right do you have to tell me what to tell next? I'm the subject; it's my story from beginning to end. I can make it up if I want to and I can tell you anything I want."

"I never said you couldn't," I said placatingly, my voice a rich, pleasant, mellow hum in the throbbing room. I have often been told that I have a singularly melodious and pleasing larynx; something which could have led me to an excellent career in public speechmaking and politics, had I not forsaken all of this for art. "I was only trying to help you get things in order," I said calmly.

"I'll get things in order my own way," D'Arcy said. "I don't need your help and I don't need being ordered what to do. Is this your biography or mine we're working on?" His voice held a thin edge of petulance and I decided that it was best to soothe him.

"Yours, of course," I said. "You are the dedicatee, I merely the witness, and I would not presume to tell you what to say or when to say it or in what manner. You lead the way, I will only follow."

"Better, then," said D'Arcy, uncapping a fresh bottle and pouring some of it tinkling into his glass. "I didn't want to think that there was a reversal of roles here. The confusion this kind of thing leads to, the hatred, the loss! No, one must enact his single destiny from childhood to senescence, never stirred by alternative. I know that you can agree to this."

I drained my own glass and poked it out for a modest refill, then sat it carefully on the arm of the chair. "Of course," I said. "Everything you say is absolutely correct."

"I was just getting on. I haven't forgotten a single thing I said I would tell you. I'm getting to it."

I took my pad from an inner coat pocket and opened it carefully to a fresh page, still feeling the thin ripples of hostility in the room but now receding, receding. "Yes," I said, "I'm waiting."

As I was saying (D'Arcy said), the gaps in my sexual education were immense and could seemingly only be filled by the girls in the magazines themselves; girls who, costumed by bare flesh and the invidiousness of their spirit would possess that utter knowledge of function and reciprocity which I so desperately needed, but girls whose means and whereabouts and interiors I had no more knowledge of than I did of the intricate, poisonous physiology of self. It was perfectly apparent that there were women about in the world—did I not see them all the time, these swaddled, irretrievable objects? And that many of these women had breasts and nipples, steaming vaginas and heavy thighs but all of it was so carefully sequestered, so remote, so distant that it could as well have not existed for all the good it did for me.

I risk misapprehension here. Let me explain. I was not interested in copulation nor interrelationship in a sexual way with women who—stubbornly—I still perceived as adjuncts or objects rather than subjects. I was only in search of the revelation of a mystery, a revelation that could only be accomplished were a woman to talk freely and frankly with me. What did they do? What did they get out of it? How did they masturbate? How mutual was the masturbation of intercourse? What was intercourse, precisely? Did one play with the breasts before, during, or after emission? These were the questions which concerned me. I suppose that these are the questions which plague the career-rapist, and that in subtle ways I had a good background toward a deviate's professionalism ... but my opportunities being as restricted as they were and my outlets so plentiful—for I had not ceased masturbating, not for a moment; if anything the tempo and pulsing of my hands and joints had increased through all this time—the idea of conjoinment violent or otherwise never occurred to me. In certain circumstances, no doubt, I could have proceeded in this fashion indefinitely, gone through all the years suspended between curiosity and fulfillment, at a kind of wasteland of the psyche until (if all things had gone this way) you would have seen me now in my 38th year, mild D'Arcy, gentle D'Arcy, confused D'Arcy sitting somewhere on a sofa wiping his glasses with a shirttail and still perpetually trying to assemble what all of it was about. We have seen plenty of men like this; their slack mouths questing, their dull eyes brightening—but never enough—as they enter into the presence of women; these men who roam in small, chattering packs outside the hotels in which public dances are being held, these men who are still trying to find an identity at some post-puerperal stage and thus are in no position to affect the identity of others. You are one of these types yourself, my friend, if I may be frank. You have sublimated most of this into the so-called "creative" or "journalistic" drives which, along with a heavy, frowning beard permit you to seemingly negate the reality of your interior, but believe me, I know what is really with you—as a refugee from that estate myself I have that kind of attuned sensitivity known only to homosexuals or convicts among one another—and I fail to derogate you; it is perfectly all right with me, in short. I know your suffering, your limitation, the thoughts which pass through your representation of a mind when you pass or witness an attractive female; the ordeal of dread and loss which occupies you when you try to imagine the contact of warm flesh, sliding breast, gentle pressure. It is not pleasant to live in a state of perpetual hysteria to be touched off by the first wandering thigh or shoulder in sight. Spite alone could blow your fragile balance to shreds. But, as I say, this is perfectly all right with me; I regard you without amusement and with much solemnity.

The province. We were getting to the matter of the province. I was seventeen then, seventeen finally, when I accompanied my parents to a dismal seaside resort several hundred miles from the city in which we dwelt. It was the first vacation for all of us in some time; my father's harassments in the "accounting business" and my mother's ambitions to "cut expenses" had kept all of us safely swaddled at home during the summers until, this preceding spring, my father incurred what he said was a "heart attack," which the attending doctors called instead a "warning of an impending heart attack," and with the first flash of mortality spiked deep into his chest my father decided that he, that all of us, were "entitled to get away." Our "entitlement" consisted of being removed to a development consisting of several bleak bungalows and a central dining area, half of it facing a rather polluted lake, the other half some blasted farmland, and my father joined us here on weekends, otherwise living and working in the accounting business in the city. I was not pleased with what I took to be a kind of exile but my mother had activities to occupy her most of the time—she was a restless card-player and also found that she and the "social director" had gone to the same school a long time ago, although at different times—and this left me with most of my own time unpressed; long swims in the dreary lake and walks through the farmland, a drive-in movie theater some miles away which had a bus line of its own, and all the time I needed and could possibly want to masturbate. I was greedy, desperate of my masturbatory prerogatives, and I had never had so many as I did at the beginning of that summer. All in all, not precisely discontent, I worked out an enclosed existence and, taking it for my destiny, passed into a period of self-absorption.

This period ended abruptly only a fortnight after our arrival, however. The social director—a widower—had a daughter, Marie-Jean; and Marie-Jean, a lush but equivocal seventeen, had nowhere to turn for companionship other than to the guests and the children of the guests. It happened that I was the only person in the entire camp between the ages of 15 and 20 with the exception of herself. Fate took us.

I see you poising nearer, my friend; I see your pencil raised to take a particularly vigorous series of notes, the high twitch of your eyelids intimates a kind of involvement I have never seen from you before. Rest assured that you are correct; I am about, at last, to talk to you of D'Arcy's inaugural into the universe of copulation. But in time, in time. It took time that summer. Marie-Jean, it appeared, did not like me very well at all. And unversed—oblivious is the word— as I was in the intricacies or even simplicities of summer-seduction, I was unable to deal with that dislike other than with a reciprocal hostility of my own. The first time she went into the lake where I was already paddling my feet and looking skyward, I asked her how she could bear to dwell in a place like this and why her bathing suit was so tight and yet ill-shaped. It was not a propitious meeting.

As it turned out, she did not live here year-round; she had little more connection with this "resort" than I did. As it developed through our conversations, her father was a teacher of mathematics in a suburban high school who ran the resort summers to "make a buck," and whose loathing for the scenery easily approximated my own. A bizarre promotional genius, however, accompanied by the services of a professional photographer, had resulted in a brochure whose misrepresentation of the property was as profitable as it was marginally legal ... and this explained his presence there as well as that of Marie-Jean, to say nothing of my own. Marie-Jean and I did not get along well together from the start.

There was no way in which we could have. As I realized later, she had seen, practically from our first meeting, that she was going to have to have a relationship with me because I was the only vaguely accessible male within several square miles of the area that summer, but the imminence of this relationship did not please her. It was a question of needing it more than she repudiated me. What I am trying to say is that Marie-Jean, short, well-developed, insular and suspicious little Marie-Jean, was a thoroughgoing slut. Her sexual history, in its way, was at least as rich as my own.

We found ourselves sequestered together in the dining room

during meals; we found ourselves, of necessity, spending long afternoons together. My masturbatory exercises and schedule were completely disrupted by this but the alternative—leaving her— was worse for several reasons.

In the first place, I was as sexually curious as she was needful and it became apparent to me early on that she was accessible to me in a way which no female had ever been. I wanted to find out what it was about. In the second place, her father took to our relationship with an amused tolerance which soon escalated to indulgence; he interpreted Marie-Jean's sexual itch as the need for a strong, warm relationship, and he began to insinuate himself on the edge of our relationship, granting my mother special attentions in and out of the dining hall and urging Marie-Jean and me to "see a lot" of one another. The poor man! He was, I realize in retrospect, so resigned to his daughter's sluttishness that he thought of it as normal adolescent behavior. Perhaps he was even correct; this is a difficult thought which I have had recently and which almost impossibly mars this explosion of retrospection. If he were correct—if Marie-Jean were a normal, healthy, and affectionate if slightly misguided juvenescent—it would force me to make the most violent recalculations and reassessments of the affair and my role and this would topple my entire strategy. I had best pass the issue.

I want to describe the first time I made love to Marie-Jean. It occurred several days after our initial meeting and the phrase "to make love" is wildly inappropriate since, of course, it was nothing of the sort. Better, then, I want to describe my first joint masturbatory experience.

"Let's stop the car," she said, and as she said this hit the brakes and moved us slowly, gracelessly, off the panels of the road into the ominous gravel at the side. "I want to get out and walk a bit." She elevated the emergency brake and put the keys in my pocket, tapped them proprietarily. "It's getting stuffy in here."

It was the second of our automobile excursions; Marie's father owned a disreputable sedan and although she had no "driver's license," she was permitted to travel with it due to the barrenness of the country and certain relations which her father had with the local chief of police. I had accompanied her on the second of these trips almost gratefully; the alternative was sitting by the water with her and arguing almost with a frenzy about everything. We agreed on nothing at all. And there was no way that I could be free of her presence in the afternoons.

No, the car at least gave the impression of motion; a sense of displacement as we spun through the grey, blasted country jouncing merrily over stones in the road, our heads whirled back and forth toward one another by the impact, this fragmentary contact given the illusion of intimacy by the rattles and trembling of the car. It was far better to move than not to move because it delayed confrontation while giving its illusion. Her tight, bare arms, hovering over the wheel, the strong profile of her large breasts thrown into occasional violent juxtaposition with the machinery, the glint of her chin as she raised it, now and then, to peer upwards through the windshield, enticed me into some approximation of connection and when the car came to its abrupt stop it was with some difficulty that I was able to dislodge myself from the seat and stagger to the side of the road, cling to a post for momentary support while she emerged with a more spritely gait than mine. I had been imagining myself in the act of masturbating to her photograph.

She came toward me, almost jauntily, and took my arm, held it loosely and guided me toward the fields. "Let's walk," she said. "It's nice here; the stink isn't so bad in the afternoons and all of them are back in the barns. Besides, I'm tired of driving."

I let her convey me and said, "It always smells here. That's the worst thing about the country. There's no peace."

"But there is," she said, looking at me sidewise. "There's a lot of peace for your mother."

"Is there?"

"Don't you know what's going on between her and father?"

"I don't care," I said, dodging some wheatstalks and then carelessly tripping so that I fell headlong, having to brush some eager gnats off me as I regained my balance.

"She and daddy are going to bed together."

Actually, I had suspected as much—the fact of adult fornication having long since been impressed upon me by media if not my interior. But I felt it was my position to defend. "She is not," I said, "and besides, if she is, your father is making her."

"No he isn't. He never has to make anybody. He told me that once; he can't keep them away from him. No, your old mother and my daddy are right this moment in bed or close to it. Doesn't that make you feel strange?"

"Why should it make me feel strange?" I asked; and indeed it didn't. Sex was an abstraction, my mother was an abstraction, the two compounded moved to the level of utter unfeasibility. But it seemed to affect Marie-Jean profoundly for her mood shifted down from gaiety to one of solemnity as her hand dropped from mine arid she moved more quickly away from me, forcing my untrained feet to a half-run through the stalks of grass.

"Well," she said, "we ought to show them. We just ought to show them what we feel about that."

"What do you mean?"

"Forget it," she said and indeed, although I persisted, she would say nothing else. After a while I took her unresisting hand and stroked it, noting the soft leverage of her palm, the way the flesh of her elbow blended into her upper arm, the way that arm became the shoulder meshed with the soft, interesting roundness of her breast. Looked at in that way, women could be vaguely exciting, I thought, particularly if the thrusting and thrashing of masturbation were imposed upon them. I found my arm heightening to grasp her, found my body, somewhat to its horrified fascination, pushing her against me, found that our walk became stumbling and eventually graceless.

"You don't know a thing, do you?" she said. "About how to handle a girl or like that, I mean."

"How could I?" I said frankly. "I haven't had that much experience."

"I didn't think you had." She made an intricate gesture, showed me how her waist could be drawn against my arm in a position that enabled us to walk without colliding, move without scraping against one another. It was more practical but I felt the vague excitation fade. Besides, I had another thought.

"The car," I said.

"What about it?"

"It's parked out on the road. Will it be safe there?"

"No one ever comes along. Besides, what if they do? It's an old car and no one could care about it less."

"Well, if it were stolen we would have to get back another way. And what would you tell your father?"

"He doesn't care."

"But still, what would we tell him?"

She gave that indulgent shake of the head more characteristic of women, perhaps, than any of the other "secondary sexual characteristics," and examined me darkly. "Sometimes," she said, "I ask myself what I'm doing. Why I'm bothering. Really I do."

"Bothering with what?"

"Oh, never mind," she said. We were at a halt now in what seemed to be the geometrical center of acres and acres of farmland; cattle at some vast distance from us reduced to minuscule proportions, stooped over grass, the sun unevenly glaring between clouds over us, the thin stem of a farmhouse sending out clouds of irrelevant smoke through the meadow. There was the feeling of entrapment in limitless space, a feeling which I have heard ascribed to psychotics or those on the borderline of function. The impact of this vastness as I took it in was such that I had to kneel, almost in the penitential posture, my hands slipping gracelessly to the ground as I tried to pretend that I was examining grass stalks. Within me fluttered the first forecast of a genuine panic; the kind of panic I had not undergone for a long time and surely not in any circumstances like these.

"What's wrong with you now?"

"I just felt dizzy for a minute. I'll get right up. It's sure a nice-looking big place, isn't it?"

She shook her head and inhaled poisonously. "Maybe we should go back. You could get some tea and go to bed. We wouldn't want you getting sick your first summer in the country."

But, recapitulating phylogeny again, I had made it from knees to hands and knees to feet alone to an upright posture and stood in a position of careful equivocation, my face sidewise to the sun, squinting against the bright flickers of light which I perceived in the meadow. Marie-Jean looked at me incuriously and then must have seen something.

"I think you've got a little stroke," she said. "Heat stroke, I mean. We can get you under that tree."

"Heat stroke? What is that?"

"It's when the sun boils your brains."

Now that my condition had a name, a diagnosis and—indubitably—a prognosis, I felt myself on the verge of recovery already. Limply, I permitted her to lead me to a large apple tree which overhung a near corner of the meadow, a corner formed by the joining of two small patches of wire fence. Why the fence was there or what its purpose was I never gathered, but as I reached a hand out to touch it, she snatched it back with an exhalation of absolute fury. "It's electrified," she whispered. "What are you trying to do to yourself, anyway?"

I wasn't sure. I permitted her to pat the ground underneath the tree where I would lay, then I sat down at full-length, hands supporting me behind my back and considered the mischievous sun.

She sat beside me and sighed. I sighed back to show her that I was responsive.

"Do you know this tree?" she asked.

"This tree? How would I know it?"

"I thought maybe in your other life you would have known it. Everybody has another life, you know; there are two parts of us and they never meet, not even for a second. Somebody, somewhere right now is just the same person as you are, thinking the same thoughts that you do, but you'll never meet. He might be a mile away or in China. But he could have seen this tree. My other person must have seen this tree because I can tell you how many apples there are on it without even looking."

Her mysticism fascinated me. It was a new way of looking at things. It might even function as a kind of explanation for my masturbation: what was my other self doing at this precise moment? Was he readying his supplies, readying his guns, readying his hands and possibilities in a litter of magazines preparing to turn loose the jets? The metaphysics were intricate, granted their efficacy they would explain everything, even the violent turning of moods. "How many apples are there?" I asked her.

"Fifteen. Two of them are rotten and eight are very small. The rest are pretty good but you can't tell the difference from the outside."

I turned to count but the sun was dazzling; I decided to take her on faith. "Where would your other self be, now?" I asked.

"Oh, I don't know. Maybe somewhere in a bazaar in Bombay or Paris or something like that. What's the difference; it really doesn't matter. I know this tree in a different way, I've seen it myself."

"Your other self?"

"My own self. I was here last year, right under this tree. I was with a man and we lay under it for a long time."

"Oh," I said, and asked pointlessly, "Who was the man?"

I thought she would slap me. But the impulse must have dissipated as soon as it had come because she only sighed, very deeply and stretched out, her arms behind her head, her small eyes well-shielded by huge dark glasses. In this position her breasts upthrust slightly and then, as if in reaction to new stresses of physics, began to settle slowly upon her body, diminishing and flattening, the more vigorous outlines receding as her dress became fuller. It occurred to me that she was not wearing a supportive garment and before I knew what I was doing—the sun had boiled my brains as well as stricken them—I had reached out a childishly curious fingertip and had begun some idiot strokes near the center of the outline in verification. She groaned slightly and twitched, then permitted me to continue. Her eyes closed.

"You're not wearing anything."

"Yes I am. I'm wearing a dress."

"I mean under the dress."

"What's the difference? Do you mind?"

"Why should I mind? Those are your breasts."

"Yes," she said, "those are my breasts. What did you think they were, anyway?"

"I didn't mean that. I never touched a breast before. I mean, I never touched anyone's breast."

She quivered and I thought for a moment that she was going to sit upright. But I held my palm flat against her chest and the pressure must have convinced her otherwise. She licked her lips, her small chin hard as she turned her face sideways toward me. "Why?" she said, "Why do you think I'd want to know a thing like that?"

"Well, I was just telling you—"

"Why were you telling me? What's the difference? Who cares and who wants to know? Is there something really wrong with you?"

That made four questions in succession; it was difficult to be systematic, particularly since the slow grazing of my hand had continued unstopped and had begun to produce for the first time an answering pressure in my groin, a feeling of ominous potential growing, growing; a blind animal in the pocket of my trousers poking for an exit. It was a feeling similar to but yet entirely unlike the symptoms of self-abuse, and I was entirely discomfited by it. Her last question seemed easiest to answer so I said, "There's nothing wrong with me as far as I know. I was just being honest with you. What's wrong with a person being honest?"

"Squeeze harder. Squeeze harder around the tip. I want to feel your fingernail."

"Can't anybody tell the truth anymore?"

"I want to feel your fingers digging all around me now. Yes, like that. I don't care, hurt me a little bit."

"I just wanted you to know where I stand."

Her breathing was moist and ragged. "I've got to get my dress off," she said, sighing and getting off her back, putting her hands behind her to work on the zipper. "I've got to get it off right now. Damn you, damn you; why do you always do things like this to me? Isn't it enough that I'm made this way that these things have to happen?

Don't rip it, just get it off gently. I can't come home in a torn dress."

No tailor or dressmaker, I did my amateur's best, got the fabric down to somewhere between her diaphragm and navel and she did the rest, moving the material in slow jerks—the dress had been very tight—to her waist. I looked upon her. I looked upon the breasts of woman for the first time. My mother's did not count, let alone the ones in the magazine. For the only time in my career I sat stricken, soundless and astounded, studying, almost with a medical precision, what was nude before me.

In retrospect, it is quite clear to me that Marie-Jean had bad breasts. They were full, yes, but of that premature pendulousness which seems to afflict the one unlucky schoolgirl out of ten; breasts that could already have nursed a battery of quintuplets, breasts that had the odd, wrinkled convoluted look of having been assaulted by an army; the nipples drawn in upon themselves, mysterious, dried, giving a bluish overcast to her flesh. Free swinging, they might have touched her navel, although this was something not to be determined; using her own feminine cleverness she had immediately settled again upon her back where her breasts fell out expressionlessly to the two sides, looking as any woman's might have in that position, telling nothing. She raised her arms and drew me to them wearily, almost as if she had resigned herself, with a kind of foreknowledge, to a disaster before it happened. I brought my lips to her nipple with precision. I encircled it, holding back my teeth so as not to nip her. I drew her into me and I began to suck rapidly, mechanically, wondering idly all the time with a high, removed consciousness what my Other was doing at this precise moment, who he was coupled with: was it Marie-Jean's other? More likely he was masturbating, I decided. I heard my own moans with a clinical ear; they were similar to those I made when accosting the magazines. It all appeared to be the same thing.

"Fascinating," I observed to D'Arcy. "Your initial sexual contact and the way in which it was inaugurated. Truly, in retrospect, the auspiciousness, the sheer auspiciousness, of all this is absolutely astounding!"

"Will you keep quiet?" he said harshly. "I was only pausing for a moment. Can't you see I'm talking?"

"But of course—"

"Sometimes," D'Arcy said, "you can be damned offensive. Damnably offensive. Remind me of that afterwards if you will."

I entered a timeless space, dreaming, dreaming. There is a blankness; I do not know what went on between the time my lips first touched her breasts and the moment, some suspended eons later, that I felt the urgent flapping of her hips, felt her hands descend below my belt level and begin to fumble with both my genitalia and hers. Her voice absent for so long, returned. "Get it off," she was saying, "and hurry for God's sake. Hurry, hurry. And don't stop biting. Keep it up. Faster, faster."

How I managed to dislodge myself of my lower garments while not breaking that fragile upper contact I will never know. But my masturbatory experiences had stood me well: how I was able to simultaneously fumble the pages of the magazine to the proper picture and at the same time encourage and whip out my jetstream is similarly a mystery. But, finally, I was bare below the waist, pressing my heaviness against her, against the rough fabric that lay between her legs as she moaned and twisted her hips and with several tearing sounds got her own garments down. Body to body we clung to one another and she seized her breasts in both hands, now apparently uncaring of the consequences of close examination and slammed their blue-tinted network even deeper into my frantic mouth and I felt the rising, the idiot rising against her. There was a wetness, a dripping, slippery wetness in the joining of thigh to thigh and I suspected that it had something to do with what we were doing to her breasts. I kept it on. It was perfectly all right with me. I wanted to make her happy. I didn't have the faintest idea of what to do.

No idea whatsoever. She spread her thighs wider and wider and I tumbled between them, feeling the grittiness of her hair bouncing up and down against mine; she seized me with limp fingers and attempted to direct me toward the orifice, and still I had no idea of what she wanted. Entrance was the answer, of course, but if I achieved it, how was I possibly going to satisfy myself? And what did it mean to her? What was getting inside there going to matter to her thighs?

She answered by screaming somewhere in her throat and forcing herself further up against me so that it was either to make the connection or to fall off completely. Balancing myself gracelessly, trying to poise between one and the other, I fell off indeed, sliding off her thighs and legs to lie beside her, still squeezing and manipulating her dangling breasts, now even the more violently to make up for my *faux-pas*. But she fought me; she fought me bitterly; her breasts no longer an offering but a withdrawal, and as I tried to maintain the contact by closing my mouth tighter around them, even a hint of teeth, she brought both her hands up to them and dragged them away inch by inch until she were separate. I heard her voice. It was apparent that she had been talking for a long, long time. "What are you doing, will you get in there; are you crazy or something, and a pervert, too? Don't you even know where it is or what you're supposed to do? Stick it in there," and then she cursed me with words that I had never known were available to women, were available to their gentle consciousness. Uneasily I attempted to wheel back over her and felt her fingers fumbling on me, then, with great difficulty and a kind of heavy, wet sobbing noise, an insertion of some kind must have been made because I felt my organ, as it were, being dragged up a clinging tunnel, much wetter than my hand and much tighter but at the same time not as well contoured, not as responsive, certainly, to its familiar needs as the hand had been. Her voice and words had passed, for the two of us, beyond comprehension and she must have stopped then, the movement of her aborted larynx being transferred down to her hips which stamped and thrashed.

I didn't know what I was doing. It occurred vaguely to me that Marie-Jean was masturbating, was using me to masturbate with instead of her own fingers—assuming they used their fingers; I hadn't the faintest idea of how they functioned—but if this were so, it imposed upon me the storming necessity to finish myself. But I had no idea of how it was done; impossible as it may seem, I was utterly unprepared to come off in the tent of a woman. Her breasts, forgotten and almost contemptible, sagged under my astonished eyes and then she began to moan in a voice I had never heard before; both low and simpering, idiot and uncheckable it sounded as my own mother's did when she was in the presence of small animals. This final horror unleashed a frenzy of bucking and churning and so, in a sense, I did the best that I could for her; I did what I knew.

And as I did so I felt a strange detachment, my prick, aimlessly colliding with that long, empty tunnel seemed no longer a part of me, no longer truly grasped by my body, but only an appendage maintained at some great distance from the flesh: wholly irrelevant, wholly lost. What sensibility and attention there was seemed contrived in my skull alone, my eyes looking incuriously on a patch of grass some feet behind us, a burnt-out section where small holes suggested the infestation and passage of vermin and I fixated upon it with fascination, then, as I compared the scurrying of the vermin into their known depths with my own infestation in the nether regions. She began to slap my face raggedly, irregularly, her small palms colliding against my cheeks and began to talk again and for a moment I had no awareness of what she was saying but then meaning coalesced and the words flickered into reason: *do it, you bastard*, she was saying to me, *can't you come, can't you do anything but flop there, finish, finish, finish*, and her fingertip grazed, my lip and tongue and her other hand, drawing me down again in search of her breasts was only able, because of her spasmodic movements, to mesh me with her breast. To return there was to recapitulate something that was already far gone; I thought, biting, that it was pointless because I'd already been there before, nothing that had been known as I had known her breasts could ever be known again but as she shuddered and spread the flattened surfaces with her other hand so that I could take in more and more, a great flame of revelation opened up before me and suddenly I understood. I understood everything. There was a whining and whickering in my loins, the first sludge of damnation pressing and pressing, and I saw what I had to see. I knew everything.

You beat off inside them. What you did in your skull was your own business; there was no way they could possibly know what was going on in there nor could they care—because the sensibility alone was inviolate—but what your skull permitted you to do you did and only results counted. Perhaps it was this way; perhaps it had always been that way and I had never understood, all those years of history, all those years of frantic scuttling on the periphery all wasted, wasted, because at last I understood the meaning of it all: *it didn't matter as long as you had the results. All that they wanted were results; the rest of it was your business.* They didn't care. They didn't care. They had their own problems; they had their own skulls. No one could ever know what went on inside them and it didn't matter.

I saw it all.

I was a night-creature, a stifled bird circling darkly at an immense height over the prairies; I was a scuttling rodent traversing the fields; I was a prowling mammal seeking his mate over far distances: I was all of these and others as well as her arms bit and tore at the back of my neck and I felt myself sliding through the ring, through the center, to the core. In that explosion of mystery I found the dark center, reaching toward it, distended at enormous length (her breasts and nipples batting against me) reaching toward a final discovery which would be as placid and immutable as the face of the moon (my tongue fell from her breasts, my face squeezed into her shoulder), a revelation beyond insight that would justify all of it (*unh, unh, unh,* somebody went) and would blow me free at last from my accursed history (*uh, uh*) into a cavern of final knowledge where all things would be glimpsed (*uh*) and ordered, touched and seen and I was reaching, reaching, moving toward that final dark target, that center and there was a pulsing (*uh, ah*) and a long, whimpering slide ending with a convulsion and thrashing and bucking and moaning we moved twitching on the grass and that was the way it finished, the last drops beaten off and out, the last inch of conjoinment made, and then as it subsided to a whickering and pointless decline I felt the most convulsive shock of all, a shock which drew me out along all the fibers of my being, dividing and imploding me, causing all the fragments to jar out scattering and I kicked and thrashed again in something close to pain and screamed into her cheek as she fought and fought and finally threw me off her.

I lay on the grass panting.

"You silly bastard," Marie-Jean said to me, "you silly, silly bastard, you went into the fence."

I turned on my stomach and inspected the grass as the shuddering went through in little rivulets and ripples, pinning me to the good, green earth of home, the tested earth of pain and knowledge.

"Can't you *ever* watch what you're doing?" she said.

"Don't you even know *what* you're doing?" she said.

"I must interject a comment at this time," I said, putting aside my pen and leaning toward D'Arcy. "I hope you'll forgive me but obviously I'm not in a position to interrupt a recollection here; that recollection is obviously complete. It seems to me that this first sexual contact of yours was not as masturbatory as you may feel but did, indeed, in most ways resemble the initial contact of most males. After all," and finally it was a relief and pleasure to express myself uninterrupted at some length; D'Arcy was fascinating, the most fascinating and provocative man in the whole sexual history of the world but sometimes he *did* have a tendency to monopolize the focus entirely; even beyond a biographee's license, "after all," I repeated, "this is a strongly masturbatory culture as you yourself pointed out earlier, and the sheer transition from masturbation to copulation, then, can be rather a difficult one. Granted all of this, granted the masturbation-orientation of your early pubescence and middle-adolescence, in short, we can only say that you functioned commendably under the circumstances. I see no reason at all for the overlay of guilt which seems to accompany these reminiscences, this particular incident. The important thing is that you did well by her.

"The important thing is that you did well by her," I said again, leaning forward to make the point more emphatically, "as far as she was concerned you performed as a male in a masculine way and toward the accustomed end. The business of touching the electrified fence at the conclusion, as a matter of fact, might be interpreted as sheer metaphor rather than disgrace; you had found an objective-correlative, I am trying to say, for the feelings and sensations which had passed through you prior to that electrification. Now, if I might go on even further to say that her comment was by no means a deprecation but only that kind of whimsical comment which women, the best of women, the most experienced of women, tend to make after the act of intercourse, well then we should see that there is absolutely no reason for you to place capsulization upon this rather than upon the place where it really should be, which was the satisfactory and apparently mutual orgasm which you incited. So I think that we can thus put the incident in its proper place. Don't you?"

After a pause during which D'Arcy made no comment, I said, "After all, you must not be so self-deprecatory. There is really no reason for it. Don't you think that what I have said makes a good deal of sense?"

And when he still said nothing, I put the question to him in the strongest possible terms. "Of course, I might be entirely wrong about this," I said. "Tell me what you think of it."

But there were to be no more answers that evening, no more recapitulations, no more discussions. For, his fine-boned head sinking slowly upon his chest, his chest moving nearer and nearer in slump to his knees, my friend, my dear friend D'Arcy, my testament, my vindication, my pursuit, had fallen into the rosiest and most gentle of slumbers. His head bobbed unevenly in his clasped hands.

I stole from him as silently as possible, not wishing to embarrass him with the knowledge that he had not listened to what I had been saying, and I found a nest of my own.

SEVEN

Today I had a long discussion with one of the doctors in this institution. It occurred within the sacristy of his office, within easy earshot, I suppose, of guards and attendants, and I have no doubt that every word I spoke was recorded to be discussed at the administrative level sometime later. But it was an extremely fruitful discussion nevertheless and bears upon the present project. I find it very difficult to function under these circumstances. I wish there were a little less persecution hereabouts, to say nothing of the dim shouts which infest the corridors at the oddest hours.

He started out—a thin, pale, almost desiccated young man who wore the faint mantle of obsession with that casual grace which only the truly accustomed can bear—by asking me how I felt about the institution in general, and my ambitions in particular. "It's only a matter of time," he said, rather vaguely, "until this comes to a head, you know. We need as much information as possible preparatory to making our final decision."

"Final decision for what?" I asked reasonably enough, lighting a cigarette with a magnificent gesture and throwing the match with a *ping* into the ashtray with a graceful generosity of motion which fully encapsulated my contempt for the institution, its occupants and this particular, most unpleasant, personage. "That is the question I'd like answered at the present time."

"Well, you know," he said rather vaguely. "Decision to do this, decision to do that. Disposition I guess is a better word. Are you getting along more satisfactorily with your roommates these days?"

"I have no relationship with my roommates. I have no desire to pretend that I do. The question you should ask, assuming that any question is in order here, is how I am getting along with myself."

"Well, then, how *are* you getting along with yourself?"

"Splendidly," I said, a bit stiffly. "I have never been more conscious of my interior depths, never have I functioned more in accordance with my secret because most basic needs. I have reached that moment of blending, you see, in which ambition can be almost instantly translated into accomplishment; this being the major function of the human psyche, I would say."

"Ambition and accomplishment. In what way?" He took one of my cigarettes absently and began to toy with it, looking, perhaps, for traces of some drug which would render explicable my buoyancy. After a moment or two of shredding, he took one of my matches and tried to duplicate my own lighting-gesture, failed miserably, and with a subsiding puff of embarrassment settled back into his chair. I could not resist the juvenile impulse to giggle; a lapse of dignity which is always permissible during moments of cosmic amusement.

"You remind me of my friend D'Arcy," I said.

"Oh? How and in what way?"

"You have the same gestures. The same flick of wrist, the same intensity. Also, the same imitativeness. This is not to mean that D'Arcy was a slavish follower; it only means that he found some of my gestures wholly admirable and tried to emulate them."

He ignored this promising line of speculation which would have led to a discussion of that peculiar role-reversal which seemed to come over us in the last days (why did D'Arcy find himself subsumed by the personality of his biographer?) and said instead in a most pedestrian fashion, "this D'Arcy. We've been hearing a lot about him recently and I note from a careful study of your case record," and he patted a large, grey folder on his desk, an irregularly shaped oblong from which protruded in violent, contradictory disarray greasy papers with the suggestion of typing on them; it was depressing to think that all that they thought they knew of me might be within those confines, "that the name of D'Arcy is quite prominent. Perhaps you'd like to tell me a little more about him."

"Not particularly," I said. "D'Arcy, after all, is not confined here. I am. Under the circumstances—to make him a tenant by proxy, I am trying to say—it would be irrelevant at best, destructive at worst to concentrate upon him unduly."

He put his hands behind his neck and sighed, tipping his chair back at a disastrous angle and recovering only in the nick of time. The brief flare of panic before the recovery brought his face to light as I had never seen it before; it was the face of a juvenescent so swaddled in his role as no longer to be convinced of his identity and I wanted, somehow, to apprise him of this, show him that I had credentials and tools of insight at least the equal of his, but before I could say anything, he said, with a hint of asperity, "Why do you talk that way anyway? I mean it's off the record but I really like to know."

"Why do I talk what way? I'm not sure I understand."

"Your rhetoric. The jumble of your sentences. I mean, why do you find it necessary to speak in the most tortuous fashion? Nobody here talks like you. It's difficult to understand a thing you say. Frankly, you talk as if you come from the pages of a bad old novel. Why do you find it necessary to hide your tensions behind these convolutions?"

"I am entitled to the way I speak," I said, as grandly as I could, "and you are entitled to your opinions on it but I think, frankly, that your comments are ill-meant and ill-spoken. *I* didn't ask to be brought here, after all, and *I* didn't ask for this interview. I'll be very happy to go at once to my quarters if you will only say the word. I might point out, however, that the biographer, one overtaken by the biographical obligation I should say, cannot be blamed for a rhetoric which in many cases is not his. Language has the aspect of a chameleon after all."

Having been so undercut—on the horns of his own processes, so to speak—my interrogator was left with nothing to say, nothing to pursue. He commenced therefore, to ask me some of the more conventional questions about my youth, predilections, and sexual outlook.

I responded as well as able. There is little reason for me to dissemble on these topics because, as I have been trying to impress upon these people from the first, I am not the relevant party; I am but the extension of D'Arcy who is subject to my object. To take an unnatural (or even routine) interest in my own habits and background is as sensible as it would be to investigate the fisherman who caught the fish for the more Freudian implications of his act. Indeed my very presence in these corridors is the outcome of purest accident; an explosion of coincidences and incidents so pointless as to reduce everything which followed to anticlimax. It is hardly possible to say at the present time that I have an identity in fact; most biographers do not. I therefore responded, as I say, freely and frankly, even embroidering some recollections for his greater interest. Uninterrupted except for certain cues I must have spoken upwards of an hour and three-quarters, describing juvenile impressions, juvenile repulsions, juvenile intimations, telling him the flat truth or that representation of it which seems to render the Profession content, all the time intricately disassembling into several divisions small sheets of paper which had been thoughtfully placed before me for diversion. It was not so much reaching a point of conclusion, eventually, as it was equivocation; what I had left to say seemed merely to be a reconstituent of what I had already said. So I slid down into my seat and looked at him, aware only at that moment that his face, in its whitened, flattened intensity, seemed to be floating against the background of the walls; a fish suspended in a sea of board. The second thing I noted when I tried to apprise him of this was that I literally found talking difficult; my larynx and vocal cords having been swollen to outsized proportions by my reminiscences. So I settled for clearing my throat in a noncommittal fashion, and settling again upon one of the pieces of paper, making it clear to my interrogator that it was his turn to speak; that I had nothing to say.

"That is fairly interesting," he said finally. "Particularly the episodes of torture. I hadn't realized that your background contained incidents of this nature. I would have thought—"

"Backgrounds contain whatever their fullest potential is toward containing," I said, aware with a distant pleasure that I had gotten off what one of my roommates would call a *mot*, "and nothing else. There is no irregularity other than in the ear of the auditor."

"But what you say happened to you; surely it must have been highly disturbing. Don't you feel—"

"I am utterly divorced from my history," I said, folding my hands over my belly in a parody of his own pose. "I exist merely in terms of my apprehension, my role, so to speak. I told you that everything I said would be of the most impudent irrelevance—"

"Tell me," he said, apparently musing. "During this particular cellar incident you described: the business with the tar and the three youths, didn't you feel—"

"I am tired," I said. "Unless I am wrong, we have exceeded the statutory limit of these conversations by almost twice its length. I would far prefer to rest."

"You don't have to show hostility, you know. You aren't the only person who ever wound up like this. You can't withdraw from everything; sooner or later you have to come to grips—"

"I am not in the least hostile," I said, noting my even pulse, my placidity. "I am only at an end and I think, unless you feel very differently, that we should adjourn."

His face took on the bleak, frustrated look of the juvenile it was shielding; then moderated toward a slow, confident smugness. "Well," he said, "there's always tomorrow, isn't there?"

"If you wish."

"Tomorrow will be another day."

"It always has been."

"You realize that this works two ways. I've given you a lot of extra time today. I happen to find you a uniquely fascinating individual, you understand. Uniquely fascinating."

I gave a modest shrug. "There's nothing particularly interesting about me. I am only D'Arcy's *ficelle* as I have said time and again. Surely, D'Arcy is the one you would want to investigate."

"But D'Arcy isn't here, is he?"

"No," I said, "He isn't."

"Not even the littlest piece of him?"

"I doubt it," I said. "Surely no such crusader, such a pervading force as D'Arcy would be found in such an institution, let alone be confined to it for any period of time. I am highly submissive ... That's why D'Arcy is the man you'll want to investigate."

"But we can't, can we?"

"No."

"Because he isn't here."

"That is perfectly correct," I said. "He is not here."

"Well then, where is he?"

"I don't understand."

"On the contrary," he said. "I think you understand me perfectly well. If this D'Arcy is, you say, nowhere here, where might he be?"

"I can't answer that."

"I didn't think you could."

"I have no idea whatsoever where he might be. It's not my affair, after all."

"Why?"

"Because I was merely his biographer. I was taking down his biography for publication. When our work was complete there was no reason to continue our relationship. Despite its affectional overtones, it was purely business in origin; I can understand that now. There was no reason to presume there to be more in our relationship than any one between customer and client. I mean, serviceman and customer, of course. After that work was done he went one way and I went the other. Being here intervened."

"Where is this book, this biography? Have you published it yet?"

"No," I said. "I'm in the process of writing it."

"Oh, so that's how you spend your time here."

"Some of it. It's hard work, though, so I need breaks in between. Can't anything be done about my roommates?"

"We'll see. So you have no idea where this D'Arcy might be now."

"None whatsoever; no more than he would know where I am. I think one of my roommates is not a patient, you know. I found out his secret the other night."

"Ah," he said. "What secret?"

But I saw, at last, that I had gone too far. Not immutable, not locked in the cell of self but all too frail in the presence of attention I had exceeded my limits, the limits of a reasonable, sane man. "Forget this," I said, standing and rather grandly bringing my clothes around me so that the effect, had I been properly garbed, would have been Victorian rather than vaguely disreputable. "I'm going to go, now."

"But don't you want to tell me about your roommate?"

"Not today," I said. "Not now. Some other time. I will not discuss it."

"But this secret you said you had discovered."

"I want to leave now," I said, strongly. "I definitely want to leave now and if I am detained there will be a scene."

"But what about D'Arcy? Weren't you going to tell me something more about D'Arcy?"

"No," I said. I went to the door and began to pound upon it with my open hands, howling at the same time for an attendant. Hastily he came to my side and with the use of a key opened it and allowed me, somewhat reluctantly, to move hastily into the corridor. His face held a wistful, pathetic glare and I could not resist laughing.

"Are you laughing for D'Arcy, now?" he asked.

Not wishing to hurt his feelings I said, "That's exactly right. I am laughing for D'Arcy."

"Why? Why?"

But I had had enough; I was no longer confined. I commenced a gazelle's trot down the corridor, gathered into myself. Behind me I could hear his shout, *why? why?* increased in momentum as my own speeding along to intercept me, but I was faster and evaded it. *Why? why?* he shrieked, and there seemed to be other questions as well: questions like *Who is D'Arcy?* and *Why are you doing this?* and *Where did D'Arcy go?* and *Don't you understand that your childhood—?*, but I was gone now; I was gone way out of sight; I was beyond the catching, speeding around corridors as fast as night, squealing through the hush of the hallways like the coming dawn, into the space of my own vacant room where I closed the lockless door and leaned against it for some time listening to my laughter ripple down the scale past sobs to silence and then at last I was ready to remove all my garments, put them in the wardrobe and resume once again my biography of D'Arcy. With luck my roommates, both reporting in on me, would be gone for several hours. I would have thought far more about the nature of the interview and certain intricate elements of luck but as always the seizure of recollection came over me and left me quite committed, quite drained; unable then to pursue all but the most rational thoughts for the next several hours.

EIGHT

"I am in an increasingly foul mood these days," D'Arcy said the following evening, once again holding the inevitable chilled tumbler of wine. We had passed most of the day in slumber, awakening only in the late afternoon to go in search of a modest meal and replenishments for D'Arcy's wine bottles and now, the last exhausted output of the sun streaming in through his windows, we had both succumbed to a late-afternoon spell of contemplation. His mood still seemed as sullen, however, as mine was generous, leading to some trepidation as I replied to him.

"I hope it has nothing to do with me," I said.

"Well, in part it does. You are, if I may speak frankly, a rather repulsive person; parasitic, demanding and utterly without insight. But since most people follow this pattern in one way or the other, I cannot say that this is the prime source of discontent; I have fucked many a woman stupider than you and whose cunt was no clear compensation. No, I think it must be your wretched biography that is doing this to me. That would be the explanation."

"My biography? But it was your inspiration."

"No," he said with vague unease. "It was yours. I was perfectly happy to allow my history to be its own biography; accept judgment in preliterate terms. But you wanted to structure and systematize it all through the written word."

"I have had your utmost cooperation," I pointed out to him. "Not at any point have you refused to continue."

"That would explain the foulness of my mood. No man's life should be exacted out of him the way we have done in the last few days. The putrefaction, the corruption, the small swinishness and greed! I had never before realized the essential triviality from which my greatness springs."

"But it is your greatness," I said, "and is thus inextricably bound to origins. You can hardly separate the one from the other."

"No one can justify this," D'Arcy growled. "Hardly on spiritual grounds."

"All right," I said, judiciously enough, pouring myself some rich burgundy from an available decanter and resisting a mad urge to upset the remainder of the contents on the carpet; it would have served him right. The obduracy, the self-indulgence of genius! Often one wonders how anything ever gets done. "Do you want to call a halt to the project? Is that what you indicate to me?"

"It would be impossible," D'Arcy said unhappily, standing to look at himself in the mirror, the reflection casting back dim fire into the room from the one bulb centered over the wooden frame. "It would be a coitus interruptus of the soul, as they say. We had better continue."

"Then consider me as ready."

"But nothing compels me to think of this as a happy project, nor to cease my resentment."

"Most great works are unhappy," I said.

"And great workmen." He sat. "I believe I had finished my discussion of that afternoon with Marie-Jean which I foreshadowed at the beginning, the very beginning of these reminiscences. I left us lying in the field, my still shuddering frame suspended only several inches from the tingling fence itself."

"That would be right," I said.

He paused to contemplate for a while and then went headlong into his narrative. Before he did so, however, he made a rather astonishing remark, one which to this moment I simply cannot interpret:

"I haven't been fucked in so long," D'Arcy said, "that I'm beginning to doubt that I was ever fucked at all. There's such an accretion built up back from my testes that I may be mistaking simple semen for recollection. But when you do it, it all comes out the same way."

I would like to say (D'Arcy continued in the face of my stupefaction, and gradually I became caught up with his narrative, the wine decanter between us now being used at a fearful pace) that my first fuck utterly changed my life; vitiated me of sentimental ignorance, made clear my position in relation to the abstract carnality I had so shockingly (and with such fulfillment) faced, but this would only be an idealization of the matter. The incident was obviously crucial; in fact absolutely central to the astonishing events which followed and eventually culminated my journey ... but the transition far from being abrupt was so agonizingly slow that the untutored observer would not even have been aware that a transition had occurred.

I sat awkwardly, uneasily beside Marie-Jean on the return home. From time to time, I would try to say something; offer a remark which would both normalize our relationship and yet intimate that I knew the import of the events that had occurred, but everything I said seemed more disastrous than the last, and all remarks I made being met with a pout or a sneer I soon subsided into a sulk of my own, watching the insects mash the windowpane with a rustling sound; seeing the endless shoreland of the country plunge toward and then recede from us; all unchanged in the action. "I guess that was good for you," was what I had said, and also, "You never really know what it's like until you do it, isn't that the truth?" and "I guess things were pretty silly when I backed into the wire but it really wasn't my fault you know, the damned thing was too near," all of this said with a disaffected post-adolescent's giggle while I looked at her unyielding profile locked in frieze above the steering post, her stunned eyes, from that aspect, seeming to take me in as merely another bit of countryside flora as she drove, the grey roads whickering, the sun receding behind us, my drained loins panting out their own measure of discontent. My state of mind, to be sure, could not be seen as an entirely stable one. Nevertheless, there was potential, at that time, for exiting from the situation without disgrace: I had functioned in a not entirely inappropriate manner and my secret—for Secret was what I now suspected it to be—was sheathed within the cove of that efficacy. But matters were not left at that point. I never left matters at a proper point. I felt constrained to tell Marie-Jean that my first experience with sex had been so pleasant that all I could hope, at this time, was that there would be another such engagement shortly.

"Why?" she said, bypassing a truck dangerously with one elbow dangling at a careless angle over the wheel, the other making flickering motions as she went for a cigarette from some obscure feminine place. "Why would that be? Why do you want it again?"

"Well, it was very nice. Pleasant I mean. I thought—"

"It will never be again," she said, finding her cigarette, and jamming it between her lips with awkwardness but a good deal of certainty. From one angle she was able to eject flame, at the same time curving the car to narrowly avoid two solemn cattle who had come to peer at the road from an incautious point. I felt the jolt as a series of small shocks radiating through my thighs and up through my limbs, a slow poisoned dripping, a series of intimations against a discovered doom. "It will never be again," she said.

"Why not? Do you want me to hold your cigarette for you while you drive? Look out, they have wagons and stones all over these roads."

"Because a purpose served is a purpose earned," she said obscurely, narrowly missing an abutment and wrenching the car back to the highway with what seemed like renewed determination. A truck scrambled past, a dim face floating in a windowpane seemed to be addressing us. "And a purpose earned is a purpose finished," and that is all I could get out of my Marie-Jean, my darling, my familiar, my first ally of commitment, all the way home. We rumbled through American roads, American interpasses, American cloverleafs in that sullen and perfect silence which I was always afterwards to identify with the postcoital shock, and back to the resort with the smashed bodies of dead flies clustered on the windowpane arranged in a pattern of tribute that seemed almost floral. We pulled in front of what had been jocularly entitled by the host the "Homing Area" and got out of the car silently, Marie-Jean kicking a few of the fenders seemingly to verify that the car was still connected and then brushing off the flies with a series of absent gestures which dumped the majority of them into the grill. I felt it necessary to accompany her into her home; it was, after all, a "date" and even a "first date" had certain responsibilities. The light bones of her elbow rested lightly, cohesively in my hands, as we flung open the doors with a series of booming sounds and entered into the indescribably musty area of the "happy room" itself, a room dotted with numerous grey couches which the host had specified for the comfort of guests during "social hours." It was in such circumstances and in such a position that we discovered my mother in the violent embrace of the social director himself, the two of them locked to the rear cushions of the largest couch of all, their bodies fluttering and trembling much as our windshield flies had been doing on the moment of contact. They were entirely naked and I noted with a kind of wicked precision the beating of limbs upon one another, a series of motions which alternately hid and exposed all that my mother had to offer anyone. Marie-Jean gave a dull sound which emerged in the quick attention of the room as more of a thump than squeal and pelted toward the stairs. I was left to bear the confrontation. Under the circumstances I think I did very well. And my mother's behavior, given the complexities and difficulties of the situation was wholly admirable, so well-timed and relevant as to be almost purely metaphoric. I might note that for a woman in her middle 40's (or perhaps it was late 30's; she always shyly disassembled in this area and would never show me my birth certificate) my mother was interestingly constructed although, by no means, on a level with the girls in The Magazine or, for that matter, in the magazines.

"I thought you and the little slut were getting laid," is what she said. "What are you coming back this early for?"

In the fine surreal tension of the moment—a surrealism exacerbated by my realization that it was true, the implications I had felt to lie under the surface of human behavior were all entirely true: *everybody was doing it, no one was not doing it; there was nowhere you could go and no one with whom you could deal who was not consumed by the treasure of the idiot's gift*—I said, "We did. But we finished early. I touched a high-tension wire."

My mother giggled thinly and at that moment, the social director himself appeared, his body sliding slowly, like a panel of wood, from under the breadth of my mother's embrace and he peered cautiously past me, into the surfaces of the room as if they would tell him all that he needed to know about the ramifications of human behavior. A bridge table, near the corner of the room murmured sympathetically and then collapsed gracelessly to one side of its legs, apparently affected by the penetration of his gaze and wanting to make some comment, no matter how lenient, upon the situation.

"This is impossible," he said. "This is clearly impossible. How can I be in such a situation?" My mother stood up uneasily, crossing her legs and began to forage under the couch, perhaps in search of her clothes. Her exposed rump seemed to me, then, to solidify all the horrors through which I had passed under the wires; I turned my eyes lest an insolent gleam destroy us entirely. "Perhaps you should ask yourself that question," she said. "The boy isn't able to answer you."

"You had my daughter," the social director said. "You possessed my daughter. My Marie-Jean. My only child. You parted her and went inside. You drifted into her. You sullied her. And now you come back to confront me. My daughter. My single child, my only substance."

"I didn't mean to," I said. "It just happened."

"Leave the boy alone," my mother said, extracting various items and articles and beginning to get into them piecemeal; she looked like a woman in a clear state of transition, perhaps being forced to a new level of feeling as she drew on concentricities, layers of silk, poise. "I told you she was a little slut, didn't I? Didn't I?"

"Why I could kill you, you dishonoring thief," he said, but made no move to leave the couch and do so; his eyes seemed blank, rather, suspended in a kind of confusion, a fine, flickering greyness catching the dull light of the room off-angle. "That is, if I wanted to."

"It doesn't mean a thing to me," I said pointlessly. "All of it. I mean, I see it everywhere now and it all comes down to the same kind of thing. What does it matter? What's the difference?"

"I bet you liked it too."

"Oh come on, now," my mother said, brushing him tentatively with a finger while at the same time she began to arrange her dress on several levels, patting it in accommodation to her body. As I equated her developing appearance with what I now knew to lie beneath it, I felt a shock of collision, a fine, vaulting insight, one which I would not be able to correlate for several years but whose apprehension, at that time, I must have fully possessed. *It was all the same, underneath.* "He's incapable of liking anything and he's really too confused now to put his feelings in order. A disaster is a disaster, why can't you face facts? I'd finish you but the whole thing would be ruined."

"My only daughter."

"If I *did* finish you, you'd hate me for it anyway," my mother said calmly, drawing on the last rudiments of her apparel, "and then you'd start on *me*. Well," she said with a splendid shrug, facing me, "I guess our vacation is over. Shall we go upstairs and pack?"

"I haven't even said goodbye to her."

"To who?"

"To Marie-Jean."

"You've said goodbye in the most appropriate manner, sweetheart. Anything more would spoil the effect."

"Oh, you bitches," the social director said, stretching out full-length on his back and rubbing his eyes. "Oh, you bitches. Isn't there any end to it? You try to start a business to make a few dollars and—"

"We can probably be home by this evening," my mother said, taking my hand in a tentative grasp. "Maybe a little earlier, it all depends. Well," she said, facing the social director, her profile now a jut of positiveness. "Well, we'll need transportation to the station. Also, there's the question of what we owe you? How much is the bill?"

"You just try to keep afloat and look what happens to you," the social director said. "The little bitch. Of course, she was just as bad in the city, I must admit that. I thought that the country would be a healthy influence on her. But instead she only does it in fields. She probably does it in cow flop. That shows the country for you."

"I said we'll need some transportation and we'll have a bill to settle," my mother said again. "I must give you credit, though, baby; before this little scene just now I was having some real doubts about your manhood. All those problems and those things that happened upstairs. I was beginning to think that your genitals were underdeveloped or that you were a sex freak or something. I can't tell you what a comfort this is. Of course it could have happened in better circumstances. Will you get dressed, damn it?"

"I am dressed," I said.

"I didn't mean you. You were probably dressed when you were doing it, if I know my son. Don't I know my son?"

The social director heaved himself up. "I can't understand it."

"Three and a half weeks. You'll give some sort of a reduction because we didn't eat breakfast; you promised that. But you can bill us for the ride to the station. Come on, we'll get packed," she said, and without even checking in verification, she left the room. I stumbled gracelessly after her, paused at the door; found that the social director and I were meshed in a long, wandering look. He covered his genitals which I took to be a healthy sign—we were, at least, responding to each other in an area of acknowledgment, now, and no proposal—and shook his head several times apparently in quest of some sort of equilibrium. "Your mother is a strange woman," he said. "A strange woman." He began to nestle a hand under the couch, apparently in search of his own garments.

I couldn't take it again. The spectacle of the social director, like my mother, drawing on an attitude along with his clothing and moving to some kind of firmness was too bewildering to anticipate. I left the room hurriedly, in search of the stairs, in search of some kind of flight. It was clear that unusual things had happened to me this afternoon, but I was not sure of their quality.

At the height of the landing I found Marie-Jean, her body poised in a full-scuttle between bedroom and bathroom, her hair askew, her breasts extruding from the undersized bathrobe she was wearing. She gave me one wild look and a crow of despair seemed to come from her but as I reached to touch her—to assure her of I know not what—the crow moderated to a scream and she retreated, her eyes sweeping me, into the cove of her bedroom and slammed the door emptily. Inside I could hear bursts of sound that could have accommodated any kind of human reaction.

My mother came into the hall tugging a large valise from which fragments of clothing protruded uneasily. "You," she said. "You better give me a hand with this. Are you ready to go? And why don't you say goodbye to the girl; she was nice to you. I wish people were as nice to me as that dear girl has been to you."

At this point in the recitation, D'Arcy paused for a long time, shifting on the web of his seat, his fingers outstretched but not touching the curved wine glass which lay before him on the table. Hesitant because I did not wish to interrupt his narrative or the thoughts which preceded it, and because I had already been lectured roundly on imprudence, I said nothing, but after some while it became apparent that he had, for the moment, nothing more to say; that he was, as a matter of fact, waiting for me to say something to him. I balanced my notebook idly on my knee and looked at the open, pleading intensity which had flowered in his eyes, then out through a window, trying to draw some shred of propriety against what I had envisioned.

"Well, that must have been most shocking," I said finally. "Most shocking. Of course it didn't necessarily have to be. It all depends. I'm just trying to get it down in as finished a form as possible. I have no right to judge your reactions; you're entirely right to have admonished me on that.'?

D'Arcy's eyes glowed feebly, then he took the glass and raised it midway to his lips. "You could understand—" he said, and then said nothing for some time, apparently trying to frame his reactions, "well, if you could understand, I'm sure you would."

"Surely," I said, and again, "surely. It must have been stunning and dislocating to have come back from this crucial engagement and to have found that during this time—"

"You fool," he said, "you blockhead. You don't understand, do you? That I would choose a petty, compulsive idiosyncratic to subsume by identity, to make clear my course to the world, oh that—"

"I'm only trying to make an inference—"

"You'll never understand. I see now the pointlessness of this episode as I have never seen it before; it is enough to make me shriek, to tear me into little ravening pieces. But we will go on, won't we? The commitment is too general, the history is too sweeping. So we will carry out the little farce to its conclusion."

"I have no idea of what you are saying to me."

"Oh, you fool!" cried D'Arcy and for the first time in our relationship I realized then that idol, object, prince as he was he was also human, all-too-human, possessed of suffering and blood, capable of a shriek. "You'll miss the essential point unless I give it to you, then, unless

I furnish some kind of psychological handout to permit you to stay in the receiving-station. The full horror of the instance is this, then: that all through this there were two parts of me; the transmitted recipient and the transmuted whole; the witness and the commentator and that as always they were never joined but riven, riven, and the transmutative part, the part which dwelt in the soul and controlled my odyssey, that transmuted part which has been the rock-foundation upon which all else has come, that transmuted part, I tell you, was observing all of this coldly, coldly, with utmost necessity and the need to re-evoke because now, you fool, you incompetent son of a bitch, *now I had something entirely new to masturbate toward!*"

  Began, then (said D'Arcy after a further pause during which he observed the rolling of my eyeballs, the frantic flutterings of wrist-and-conjoined pen with which I took down this amazing revelation, the slight crouch of shoulders and knees with which I attempted desperately to literally entrap within myself this insight so that never again would I miss a point so crucial; the slow, burning density of shame which passed from my forehead downward like a shroud, while all through this he rubbed his hands slowly, confident, at last, that he had made a point too central for the world, our eventual locus, to miss) the most frenetic period of my career; one in which all the latent implications, education and history which had been fed incautiously into me through adolescence began to find a point of connection, of that utilization of background which is the hallmark of the middle-class as we know it; nothing wasted, everything gained. Shortly after my return with mother from the farmlands—my father had been warned by telegram that a small plague had infested the general area and that we were leaving immediately; he was not to come to join us on the weekend nor was he to have any comment whatsoever other than to await us and our explanation of the terrible illness—it was decided that my education at the "special" school had reached a kind of completion and that it was now time for me to leave my family and to voyage, for the first time, on my own. My mother was insistent that I leave the household; I had been "cooped up too long in this hothouse," is how she put it and now it was time for me, for any young man, to "spread his wings and try life." Catalogues were consulted by the thousands, our mailbox became insufficient to encompass its daily spray of leaflets, enticements and application forms, and the mailman came personally to drop off a small density of brown envelopes with a sullen expression heightened by a tint of knowledge which, as he explained to mother, was that they were trying to "send me away." In less earnest circumstances—if mother had not felt that my education had been sorely lacking for almost two decades and now desperately needed to find its fruition—the "application procedure" might have been an unpleasant but provocative interlude lasting through the remaining months of the summer and into at least the middle of the next school year. But mother refused to send me to "that place" for even the space of a week; it was absolutely vital, she insisted, that I get out of town with the opening of the school year, so that I would have ample time to adjust to a life away from home. After all, she pointed out to my father, life was mortal, she was mortal, everyone was mortal; it would be catastrophic if anything happened to them before I had had the experience of foraging for myself, even if in a controlled environment. A school no less "special" than the one I had attended was selected procedurally, its major benefit, to my mother, being that it was some 600 miles from our home; huddled between two dismal mountain slopes —they were called "giant peaks" in the catalogue—this school accommodated some 300 of the most "special" children it could find and, to its further benefit, was co-educational. Mother said both within and without my father's presence that I would find this a particular lure since a huddling with baffled and troubled members of my own sex for long years had made me "shy." An enormous deposit was mailed, five large bags were sent up on the railway and at the beginning of the next month I was given a large sum for self-sustension for the full year, an airplane ticket, and was guided to the airport by mother's careful directions. It was important, she said, that I "practice" being on my own as soon as possible. I was instructed not to come home for the holidays—large presents would be sent me air mail—and to keep my correspondence to a minimum, and then to be addressed only to my mother at home; it was important that I "branch out" as soon as possible. It is entirely likely that I came nowhere near my senses until the moment when I entered the private room in the large dormitory that was the main function of the school and realized that for the first time my opportunities outstripped my capacity. I was no longer a virgin and I was alone.

All during this period I had been masturbating, of course; masturbating with an intensity, a skill, even a sheer exuberance, which I had never before possessed. I had ample material with

Marie-Jean for one thing and for another, the climactic interview in the parlor of her home was always sufficient for at least one major climax if all else failed. Throughout that tortured month preparing my exile I had spent the larger part of my waking time either in my bedroom or making frantic plans to get there, my turgid, plaintive organ centering my being as firmly as a bolt of electricity can short-circuit an appliance. Often, the connection between fingers and prick seemed so fragile that there was a kind of suspension in the act of connection, a feeling that my hand was fleshless, almost transparent with need and so that at this time I discovered pillows; they were both more and less resilient than skin and duplicated to a degree astonishing, the feeling of Marie-Jean's slippery greeting as we had meshed. Also, there were sheets, towels, pillowcases (entirely different than other linens because the hole, when tightly bunched, could simulate very interestingly) and rough bits of paper which I now kept in my desk ostensibly out of a discovered ambition to write. The masturbation had become so intense, the climaxes themselves so highly distended, that I had little idea of what was going on outside of them. Marie-Jean might have told me but after one limpid, one-line letter in which she had asked me to kill myself, from her again did for a time.

I had smuggled my collection of magazines virtually intact into the dormitory; openly as well, simply by removing the covers, tying them all with string and sprinkling a little dust over the top and bottom copies, I passed them in my own mind and in the minds of all possible sightseers as "research materials." Nevertheless I had been frightened during the plane trip that an air current or a malevolent stewardess might have dislodged them from their precarious balance on the rack above my head and sent papers containing dismembered breasts, open mouths and speckles of dried semen to a final and terrible destiny all over the continent. But no such thing happened and it was with a feeling of inequitable relief that I dislodged the string behind my barred door to find that they, like I, had survived their journey with the contents askew but essentially intact. For sheer happiness I took out a favorite copy of The Magazine and rolling it into a tube (for old time's sake) inaugurated my narrow bed with the first of what I thought would be an imploding and protected series of joy, all cascades, all foam, white and purified as the first touch of loss. But I had mis-estimated the quality of my environment, to say nothing of my colleagues.

May I leap ahead rapidly in time, modestly discarding the

expository necessities, leaving the bridgework to the biographer who, if possessed of intelligence as you are not, would be able to work out the transitions with a minimum of wordage and a maximum of insight; the transitions being the most painful because least necessary part of all biography. I am poised over the girl in the heat and cove of my room under the doom of a November rainfall—the girl is somewhat older than I am and tragically overdeveloped, her large breasts, fascinating in armor, in a kind of flat, aimless repose with clothing removed, stretched out aimless to her sides and under her arms, the nipples almost invisible under the distension, to say nothing of my clasping mouth. She is muttering faintly, probably about the weather, while with a kind of desperation I try to find her opening, at the same time making polite comments about the disorder of the room, my embarrassment at her seeing it in such shambles, until finally with a moist clamor I feel myself sliding into her, sliding into her, and her arms go reluctantly around me, severing the connection of mouth and breast—which had never been that interesting anyway; I had been doing it only out of a sense of propriety—and with a series of horselike bucking movements not to say whinnies, she begins to carry me, carry me over the sliding eaves of her need.

I feel myself growing inside her and at the same time moving away; all this time birdsongs moving within my head, proud eaglets struggling to churn away from the surfaces of the sea, and the rain comes down unevenly, unevenly, so that I feel myself surrounded by a kind of disorder on all levels as I lie submissive at last in her embrace, feeling the slow steaming and then, as one particularly violent heave of her round body sets my magazines on the shelf above my bed to a kind of scuttling underneath their rubber band, I feel myself turned to them, turned to that attunement, and in a kind of explosion of feeling, all legs, all memory, I am devoured into her and expire slowly, reaching at this time for her breasts to support and inspect them. The feeling at the moment of orgasm has been that of girl-as-giant-fist clasped around my genitalia but underneath that has been something else; a profound undercurrent of woe, perhaps, an unscholarly feeling of mystery destroying the personality. When I came from without her limbs again with that peculiar slurping which seems, I have since discovered, to be the comma of intercourse, I lay atop her having no idea of what to say until finally she dislodged me and sat up, her breasts assuming their normal (or abnormal) proportions again, falling hugely to the area of her navel where she inspected the nipples carefully, apparently for lustre or change of color.

"You really bite, don't you?" she says—all post-coital conversations have now, for me, assumed the aspect of the present tense; this is one subgenre which, because of its hideous sameness, is always of the moment, "you could have hurt them if they weren't so tough."

"Well, it was nice of you to come to the room," I say, because there is nothing else at the moment I can think of and at that moment, the magazines which have been precarious enough, shift on their perch and topple, in a slow, drooling wobble, one by one to the bed, between us. I shrug and reach toward them, hopeful that it will be seen as a kind of joke.

"Are those those girl magazines?" she says, chewing on a fingernail and reaching the free hand out to caress them. "Oh yes, they are. That's what I thought they were. You see them all over. You keep them too?"

"Just for the articles."

"Oh, a lot of the boys use them to jerk off. You'd be surprised how many use them that way. The shy ones, mostly. Do you ever use the magazines to jerk off in?"

"Not really," I say, assembling them hurriedly and trying to get them back on the shelf without exposing my genitalia which have hardened in idiot need to the coincidence. "I don't think of them that way."

"Oh that's perfectly all right. There's nothing shameful about it. A lot of the fellows who can't seem to get laid use them all the time. Can you imagine anyone not getting laid around this place?" She ventures a tentative laugh which becomes, eventually, a giggle. "It's possible, of course. You're not very good, you know. You need a lot of practice."

"It's not my fault. You rushed."

"Who rushed who?" she says, inspecting the other breast carefully, putting a finger in the nipple as if to test it for responsiveness. "You asked me to come to your room and have a talk and the next minute I have my clothes off. All of my clothes off. Not that I mind, of course. What else is there to do when it rains?"

"Well," I say, still in that slow stun which seems to be the inevitable consequence of the aftersex and feeling now too that familiar combination of dread and eagerness which means that the real implications of an event may lie entirely before me, "I guess you'd better get back upstairs."

"Why? They never check after seven o'clock anyway. I might as well stay here all night."

"But in the morning—"

"Who's going to look? It's a progressive place. You've got to work with it; why fight things?"

I take her clothes from under the bed where I have casually tossed them with a social director's ease; where, poised like an arrow, I had hidden her garments in the same gracious gesture with which I had bent my mouth to her breasts. "I want you to go, though. I want to be alone now."

"Oh well," she says, "that's different. If you want to be alone, I can't stop you. Just don't ask me back again."

"Why not?" I say, finding my own clothing in the form of the shapeless bathrobe in which I had greeted her and belting it snugly. "It isn't anything personal."

"You could have some conversation too. It isn't all sex."

"What isn't?"

"Sex," she says. "It isn't all sex."

Somehow, I get through the moments between her nakedness and her entrapment, somehow I guide her without lapse of courtesy to the door, smooth over things, justify the equity of our act, our relations, the role they occupy in some larger scheme. Somehow, I enable her to pass through the door without disgrace, looking at her large rump dwindle in the hall, her step, a series of diminutions. I stand like a bird between heaven and hell; then opt for the latter with a bound, turning the key in my privates like a deep wound, moving out to cover all the inner and outer spaces. I seize the magazines and spreading the largest and most culpable all over the bed, I expose my organ from the (conveniently falling askew) bathrobe and holding it with both hands in a frenzy of disgrace I pull and pull until the last grey waters of consciousness have passed from inside to the outside of me and then I fall into a collapsing sleep, unstifled by groans, the magazines acting as a pillow for the precious rectal cheeks.

The name of this girl has been Carole and Carole is only one of the ten or so girls at this very progressive institution with whom I have coupled; there were Vivian and Portia and a girl named Helen with sloping, almost concave buttocks, and Marcia and Grace and Carole herself who dwelt in a double room above me and had found me interesting.

The true tenor and possibilities of this new residence had been unknown to me for the first several days; when they became appallingly clear in the context of the mixed-sexes dormitory and the caliber of most of the personnel, it was still several weeks before I could act upon it. For me generation had always been an unequivocal, inward act rather than the frantic outpouring which seemed to be the *raison d'etre* (can you spell that you idiot?) of this place, and when it did finally become clear that there was but one justification, one underlay, it took my atrophied skills a little longer to adjust. But now I was locked into the scheme of things: by day abysmal "classes" instructed by confused personnel, who seemed to be transfixed by latent possibilities which they could barely apprehend and of which they could never partake, functioned as a suitable bridge to the afternoons and evenings, and the evenings were full, rich, rooted in that causality which is the token aim of the most progressive of all education. While Carole had been correct in saying that a surprising number of my colleagues were probably masturbators, it was wrong to attribute this to sheer lack; one of the prime benefits of this institution as it contributed to my self-knowledge was to give me the apprehension that there were many like me: those who preferred rather than submitted to the sacred self-abuse as the rounding-out of the full man. No one of us could have felt simple lack there; the male-female ratio had been contrived by a demon in the administration office to function at a constant one to one and as an occasional girl would leave the school in a fit of depression, insanity or pregnancy; as an occasional male would find this astonishing gratification of all forbidden fantasies too much for his cautious consciousness to assemble; a member of the same sex would be brought in, almost instantly, as replacement. It appeared that the waiting list for this institution was incredibly long; it numbered in the hundreds or, perhaps, the thousands, there would have been no way of explaining how she had maneuvered me in on something less than two months' notice had I not found out that one of the executive personnel had the same middle and last names as those of the social director, which cleared up part of the mystery. The girls were viable, cooperative, almost instantly gratifying, so much so that it was hard to believe that they, like me, were paying students; it was as if they had assumed a kind of staff function. I found out a great deal about the intricacies of female flesh during that splendid period; all the time holding my rod firmly in the final embrace behind locked doors to bring to my researches the final order of insight which could only be achieved by reinforcement-through-masturbation. Now I can construct for you a series of vignettes, picturizations, actually, which taken in toto can approximate a picturization of that period although, alas, it would be little more than a metaphor; insufficient data always leading to this conclusion. The name of this school was Rock Point and like the other resort it sat somewhere in desiccated heartland, and the two peaks which gave it its sole appeal held it clumsily, as two uneven palms might grasp a cup, as two frantic, grasping hands might catch a breast and squeeze its length away. Rock Point was privately supported by what was known mysteriously in the catalogue as "friends of the institution," which endowment, added to the handsome sums paid for tuition and other benefits, enabled the school to have purchased the small cemetery lying directly on its westward flank. It had commissioned this cemetery as a "historical site," so much of what occurred seems to have taken place within its confines.

I am holding the girl named Vivian close, close in the small shelter I have made of chest and huddled thighs and she is burrowing beneath me eagerly, seeking my privates, her free hand caressing me aimlessly in the area of the nape of the neck. We are clutched to the right of a small gravestone, the northern drizzle coming down slantwise and I feel the guilt once again surging within me that I had not taken her to my room, and insisted that we get a "breath of outdoors" despite all signals to the contrary and had subjected her to what can only be a complex humiliation, her body dampened by the unrelieving blanket of rain which I can feel chill on my exposed, upturned buttocks. But she does not seem to mind for all of that; she is embarked on a complex, careless journey of her own, her hands gripping and squeezing with amazed and growing discovery; her mouth also enlarged and slippery under mine as her tongue whickers inside. *Wet, wet*, she is murmuring, her upturned body careless in the slick moisture and I am reaching as best as I can, squeezing as best I can, while trying to make that difficult contact. She is open before me, a furnace stoked by its own heat, unneeding of operation and for an instant, trying to make the contact, I can feel the foolishness; the sheer pointlessness of it all as I try to burrow inside her; the position always striking me, somehow, as irrelevant and pointless, the supple ease and graciousness of the masturbatory turn having conditioned me. Her mouth presses against mine, unyielding rubber and I reach forward with my loins to find her slender flame; as I do so we slide, gracelessly into the very stones of the gravesite so that the crown of her head touches and obscures some chiseled letters. "Oh, oh," she mutters, "never anything like this before," and I feel her rising to greet me, her slight, superfluous breasts trembling and puckering with the cold impact of the stone and still fighting, still pillowing within her, I reach a damp palm up to grasp the gravestone for support and feel the hollows of the letters pressed against my hand; apparently it is the word BELOVED although I cannot be sure. "Inside, inside you ass," she is muttering to me—all of them curse at the moment of gathering, I have learned this; their revulsion at the act being so deep that even the Magazines themselves could hardly explain it, make it comprehensible—and as best as I can I point myself within her, reaching the other hand also for the gravestone because without that clinging support surely I will fall from my kneecaps and strike myself a blow in a more vulnerable spot from the stone. So as I move over her I am not touching her but the polished slickness of an epitaph, eyeing her nipples with rolling eyes, the eyes distended and flattened against the palm of my skull by the enormous effort I am making; the seriousness of the commitment. I feel absent flashes of fire, a rumbling below and my glazed eyes, fastened upon the stone, close; now I see the images of The Magazine itself and the images are less what is upon the page, the familiar dismemberment and narrowed focus upon breast, thigh, buttock, but rather upon the pages themselves, their uneven glossiness, the slickness of their feel: the Words written under the pictures that are themselves part of the picture and as her nipples rise up toward me in a trembling of gratitude I bend slightly, my eyelids still fluttering and put the last inches into her; feeling then the steaming and rising, the entrapment itself and my palms graze against the stone, entrap the stone, feeling the stone itself and yet at that moment it is probably not the stone but the very pages of the Magazine that I am feeling and so I come that way in a small spot of gloom, a cove of misery too deep to be reached let alone filtered by the bucking motions of thighs, the sound of cries in the air around me, the rain sifting down. "Come on," she says, grabbing me when I have worked out the last agonized spurts, "come on now and come you bastard," and this works me through the storms and stones of another orgasm, my palms falling from the slippery surface of the epitaph and I crumble on her quite helpless, quite drained while in an orgy of pragmatism she draws me over her body to cover her completely while one semi-detached hand, possessed of its own cleverness, begins to search for her pants.

I am in the cemetery again on a late-winter evening but far from the gravesites this time with a huge-breasted, tiny-buttocked girl named Jane who says that she has always wanted to do it open in the cool air, tickled by trees. The tree we have found is a wispy remnant of some crazed itinerant's mission, its leaves rustling dimly around us and somewhere in its very center, protected against all elements, we huddle, the two of us quite naked this time while the huge, glowing surfaces of her breast flop a merry drum against my chest, my lips having found fuller purchase on her forehead where, discovering a full fold of skin, they suck and suck away. She is not cursing to me but singing this time; singing one of the popular tunes of the era in a voice which both transcends and subsumes its banality; the song is all about love and Jove, heart and start and her voice, an unpleasant contralto, lifts to the uneven pounding of my thighs. I have caught her hole the first time out for once; the practice of fucking outweighing its disadvantage in some cases, the tiny hole possessing rewards which the more easily found (because instantaneously adjustable) closed fist could never provide and as best as I can, I am fucking away my private fuck on her, listening at the same time to the toneless melody which, absurdly, shifts now and then to a whistle, searching for her breasts with thumb and closed forefinger, and what she is singing blends, finally, into the better part which is what she is not seeing and so I come that way, poised bird against her huntressy determination, flicking seeds from my bill into her pouch and she clasps me in an orgy of gratitude as my magazine-inspired sperm greets her ripening and eager Egg. "Oh boy," she says, "oh boy, oh boy, oh boy, you're all heart; that's what you are; a Jove of love." My throat, crackling with retrospection's saliva, would tell her something, but I am obviously speechless.

Surrounded by darkness above and below, I am suspended on my bed, hands and knees to full flight, moving eagerly in the ascension and reversal of love, locked into a cell of sensation so private and interesting that I could as well be alone but underneath me is the girl named Margaret, her body spread like drifting water, porous on the surfaces of the bed and she is accommodating me; accommodating me as best she can in her slippery hole, her hands working idly on my chest. Margaret is one of the "less advantaged" members of the student body; she supplements her scholarship and meager allowance by doing "housekeeping" tasks in the dormitory, and it is in such circumstances that I have come to greet her, her mop, broom and housedress to the side of the bed, her industry forgotten as we move in another, intricate kind of cleaning-gesture. I have then, it seems, done it to the housekeeper here, as well as everybody else, but the housekeeper is 17 years old and is mumbling to me in a credulous voice: *this is terrific, this is really terrific; I didn't know you guys had beds like this; you couldn't imagine what we girls have to sleep in; I could lie like this forever.* And so she could, but I am pursuing her with unprecedented industry, unprecedented business, her breasts so superfluous in the welter of sensation I have aroused through our joining that I am barely conscious of their presence or appearance. *This is really the lap of luxury* she advises me as her thighs thrash in confirmation.

Above me, the cheerful, rattling *thump! bump!* of my magazines in their locked pouch indicates perilous movement on the shelf, the possibility of collision, disaster, falling action at any time and the knowledge that these magazines could truly fall, right into the cup of my exposed buttocks, bringing a kind of triumphant finale to my researches, fills me with ever-quickening excitement; I can imagine how they would feel clouting me slowly like a large covey of emergent insects and the explanations I would have to give—oh, the explanations!—all of this sending me even further and deeper into necessity's groin and her arms gather listlessly to drag me in. *I have to finish off the other rooms soon,* she reminds me behind her closed eyes, *otherwise I'll lose my stipend*, and I moan to her in a burst of cooperation and feel myself open and open above her, a reciprocal opening below; breezes seem to drift over my buttocks and I get it inside her to its fullest length, feeling her fingers scrapple on my shoulders and the tube of her gathers around me all ferocity, all obligement and I finish then to a feeling of slow scattering, thousands of sheets of paper drifting down around me; fall upon her in the rigidity of the corpse itself imagining how it would be indeed if all of this texture and stock, photography and art would came down over the hushed and tenanted spaces of my distantly bartered grave.

I am at a "drive-in" movie with tiny-buttocked Jane again; this time she wants to do it in a new and novel way during which she can examine celebrities and because of her help and attention I am in poor position to protest. There is no way in which I can tell her that the trunk of the rented car which we have jointly taken (but which I must pay for and which Jane must drive) is jammed, almost to the top, with magazines; a hasty room inspection during the morning had determined that these would have to be out of my premises before was conducted what was called there the "mid-semester audit." This procedure, nominally to determine whether or not students were living up to the health habits and ways of the institution was actually, I long suspected, in search of prophylactics or the remains of aborted fetuses but I judged it unwise—oh, the cunning now that I had at last learned what they really meant!—to have my magazines for discovery; masturbation was the one excess which the school, even in its convocations, would never imply. (*We must learn to love one another*, had been the suggestion of the Headmaster during the mid-Christmas assembly, *even if some touching is required in the process*; he had said nothing about Loving Oneself). So the magazines, carried from class to class in a large imitation leather briefcase with a self-locking clasp, had been unobtrusively tossed in the rented trunk during the conclusion of the rental process; now as I jounced and bounced my lonely way above Jane's watchful breasts I hoped that somewhere in the rear there was no suggestion of reciprocal, less joyous, bouncing of the hidden and more important load. Before my stunned eyes had drifted the slight convexity of the screen, huge images locked with one another in two or three colors, suspended above us, and in the soundlessness acting out scenes far more intricate and beautiful than we could ever conceive, but now I had turned down upon her again, making rough work of the entrance because it would be quickest and the quicker fruition would lead to quicker retrieval of the magazines, but she wanted it slow, begged to me in her small popular-singer's voice to extend it as far as possible, all the time her eyes rolled to the screen where she absorbed the images in a kind of placidity and contentment which I could only dimly apprehend. Her mouth, working on some gum, chewed evenly, her eyes calm and bright surveyed me with an owner's pride as I jabbed and jabbed at her slender receiving reed and then, hastening over her, my eyelids clamped and fluttering against her breasts, I must have had an accident; I must have jabbed something with an elbow because the speakers suddenly flicked on, both of them and the voices began to boom and shatter in the car, words of love and rage tumbling over one another in unbearable volume and I reached out my hand, trembling, to smash or reduce the sound but found it stayed by two tentative fingers she had raised to stay it. "No," she murmured, "leave it on; it's nice," and I fought with the cripple's weakness to free myself of that clasp and shatter the sound, but, confident of what her thighs had done to take my strength, she merely held the pressure and said again, "It's so *nice* this way; what do you want to spoil all the fun for; it's just like they're right in the car or we're up on the screen, isn't that more exciting?"

And confined now by a small and terrible rage, a rage which exerted a pressure which screamed only for Justice—whatever that must be—I found the resolve she wanted, which was only the resolve for perishment, for completion, for a connection so rapid as to lead to an immediate withdrawal, which would be the end of shame, but with her clever, fluttering box she held me off for a long long time and so I was forced to listen to strings and horns, shrieks and giggles, sobs and *scenis obligatoria* while my reluctant weapon ground out its few spurts of enthusiasm and I came mumbling against her, as contrite, humbled and profoundly embarrassed as any character in the *commedia* she was witnessing. Throughout she took me with a massive and almost sympathetic air of contrition, her thighs grinding against my organ, her hole exerting the last inch of pressure against myself and at the apocalyptic moment, as through memory I raged and bucked thinking of those lovelies in the trunk, her thumb rose to her mouth and she sucked it earnestly, her eyes averted as I spent into her. Finally free, I was able to turn down the sound, still clamped within her and as I did so she sighed and looked at me as if for the first time, her fingers winding, winding below to complete the circle of causation.

"It's really a good movie," she said, "you know that? There's so much sense to it, just good common sense. What did you do down there? Did you finish? I wasn't sure."

"You weren't sure?"

"Well, I wasn't really concentrating on the movie and like that. I mean, I hope you had a good time, I didn't want to stop you or anything like that. It's just that I'm not really in the mood."

"I guess I finished," I said. "Do you want me to go outside and pick up anything? You want something to eat?"

"Well, that wouldn't be a bad idea, I guess. I'd want some hamburgers and drinks and so on. Maybe some candy. You sure you won't get lost outside and not be able to come back? I'd hate to have to return this car alone; I'd owe the whole thing."

"I think I can make it."

"Make sure you remember what row we're in and what number car. That's the best way of doing it."

Still within her, I tried to withdraw. "Okay," I said, "but I have to get my pants on." For a fine, slender moment of panic I thought that some of the horrid blue-covered texts in my parents' dresser which I had once read had intimated the truth after all; that I was in the grip of *glans penis captivus*. The harder I tugged, the more snugly the conjoinment seemed to fit. Finally, I lost my balance and tumbled on top of her, her little jaws still earnestly compressing and contracting the gum. "What's wrong?"

"I can't get out."

"What do you mean, you can't get out?"

"I mean, it seems stuck in there." I guided her unwilling hand down, let her fondle the dilemma. "You see what I mean?"

"Oh," she said, "that's just the thighs. Nothing to worry about at all; I'll just move my legs a little." I felt her grunt underneath me, her body heave. "Of course it's difficult to move because you're on top of me."

"Well, I can't get off you, can I?"

"I know that. Gee, this is really kind of embarrassing." Her fingers pinched, brought a glimmer of pain. "Try it now."

I tried, seemed to be on the verge of a small but boisterous withdrawal, but felt the pressure even harder, somewhere near the tip. "No, that won't do it."

"Jesus, I'm getting all out of position. I can hardly see the screen. We'll miss the whole movie and all."

"I've still got to get out of there."

"Couldn't you just kind of lie around and nap for a little while, until the picture's over? Then we can both work. It isn't anything to worry about; this has happened to me before. I have a very small, nervous thing."

"But I thought you wanted me to go out for some food."

"Well, yeah. Yeah that's right too. Okay, now. You know, once a boy got caught inside for an hour. Boy was he mad! He didn't know what to say; we just had to wait until he got small enough to get out. That wasn't you, was it who got stuck?"

"No, this is the first time it's happened."

"Oh. I guess I was thinking of someone else. All right, try it now."

"I can't. I can't move."

She giggled. "This could be very embarrassing. I told you, you'll cool off and get out if you'll only relax. Why don't you put my breasts in your mouth and just relax on them? Boys seem to like that."

"I want to get out," I said and at that moment, the Singing Strings, all 106 of them, apparently in some unprecedented cinematic transition, broke out into an unmuted throb, a series of pulses so sharp as to break the tenor equipment of the speaker and fill the car with rattlings of sound.

"My God," Jane said, "someone's trying to come and see us. We better really get out of here. Can you drive?"

"It's just the speaker. Now let me do this." I felt myself overcome by rage, but as profound as that was, the pain was still there at the rock-center of the scene, flooding into my organ, making it even more turgid, things more rigid. I managed to get both hands in position, squashing what little there was of her breasts with my upper arms and seized what I could find of my organ, pulling and pulling desperately. She gave a high wheeze, somewhere between a shriek and a sigh and began to settle under me like a blanket.

"God that's lovely," she said, "I don't know what you're doing there but it's just lovely. More, more."

"I'm trying to get out."

"With the fingers, squeeze around that way. Oh, God, that's really terrific now. I can see the movie and everything. The speaker is broken. The movie is good. You've got to squeeze more. Oh, I'm coming, I'm coming. That's it. That's it. I'm coming."

And come she did in a series of thick waves and flashes of thumping which somehow disgorged my prick at her moment of climax and left it, sopping wetly, on the shiny cushions of the rental car. The speaker clattered in the blackness and, rubbing my fingers in her hole, I obliged her to an orgasm. She fell back, her eyes gripped by the screen.

"That was good," she said. "That was really terrific."

Speechless, I used a shirttail to clean off the residue of my orgasm, managed to adjust my garments without undue rolling, poked an elbow against the window painfully and subsided in the seat, watching several ballerinas on the screen attempt to persuade a choreographer that they were usable. I was quite incapable of thought.

"Well?" she said when the ballerinas had made their case and, embracing one another, had vanished in favor of an operatic singer who appeared to be having romantic difficulties with the choreographer, "what about it?"

"What about what?"

"Aren't you going to go out and get us something to eat? You said you would, you know. I'm hungry. I fixed you and all, the least you can do is bring some food back."

I managed to get the door open and inspecting her for a considerable time—she had heaved herself to a sitting position and was working halfheartedly on her brassiere while searching the dashboard for a fresh piece of gum—I got out into the dirt of the enclosure itself, standing uneasily on the ragged ground, trying to find my balance. Now, in the speakerless silence the screen had assumed a kind of beauty, its figures in being devoid of noise seemed to lack context as well. Moving in a sea as mysterious and as possessed of its fulfillment as I had moved in my sea sleeps many years ago. I stumbled away from it, my back to the screen, my eyes to the moon, feeling a special tendril of fiery knowledge cross between my smuggled goods in the trunk and my exhausted loins as I trudged to the food counter.

And, too, I am with Marcia the redundant in a classroom this time in the pitch of a winter evening, the two of us huddled over the desk, quite naked, her eyes roaming the ceiling while I inspect her nipples with microscopic urgency and work on the alternating surfaces of her stomach and thighs with a woe compounded out of lust and fright. We have no business doing it in this building, but she has assured me that faculty and staff themselves are aware of the student need to disseminate knowledge in its oldest form in the very seat of learning and that to copulate in the classrooms is, in the last analysis, only to join in the hidden and therefore more necessary, purposes of the institution itself. I am sliding, sliding, all lost in the glistening wetness, my tool a tangle, my eyes bulging and behind them I am playing the pictures and images while I work at her with a fool's persistence.

"Higher, higher," she mutters and for a moment I think she means a greater thrust and I attempt to spread her deeper and deeper yet upon the desk but her frantic, tickling fingers below tell me that there is something else she has in mind and I find withdrawal forced, a sudden retraction, a sudden drawing. Pouring sweat and mingled juices, my prick looks for a better home and she guides me with her hands to the cleft between her breasts, centering me with an indulgent palm while with the other she tugs at a breast and then, the first hand freed, takes the other in her hand and forms for me a tight channel, a wedge almost, through which I guide the small, desperate prow of my ship.

And it is as close, then, as close as I can ever come, before or since, to the sensation of the magazines, for here it is all before me, her breasts, held in that full, cupped aspect, almost dislodged from her body, her face a disordered irrelevancy behind the spread of her hair, and I feel myself reaching, reaching, grown to enormous size and power within her and she reaches forward grateful lips to touch me with teeth-and-tongue, adding a slow insistence to my rhythm. I can see vaguely below her cupped and held breasts the shuddering of her thighs and trembling of that nervous skin caught between them but it means nothing to me; I am surrounded by breasts and breasts, nestled in them, lost in them and as she increases the tension on them to make a cylinder I feel myself lengthen toward a final extension and come easily, gratefully, missing her withdrawn face, my hands reaching to touch the side of her breasts with appreciation while she mutters encouragement to me and I leak out the last drops.

After a long time I fall away from her, my buttocks brushing chalk, sliding to a stop on the wood and she looks up at me easily, her eyes glistening with an emotion come close to tenderness. "Oh, wasn't that wonderful?" she says, "When my breasts are held that way, they look just like all the breasts in those magazines, don't they? Don't they?" I tell her this is so and bury my apologetic prick in her bush, waiting for the lights to come on, waiting for the assailant to come.

Somewhere in the middle of that year—I am not sure when and it hardly matters—I received a letter from Marie-Jean, the only piece of extra-familial correspondence which came into my mailbox that year:

"… I obtained your address from my father who with no difficulty attained it from your mother. I guess you suppose you're lucky to be up there, ha, ha, but I wanted to write you this letter to tell you that although you are gone you are not forgotten, at least not by me although you would like to think so. For what you did to me I can never forgive you even though you can forgive yourself so easily for a thousand things; I want you to know that Marie-Jean thinks of you all the time and that Marie-Jean will never relax kind for what you did to her. What form that for a moment until she has paid you back in payment will take and when it will happen is none of your business; it could happen at any minute or not for the next 100 years but it will happen and it will serve you right. Not only did you dishonor and shame me, you dishonored and shamed my father by having your mother take up his time only because then you could be safe in taking me into the cornfields. My father is a fine man, an innocent man, a widower who means everything to me but is not a man who knows people of your type and your mother's and thus could not deal with you or protect himself but I can protect him double and I will. No matter what happens to us there will be a time of getting even. I do not want you to answer this letter as if you do I will find it necessary for me to tear it up …"

And yet another fulfillment: straight as an arrow, proud as a blade, I am hunched on the main quadrangle of the "campus" itself, giving it in this noon of the night to the proudest, most preposterous of all the bitches I have met this year; a girl named Elena with breasts which thrust up as squarely as they thrust out, breasts whose resilience increases out of clothes, thighs whose slight flabbiness only made more needful and urgent those muscular exercises which comprised her special contribution to the craft of copulation, her feet pointed at the moon at the same angle that my buttocks were and there was, around us, no intimation of substance or of presence, only the two of us in the spring night, the campus hushed around us, all groans and quivers in the cathedral or the cemetery. It was Elena's special innovation to do it in the center of this quadrangle itself at safe hours; expressing, as she said, her feelings for the environment in the best way possible and she was extremely difficult, not out of prudence, but by virtue of sheer weight of numbers; there was always a waiting list of 30 or more for Elena's embrace and there was no way to hasten one's progress on that list because she was strictly fair about the process; so fair that some escorts, having painfully waited out their ascension, wanted to do it a second time but on another night and Elena felt that not to give an option would be to render herself a bit of a slut. So it was a question of patience, patience, but in the last analysis she was worth it; the most "special" of all the special people who inhabited the campus, she conceded darkly that she had been there for five years and had worked with difficulty to her position of queen ex-officio; a position whose only benefit was that she was able, in essence, to talk for the student body at the occasional faculty confrontations which were part of the progressive spirit. I had waited and waited, working out my time with the Janes and the Viviennes, waited for so long that it seemed to me that Elena was a hoax and the waiting list was a ploy, but one night she called me in my room to say that she was finally able to take me up on dinner the following evening and now at last I had her; I had the queen on her campus itself, and it was almost worth it because she not only did not block out my fantasies or twist her body unconsciously against them as some of the others had but rather, with a tenderness and understanding I had thought impossible in women, had seemingly understood almost from the start what I wanted and had allowed me to stretch out not on top but alongside her, a fist held in readiness, while she dwarfed my organ in her bulky pouch and produced her breasts, one by one, for me to nibble. I was as loose, swinging and free at ease as if I had been doing it into a magazine; her body, a long, coiled tube, seemed ready to spring to my convenience at any moment. So we sighed and mumbled the night away, our limbs tumbled like glass on the shores of that campus, her breasts bulging hugely and contentedly against all my surfaces and until the sun came we lay there, every confrontation a joy, every joy a refreshment and then, as the sun began to moan darkly in the distance she came upon the oldest, coldest and boldest variation of them all; what she did was to take her breasts in either hand and pointing them toward me, she—

My voice was thick, seemingly unattached to my frame, the frame distended at some impossible distance from the chair but I had to say it. I had to speak. And so I did. "No more," I said, and broke my pen in two. "No more tonight, D'Arcy. We will continue tomorrow."

Still in flight, his high voice cadenced and fluttered against the panels of the room but now, with the necessary biographer withdrawn the words meant nothing, and no sense; no form or reason. It wandered on pointlessly, reduced to the verbal rhythm of its constructions, stopped on an obscenity and then glided to a halt. He cleared his throat. He pulled at an ear and then again on his beard, his eyes wide and full. Then he turned to me.

"You stopped me," he said.

"I had to."

"I was talking about the key event of that important year and you stopped me. You who said that all he wanted was the full information underlying my 'immortality,' my 'quest.' *You stopped me.*"

"I spoke. I had to. There will be no more of this this evening. In another time."

"But you bastard," D'Arcy said, and his voice was a shriek, "if you could stop me in the middle of what I was saying then, it indicates that you have no understanding, absolutely no understanding of everything that I'm trying to do. How could you? I don't even remember—"

"I understand very well," I said sadly, "and that is why I stopped you. It doesn't change the reality of what happened, D'Arcy. You must avoid this falling into the biographical fallacy. It still happened; it doesn't make it any less viable."

"Aha!" he said and a kind of sheer cunning drifted down from his eyes toward his intense mouth, his crooked frame. "All of a sudden, we talk in polysyllables. No longer are we the fawning, respectful, careful biographer. All of a sudden we are something else."

"I am the same, D'Arcy. Only you have changed. The reality remains constant. It is only your way of seeing it which has altered. Everything is as it was. This wine had made me very sleepy and I must rest."

"Since when do you do this to me? Since when can this happen? I renounce you, you son of a bitch bastard. I don't want a biographer anymore. I don't want any part of you. The biography is finished, it is over. Leave my house at once."

I laughed softly, so as not to disturb him at all, trying to make my chuckles and gasps as soothing as possible. "I can't leave your house, D'Arcy," I said. "You know better than that."

"You can't *leave?* What do you mean, you can't leave?"

I closed my book with a snap, tossed the broken pieces of pen into the fire and closed the decanter. "I must rest," I said. "Tomorrow. We will continue tomorrow on more progressive territory. This line of reminiscence was doing neither you nor me any good, D'Arcy. We must consider it from a different angle tomorrow."

He ran his hands through his beard desperately; gestured then, as if he would strike me. But as I caught him, then, with the full cold light of knowledge in my eyes, pinning him in frieze against the mirror, he must have thought better of it because his hands fell from his face, dropping to his sides and something seemed to go out of him then, all of it seemed to drift away leaving only heat and loss and he stretched out fully on the bed then in what might have been an imposture of sleep except that in a moment his eyelids were fully down and his blank face inspected the ceiling incuriously. I sighed, a gross sigh mingled of pain and pity alike and uncapped the decanter quietly, poured myself a final glass and finished it slowly, wondering.

In sleep D'Arcy's face was robbed of all but that feral knowledge which had come so late to him; a heightened, compressed focus of the features seemed to imbue him with an insight far beyond his gains and as I watched him I felt drifting out of me, as smoke rings, the first apprehension of the final disaster.

NINE

This morning, finally, there was a conference. It came only at my frantic repeated requests to the attendants; insistences and threats aided by vague Greco-Latin mumblings of *habeas corpus* and *kyrie eleison* and *mens sanal* and *obiter dicta*. But finally they came, the three of them, and escorted me into the large room of which I had heard my roommates murmur, the room where issues were settled once and for all in this institution, and in this room there was the doctor with whom I had spoken previously and a large, thick, squarish man who wore an expression which I took to be vaguely legal. The attendants placed me in a chair before them and left, slamming doors roundly, and I permitted myself to light a cigarette before them without permission, looking at the water pitcher on the table which seemed somehow reminiscent of D'Arcy's *decantrum*. Under the circumstances—considering the history, that is—my control was superb, my sensibility and countenance icy. I could tell that this was truly the room of last opinions because I could feel myself slowly coming together in there, the first time in many, many months that I approximated, in spirit and in essence, that fine, high purpose with which I had started so long ago, my tragic adventure.

"My name is DeSoto," the legal person said with one eyebrow faintly raised. "I am here in answer to your requests which, I understand, were frantic and constantly repeated; I am here only to show you that this is not an institution of retention so much as it is one of crystallization."

"That's it," the doctor said. "You caught it, you really caught it." He moaned with satisfaction. "That's exactly the way he talks."

"The way who talks?" DeSoto asked.

"This one."

"I certainly do not," I said. "My speech is littered with archaicisms on occasion but it is neither convoluted nor that agonizing jangle of semi-imported words which my roommates substitute for communication. I am delighted, however, to finally have someone before me."

"That's my job," DeSoto said. "Now, the question is, what do you want? What brings you here? I'm an extremely busy man and there are many people here to service, you know; this feeling that all elements here are peculiarly molded either for or against you is one of those obsessions of which you're going to have to rid yourself before we can be expected to be entirely sensible here. So why not tell me—"

"That's no way to get at him," the doctor said. "He can convolute with the best of them. You have to be direct, direct."

"What the hell do you want?" DeSoto asked blandly, and put his other fist carefully on the table, from which fist extruded a gleam of chromium which I took to be a prosthesis. "Level with me."

"Many things," I said. "In the first place, I know on direct evidence that at least one and probably both of my roommates are not confined here but are staff members whose sole function is to spy on me and to report my movements and convulsions to their seniors—"

"The usual systematization," the doctor said. "You know what that represents."

"Never mind," DeSoto said. "He's asked for a hearing, we can grant him that at least. Why are they reporting your movements? Why are they spying on you? What's the particular interest in your movements anyway? I'm a responsible official, you can tell me this in complete confidence."

"It's not necessary," I said, frankly enough, charmed by the refreshing honesty of his manner; at last a sensible, if not a cooperative man's attention had been granted me. "That would be a question only the institution can answer. I can only say that there seems to be a most particular interest in my functioning and my idiosyncratic behavior; almost as if an elaborate biography of me were being planned which biography would require such *minutiae*. Nothing I do here is that interesting except for the writing, of course, but there's no way of getting hold of that because I keep it in a very private place. Otherwise, it's just a question of lavatory habits and sleeping and that kind of nonsense. I don't pretend to understand it."

"Comes and goes," the doctor said. "Like I was telling you, they come and go. Sometimes they're here and sometimes they're there. It's a cyclical kind of thing. Now, in a case of this sort the cycle—"

"Biography?" DeSoto said, not without interest. "Why would someone want to write a biography of you, particularly here?"

"The biographer's instinct is a sheer twitch," I told him, reasonably enough. "I have it myself; I can't pretend to explain to you its origins or its purposes. It is founded in the obsession to be subsumed completely in the life and thinking of another person; a kind of supercession of the will, a denial of self for the better, richer alternative. It hits most people at one stage or another in their lives; perhaps in a state of acute depression when they want to flee the hated and therefore hateful self. It is entirely possible that one of my roommates or someone higher in the institution—"

"But why you?" DeSoto repeated again, quietly. "That's the question on the table, so to speak. What is so exceptional about you? Not that you aren't exceptional of course; every person is exceptional and not only to himself, but in the present case—"

I folded my arms rather grandly against myself and raised my beard to him. "I don't have to answer that," I said. "That wouldn't be within my province. You would be obligated to. That is why I called this conference. I think that it is time to terminate my residence here. In short, I want to be discharged; I want to walk in the park again, I want to see women—"

"But listen," the doctor murmured, apparently only for DeSoto, "we go through this periodically, I'm telling you—"

"I'm telling you that I am conducting this discussion as provided by law," DeSoto said, and turned back to me. "You say you want to see women, do you?"

"Among other things. As I would want to glimpse all aspects of the normal, civilized, transitory existence, I would certainly want to see women. There are other things of course."

"But this biography you say you're writing. The one about your friend D'Arcy. What would happen to that if you left here? You'd probably abandon it."

"You told him," I said to the doctor. "You told him all about that."

"Of course I did. Did you think I wouldn't? What's the difference? You were the one who built up this biography—"

"At any rate," DeSoto said roughly, "that would certainly injure its development, wouldn't it? Don't you think you're better off in a quiet, stable, unpressurized environment like this one, where you could—"

"I'm not that interested in the biography anymore. I've just lost a certain kind of interest in it. It'll get written; if I don't do it, someday someone else will. D'Arcy is that important. But I don't feel like being involved in him anymore; I am feeling, rather, that my own identity, long-neglected, long fallen to ashes under the mire of obsession, is ready to flower once again and I would like to find it; I would really like to find that identity. I am not saying—"

"But this D'Arcy is so uniquely important to you," DeSoto said, leaning forward, a flicker of intensity now passing across that *habeas corpus* face, "do you think you should really neglect him; leave him to wither, so to speak, and besides, were your—ah, ah—your detention to cease there would be other problems; problems which you—"

"That happens to be the way I feel," I said. "A sense of mission can be equated with purpose only so long as that purpose can be said to exist, but when it is misdirected, it is usually unrecovered."

"Well, tell me then," DeSoto said, "were this detention to cease, exactly what would you do? What would be the quality of your life? Surely you've made plans."

"In a sense I have," I said. "I would want to find a room, a quiet room with an overhanging balcony somewhere where the sounds of women and birds commingling in the dawn; perhaps the slapping of pond waters and the murmurs of children as well, a room where I can both glimpse and yet withdraw, see and yet be not part of what I witness; gather in the slow storm of life as I pace out my own days. The room would have a mirror and tight shades for moments when I wanted to rest and there would always be a decanter of wine, the finest wine beside my bed where I could reach for it. There would be periodicals and music and once, perhaps in a great, great while there would even be a prostitute; not an exceptional prostitute but an ordinary working woman of the commonest and therefore most lasting type. And she would come to me unhuddled in the shroud of clothing; her breasts frank before me in the casting light of noon, her nipples square and open and neither the height nor fullness of those breasts would matter as long as there was a touching, a clinging. And we could lie together, flat, stomach-to-stomach in the stillness of that room for a long time, our loins misty with their need but separate, separate and after a long time, with a beautiful and lunging spontaneity, she—this whore, I mean to say, for she would only be a whore; this is the crucial part—would open before me and I would ease in by her side, just the first inch of me touching the wet lips drawn together puckered like a young girl's and they would part just a trifle, enough to allow me a kind of succession of connection until finally I would feel myself gripped fully in that gentle and ancient embrace and then, palm-to-palm, lips grazing one another we would move together slowly, the tube of her rolling and unrolling around me until finally with a whicker of sunlight I would emerge through the other part of her and climax. And then there would be other things to do; good wine and good books and even some writing if I care to get it done, perhaps on D'Arcy himself. I might even return to D'Arcy."

I admit that I had bemused myself, let alone my two auditors and it seemed only after a very long time that DeSoto, rubbing his palms together, spoke slowly and in a different kind of voice to the doctor. "Remarkable," he said.

"Simply remarkable."

"These cases always are. The unusual reality—"

"All I can do," DeSoto then said, "is to take it under advisement. Your request, I mean; the way you feel. I can't say yes or no. But we'll discuss it and inform you of our decision."

"Discuss it with whom?"

"The staff. We'll probably have a full staff meeting as we do every so often and discuss you and a few other things."

"You mean my roommates," I said. "My roommates will be part of that meeting, won't they?"

"You roommates are fellow residents like yourself, not members of the staff, so they will not be present. Only qualified personnel will be. Isn't that right, doctor?"

"Oh, that would be correct. In the event of such a meeting of course. There are imponderables—"

"I flatly refuse to consider their presence at any such convocation," I said flatly, looking at DeSoto who in the last analysis I had judged to be an entirely sensible man; an external correlant, perhaps, to that fine rationality of my own which had swept over me like a cloud the first time I had glimpsed the markings on my roommate's wrist. "They would see the man *in extremis* so to speak, rather than in the conservative public posture and no man has any right to be judged outside of how he appears to be. I must be quite strong about this."

"But the question of living arrangements," DeSoto said, "perhaps you are a shade—ah—overambitious in your tastes. It might be better—"

The doctor put a strangely tentative hand on DeSoto's shoulder, turned it into a sweeping gesture which glided from chest to waist to calf and ended with the two of them facing one another in attitudes of mutual bewilderment; clowns locked in puzzled confrontation. "I think we've had enough," the doctor said. "There's little point in continuing this."

"But I haven't made my position clear," I said. "There are certain elements which certainly must be justified including that of sleeping arrangements; if I am only given a chance—"

"He can go on for several hours," the doctor said. "Once unchanneled, there is no end to it. I tell you this from experience."

"Well," my familiar said, shaking his fine-tooled head, looking at me with an expression into which the first edge of equivocation had passed, "perhaps we should terminate this interview now. Next time—"

"But I wanted to discuss this matter of women as well as the diary and the plans I have for my estate—"

"Later," the doctor said. "We can do all this later."

"Well then," I said, "how about tomorrow? We can sit down again tomorrow and discuss the sheer mechanics of my release."

"That would be at the discretion of the staff," DeSoto said. "Of course if they were willing—"

I felt my reasonableness, that strange mood which had come over me during this interview, subside; it went away so rapidly that it was with a feeling of violence that I confronted the aspect of being drained; all parts of me running out, all conscience, all connection, all possibility. I fondled the table in an enormous embrace trying to recover my aplomb, then stood shakily, facing them. It was evident that I was at some kind of an emotional crisis because the phrases and rhetoric, instead of coming easily from me, much as if they had been pre-arranged and I was only giving meek and humble voice to them, seemed to have an odder, thick consistency, much as if they were being made on the spot and manufactured for causes more obscure than those for which I generally competed. I fastened upon DeSoto, seized him so to speak in the glare of that emptiness and said, "You can't do this to me. I cannot take it anymore. I have been here for days and days, possibly weeks, entirely cut off from an apprehension of history; entirely severed from the promise of out-come and I tell you now that I can no longer bear this cheat; I have not circumscribed the awful facts of D'Arcy's life and my own so that I could be systematized to extinction. I tell you now that there are drastic undercurrents here; drastic intimations, I tell you that I will not be humored anymore or reduced to a kind of functional implosion of all possibility due to your devices; rather I must seize, seize, I must transcend all of this, I must renounce utterly with the one hand and yet grasp utterly with the other; I must find reason or failing that a kind of apocalypse but there will be no more of this. I demand my rights, gentlemen! I demand that you desist! I demand my most immediate release, a pardon, a sheet of paper stating that I have done no wrong! I demand this standing on my record and on yours and I can promise you the most dire consequences if this is not immediately accomplished!"

Even from the depths of the sudden emotional distress which came over me—a distress which caused my eyes to peer suddenly through that bridge of water and retrospection which is, perhaps, all they can know of feeling—I could see that this speech had impressed DeSoto strongly if not the doctor. He looked at me, stricken with that kind of communion which will affect even the most officious of men when he realizes that what has come before him dwells other than in abstraction, and he raised his hand as if he were to say something.

But it was the doctor who spoke first. "Oh you poor bastard," he said, "you poor, poor bastard. You poor bastard."

I wheeled upon him desperately for explication, my own hand raised as if to guide the doom-ridden lightning toward him. But he only said again, "You poor bastard; this is just terrible. Terrible, terrible."

DeSoto turned upon him. "I don't really think there's any need for this," he said. "The patient wants release; he has just delivered a very affecting statement to that effect and you—"

"But you don't understand either!" the doctor said wildly, his eyes glinting from one to the other of us, a fine, high madness in them and beyond that a streak of woe which would have caused me, in other circumstances, to reach out my hands to touch him. "I thought they explained to you! I thought you read the records! Surely you could not have come in here not knowing!"

"I really dislike this," DeSoto said. "I am an examiner, a judicious, state-appointed examiner; I make my rounds, do my job, collect my benefits and try to think of the future as little as it thinks of me. If I am put into wild inextricable situations, they cannot be my doing; causation is beyond a man of simple talents like myself. I don't know what you're talking about."

The doctor backed against the wall, his palms touching it, his wild, flickering stare unabated and as I looked into it, then, I saw what he was trying to say; given rhetoric and substance by desperation his message pierced out at me unevenly from his ragged face and hit me with a dull impact, somewhere between orgasm and the pain of withdrawal. I couldn't take it; I felt my breath drawn unevenly into my lungs; felt the churned pulsing as my heart tried to make sense of it, felt my knees cave and went into the seat. The folly, the desperation came over me then and if I had had the strength I would have whipped my prick from my pants and ejaculated for sheer horror.

"Every time the same thing," the doctor was saying, "the same thing, the same confessions, the same pretensions, the same demands. No change; no change, perfectly contained fugue, perfectly contained I'm telling you; circular in its essence and unbreakable because we can't touch it, we simply can't touch it and yet reasonable, reasonable—"

"What the hell is it?" DeSoto shouted, grappling the doctor finally by his damp lapels and half spinning him toward me, toward the center of the room, the pressure he exerted causing DeSoto himself to fall back and half crumple into the wall, then unfold in a gesture of reception as he waited to hear from force what silence could not have given him.

But it was not DeSoto to whom the doctor spoke. "You poor bastard," he said to me, then, "you've been here for seventeen and a half years."

TEN

"There remains very little more to say," D'Arcy said slowly, examining his glass. "And I, most particularly, am delighted that this is the case." He tossed the glass, with a little of the wine still glistening, to the floor where it bounced and then spread its putrid contents over the rug. All the emotion seemed to have gone out of him under last night's explosion and out of me as well for I only sat idly in an approximation of the scribe's posture, fondling my pen and putting it occasionally into a large gap in my teeth where it tasted vaguely like rubber.

"But the whole biography," I said, "the whole sweep of it; we have barely understood you past your 18th or 19th year and yet you say that you have arrived near completion. I fail to understand this." Under my reasonable dialogue was an urgent clown's voice counseling me to smash D'Arcy, to leave my chair and render him senseless on the rug next to his wine glass but I was tired, tired, the action was as irrelevant as unperformed. And the end was near; for whatever reason the biographer's journey was almost done. So I said, "Of course you must have your reasons."

"Of course I have reasons, you oaf," he said, but there was no malice in the word, only a vague kind of endearment. "This is a seminal biography; we are talking of the seminal, the basic influences which went into the composition of the whole man. Once he has been set on his course, unalterable, there is merely a gentle flowering of possibility. No, almost everything which happened between the incident I am about to describe to you and the present time is as predictable as it was delightful; the influences being locked into place guided it as smoothly as you can send your pen through curled sheets of white paper. After this, there is little more to explain; you will know why I am what I am and you may go back to the dismal hatching-place of your rooms and try to make an art out of it."

"If I want to," I said. "Frankly, I have been thinking more and more of going to the sea at the completion of these dialogues; finding a white, enclosed bungalow somewhere where I can rattle around in two or three rooms performing meaningless tasks, consoling absent but soft local women while the waters slowly but necessarily overtake me, bringing me back, bringing me back. I have thought of this more and more often; the harsh perpendicular made by sand and sun in the early morning, the lone beach wanderer caught in the middle of this geometry, the whisper of fishes in the warm wet sands below. This strikes me as a more useful course; I may be getting out of town shortly."

"That would be your choice," D'Arcy said. "I have been thinking oddly not of water as a place of retirement but of fire; a slow, broken schooner journeying from this city through the mists of the equator itself, the sun turning slightly at midday to slam the boat against the heated plane of glass that is the sea, the slow, parched suffering of the equatorial voyage; the scent of the hard, flat pine boards of the deck as I drag myself suffering in search of some vegetables to conquer my scurvy. Of course this is all a matter of individual choice. What we have concluded is that the present situation lacks leverage."

He poured a small serving of wine into his carefully cupped palm and drank it that way, considering me. "I want to tell you now of the motel and the splendor, the reaching and the drawing, and the apocalyptic moment which happened somewhere between the wiring and the horror under the sheets; I want to tell you all of this and be done. We never should have started this." He gurgled up the last of the wine, rubbed his palms absently against one another and settled back into his seat, gesturing at the same time that I could have some wine as well, if I wished.

"No," I said, "there has been entirely too much drinking here over the last few days."

"And other things as well," D'Arcy said almost agreeably, and searching with increasing eagerness for his cigarettes, he then began:

I returned home that summer (D'Arcy said without pause, finally grasping his cigarettes with a sigh) in that state of slow, glazed apprehension which can only afflict those who have seen too much combat or too much copulation; my loins drained, drained, my perceptions hardly equal to what had happened to me, that summer of pause eagerly awaited as a means of necessarily and finally integrating the two. Even the prospect of two more full years at the school, commencing that fall, could not disengage me from the feeling, as I came home that summer, that I had already bypassed the possibility of transition; short-circuited myself into a kind of final disaster. Surrounded by trunks bulging with fresh copies of magazines I had purchased at the railroad terminal, holding two fresh copies of The Magazine itself on my lap I passed that journey in a slow orgy of pinching and rubbing, my compliant prick trying to remind me with its idiot's sense that there were, perhaps, better times ahead.

At home I found the situation to be relatively stabilized: with my acquired sense I soon found out that my mother was having a series of new, vagrant affairs with various uninteresting men who hovered on the edges of commerce in the city; likewise that my father, long since having abandoned himself to the possibility of these affairs if not their actual occurrence, had found interests of his own in an obscure but refreshing way which kept him away most evenings on what he termed "private business." It was surprising how all of this was clear to me after one short year at the school; what had been abstract and removed a year ago because "adult" actions were always somehow both more and less rational than those of children was now almost translucent; my new insight—*that everybody was doing it, that there was no one, anywhere, who was not doing it; that all of it came down to the contact and the coupling*—rendered everything explicable and therefore somehow shameful; I had thought that adults, perhaps, functioned on impulses less bizarre than those which guided my own pale thighs and fist in the darkness. But the adjustment was made easily and I landed my bags and parcel of magazines in my own room without incident, explained to my parents that I was anticipating a contemplative summer and closed a door which, although somewhat figuratively, I intended to close for three months.

I might have made it, too. This is the important point; one which cannot be dropped from your recollections, you ass, when you get into your vile bungalow and begin to rattle around in search of that common sense and discipline which has long since deserted you. My fist was strong, my heart resilient; my perceptions cooled by the extrinsic ardors of the years, I might have managed to tie it all together and yet emerge a whole man. I had the magazines, tubelike (I had discovered how to wedge the pages into one another for an even tighter grip), I had no dearth of interesting things to jerk off to with my recollections of the year just past, I had not even guilt or guile because I had proved time and again—*had I not?*—that I was perfectly capable of doing it. If I preferred masturbation this was very much my business; my mother seemed to prefer a little adultery and my father a streak of perversion; it all came down, then, to the same thing in the long run. Between meals and long roaming excursions to the park; between easy sleeps and the idiocies of a "preparatory course for adults" taken in a local high school, I might have suspended out the full weight of that summer and redeemed, returned to school that fall to fuck and think in equal parts, the two sides of me ever-reconciled. But that was not to be. Such things are never meant to be. Stability is the ultimate imposture; only change exists, implosion, violence, the severing of parts; not even the masturbator has his cove. In the middle of that July I was rewarded by an unexpected and wholly peremptory visit from my little Marie-Jean.

It was the slowest and most promising of summer afternoons; my mother had gone into the center of the city for what she said would be a detailed Christmas shopping expedition which might keep her out, searching the bargain stores, until midnight; my father was performing obscure accountant's acts at a firm so small and in such legal trouble that it did not even have a telephone. Before me in a small pouch lay my magazines, tacked upon the wall were two severed breasts, a thigh and my most precious ornament, a full, closed vagina which I had transcribed, on tracing paper, from the pages of a nudist magazine. (I would not add such magazines to the permanent collection; they struck me as peculiarly perverse, insulting because of all that denial centered by that one desperate purpose.) My prick, recharged by 6 hours of morning idleness stood at ready, my slow pounding fist beginning to describe delicate circlets around the head. At that moment the bell rang.

Facile as I could only have been made through five years of such adjustments performed with a maniac's ease, I placed the magazines back in the pouch, removed the tackings from the wall and restored my reduced prick to my pants pleased that even this organ needed no signal from me. All of us were cooperating, all of us were in place. I went to the door and opened it, ready for any kind of engagement and found Marie-Jean looking at me, her eyes shrouded by their heavy lids, her sleeveless dress glowing orange against the colors of the dismembered sun. She had improved slightly physically in the past year; her sexuality was no longer a mere suggestion under her carefully contrived attitude but had somehow, instead, filtered into the attitude itself, causing her large breasts to press urgently against the compound of silk and memory that covered them. She looked at me without speaking, then walked into the house and almost with a possessor's appropriation, kissed me gently on the forehead and slid down into the nearest of chairs.

"You look well," she said. "That place has done wonders for you. I wish something or somebody had done wonders for me. I didn't know you lived in a place like this; it's pretty awful, here, but it's not your fault."

"Listen," I said, vaguely stunned, "I don't know what to say. I thought that—"

"Oh, the letter," she said, almost charmingly. "That mean letter I wrote you up there. Oh, I was just envious because you had gotten away from home and were living a nice life while I was stuck at home with Daddy and his bedsprings. I wasn't really mad at you; I kind of missed you. So since we're in the city for some kind of a convention or something, I thought I'd drop by and say hello to you, kind of apologize for that letter. You look very well. I bet you were screwing like mad up there."

"Not really," I said astonished. "It's—"

"Oh, everybody knows about that place. The miracle is, how did you get in? People wait for ten years, sometimes, to get there and when they do, they have a way of never leaving, even when their time is up. It's a great place; very expensive though. I guess you got your share of it, huh?" Her eyes measured me, then flicked to my father's scotch decanter on the table. "If I may—"

"Oh yes," I said, grappling for it and handing her a glass from underneath the table, letting her construct her own. I had the fanatic's intimation that if I would only leave her alone, give her as much to drink and hear as she wanted, she would leave in good time, and leave me to my devices. The important thing was to be obliging. "You look well yourself," I said pointlessly.

"Not as well as you. Of course, I haven't been fucking in and out like a big machine all year, either. I have to take it where I can get it and most of them don't want it." Her eyes flickered. "I bet you've come a long way since that day. Technically, I mean."

"I don't know what you're talking about. Everything is the same as it always was."

"*Nothing's* the same as it *ever* was," she said intensely and finished a medium-sized glass of scotch at a bound, went to the decanter again but poured less and moved back knowingly against the cushions. "Anyway, I came to tell you that there are no hard feelings at all and in many ways I admire you. Let's go to a motel."

"What?"

"Let's go to a motel and shack up. I'd like to go to bed with you again; it's been months since I got anything decent at all inside me and at least you were big; now you're probably better. There are some awfully nice places on the highway coming in; Daddy and I passed them all to wind up at this disgusting hotel. Clean and neat and the air conditioners don't make any sounds at all, I bet you."

"But look," I said, or rather some demented dwarf within me said, "we don't have to go to a motel. We could do it here, right here." I didn't want to go to bed with her, the thought of it sending me into a storm of revulsion, a welter of loss, but there was no way of getting rid of her without being cooperative. That was the idea which afflicted me and which made everything possible: I was only trying to be cooperative. "It would only take a few minutes and nobody's coming home for the rest of the day," the dwarf said.

"It isn't the same. Motels are really nice; you know, they're simply made for fucking. All the time I was wondering what the hell motels were for when there were so many other nice places you could go to and what the hell was there to do anyway except look at television, but the first time I went to one around Christmas it all came to me. They're the hottest thing going. There's nothing you can do there *but* fuck." She put a hand between her legs, stroked her genitals idly. "It makes me hot just to think about going to a motel with you. Don't worry, you don't have to pay. Daddy gives me all the money I want and I saved up on my allowance for this. I'll take care of everything."

"But listen," I said, "couldn't we do it here? It would be the same thing and I told you no one's coming home here all day and you could save the money. I mean, *I* could save the money; I wouldn't let you pay."

"I don't want to fuck in any old house," she said, "let married people fuck in their houses. Young people can do it in motels. Don't you know that when some married couples have problems that way they take them to a motel? It's a sure cure."

I had no alternative. I could have asked her to leave, of course; in the long run, I understand now, it would have worked because I could have left her with no alternative. I could have spoken of relative impotence; I could, for that matter, have laid my reduced prick out on the table and jerked it off for her. All of these would have been better or, at least no worse. And yet, in the last analysis, of course, it would have made no difference at all.

It would have made no difference because we are what we are; there is no changing, there is no alternative; the compound of disgust, reflex and beliefs which all of us become is based upon the careful selection of only those experiences which will adjust the compound in a certain way. So nothing I could have done or said would have made any difference, would have changed the situation at all; even the memories of the throbbing wire, colliding with my bruised wrist changed nothing. The magazines lay safely upstairs; there would be better times ahead. And her breasts under the dress were the breasts I dreamed of, in and out of my slippery orgasms.

"All right," I said, "the hell with it. We'll go. But I'll pay. I insist on paying."

She rose from the couch, solid as rock and as unyielding and touched my elbow. "I know a little place, a very nice place, where we can save lots of money," she said. "There's no need for you to spend a whole lot."

It was settled. In a spirit of assassin's pact, we looked at one another as I circled the house picking up necessary objects, cleaning away unnecessary residue, denying her presence or my own impending absence as best I could while she followed me, her graceful thighs touching my buttocks gently, her hands murmuring something tuneless on my body. I took her by a firm, roseate upper arm and guided her to the door, swung the door open, put her outside the door, put myself beyond the door, closed and locked it and we went to her car, a small, ominous sedan parked on the other side of the street. When we got there she handed me the keys and indicated that I could drive and I shrugged—it was a minor skill I had picked up during the winter at the school but was still unlicensed—and decided to risk it. We got into the car. We closed the car. I started the car and we drove.

We drove once again through the familiar, ever-recapitulated landscape, the radio on this time giving the form of a musical comedy to our humble journey, the flat, grey roads which led out of the town lying in their smoke and ashes as cars fore and aft wandered past us, probably on better journeys. Out of town, Marie-Jean guided me to one of those small, dismal highways which leads either to a journey's end or beginning, and straddling two lanes cautiously I went to fuller speed, feeling for the first time her capped fingernails grazing my thigh, heard the slow mutter of her voice as she mouthed the words of the song and turned against me, nestled into me, implanted her breasts into my shoulder, a soft, squeezing pressure held out against the hard asphalt of the road which reverberated through the wheels to my stricken hands. "I'm hot, aren't you?" she said and again, "I really want a fucking, don't you?" and I finally said yes and she quieted against me with the rolling of the roads, then, still pocketing her hand in my lap.

We drove in suspension like that for a long, long time; hearing newscasts, advertisements, music, advertisements, several bulletins, transcriptions of interviews, battling with the misty aspect of diseased trucks that wandered by us, and as the soot and heat steamed up from the road I felt myself to be literally transfixed into a station somewhere between consciousness and passage, locked in an endless gloom with only a small spread of light at the farthest corridor to tell me who I might be or where I might be going. Her mouth slid down, dreamlike, to my lap and began to explore me tentatively; I thrust like a lunatic against her, dreaming of tubes, until I realized that there could be no contact and that it was only a cheat; her breasts moved higher to touch my neck and I sensed, then, a suspicion of skin as if she had bared them for me and was more than grazing, but I would not look. The sun, contrary to astronomical evaluation, seemed to rise higher and higher rather than settling and the interior of the car ticked. "It's only about a mile away, now," she said and I was shocked at the presence of a human voice in the car; we had been suspended so long by radio and by the sounds of the highway that the reality of direct, untranscribed human speech seemed to be something entirely new. "No," she said, "I was all wrong; it's right here, we made it." She pointed toward an agglomerated pink structure, several boxes nestled unevenly upon one another in a row to our right a few hundred feet ahead. FARMER'S HIGHWAY REST, it said. "That's it."

I took my foot off the gas pedal with surprise that I was capable of movement at all and with a feeling of physical wrenching slowed the car and curved it into a grey, cobblestoned path, stopped it before a dreary, central box that bore a sign in red and white: OFFICE WELCOME. "You're supposed to register; the man always registers," she whispered to me but for a few moments, stricken by the accumulated tensions of the voyage I was unable to move, in a kind of shock that there was, after all, an end to transition, but then Marie-Jean did something urgent to me and I found myself able to move. I heaved my way out of the car, leaving the keys dangle and stumbled into the office.

A rustic before the counter, all spangles and checks between the scarred wooden surface, wanted to know if I was interested in a "special" or a "regular"; I told him that it made no difference and he gave me a special; he then asked for my license plate which I gave him without trepidation and finally wanted to know if I was married. Strangely, this question which is the punch line of every good and bad joke about motels which I have subsequently heard, within them and without, struck me as entirely routine, legitimate and matter-of-fact; I told him that I was and that this would be the second night after our honeymoon. He seemed to lose interest at that point—not that he had any particularly in the first place—told me that his name was Elmer and that he raised tomatoes in addition to eking out a very modest life with this motel, and made me sign two cards. He asked me for ten dollars, I gave him eleven to show my appreciation for tomato-growing and he handed me the keys to unit 27 which, it appeared, was on the ground level of the "third barricade." I thanked him, returned to the car and tossed the keys to Marie-Jean. She gasped.

"Did anything happen?" she said.

"Yes. We got the room."

"Oh. I was so worried. Everything's all right then?"

I had never been to a motel before. "What could be wrong? I thought that you loved these places."

She had no answer to that, moving away from me slightly as I brought the car awkwardly before unit 25 and told her that we could probably walk the 8 feet to our own cabin. She nodded and said something about baggage and took an eyeglass case from the glove compartment. "That will have to do," she said.

"What's the difference?"

"The police watch these things," she said, astonishing me. "They're so hot that the cops have to watch for them. All kinds of things go on in these places; I'd hate to tell you."

We got out of the car, myself stiffly, Marie-Jean with at least as much distress as I had experienced the first time, and she handed me her eyeglass case which I put into an inner coat pocket. Her hand brushed mine tentatively, then moved as if flight and commingling were somehow antithetical and we went to unit 27 which appeared indistinguishable from 26 and 28 although, perhaps, bearing a slightly more used appearance. I had some difficulty with the key, jabbing it over and over again at the lock, trying to force an entrance, and then made it all in a rush and we staggered into the cool, damp cavern of the room, the sound of birds and of television sets overwhelming us in the darkness.

"It stinks," Marie-Jean said and closed the door behind us, went to the window and began to experiment with an ominous device encased in tin which bore a warning DO NOT DISMANTLE. I found some lights and turned them into an uneven glow which filtered through the wetness of the room and the device in the corner began to hum. Marie-Jean tucked the shades even tighter into the windows and then put on the television set in the corner where some kind of a sporting tournament seemed to be in progress.

"They charge you a quarter an hour for the sound," she said, "but we can beat them because who needs to listen anyway?" She adjusted the dial, her earlier spirits almost completely recovered and went to the door where she pressed a small button which, she said, locked us in and the world out. She shrugged and faced me. "Do you want to fuck?" she said.

"All right. If you want."

"That's why we're here so we might as well."

"I don't care," I said pointlessly. "No objection." I watched her take off her clothing then in a feeling of total suspension, her breasts which hung from the release of her brassiere somehow not her breasts but those obscene, semi-detached cylinders which I had hung on my walls, the nipples not made of flesh but of paper, the glossy thighs emerging from the tube of her unrolled pants much as my detumescent prick might have scattered its last wandering shots emerging from its snug home. In a continued mood of abstraction I took off my own clothing, watching the sporting tournament where several men appeared to be trying to surpass others with the exercise of their limbs, then stood before her in the cooling, damp breezes of the room feeling like a dwarf suspended in putty, everything an abstraction but the central aspect.

"You've gotten bigger," she said. "Screwing will do that to you." She lay down on the bed and for the first time before me, then, a woman exposed the full flower of her thighs, that moist, reaching cove where all ceremonies end, the dampness and bleakness of her hair commingling with the preparatory juices that already seemed to move idly within her. "I'm pretty hot, you better come right here," she said.

From this angle her breasts had flattened out to near invisibility, becoming a part of the bedsheets rather than her body; her thighs too had spread to a plane of dwindling; only her huge, strangely muscled orifice itself lay before me, an unwinking eye, center of all things, blinking and winking with its special knowledge. I had never seen a woman that way before; I had never conceived from the magazines that they looked this way and in all my previous experience it had only been the weapon's knowledge, never my own. What my genitals knew then, my sensibility was first attuning to and this filled me with a feeling of horror: how had they stood it? How had they managed? Was that all there was to it? But the body, on its own faithless round, had already moved beyond me, moved to the bed and I pushed myself upon her, feeling the wetness of the contact above and below, heard her sigh and begin to turn against me. *Fuck me, you bastard son of a bitch*, she said. And in the slow, gathering wandering that came from that, the last battle began.

I rolled with her in an anxiety of pace, trying to order myself above as we were ordered below, the small, slow connection of organs working on various levels of wetness and as I did so, I could hear her murmur, unsilenced in the blankness continuing at rising pitch: *fuck me, fuck me*, and the joining was accomplished rapidly, so rapidly that her grasp of need was met with my own breath of astonishment as the conjoinment was made, and slowly then I rose on knees and elbows above her, a small heightening, a feeling of ascension and I began to work in her, feeling her tube shudder and close under me, her tube reaching to clamp me and I began slowly, my erection already accomplished, to work on her, hearing her vague mutterings not as words but as a collection of emotions refracted through my own despair. *You can't do it, you can't do it, you son of a bitch*, is what she was saying or what I took her to be saying and the distended pupil of my left eye, caught on the wall, swung idly over to the television set and I glimpsed then the apotheosis of sporting event while under me a different series of events took place: she was so moist that she expelled me, dripping on to the sheets and I had to begin entrance over again, this entrance somewhat more difficult because the wrenching and tumbling of her body made that accomplishment almost irrelevant to the higher need.

I got it in, finally, my bulging eyeballs receding from the television set to her breasts, flat against her body and gleaming with perspiration, shoved up against me and in other circumstances it might have ticked me into orgasm, severed as they seemed to be from the rest of her body, the nipples little more than commas impressed against the sleekness of flesh. But she was talking again: talking too much and too frantically and I felt my quickening recede, felt my impending orgasm diminished and the screen shifted and began to play a biscuit commercial while in a small explosion of attention I let my two hands wander over her body, balancing desperately on my knees as I did so and I heard her cries begin to mingle and to find words again.

"Inside, inside you bastard," she said, and I tried to go inside but there was a retarding slickness which sought to expel me again and all that I could do was butt up it helplessly again, feeling myself drawn into those waters. "Come on," she said, "what are you waiting for, can't you even do it?" and I felt then the drawing, the drawing itself. It was as if she had turned herself inside out to accommodate me and now was turning back again and I could feel myself sliding damply, wetly, desperately up to her core and at the same time there were frantic thumps on the ceiling and cries of children; a family was heading out for the highways, apparently. The thought of these consequences, all the eventual consequences of my own emission strewn aimlessly all over the landscape kicked me into further determination and I began to work over her in earnest, freeing a hand to grapple with her breasts while I bent slowly in a kind of inclination. And still the orgasm was retarded; I wanted nothing more, then, but to finish as quickly as possible and withdraw: to return in comity to that car and giving her the wheel that time permit the reversal of a journey which would leave me spent but not undone hovering over my magazines in the evening's glaze, but she wouldn't release me and I realized then with a kind of primal and final horror that she wasn't going to release me; that she wanted all of me, all of me inside her. That she was drawing, drawing me from the very center. And I shouted then, a shout somewhere between pain and dread but she clamped and would not let me out and forced me, busily, to continue with the grapple.

I think I saw it all, then, you son of a bitch, working over her as I did: I think that in the center of her cries and moans, her lunging and despair, I saw the totality, the sum, the oft-evaded center of everything which had happened to me already. I think I must have seen that she was not a tube but a girl, that her breasts were not severed but rather attached by muscle and blood and extension to the drawings of her breath herself and that finally, denuded of all but need, I was being forced on that last journey defenseless. But I must not have seen it too well; I must have gripped all of it only through retrospection for what I tried to do, putting my palms flat to the wall and raising myself above her was to seek a kind of withdrawal. I wanted to remove myself from her. I wanted to tear myself free, tear myself into some small space where I could consider what was happening to me; what had happened to me for a long, solitary time but she wouldn't let me, the pulsing was both outward with her thighs and inward with the mechanics of her cunt itself and I was helpless, I was helpless. And now, as I poised above her, broken arrow, trying to work myself through the blank space of the final seconds with this girl and behind it all the dull realization that it would never happen, that she had brought me too far and therefore beyond the possibility of function, something must have smashed within me, scattering its fragments throughout and I heard her; I truly heard her then, crying with her full voice in the darkness.

"You're going to do it, now, you bastard," she was muttering to me, "you're going to really do it; you're going to do it with a woman not yourself, you're going to force yourself into a woman, not yourself, you're going to come into a woman, not yourself; you're going to break through, you son of a bitch, into free high ground." And she said this to me, all sprinkled with obscenities which I cannot recapitulate, let alone bring myself to utter, I felt the rage within me: the One, free final rage; a cooling rage that removed the last elements of my turgidity and left me in control in some dark space above her; a taloned bird swooping in the night, a plunging beak moving to grab her. "You will, you will," she said, "I'm a woman, not a god damned picture," and I had no way of knowing if she was saying this or if the dwarf's voice inside was addressing me but it was all the same, all the same. I felt myself retracting, sliding out inch-by-inch, all the time playing the idiot's game of bucking and necessity so that she would not know what was not happening inside her. And so my chest pummeled hers, my uninterested hands sliding through the gift of her breasts and her mouth opened; she passed beyond speech, she passed into a different time.

And I was an eaglet suspended above the lost dominions of the sea; I was a roc, that legendary, frantic bird, scuttling over an egg on an abandoned island, I was a sea-creature, suspended in the aqueous death: I was all of these both far above and below of her, struggling past the network of my sensibility and then her voice cried out in sheer, grave horror that struck me like a lance and brought me past all of this: "You can't do it, you son of a bitch!" she was saying to me, "you can't do it to a woman, you need your pictures!" and her voice was as I had never heard it before, strained and low.

So I poised above her, then, poised above her in the astonishment of flight, her body wide and open before me, her breasts small, encompassed flowers and as the last piece of me slipped free I found myself, by that individuality, thrust into the oldest, coldest and finest insight of all and on the television screen two of the sportsmen began to struggle with one another with clubs and somewhere above us there was a splashing of water and the very eaves themselves groaned; the machine in the corner giving out drafts of fresh air, and suspended at that height above her I brought my fists down once, twice, three times, violently upon her throat, feeling her spread at last and those juices of completion surge forward from her.

I brought it into her then with all the cunning force of accumulation, plunging my need into hers, severing her from herself so that, like me, she flew at some fine, high, dreadful angle from her history, raising to crash again and again, thighs and before me, fell all the way back, her eyes open and shoulders working in dreadful comity and she fell astonished, her head split with the general cleavage, her body open and pulsing and the grey flickers of the television set passing over her: I put it into her once, twice, and again and then, for the first time, as if I had put a twenty-five cent piece into the television set of sensibility, the sound came on. I heard the screams. I felt the rush. And in that last high twisting, I began to understand what had happened to me that afternoon.

And so, falling now, falling before her, falling before all possibility, my head in the penitent's crouch between her knees, my tongue in the penitent's curl in her cunt, my body in the penitent's curve in the snow and redness of her culmination I lay there while the full sounds of the afternoon passed over me for the first time, the full meaning of her body passed through my clutching hands for the first time and the uneven pounding and shouts outside of the diminishing door might have been a true and final counterpoint to that mutuality of need which had sent all of us to the FARMER'S REST that afternoon, past the sunken highways of our destiny.

D'Arcy fell as he said these last words, fell lengthwise to the mottled rug and then rolled over on his back, his eyes sunken and huge, focused on the ceiling, his chest falling uneasily. I put my pen shakily into the pages of my notebook and looked at him. I could feel the sweat dart out on my palms and with it a feeling of apprehension, almost as if someone would break through in the instant past the walls of the room and discover us in this confidentiality of loss. But after some time I recovered my voice and said to him very quietly, "I'm not going to pick you up, you know. You're going to have to get up from there yourself; you. You'll have to do it."

He said nothing, attempted to make a sound, his voice a croak in the room. I considered him. I was in no hurry, finally. There was nothing before us but completion.

"I said get up," I said.

"Oh God," he muttered. "Oh God, God."

"None of that is going to do you any good, now. You're going to have to pick yourself up from the floor."

"I can't," he whispered. "I think I injured something."

I closed my notebook and put it carefully beside me on the table. I would need it later; it was the only record.

"You killed her," I said.

"I didn't say that."

"You killed that girl. You killed her in that motel. That's what you were trying to say to me. Wasn't it?"

"I don't know." He scrambled at the floor, rolling to his stomach, managed to raise himself to his knees. Hated D'Arcy. Destructive D'Arcy. Killer D'Arcy. "What does it matter?"

"And they found you there. After you had killed her."

"No, no, it wasn't like that. It wasn't like that at all."

"Then how was it? How did they find you?"

"No," he said, "no, no."

"I have to finish my book. How can I finish it unless I know? They found her corpse under your thighs."

"It wasn't that way."

"Her corpse was already stretched in the strophe of suffocation, her eyes full, wide and bulging, the blood running down the two of you, the broken limbs, the broken glass. You shrieked with laughter as you opened the door to their pounding; you trembled with a fanatic's glee as you showed them her body."

"I tell you it didn't happen that way. You couldn't know. How could you know this?"

"And you struggled not against their embrace—against the wedge of Elmer's shoulders, that is—as they took you away, leaving the car still insolently parked off-angle from your cabin."

"No, no, no, no. No, no."

"That's what you did," I said.

"I didn't mean to. I didn't understand what was happening until it was too late. I didn't want a girl. I didn't want a girl to be that way. There are ways and ways."

"You wanted her to be inert and glossy, as everything else you had fucked and she wasn't. So you killed her then and left her corpse to Elmer, willed your history to possibility."

"I didn't mean it to be that way. She didn't understand. None of them understood. She forced me."

"And they took you away and in time took the battered corpse and took it on a different journey."

"Yes," D'Arcy gasped, struggling to his feet and trying to reach the decanter, finding it and funneling it into his mouth with a desperate gesture. "That was the way it was."

"I know."

"I must drink."

"Drink," I said. "Drink, drink, drink. Drink your life away, D'Arcy, for your journey has now begun."

He held on to the decanter stuffing the neck down his mouth, ingesting the fluids and I let him, seeing the silt rise toward the top, seeing the workings of the cords of his neck. It didn't matter, now. None of it mattered. I took my pen and gripped it. He put the decanter down with a gasp.

"So that completes it. That's all that there is to say. Now you can leave and write your book. Go to the sea."

"Not yet," I said. "Not just yet, D'Arcy. There is one more thing I must do before that."

"What?"

"You know what it is," I said.

I raised the pen and advanced toward him.

And with a fine distancing stroke, a triumph of leverage and patience and luck, I drove the pen point smoothly, inevitably through his temple and deep into his brain. It penetrated to the clip, only a faint streak of color remaining outside to give any indication that the pen was there.

"That's what I had to do," I said. "You left me no alternative."

He fell slowly before me; collapsing in pieces, bits of him strewn before the others and tumbled in a heap, his mouth opened, his eyes wide and pleading and desperate in the cave of his face. He seemed upon the point of saying something but he had absolutely nothing to say.

I knelt before him. "I don't like this any better than you do," I said, "and I can't get over the feeling too that it has all happened before. But what is there to do, D'Arcy: tell me, my friend, what else is there to do?" My voice broke. I could not help myself. I had really cared for him after all. It was not his fault.

The old feeling, the old admiration returned; the old courage and determination. I reached before me and put the book under my arm. "Don't worry," I said to him as he lay so slack, so drained, so broken on the carpet. "This is not where it all ends. There will be other times, other places, D'Arcy. We will meet again."

I stood then, went to the door, looked at him for the last time and then on an impulse returned to pick up the scattered decanter, turned it above him and poured the last streams into his hair. It lay there redly, glistening in the black surfaces.

"There will be other times," I said to him again and went to the door, opened the door, looked at him for the last time and stepped out into the hall, pulling the knob before me. Down the stairs, all the way, I felt terror at leaving my biographer's commitment to once again confront the surfaces of the world, but as I came out into the air the apprehension vanished, dwindled to a slow, modest appreciation. It was really all the same. Outside, inside, it was all the same. It was a cool spring day, much as it had been in D'Arcy's apartment. I walked through it gracefully, jauntily, eyes toward the sun, pushing the ancient frame toward that final time of resting when the biography itself could begin.

June 1968
New York, New York

Afterword:
The Man in the Glass Booth

"No true history of the 20th century can be written without an account of my friend Ernie" Schwarz-Bart opens *The Last of the Just* and the same could be said of Maurice Girodias and 20th century publishing. Girodias (1919-1990), the son of the first publisher of the Paris Olympia Press was caught in the French occupation, changed his surname (as brother Eric did not) and essentially waited out the occupation underground; when he returned to publishing as his father's designated successor it was with a political program to supplement what might have been his father's rather simpler ambition to publish pornography of compensatory literary interest in English for tourists in which pornography's indelicate reputation made it of unusual interest to foreign seekers of the truth. Jack Kahane found Henry Miller among some other celebrants of copulation but was less interested in literary than commercial outcome.

His son, who must have exuded an air of weary, fallen aristocracy in his 20's might have had the same goal but after the ravages of WW II and years of what must have been unending anxiety and fermenting anger was driven by ideology which he once explained to me. "Government wants to repress freedom, personality, choice, individual expression but the people instinctively resist this so Government learned that the best means of repression was to campaign against pornography. Who will openly defend pornography? So they clamp down on that which is acceptable to most of the reading class and then, having established the right to repress they go after everything else. The first thing a Government on the march wants to cancel is public expression of sex and when you have that approval you go on the march."

Girodias then in that weary elegance of which I have written decades ago (Introduction to the *New Olympia Reader*) embarked upon a weary and shuffling postwar crusade; revived his father's Olympiad, created the Traveler's Companion imprint and in 1955 acquired a novel which was deemed unpublishable by the 30 or 40 publishers to whom it had been offered. Girodias shrugged, paid a one thousand dollar advance to the agent who had had nowhere left to send it and found himself at the center of a scandal and controversy which utterly changed publishing and very possibly the modern sensibility. *Lolita* made everyone but Girodias wealthy (and respectable); he was never able to sequester the English language rights and while Putnam and Walter Minton made out comfortably on a novel essentially pirated, Maurice had nothing to console him but fame. Ultimately he was more distressed by the failure of the Parisian nightclub he had spent far too much to sustain and he fled with his usual dignity to New York City in 1967 where he presumed to begin Olympia America on a shoestring, a smile and an elegant weariness which by this time had become almost monarchial.

It is then April of 1968 which was when the first Olympia America titles were published in paperback with one faint hardcover title, Robert Turner's *Pretty Thing* when Maurice's odyssey and mine intersected, first gradually and then in tight fusion. ("Just like the sex, eh?" he might have said.) He called for manuscripts from writers who would in that cascading year of collapse willing to enlist with him in the new resistance; Vietnam was the flashpoint for an ideological, raging protest the governmental response to which confirmed his theory of literature as the central agent of resistance.

In the garden apartment at 216 West 78th Street I was certainly paying attention, if not to Maurice's ideology but his finances. I was writing literary novels for Harry Shorten published under titles like *Nympho Nurse* and *Instant Sex* for advances less than half of Maurice's presumed offer and furthermore *Lolita* was being evoked as central to his history and at least possibly, then for his program. "He wants *Lolita?* I thought. "I've read *Lolita*. I'll give him that," and in that kind of storm of misguidance which characterized my self-administered career advice through the decades, I wrote the first twenty pages of what was first less floridly titled *The Oracle* and mailed them to the Gramercy Park brownstone the bedroom of which was Maurice's first headquarters. Four or five weeks later a contract was offered. "Okay, he *does* want *Lolita*" I thought in affirmation and wrote the damned novel in two or three weeks: unreliable narrator, shifting perspective, doubling of narrator and protagonist with a big reveal implied but never quite enacted, awkward, plunging sex scenes, and of course self-service as the narrator's central sexual expression. Mad, tilted comedy as the Oracle at a crucial instant, flogging himself in a barnyard, inadvertently touches an electrified fence. This is what Girodias addressed when he summoned me to Gramercy Park a week after the manuscript had been mailed.

"Well," he said, in summary, "This is not your number one bestseller but it is amusing and I guess I can publish it. As a favor to you. Now I want you to do a favor for me." He proceeded to outline *Screen* which he promised would be the bestselling and most scandalous novel of his time. "I know you are the man to do it." Later I learned that he had offered the central conception to every writer who had passed to or by Gramercy Park over several months, all of whom had politely or impolitely refused. That central conception seemed actionable to me. "I will protect you, I will assume any legal expense" Maurice averred. I wrote the novel in less time than *Oracle* had taken. The rest of the story is in my Afterword to the reissue, kindly published by Stark House a few months ago. *Screen* in its subterranean way has hung around for half a century and without ever quite surfacing into the culture above ground has found a quiet readership over the years. (Gene Wilder wanted to star in a movie adaptation but the saintly producer, Sidney Glazier, could not raise the money.)

Oracle did not incur a similar fate; maybe the Nabokovian pastiche (at least in technical terms) was all wrong for the mass audience Girodias wanted; maybe the fact that every USA publisher with whom Girodias had been involved was waiting with avidity to destroy him, maybe I was not sufficiently Nabokovian; if you want to do that kind of job you'd better know, as Donald Westlake might advise, to have a getaway car and know where it is stashed.

But here it is, nonetheless. The Friday after the Wednesday on which I had delivered the novel I went out to dinner with my wife talking about it incessantly. "I have written the novel I always wanted to write, just the way I wanted to write it," I said. I was 29 years old. "I am at peace. If I go right now, at least I have done that." Fifty-two years later I still have done it.

August 2020: New Jersey

In My Parents' Bedroom

by Barry N. Malzberg

For My Wife, Joyce

"… Me next to sleep
All that is left to Eden."
Delmore Schwartz: GENESIS

"There is no such thing as a free lunch."
—old aphorism as quoted by
Michael Malzberg, circa 1949

ONE

The home in which I grew up has become a museum and, with a group of others, I am now on a guided tour. Exactly why I have chosen to do this and why the house itself has become a collection of artifacts is something which I do not know; perhaps some of this will come clear later, although almost everything in my more recent experience militates against my belief in easy answers. The fact is that I am tired, very tired, and hope to go to sleep at some point along the tour, possibly on the couch which I remember as having been in the living room, adjacent to the grand piano. I doubt very much that I will be missed because the other tourists are most excited about the tour and have no eyes for anything except what is before them.

I am with a girl and our hands touch lightly now and then; she is blonde and wearing a dark raincoat made of thin material which does good things for her body. I seem to have some distinct memory of this girl, of having in the recent past gone to bed with her and ex-changed words of love and remorse but at this time her name escapes me as well as the exact circumstances of our meeting and our relationship. She apparently feels close to me because her face is always on mine when I turn toward her and her eyes seem to light with that sense of rising intensity which, I have been led to understand, indicates that a girl is on the make. The fact is that I know very little about women, far less than I would have dared to hope years ago, and this girl's conduct, to say nothing of her antecedents, is a mystery to me. Nevertheless, I am moved by her—there is a real chance that I might even be "in love"—and I hope that as the tour proceeds I will learn more about her and what we have done together and what we may hope to be in the future. She seems to be about twenty-three years old with the tender, slightly naive expression of a virgin past her long-sought deflowering, and I hope, although this is unreasonable, that I have brought nothing but joy to her in the course of whatever relationship we might have known.

But there is little time to think of her now and little inclination as well, although her fingers are rather tight against my palm and seem to be full of messages. If I do not know what she is doing, then, she does and I am somewhat relieved to know that at the least she is not discontent with me. The tour guide, an old man with baggy trousers and a face wrinkled by sun into the color and dimensions of a rather forbidding plum, has led us through the doors of the house and into the large vestry which precedes the living room. There is more than enough room for us to gather around him there in a tight mass and as we do so he takes from his pocket a large notebook with paper coming unevenly from it at all angles and, opening it, begins to talk to us in a high voice, his eyes not so much on us as deeply withdrawn, caught by some intricacy of webbing in the shattered wall which lies to our rear. He seems faintly nervous and occasionally tugs at an earlobe, scratches his stomach as he talks and it occurs to me that this is probably a very cheap guided tour—the kind of thing which is put together by small men working on margin for the titillation of tourists who would not understand anything else—and that the house itself may be a very minor grade of attraction.

"This is the Westfield home," he says, "restored to its present condition by a large grant given by the National Council on Ruins and Relics and currently supported by a series of government grants which permit it to be open to viewing five days a week as well as on holidays. The Westfields, of course, were a family of moderate circumstances living in New York in the middle of the twentieth century, whose tasks and deeds have long since elevated them to genuine significance in the historical survey. The home itself is an excellent example of the architecture of its time and, indeed, contains many points of interest to say nothing of the complete furniture collection and that of *objets d'art* which are considered to be very fine examples of their type. All in all the home can be considered to be one of the most interesting exhibits available on the life of its time and I think that you will enjoy our walk through it this morning. Refreshments will be available in the kitchen after the tour has concluded and, throughout, the facilities of the bathroom will be available to those of you who need it. I ask you to use routine caution in the course of the tour and not to touch any of the objects or furniture without permission and then only very carefully; most of this material is extremely fragile and its condition under stress could not be spoken for. I suggest that we all go through the vestry one by one, trying to wipe our shoes off on the carpet, and then re-assemble in the living room, before the grand piano, where we will begin our tour. The tour itself lasts for four hours so perhaps we will have a cigarette now; no smoking is permitted in the corridors, of course, and the house is hermetically sealed anyway, meaning that smoke would quickly asphyxiate all of us."

The guide seems to have taken this last line as a joke because he begins to laugh uneasily in a rising croak, and then, briskly motioning us to pass, he steps aside and does produce a cigarette from his inner coat pocket which he carefully inspects and then wets with his tongue. It is obviously his intention to compel smoking in the vestry if at all, but this is obviously impossible; the ten of us are almost shoulder to shoulder in the gripping space and whatever smoke might do to us in the inner rooms, it would be even more damaging in this confine. Besides that, I have given up smoking very recently, having cut down from two packs a day to almost nothing, and I do not wish to succumb to temptation. I am, then, on the point of trying to lead the girl into the living room when she gives me a sharp, if affectionate, tug on the wrist and looking up at me says, "Let's go outside and smoke there. It's too crowded in here and besides you heard him say it's going to be a long tour; we could use the fresh air."

There is something so soft and knowledgeable in her voice and expression—this girl obviously knows me well and thinks highly of me—that all argument is stifled. I permit her to lead me away from the tourists and the guide and we go through the clatter of the receiving door and into the small yard where I spent most of my outdoor life before the age of ten, tossing a ball against the eaves of the roof and now and then dabbling in gardening projects which never quite worked out. We stand there for a few moments and, realizing on some basic level that the situation has become awkward, I quickly hand her one of my own cigarettes—although I have almost quit smoking I cannot bear to be without them should something terrible happen—and light it for her.

"That's better," she says briskly, tossing her head and blowing out smoke vigorously. "It's really stuffy in there but it's nice out here. I'm glad we decided to come though. The Westfield is one of the main spots."

"I know," I say and the fact is that I *do* know. Moreover, it is not as if I am amnesiac so much as that I do not care for the moment to seek perspective. It is like those thick, strange moments of emergence after a pleasant dream when reality hangs over very heavily and could be subsumed but it is far more pleasant, for the instant, to languish in the possibilities of fantasy. It is probable that I know who this girl is and why she cares for me, that I know why I am on this tour and where we will go afterwards, but it would be too much of an effort and besides it is all too confusing for the moment, better to simply take it on its own level and let it make its own sense. I am aware, of course, that this is probably a rationalization and that I fear disaster if I really try to understand what is happening to me, but my talent for speculation, at least since I gave up cigarettes, has diminished and the girl is very pretty. It is apparent, in fact, in this light, that she is close to being beautiful.

"But it's going to be *so* boring," she says. "If he'd only let us walk around and touch things and kind of learn on our own it would be nice, but he's going to lead us through one of those stuffy walks and probably ask us questions about what we're seeing and he'll ruin everything. Why can't people be trusted to learn everything on their own? Why do they manipulate us so? Don't they know that we're far better than what they take us to be? Or can't they afford to know that so it goes the other way?"

At these profound questions I feel an answering response starting and would begin to talk to her but find, suddenly, that I cannot: the girl is so beautiful, her face so enticing, her breasts even under the raincoat so obviously well-constructed, and I am tired as well, so tired that it is probable that I got no sleep at all last night or maybe even the night before that. So I only nod, losing what amount of esteem in her eyes I do not know, and then, on an impulse, dig for the cigarettes and light one myself. "Yes," I say, completing this insufficient act and tossing the match into the familiar dirt where I place some earth over it, "that's all very true but there's so much to see in the Westfield that we probably wouldn't see half the things of interest if we found our own way. This way at least we'll know that we won't miss anything."

"Maybe you're right," she says, "but I don't like this guide, I don't think he takes any interest in his work and besides it's such a cheap tour. Usually you can do better than this, most of the guides are really quite nice. I suppose we should have waited but that was our schedule."

"I know," I say and for no reason then the girl gives me a touch so blank, so urgent, so full of promise that it is all I can do to contain my responses. She has placed her fingers lightly on my thigh and eased them up toward my scrotum, and as she does so there comes to me, along with a wedge of response, a wave of emotion so thick, so deadly, so poignant and so filled with memory and guilt that I literally gag, unable for the moment to stand it. She is so beautiful after all. I put my hand on her wrist and gently take it from me, rub my fingers along her bare upper arm and say, "We better get back inside now. They'll be waiting for us."

"Don't you care?" she says. "Don't you care for me? Did I make you mad?" She looks soft and vulnerable, as if I had hit her fully across the face, but there is a kind of guile underneath her assumption of pain as well and I am aware of it. It is obvious that I know far more about this girl than I am willing to concede at this moment and it lends a certain double edge of intricacy to our relationship which, I know, will almost certainly mar the day if I do not come to terms with it.

"I'm sorry," I say. "I care very much, I care very terribly for you but we simply can't get involved that way now. We have the tour to go on and things to see and things to do and certain responsibilities to fulfill; later will be time enough for all of this and besides you know I love you." But it has been the wrong thing to say because she tosses her cigarette to the ground with an anguished expression and caves against me, her hands reaching to meet around my back.

"Oh, Michael," she says, "oh, Michael, why did we go on this stupid tour anyway? We could have been back at the hotel making love to each other and everything would be beautiful, but instead we have to come out and see this and I don't even want to. I don't even care about it. It was all your idea, I'd rather be at the hotel. Couldn't we give it up and go back?"

"We already paid."

"We can turn the tickets in or go another time. Oh, Michael, I hate to see us fight like this; we're all we've got."

"Yes," I say and stroke her hair, shining dimly against my palm. "Yes, I know, but we're way out of town now and the bus is the only way back. I wouldn't know how to get back by public transportation and we really can't afford taxis." I know the route to midtown very well, of course; it is engraven upon every cell from years of solitary buses to the center, but to concede this would be, of course, to lose the argument and I do not want to lose it. I am strangely fascinated by the prospect of seeing my old home once again and the fact that neither the girl nor anyone on the tour knows my relationship to it is additionally titillating; it is as if I am walking around with some kind of strange power, a total precognition which renders me superior to them and although there is a kind of excitement in this there is pain also because they do not know the cost of these rooms. But I cannot reflect on this at the present time, all that I say to her is, "Let's go inside again. You know I love you, you know how I feel about you. I could spend all of my life in bed with you and not even find the beginning. But we came out for this tour and we bought the tickets and we ought to see it. I understand it's very interesting."

"That's your trouble," she says. "That's the trouble with all of you, you say that you could spend the rest of your life in bed with me. How about *not* in bed with me, just talking and being together, would that mean anything? Isn't there anything but sex for you?" And I understand finally that I have reached very deep water, but at the same moment she gives me the reverse of the exiting tug and thus indicates that she will go back to the house now. I decide to say nothing—anything I say will only complicate matters impossibly—and allow her to lead me back, our feet lifting small scuffs of moisture and sand into the air, a feeling of heaviness and oppression in the climate. When I was much younger I believed that the weather was somehow personal, that it was contrived only to afflict me and in truth I have never lost this assumption. Being back at my own home has only reconstituted the obsession. I warn myself to stay as calm as possible, there is every indication that this may be an emotional day and little good will accrue from expending feeling easily or for triviality.

We go back into the house. The tourists have moved, from the vestry and into the living room and are standing behind the large gate shutting off its contents from visitors. The guide is in their center and is saying nothing, apparently they have been waiting for us, the laggards, to rejoin them and there is a good deal of pique on some faces as we try to huddle into them inconspicuously. A heavy, red-faced woman shielded by sunglasses and a handkerchief held against her cheek is particularly enraged, she mutters something to me as I brush against her and then bends to whisper into the ear of an albino boy standing at her side, apparently her son. "No consideration," I hear her say. "They have absolutely no consideration, but then these people never do."

I would, if it were feasible, reply to her at that point, tell her that in the most essential sense if I were not there there would be no tour, but I decide not to; at the same time the girl's hands fold into mine again, almost trustingly, and I am overcome by such sentiment at this sudden admission of her dependence that I am momentarily incapable of speech. And then, too, the guide has begun his speech.

"This is the living room," he says. "It is an excellent example of its type, both accessible and comfortable for the occupants, and the furniture, restored to its original polish, is extremely practical both in terms of cost and convenience. The family used to spend their evenings here, watching television, reading, and occasionally playing board games such as Monopoly, Parcheesi and chess. This was a common way of passing the time during this period although they had other activities as well."

I look intensely at the living room. It is somehow comforting to see everything as it was so long ago; I have not been here for quite a long time, of course—it is hard for me in my blanket of buried recollection to know exactly, but it is probably twenty years—but everything seems the same. There is a large, reddish couch which is backed up against the far wall, to its sides are pictures and adjacent to this on the other wall is the small bulk of the television set and a straight chair. In the center is the dining table and there are a couple of other simple chairs scattered in informal positions. The flowers on the dining table are artificial, of course, but look very well for all of that, being a cluster of pink and blue which has the aspect of human flesh.

"Although the room is a common example of its type," the guide says, "it is extremely well preserved and possesses to the highest degree that combination of functionalism and anonymity which was the keystone of this culture. Observe the living room closely, if you will. It appears spare, clean, reasonable, as if it were tenanted by sensible people who spent a good deal of their time examining their lives and trying to make some sense of them, as if it were lived in by people who devoted a good portion of their conversation to considerations of their mortality, their penalties, the ultimate meaning of what they would have to eventually understand or die. Yet the fact is that this room entertained almost no such thoughts and that its occupants were often not only unaware of these considerations but felt that the room—being 'pleasant' and 'bright' and 'airy'—was a good source of 'relaxation' geared to take them away from exactly those questions which I have raised. They thought, in short, of this living room as a kind of respite from the torment and considerations of their ordinary lives, and who among us is qualified to understand that irony or to comment upon it? There are no easy answers, as any consideration of this Westfield restoration will show us, and I think that you will find this increasingly broadening as we proceed."

The guide grins when he finishes this sentence and I am aware for the first time that I do not like him very much. He is a small man, beautifully proportioned so that there is no hope of ever referring to him as a dwarf, but his features are even uglier upon inspection and there is a kind of whimsical light in his eyes which indicates that he has certain thoughts on his job and on the restoration site that his canned speeches will not permit him to concede. Our eyes meet for an instant as he passes them flickeringly over us and I feel a fear that he might have recognized me, but then they turn away, passing others, and I realize that this is only my own discontent and insecurity I am feeling and that the guide, actually, has no idea who any of us are but is merely trying to do his job in as reasonable and controlled a fashion as possible and is probably interested in nothing so much as his mid-day break or a time after that when he can go back to his own furnished rooms and, by swaddling himself in liquor, immerse himself in his own sense of restoration. As I think this I decide that I have no reason to dislike him, yet the response remains, nestling uncomfortably in my gut. I understand that I will have to work all of this out sometime during the day and this intimation fills me with gloom, not so much because I am afraid of knowledge as because I am very tired and interested only in sensations at the present time, having no capacity whatsoever for abstraction. It occurs to me from some abscess of memory that this is an old problem.

"The tenants in this 'living' room were thus not so much 'living' as merely 'existing,'" the guide says, running a small hand over the gate, "and indeed some of the eminent philosophers and writers of their time took this one step further to say that actually this was not the case either but that they were in all likelihood 'dying.' This is something worth thinking about and we will touch on the subject again, but as more information comes to bear we will be in a better position to appreciate this." He shrugs and makes a tilting gesture with his palms toward the ceiling. "Shall we go now?" he says.

"I have a question," one of the tourists says. He is a fat man carrying an umbrella looped over his right wrist, splendid mustaches flaring, an air of piggish certainty caving in over his eyes and down toward the duller planes of his cheeks. Surrounded as he is by others it is hard to gauge his weight, but surely he is massive, he talks in short puffs and with that kind of portentousness which men almost always assume when they realize that they are potential heart cases and thus uniquely vulnerable at any given time, yet are not willing to do anything to deal with the more pressing medical certainties underneath. "In fact, I have a couple of questions."

"Well, yes," the guide says, "that's my job. I want to emphasize that I am happy to entertain your questions at any point of the tour; this is an important museum and the job of the restoration is to make its contents and meaning as apparent to as many people as possible. The cause is not only educational but cautionary, and how can we do both if we do not know what is on your minds?" I feel that this is very nice of the guide although I suspect that he is only following protocol in saying this, and that if there were complaints to his superiors about a failure to answer questions, his job or at least his actual tenure might be in some jeopardy. I too have worked in civil service at some time in my past, I recall, and know of the tense ambiguities of the position, the constant conflict between guilt and revulsion which so undermines the civil servant and renders him open to cheap satire and burlesque.

"Now then," the fat man says officiously, "who lived here? You keep on telling us about the 'Westfields' but who, actually, were they?"

"That is a good question," the guide says. "I was going to delay this information until we came into the rear hallway, which was the place in which all family portraits were hung, and I would at that time have given an ample explanation of the biographies and relationships of the members of the family, but there is no harm in telling you this now and it will, perhaps, give you a better appreciation of the points of interest in the kitchen, which we would reach first, as well as the essential mystery of the dining room. The Westfields were a family of four, composed of Jonathan Westfield, a salesman of minor accomplishments, his wife Josephine who was a part-time schoolteacher in the city civil service of her time, and their two children, Michael and Katherine. Michael was the older by three years and both of them came relatively late in life to the Westfields who were, respectively, forty-five and thirty-eight when their son was born. Both of them married relatively late as well and for a while lived in a small furnished apartment in the more central city, but after the birth of their son, they decided that they needed 'more space' and accordingly rented the home which has become this museum. The relationships between the Westfields are surely interesting and surrounded by many comedic aspects, but there is so much of them which we cannot know because it is buried so far back in time and because relationships, in any event, are very tricky things to understand. We do, however, have certain facts verified by biographical data and correspondence and they can be rapidly summarized as incontrovertible. Incidentally, these materials are on view in the attic, which will be the next-to-last stop of our tour and surely one of the high points, although the footing up there is extremely dangerous and only volunteers should come on up."

"Tell me those facts," the fat man says. His eyes are more and more possessed of a certain pleading intensity and at the same time the fingers of the girl dig into my palm sharply and I inhale in a rapid squeak, which is particularly embarrassing as those eyes turn toward me. I shake my head. "I'm sorry," I say. The fat man turns away in disgust.

"You shouldn't do that," I say, bending down to whisper this into her ear. "It upsets me and we're in company now." She shakes her head rapidly, indicating that she will not listen, and it occurs to me that there are intricacies to our relationship which are extraordinarily dangerous and which I should familiarize myself with before proceeding any further. But this is not the time, of course, and besides I am very interested in everything that is going on outside: I am interested in the guide, interested in the living room, interested in the fat man's questions and exceedingly anxious to hear the answers. It is as if the guide, by laying out the facts of the relationship, will illuminate certain problems I have had for a long time and by that illumination make them disappear. Although I have never undertaken psychoanalysis I have done an inordinate amount of reading in the field and the key to most modern theory, as far as I can surmise, appears to be that to totally realize and apprehend one's problems is to vanquish them, and there is nothing that I am more interested in doing at the present time since my life, obviously, has become a very difficult, complex one. What I want to do is to kiss the girl and show her in that kiss both affection and dismissal, but I know that I do not have the poise or facility to bring it off. Perhaps if I had already possessed these facts things might have been different.

"The relationships," the guide says. "Yes, of course I will try to summarize them. We are talking of a family of four, which means that in geometrical constancy there are ten or twelve possible relationships between the members of this family or some part of them: the relationship between Mrs. Westfield and her daughter, for instance, the relationship between daughter and son, father and son, father and daughter, father, daughter and son considered as a trinity, son, mother and father and so on and so forth. This is one of the most interesting facets of the Westfield project: the way in which an almost total picture of life in the period can be built up from the simple analysis of these relationships. But at the moment let me say that Mr. Westfield married entirely too late in life to bring to his wife or children that particularity of understanding or relaxation of perspective which is the key to carrying off relationships successfully.

In the place of these missing elements he substituted compassion, but that is often not enough, not when you are dealing with highly volatile human beings and a great deal of history. Through most of his life Mr. Westfield routinely expected that he would never get married, and when he did, it was with a kind of bemused surprise. Some expert scholars have advanced the interesting theory that Westfield spent all of his marital life in a continual reflex of shock and that his failure to ever deeply accept the nature of his condition may have contributed to so many of those difficulties which have been later documented. Of course Westfield did not himself feel this way, nor would he understand what we are saying. He felt that he was a 'good husband' and a 'good father' and so indeed he was in all of those terms of reference which we would care, as strangers, to bring to him. He committed no adultery, made a fair living, took his family on trips, and for a man whose identity had been based upon solitude for forty years or more, he did a noteworthy job of shifting his entire self-image to that of a 'family man,' so much so that he could not, after a while, think of himself as being distinguishable and discrete, as apart from Mrs. Westfield and the children. Of course he had no friends other than through his professional duties, which makes of this rather a moot point. All of his free time was spent with his family or trying to get back to them."

"I don't understand this," the albino child says suddenly in a high, whining, rather dreadful voice. "I don't understand any of this and I don't like it; it has nothing to do with me, why did we come here? I'm bored, it's all too terrible, let's go somewhere and get an ice cream cone or something else." I would judge his age to be eight or nine although his rhetoric is obviously that of a child far advanced beyond his chronology. On the other hand, there is a certain irritative note to his voice not characteristic of children beyond babyhood.

At his outburst the guide pauses, of course, and turns toward him with a faintly embarrassed look, once again making that gesture of the tilt of palms. Some sun comes through the skylight, flickers off him, and in that moment of attitude he looks almost saintly, subsuming all knowledge, all rationalization into that posture. But like all things, this passes, and his voice is thin and querulous when he says, "Who said that?"

The woman with the child becomes still and grim and it is apparent that she would try to let the moment pass and deal with it later. But it is not to be, for the girl with me suddenly takes her hand from mine and pointing a finger says, "Her child said that. He was the one creating a disturbance."

The mother gives the girl a look of hatred which passes and flickers on to me and I feel such a surge of rage and pain that at this moment I could commit sheer murder for shame. But the girl adds defiantly, "She's got no right to take a child here unless she can keep him under control; we're all very interested in what's going on here and how can we be expected to appreciate it if this is going on?" And I feel a retaliatory surge of affection for her so enormous that I slide my hand down her arm and squeeze her wrist gently, trying to show her that I agree with what she is saying after all. She shakes her head and subsides against me, breathing rapidly, and I realize that this has been more of a strain on her than I would be able to understand.

"Well," the woman says. "*Well*, we'd leave right this minute if there were a bus going back, you'd better believe me, but we just have to stay now."

"I do think the child may be too young for this tour, madam," the guide says. "As a general rule we do not accept people under fourteen, we feel that they do not have the maturity or perspective to appreciate the exhibits in their truest light. It was only as a favor to you as a matter of fact that we permitted the child to come along, but if you find yourself unable to deal with this—"

"Don't like it!" the albino mutters, driven to some high petulance by the discussion. "It's boring! Let's go somewhere, Mama, and get out of here."

"Well, listen now," a slender, very well-kept young man to my rear says, "I don't think there's any reason for this at all. The child is only a child after all, he can't be expected to understand all of this as quickly as we can take it in. You ought to show a little patience. We'll go for some ice cream very soon," he says to the child and I understand then, with an intuition so enormous as to be beyond doubt, that he is the father of the child and husband of the woman but has hitherto stayed at a little remove from them because in normal circumstances he finds his life in their presence so intolerable that he finds every structured situation a divine order to be apart from them. It is impossible for me not to be sympathetic to this painful situation—so similar in ways to that of the Westfields and yet not a cold artifact, real and therefore intrusive—and yet my train of concentration toward the tour has been severely broken and I wonder if I will be able to get myself back into this again. It is a very tenuous thing after all, this concentration, and my mood of before has already begun to change slightly, to slide imperceptibly toward that sour and self-indulgent despair which I have known at so many other moments and which makes appreciation so difficult. I remember now the girl saying to me last evening as we huddled together in the spaces of the motel room, only our limbs touching, "Michael, you're really hell sometimes. You've got to stop this sulking around because it's like you're doing it because you've got an audience and you wouldn't have the nerve to do it if you were alone, and I simply can't pay the price for your dramatics anymore. Isn't that right? Isn't that right, Michael?" And at this remembrance I bend and put my lips against the surfaces of her ear, strangely hard, like pinpoints coming against me, and her odor swirls up to me as well, an odor compounded from sweat, semen, flowing, need, desire, disaster and such a multiplicity of other things that—ah!—I rebound from her like a spirit and put my arm against her waist, drawing her in. She says nothing but, by rubbing her head against my chest indicates that everything is once again momentarily well between us, and I feel myself dazzled at the complex of emotions I feel for this girl, the sheer liability of all of it. I have never been this way with myself and possibly what she said to me at some time in the past was true, that I make far more demands on others than myself because there is something inside that I am afraid of facing. It is a thing that I know I will probably have to face seriously in the near future. My career is at something of a crossroad.

Meanwhile, the flurry of dialogue around us has ceased and the albino child has curled himself into a small, quietly muttering bundle, against his mother's right armpit. She stands otherwise to the side and slightly apart from him, the contact something which she is trying to make negligible, and the lines of her face are deep and straight with the pride that she is trying to assume. It is obviously a very difficult series of relationships from which the albino has emerged and which nurture him yet, and I find myself closing my eyelids—an old habit—against further consideration. The guide, meanwhile, with unusual aplomb, has settled himself into the couch, crossed his legs and leaned back.

"Well," he says, "well, yes, let's proceed then by all means. I'm sorry I can't permit all of you to sit on the furniture while we talk but the mansion, despite the skill of its restoration, is in very fragile shape; excess use would certainly destroy everything here. Also, this room would not contain even half of you; I let myself through the gate because I can only lecture by facing all of you in the room but the room itself is restricted to personnel. I am truly sorry but then this is a difficult tour, you might be aware of some of the problems we've had in the past. What was the question again?"

"You were explaining the relationships," the heavy man says, lifting the handle of his umbrella slightly off the wrist with his other hand. "You had just finished describing Mr. Westfield."

"Oh, yes," the guide says. "Oh, yes, that's right. Actually I was not explaining the relationships—hell, that would, as I've already pointed out, be almost impossible in line with the geometrical multiplication—but giving you a brief detail of the actual personalities so that you might be able, in your own heads, to imagine the relationships which would proceed from these individuals. I was, in short, giving you a still-life. Incidentally, as we pass the courtesy shop on the way out—it is in the basement and you're free to go into it at the end of the tour—you will be advised of the many fine souvenirs you can purchase there; there is a brief biography of the Westfields whose two hundred pages contains far more material than I can give you in this brief span, and there is also an excellent album of family photographs, still-lifes and backgrounds, which give an excellent picture of the way they lived. In addition, there are records which may be purchased as well as objects of other interest. So you can rest assured that although my information may be sketchy it can be easily supplemented at your leisure." A certain plaintive note has come into the guide's voice as he says this and I wonder whether this is communicable resentment or merely that variety of petulance which overtakes limited men when they perform jobs whose consequences they do not understand and whose actions seem pointless. I decide that at some point of natural breaking in the tour I will speak to the guide separately, try to understand him as I am trying to understand myself, and perhaps then all of these things, as well as his aspect, will fall into place for me.

"In any event," the guide says, "we have discussed Mr. Westfield; let us consider Mrs. Westfield briefly now. She also married rather late, as I pointed out to you, but in her case the marriage may not have been as disastrous, as completely murderous, to the original personality as it was in the case of her husband. Like many women of her period, she never doubted from long before puberty the fact of her eventual marriage and motherhood, and indeed interpreted all of the events of her life as merely some kind of preparation and foreshadowing for this. Imagine her dismay, then, when at the age of thirty-one she found herself still unmarried and with no visible prospects; it was a condition which would have upset the serenity of a woman ten times more serene than Mrs. Westfield. Nevertheless, she persisted; although she had moved into a supervisory position in her teaching duties and although many of her best friends were also over thirty, not married and assuming that hardness and whimsicality of approach which forecasted great things from them in their jobs—although all of this was true, Mrs. Westfield, with that kind of blind faith which may be as close to the truly sacred as any of us may ever know, Mrs. Westfield continued to seek men through 'mutual friends,' through 'adult resorts,' through 'cocktail parties' and the other unique anachronista of the period, her features never raddled in public by any apperception of singlehood and doom, and then at one of the 'cocktail parties' she met Mr. Westfield himself, who had been induced to come there by a prospective customer and who could not resist the possibility of doing liquor and business together. Mr. Westfield was a used-car salesman. She was immediately attracted to him, observing him at great distance through a haze of bootleg liquor which had been subsumed into a very popular drink of the day which then and now is called the 'martini.' All of this occurred slightly before the repeal of 'prohibition,' a concept which, of course, will be a mystery to most of you here but which was one of the controlling aspects of the age in which Mr. and Mrs. Westfield grew to maturity, lending a fine air of illegality to even the simplest and most inevitable of human activities, an attitude which had many interesting implications in the conduct of these people several years or decades later.

"After some time, Mrs. Westfield found her pull to this good-looking stranger almost irresistible although, at the same time, there was a good deal of guilt attached to her feelings of attraction because it was then a popular theory that a righteous woman could undertake no feelings of sexual attraction, let alone passionate response, and yet Mrs. Westfield, as some of the documents in the attic will indicate, was a woman of almost unbearable sexuality, which led to a certain rapidity in her sexual dealings which of course had unfortunate consequences. At this time, however, she was a virgin which added, as you can imagine, not only to her guilt, but to that uneasy feeling of excitement which she interpreted as a distant warmth working through her thighs and toes and even parching the nipples of her invisible breasts, which were well concealed under several layers of the dress of that period."

Once again, the girl's hand slides into mine and this time she gives me several urgent presses of the palm, along with a certain tickling motion of the forefinger which, under other circumstances, I would find almost unbearably exciting, very much like the damned Mrs. Westfield trapped in the swirling of the cocktail party, trying to fasten some kind of sense of direction to herself so that she can garner an introduction. The girl, of course—it is remarkable how my prescience unfolds as this morning goes on; I feel as if all actions, all meaning are subsumed in my intuition and that I can assess the most hidden and therefore basic motives of individuals simply by considering them—is trying to tell me that she is thinking of us and is also trying to draw ironic contrast between the morals of Mrs. Westfield's day and our liberated own, of the morals of a day in which women had to suppress all sexual consciousness as against the present time when it is understood by all people of some college background that women are as sexually needful and deserving as men and therefore can cut through all layers of potential hypocrisy toward a clear sense of understanding. She is trying to remind me that our own first meeting embraced none of these difficulties and that indeed we went to bed after knowing one another two hours as casually as Mr. Westfield, on the eve of his thirtieth anniversary, must have ground his limbs forth toward determined conclusion, but I find it difficult to respond to the girl's pressure with my own enthusiasm, and for several reasons. A feeling of woe scuttles around in my center, familiar and accessible as the ravages of any orgasm, and I recollect that on this aforementioned evening when we went to bed after barely knowing one another, her arms were tight and still against my back as I entered her and her eyes held only a dim surprise as I wedged and sought her with my prick. Her grief, in its stillness and intensity, was as close to that of Mrs. Westfield's as either of us may ever know, and it was difficult to deal with, difficult to take even in memory although she seems to have no such recollection at this moment. It is strange, of course, how my memory comes back to me when convenient; it is increasingly obvious to me that I know almost everything that I will ever need to know about this girl and the circumstances which brought us here, and yet I will myself not to think of it, being far more interested still in what is going on outside and knowing that any final key, any unlocking of understanding, must proceed from the events of this day and not in the reverse fashion. It occurs to me for the first time that I have a fair idea of what I am doing here and what strange fate has led the two of us into these rooms. Meanwhile, of course, the guide is still speaking and I attend to him, drawing the girl's fingers over my thigh as I do so to show her that she is yet important to me. Her name I now remember is Joanne and I have known her for seven months and twenty-two days and I know, as well, exactly what her furnished apartment—in which I have spent so many nights— looks like, but of the circumstances of our relationship or the long span of time behind us I still know nothing and do not seek to. In fact, I would rather not know any of this although I am sure that I will. Her fingers claw at my pants absently, she rolls some of the fabric between her fingers, fashioning it into a phallic form, and does things with her fingernails, but I take neither caution nor pride from it.

"'Lovely night isn't it?' Mr. Westfield said to her and she replied anxiously, 'Yes, it is, yes, it is,' hoping that he would not lose all interest in her and turn toward other occupations as, Mrs. Westfield remembered, so many men had in the past," the guide is saying. Apparently during my preoccupation the matter of the introduction has been passed over and now I will never know exactly how Mr. and Mrs. Westfield met one another. This fills me with dismay because it is not one of the least things which I had hoped to learn from the tour, and the brochures and publicity guides about it which we had picked up from the desk of our motel had indeed made special mention of this as being a highlight of the tour; the Westfield home guide included a complete account of how these people had met and what had drawn them to one another. "Excuse me," I say, breaking into the guide's flat, meandering monologue. "I'm sorry, I didn't quite hear you. How did you say they met? Who introduced them?"

I realize that I am being stared at in an unkind fashion by all of my companions; not only the albino and his family, the fat man and a tiny woman who appears to be his wife, and the two teenagers in Edwardian dress are looking at me with loathing, but Joanne herself has turned, momentarily taking her palm from mine, to look at me with a hard questioning stare in which there is very little approbation. Nevertheless, I cannot allow my conspicuousness to divert me from what I deserve to know; this is an old problem which I will not allow to defeat me. "I'm sorry," I say again. "I didn't hear you but it's my right to know, they promised it in the brochure and it's an important part of the program. How did you say they met? What attracted Mr. Westfield to her?"

The guide licks his lips and swings his little legs uneasily on the edge of the couch. "I've already been into that," he says. "I can't start repeating everything, you know, if I do that we'll never get anywhere. This is the basic tour, if you want a private showing you have to come out on Fridays and pay extra and take your own guide."

"Please," I say.

The guide settles back and looks at his fingernails, opens his mouth as if to say something and then closes it. This is so grotesque and out of kilter with his easy, careful motions hitherto that the albino laughs, a swift, high bark which is instantly stifled by his mother, and then as instantly begins to sob. "I'm sorry," the guide says when the albino's moans have faded into his mother's skirt. "I'd like to tell you if I could. But this is a programmed speech, you know, we can't be expected to remember everything and I don't have the right cues. I lost them when I passed it. In order to tell you what you want to know, I'd have to go back to the beginning of the tour and start there. That wouldn't be fair to anyone else."

"No, it wouldn't."

"Maybe you can infer it from what I'll be saying later. And the tour goes on four days a week in the summer, every day except Friday, which is private. You could come back tomorrow and I'll know it then. You just have to pay a little closer attention."

"All right," I say, now merely shamed because for the first time I have become visible among the tourists, have established myself no less than the albino or the fat man or Joanne as something to be reckoned with. "I'm sorry. I won't bother you anymore."

"I don't mind being bothered. That's part of the job of the restoration staff, after all, to highlight the points of interest and be always ready to illumine them. But we can't know everything."

"Let him go on, Michael," the girl whispers to me. "After all, what does it matter how they met each other? They're both very dull people, they sound like the kind of people who would meet in the most boring, insignificant way possible and none of it matters. Besides, I'll make it up to you later. I'll make you think about other things." And once again there is that quick, deadly pressure of the hand on which is super-imposed a wink which she gives me with her left eyelid, the right tilted off-angle to it to produce the kind of pleasing unevenness associated with a grand master painting. "I love you, you see," she says irrelevantly.

"Well then," the guide says, "after some time, having exchanged those simulated 'biographies' with which people of this unique period always felt they came to 'know' one another, Mr. and Mrs.

Westfield began to feel more comfortable, by which it is meant only that Mrs. Westfield came to understand that she was safe in his presence and he that her occurrence did not of itself destroy his present and future prospects at this gathering. Indeed, under the influence of the liquor they had had and a certain restlessness which Mr. Westfield had been feeling for some time and which seemed to coalesce around the prospect of this woman who stood, hands folded before her, at his side, a certain quantity of another emotion began to intrude, one which made them suddenly restless as they considered whether or not they would leave this 'cocktail party' together and what would happen to them if they did."

"This Mrs. Westfield," one of the Edwardian-dressed teenagers said, "was she pretty?"

"That's an intelligent question and I'm glad you asked it. Furthermore, it comes within context, unlike certain other questions which have recently been raised." At this slam at me the guide permits himself a small knifing smile which apparently produces such tumult within that he bounces slightly on the couch and uncrosses his legs. "The answer to that question is that Mrs. Westfield was not really pretty but that she fell within a certain margin of sexual acceptability and a man greatly desirous of sex could, despite the unusual modesty of her garb even for the period, have found her attractive. Mr. Westfield's sex drive had, of course, been sublimated in other areas for so long that it is an object of consideration as to whether or not he responded to her in that fashion. He probably did since all the available documents indicate that he was of normal heterosexuality in his pre-marital period and merely of a certain low intensity. It is indicated that he visited prostitutes once or twice monthly when 'the urge,' as he called it, became irresistible."

"That's very satisfactory," the teenager said, "and I thank you very much for it. I think that that should settle the question once and for all of Mr. Westfield's homosexuality. He was not homosexual in the least and I have never felt that he was. I am glad to know that you have backed up that point. For if he was homosexual then his entire life could be seen only as a kind of terrible, evasive farce springing away from the centrality of his passion; indeed all of this—home, artifacts, children, incident!—would have been merely an enactment of his unwillingness to face the truth and that, of course, is completely impossible. It would render the restoration useless. So thank you again. All of this is earnest, there is no evasion in the sexual lives of the Westfields."

At the conclusion of this long speech the guide eyes the teenager strangely and indeed a subtle giggle seems to permeate the general atmosphere, loosening, for the first time, a certain air of tension among us which has been evident from the beginning of the tour as if we have used that tour only as a means of divertissement from more central and interesting hatreds. The teenager shakes his head and nods alternately, scuffs his feet and looks down at his shoes. "Sorry," he says, "I tend to get a little passionate about the subject. I'm working on a doctoral dissertation on the Electra complex in the Westfield family, you understand, and I tend to get a little passionate about all of this. I don't mean to be intrusive, of course. But it's all so terribly interesting and the main reason I wanted to take the tour was to get some first-hand information. I'm sorry."

"That's perfectly all right," the guide says. "It's good to have someone participating who is at a level of expertise. Do you find the tour interesting?"

"Oh, very much so. I don't think anyone has questioned the value of the restoration, the unique value of the Westfields, but there's just been so little constructive, disciplined work done on this material that all of it remains still to be undertaken. This is my friend, George," the teenager says, pointing an elbow at his companion. "He's a scholar too, although not in sociology; he's an eclectician. George is just keeping me company this morning." He pats his companion in an unmistakable way, inducing a high giggle, and then turns back toward the guide.

"I'm sorry to have interrupted," he says. "I just wanted to get that one little question settled and then we can go on. Please excuse me."

"Well," the guide says, "well, that's all right. That is something I was glad to answer. At any rate, after a time the Westfields left this 'cocktail party,' not precisely sure how they had so easily accustomed themselves to this as an inevitability, yet at the same time perhaps enjoying one another's presence, and then Mr. Westfield said, 'Why don't we take a drive somewhere?' and she agreed. By the way, are you here on a grant?"

"Oh, no," the teenager says. "I paid my own way in. And George's as well; it wouldn't have been right to have taken him to a place that bored him unless I at least had the *manners* to pay his way."

"Well, you could have got in at half price as a student. Remind me when we get to the exit and I'll make arrangements for a refund."

"That's very kind of you."

"Tell me more about the lady," the albino says, and is instantly muffled by his mother. "I want to hear more about the lady."

"Well, then," the guide says, and a slow hint of pleasant light seems to illuminate his features with the knowledge that he is being attended to from an unexpected source. "I was about to. The lady, Mrs. Westfield that is, accepted this offer of a ride from Mr. Westfield because she was impelled by both necessity and curiosity. Also, at this time so early on in their relationship, she had already decided that she would marry him. This is not an exceptional admission because Mrs. Westfield, having passed the age of thirty, had reached a point where every single man of equivalent age to whom she was introduced became a source of matrimonial intuition and it had already led her into a number of embarrassing situations from which she had emerged untainted by gloom because unpossessed, in these things, of memory. She quickly got into his car—it was a fine, late-model Buick of a kind rarely seen nowadays outside of the museums—and he drove her to a secluded spot in the distant woods. There, after a time I am happy to say, Mr. Westfield performed upon Mrs. Westfield the act of love, the speed of his maneuvers being in no small way impelled by the rapidity with which the wind moved through the trees, the distant shore lights played on the grass, the energetic crickets pumped out their nightsong. He copulated with her, in short, some three hours after his introduction, a record which neither Mr. Westfield nor his intended spouse had ever expected to attain nor, for that matter, one which they ever equalled again. I will not go into the more licentious facts of this copulation; downstairs in the courtesy shop are facsimiles of a series of letters written by Mrs. Westfield to her husband some months after the fact which go into a certain explicitness of detail, and similarly there are a collection of family home movies, duplicated for popular consumption at retail prices, which show both of the Westfields during their honeymoon in bathing attire; from this can be gained an excellent understanding of their physical attributes and capabilities. More than that I cannot say; a certain shyness is programmed into this lecture and in the bargain the restoration committee is not interested in the sexual lives or capabilities of the Westfields except as they reflect a certain reality of circumstance. And since—a final digression—it has long since been proven that the sexual lives of *all* the Westfields have no more to do with their inner reality than the frantic manipulations of a fly on wallpaper have to do with that fly's inner sensibility, there is needless to say going to be little material of this sort discussed today. Of course I am open for questions here."

"Questions," Joanne says. She removes her hand from mine and fixes her wrists together, confronts the guide in an attitude of demureness which I would consider stunningly attractive under other circumstances but which I can now only interpret as malevolent. "Yes, I have some questions if I might." She gives me a slow, even wink and my anticipatory prick, as if having grasped some meaning of its own, roils in response. "I thought that morals in those days were different from what they are now. Specifically, I didn't think that couples fucked on the first date but only after a long time, and usually then with a certain amount of guilt."

At the word "fuck" the guide winces slightly but recovers his aplomb long before the question is finished. The other tourists, however, titter somewhat and I feel a faint, high flush of embarrassment coming over me; it occurs to me now that Joanne has always been characterized, at least in our private dealings, by a certain frankness of rhetoric which is perhaps more forced than free, more contrived than whole, but which is nevertheless abrasive. "Fuck, fuck," the albino says and his mother clouts him on the ear. He begins to sob and the moans in the sudden hush take on a copulatory tinge.

"Ah," the guide says. "Well, that too is a question worth pondering. We have to consider the morals of that day versus those of our liberated own and it is indeed hard to draw a dichotomy because it is the fixed assumption of the restoration scholars that such a di-chotomy, if it does exist at all, is much subtler than the popular press would want to conceive. The fact is that there has always been as much fucking per capita—I use your word, young lady, to indicate I take no offense—but that it has a slightly higher visibility nowadays than it used to since it has become somewhat of a commodity. So there was nothing remarkable about the Westfields' behavior. There was never anything remarkable about the Westfields' behavior. A horrid predictability infuses all of it. Does that answer your ques-tion?"

"Did they enjoy it?" Joanne asks. "Was it good for them? I mean," she says, bobbling my elbow slightly and favoring me with the quick offered plane of a cheek grazing my suit jacket, "I mean was it as satisfactory for them, as *good* for them as it is for us? Those of us of this day, of course, I mean." She laughs and pinches her fingers into my elbow and I realize then for the first time—how obtuse I have been! but then I have excuses—that she has contrived all of this to embarrass me.

"Of course they enjoyed it," the Ph.D. candidate says, "they enjoyed it a great deal. You don't think there was anything wrong with Mr. Westfield, do you? I think that we settled that right off."

"Some Coke," the albino says.

"But what about Mrs. Westfield? I was asking about both of them. Did *she* enjoy it?"

"I don't think your question makes any sense," the Ph.D. candidate says, flicking some imagined dust off a sleeve. "Of course she enjoyed it. In those unfortunate times women were objects and those responses which were expected were elicited. Rather we should concern ourselves—"

"Some Coke with ice," the albino says, "and let's go for a walk. It's so boring! It doesn't have anything to do with anyone! Please let me go home, we don't have to stay here all the time, huh, do we?" Casually but with easy grace, his mother slaps him again and the child collapses against her, his eyes enormous. The guide, somewhat taken aback by this explosion of incident, shifts on the couch and then gets up swiftly, comes to the gate and leans on it.

"Well," he says, "really now, there's no reason for this kind of emotional display. The project is controversial of course, and the restoration, because it is so significant to all of our shared history, takes on a rather painful emotional tinge but this isn't worthy of anyone here. Can't you all act mannered?"

"Don't tell *us* to act mannered," the albino's mother says, giving Joanne a ferocious look. I understand that the situation is coming close to a danger point and, intercepting Joanne's hand which was aimed toward the child probably to give him another ferocious tap, say, "Maybe we could all take a rest for a little while. I mean, this kind of thing isn't easy for any of us. Maybe the child could get some Coke and the rest of us could stretch our legs and then we could come back here to hear more of this. Isn't that fair enough?"

The action has been somewhat provocative and indeed there is something to its definitiveness which, I fear, might reveal my secret, the fact that I have particular interest in this museum and knowledge of it. Surely tourists do not normally interpose themselves between their guides and events. But this particular guide is, apparently, at one of those moments of fatigue whose onset in the civil servant is so rapid and whose effects are so pernicious; it is the occurrence of an uncontrollable situation upon the civil servant with the attendant realization that since he has no vested interest in the outcome he can only pay a penalty either way. Perhaps I have caught him at some moment of private retribution. "Well," he says, "that's not a bad idea. It's terribly warm in here in the summer—it always was, the Westfields stubbornly refused to install air-conditioning, they felt that it was an 'unnecessary expenditure to spoil all of us,' which we have tried to continue in the restoration as well for a sense of authenticity. I'm sure the courtesy shop is open and you can probably get something now. Why don't we reassemble here in fifteen minutes?" There is a slight mumble from the thin man behind me who doubtless wants, at this moment, reunion with his family as little as I do with Joanne, but the guide, all precision at last, overrides this and says, "Yes, then, well that's a fine idea and I'm going to have some coffee myself," and leaping over the gate with a swinging bound, dodges through the corridor and into a stairwell. We hear the sound of pattering.

We stand there for a moment in that vague collage of embarrassment known to all travellers who can judge their presence only in terms of a structure suddenly removed, and then the albino says, "Coke Mommy, coffee Mommy," and this slight impetus causes a virtual rush; first the mother and child leave at a slow trot, the father follows, the fat man with his umbrella still at bay gives us an embarrassed smile and walks toward the front door, doubtless seeking some air and rain for his equipment, and then the teenagers, giggling slightly, nod to one another and move into the next open door, toward what would be the kitchen exhibit as I recollect. Joanne and I are, thus, left alone in the room and for an instant I do not know what to say to her; she looks so lovely and yet so dismally threatening in the weak light, and then she seizes my elbow in a gallant grip and presses herself against me so that I can feel her breasts on an elbow and then she says to me quickly and in a whisper, "Michael, while the rest of them are wasting their time, why don't we go right upstairs into the bedroom and fuck? I'll be on the bottom and you'll be on the top and we'll take all of our clothes off except for the ones at the very top. Wouldn't that be fun?" And the thing is, looking at her, that I am seized by such desire that it becomes a pain in my stomach, and moving solemnly with the gravity it moves toward the groin, a sinking need, a rising expectancy, and behind me I can hear the cries of the tourists as they seek their own means of passage. And in the heart of the living room, beneath the beating clock, I think that I hear a cackle.

TWO

Memory returns to me in thick, uneven, pounding waves of insight as I take Joanne's arm and guide her toward the upstairs exhibit. The idea of fucking in the bedroom of my parents has seized me with such tenacity that I can barely keep my tread straight, although at the same time I know now that Joanne is evil and that she is out to destroy me. It has always been so and I remember as well why we have come to this museum. We came to avoid further arguments. It is strange how now that memory has returned I want so little part of it.

But, nevertheless, there it is: we have been travelling together, Joanne and I, and have come at last to this strange city which, by coincidence, houses the Westfield restoration among other monuments. We have been in several cities on this latest trip, we have been in Detroit and Minneapolis and Ames, Iowa and Pittsburgh and New York City as well, but in none of them have we found precisely what we were looking for, which, possibly, was some solution to our relationship, although that is hard to ascertain. From the insides of motel rooms all locations look the same; also there has been the embarrassment of staying in all these motels without a car, the embarrassment of checking in with luggage and formality and leaving "license plate #" blank on the applications because neither of us knows how to drive but Joanne "digs motels." So we have gone from hither to yon, mostly by bus and taxi and in room after room we have enacted the same slow, deadly scene of convolution and departure and are no closer to a solution now than we were at the beginning, have come, in fact, to that point where we suspect the only sane means of continued accommodation is to turn jointly outward rather than separately inward. So I have suggested the Westfield museum to her as a means of passing the day, conceding in no way either my coincidental relationship to it (I have never, after all, told I her my last name) or my unusual, virtually obsessive desire after all these years to see it, and she has said yes because she is still at that point of relationship where she believes that to please me is to please herself. And so here we are.

Precisely who we are, from where we have come, how we got to know one another are questions which still evade me but I know that in time now, the answers will come. I know how Joanne and I have gotten here, what we mean to one another, what else matters? We ascend the creaking stairs of the house slowly, fearing a collision or plunge at any moment, and at last come into the main hallway of the second floor. My bedroom is at the rear of this hallway, of course; my sister's is in the center and my parents' is at the near end. It is toward this nearest one that Joanne now leads me. I follow, torn between lust and indecision, and when we come to the gate we pause for a moment, whether out of deference to our history or awe at the enclosure I have no way of knowing.

It is strange, strange to see the bedroom of my parents after so many years, but, of course, it is exactly as it always was; the twin beds lie close to one another, separated by the bulk of the reversible television set which lies between; at the corner my mother's vanity bureau exudes a sickly reflected yellowish light from its mirror; at the other end is my father's dresser where, I recall, he kept his prophylactics until my eleventh birthday when I located them in the top drawer and tried them on casually one by one to a disastrous (and long-since suppressed) outcome. The closet, half-ajar to reveal the cunningly restored clothing of the exhibition, also has a large mirror and it reflects that of my mother's vanity bureau, although not to a sequence of merging rooms as one might suspect, but only to blankness. Joanne gracefully climbs over the gate, catching her skirt only once in the act of getting off, and then sprawls on the bed, motioning me to join her. I do with some finesse and then we are seated together, toe to toe and only that way but it is enough. The bedspreads feel oddly smooth to the touch; age has rendered them glossy rather than otherwise and I feel that if I looked closely enough I would see the smudges of my old semen stains from the time in my early teens when I came into their room on Saturday nights when they had gone to the movies and beat off violently at the ceiling, wondering as I did so whether my mother had the same aspect as my father poked into her and whether it could possibly be enough to make it worth it.

"Did they do it right here?" Joanne says hoarsely. She is titillated. "Did the Westfields really do it right here in this bed?"

"Yes, they did," I say. "They did it all the time up until the lamentable death of Mr. Westfield, which occurred some time ago I understand, while he was enjoying a shoeshine on the corner of Lexington Avenue and East 53rd Street on his way to the agency. He was fifty-six years old. All the way until that time, however—"

"You really know a lot about this, don't you?" she says. Her mood has altered over the past hour. She is girlish, winning. Even her breasts seem sharper, higher against the fine arch of her chest. She has decided to appreciate me. Had we not been through this so many times before I would be touched past desire to submission ... but I have indeed seen all of it.

"I've made a study," I say. "I've always been interested in the Westfield exhibition. It's one of the prim artifacts of mid-century urban life in America, you know, and it's becoming clearly established as a scholarly and cultural treasure, more and more noted every year. I think that it's uniquely valuable. I'm very happy we decided to come here." This last not being the truth of course, because it has only been my persuasion, her submission.

"Well, yes, it is kind of interesting," she says, "particularly this business of how they met and the screwing and so on, but honestly! have you ever seen anything like that guide or the people we're with? They just have no understanding of what's going on. It's terrible to think that the world out there is full of people like this."

"Yes, yes, but at least they're trying, at least they want to be a part of it, they have the decency to come and to try to learn something, it's the people who don't come and the people who don't learn who are the ones to worry about."

"That boy is uncontrollable."

"Well, yes." I say, "so he is, but then the Westfields were too, at least half the time or maybe more than that they had no understanding of what they were doing. And nobody could have made them understand. But *they* thought that they were important and significant and that what they were engaged in had real consequences. You never know. It just goes to show that you never know. The price you pay—"

But I have obviously said too much, my voice breaking boyishly on the word "price" and Joanne looks at me with an unusual keenness which is only augmented by the fact that she is meanwhile removing all of her clothes as quickly as possible, first sweater, then brassiere, then skirt and so on, and the confrontation of flesh is appalling; the sheer *magnitude* of women, even the slightest of them, has never ceased to bemuse me, and at the sight of her familiar but devastating nipples spreading open in their discoloration and taking on the rather hideous hue of the surrounding wallpaper I find myself seized by a kind of madness. "What is this to you?" she is saying. "Why are you so affected by it? Do you *know* anything about these people? Did they mean anything to you?"

"No," I say, "I never knew them at all; no one really knew the Westfields, they existed to themselves so utterly that to open a door on one of their private moments would, for a neighbor, have been an exercise in horror at the matter-of-fact banality of all this pain; the Westfields were never known, it's just that I find it an interesting referent or should I say objective-correlative for certain things in my own circumstances oh your body, your body, your body, your goddamned breasts." Once again I am mumbling. The sight of her nude has never failed to afflict my sanity and she has capitalized on this from the beginning, taking pleasure in the way in which my sexual need can patently devour me and make me only into a weak self-parody, but in basic concession to her I will admit that she is a nice girl and has never used this cruelly as so many others have. She pleasures and glories herself in it as simply as a child might take pleasure in a puppy's intransigence. But the effects, of course, are always the same.

"Oh, God," I say, taking off my own clothes in a rush of fabric which must have the uneven sound, to any distant auditor, of an ill-assembled flight of birds passing at some remove. "Oh God, I really don't know if I can take it," and I fall on top of her, the flat planes of our bodies intersecting at some frantic angle of need, and then, on my parents' bed in the restored museum that was my home, I begin to make love to this girl that I really cannot get along with. It is very complex and very necessary and ultimately as simple as the albino's need although far easier to rationalize, far more interesting in the recounting.

"What if they come in?" Joanne whispers to me, spreading herself open underneath. "They'll see us, they'll see us," and her voice is somewhere midway between an avowal and a warning, impossible to understand what her real purposes are. "It doesn't matter," I say. "They will just take it to be part of an exhibit," and I work myself deeply into her, feeling her cunt close over me with more willingness than her arms will ever demonstrate, and I begin to fuck her with slow earnestness.

It is strange to be screwing her on my parents' bed, but neither disconcerting nor unpleasant and I feel myself, in the bargain, whipped on by spectres and memory; I see the honest, laboring bulk of my father working through my mother's body with its slow understanding, I see my own butterfly of a hand urging the last drops from the sphincter as I turn scuttling through the pages of magazines, I see my sister's slow glaze of astonishment as I open the door to find her copulating with a girl friend some time many years ago, and it is as if all of these voices, along with Joanne's, are helping me, speeding me toward my destiny as I work myself in a frenzy of real concentration toward a predetermined outcome, as predictable as the guide's lecture but a damned bit more profitable, and as I do, all of it comes sweeping over me—old pain, old grief, old knowledge—and I seem to hear my father's voice whispering obscenely to me, "Go to it you son of a bitch, you're a hell of a lot better fixed than I am," and as I think about that, as I wonder whether "better fixed" refers to choice of partner or only to the relative ease at with which I am able to come in almost any circumstances, I pour into her in a swoop, feeling my semen rill and surge back at me and it is as if I am fucking not only her cunt but my own emissions and very sensuous it is indeed. "Oh, God, that's good," Joanne murmurs to me, offering me a breast to bite and suck, and this too is an old problem; we have always found our answers in sex too easily to tackle the more difficult extrinsic ones. It is strange how these kinds of reflections always overtake me in the midst of what other men might call "unalloyed pleasure," but then the message of the museum is vast and personal and one cannot quite flee one's history, although it is worth a lifetime of trying. After a while I come off of her very gracefully, surrender the breast, and suggest that we rejoin the walking tour, otherwise our presence might be missed, questions raised, and an exploring company sent. Perhaps the other personnel, from the courtesy shop, will be coming up.

"Oh, no," Joanne murmurs. "Must we? Can't we just lie here for a while? You remember he told us they would be doing the kitchen first and then probably the bathroom, they have the whole first floor to do, we can stay here for a while." I point out that this tour group is so small and our own persons so evident that surely a party would have been sent long before the troupe got to the bedroom. "Oh, all right," she says with a kind of pretty petulance and stands up, begins to shuffle her clothes and gets dressed again. While she does so, I prowl around the objects of the bedroom, noting that everything is in the place I remember it to be, and then on an impulse I open the top drawer of the bureau and find that my father's prophylactics have been restored to their original place, in a small abscess to the right of the main drawer, in an area also containing his tie clasp and cufflinks. The package is open and a quick count indicates that two of the prophylactics have been used, and I am overcome by my feelings of approbation for the staff of the restoration which has obviously done everything in its power to bring to these rooms and objects the particular sense and posture which was their characteristic in life.

In the center of this first drawer, on top of a pile of socks, is a sheet of paper, folded over. I take it out and open it and glancing quickly at the bottom see that it is a letter from my mother which my father, having apparently read, has put away in his effects for further pondering. The letter is written in her familiar, crosswise hand in that pinkish pencil which was her only apparent writing implement and I read it quickly, not being unaware at the same time of Joanne's exquisite efforts to tuck her breasts into a brassiere which is deliberately two sizes too small for them, a predilection which lends her every motion in a tight sweater or dress an excursion into the deepest recesses of the observer's heart. But today, of course, her dress has been nondescript, which is just as well in terms of the scholarly curiosity which has taken me here.

"Dear—" [the letter says, my mother having apparently left a name off out of indecision as to how to put it; in our presence she called our father by either his first name or last, occasionally adding "sweetheart" when guests were present but never finding that consistency of address which might have saved so much difficulty.]

"I thought that 1 would try to write you this rather than speak it because we never seem to talk any more and I find the words hard to get out of me but it is important to say it and that is that there is something missing. There is something terribly wrong I do not know what it is. It is not so much that I feel something to be missing as that I feel something where nothing should be. I can't put it any better than that. Maybe we could talk about it. The kids are distracting of course but that's not all of it. The reason I made you leg of lamb the other night is that you said you liked leg of lamb how did I know you wouldn't? We have got to talk things over because nothing is as it should be but then everything can't be wrong either. Something has got to be done about the relationships."

Then, apparently indecisive as to whether she should sign her name or merely leave off a signature as understood, there was a small curlicue which might have been an attempt at initialing. I consider the letter for a little while—it is not, after all, that unusual a construction; I have seen many notes like this in my time and have written a few as well—and finally put it back in its original place, regretful that my father who had taken such care in its placement will obviously now never have the opportunity to consider it at what he often called his "leisure." Indeed, it speaks well for the conscientiousness of the committee that they would take care to place this unanswered and unanswerable letter among the effects, and this conscientiousness speaks well of its seriousness of purpose, the eventual worth of the whole project, for no one knows better than I that the Westfields' lives consisted only of such compendiums of the Unanswered and Unanswerable and there is, hence, some slight indication given by the committee's action that this in itself may not have rendered those lives meaningless. It is a whole new way of considering things—that the meaningless may have a scope, a structure, a beauty and a purpose no less than the meaningful—and I know that I will want to ponder it at my own leisure as soon as I have a chance.

"Well," Joanne says, taking my elbow, her body contained and straight beneath the brightness of her restored dress, "I'm ready to go. Aren't you?" And indeed I am still naked and embarrassed in the bargain as I nod weakly at her and begin to assemble my own clothing. My act of dressing is neither as precise nor as purposeful— nor as aesthetically pleasing—of course as hers and therefore I do not loiter on it. While I am scurrying through these motions I see that she is looking through the open drawer with a bemusement of her own and has indeed just finished reading the letter, which she refolds and replaces.

"Mr. Westfield used prophylactics," she says. "What is this letter all about? Who wrote it?"

"He used prophylactics because he feared any other kind of contraception and his wife objected to that interruption of coition which he had read about in a book once and was always eager to try. But never did I think the letter is from his wife."

"You really know all about this, don't you? It's uncanny how much you know, Michael."

"It means something," I say, taking the letter from her hand and retucking it in its accustomed place. "Everything means something, even this. Perhaps the accumulation of objects, of mannerisms, of attitudes is as precious a task as accumulation of knowledge or money. Only the Westfields can know."

"What did his wife want?"

"How do I know?"

"You seem to know everything else about them."

"No, I don't," I say and it is a tribute to my aplomb and my certainty of self in these remembered surroundings that I do not take her line for a hint of suspicion about the actual relation. "I know only what I can infer from this, which is only what any other intelligent person can infer. Perhaps she wanted to be understood, that's all."

"What is this with understanding? Why does everyone want to be understood?"

I take her chin and tilt it upward slightly, attempt a gesture of tenderness by kissing her nose but the delivery misses slightly and I find myself implanting the a kiss instead on the cool, resilient surface of her fluttering eyelid. "Not anymore," I say. "Not today. People aren't so high on understanding these days, only accommodation and mutual use. But in the time of the Westfields— which was thirty years ago, you know—understanding was to them what sexuality is for us, it was the only way in which they could communicate. They always accused one another, these people, of not 'understanding' one another or not 'caring' enough, which is quite a different thing, you understand, and their most intense moments with each other were moments of self-revelation, which is kind of criminal when you come to think of it because it's all so confused. But 'understanding' was for Mrs. Westfield what a 'relationship' would have been for us three or four years ago or what a 'good thing' would be today, and we must have respect for that. Just because the language was different doesn't mean that they didn't feel the same. Just because our past seems a little archaic," I say with a feeling of rising expectancy which for me always indicates the beginning of what I later take to be an "insight," "doesn't mean that it doesn't have as much passion and terror as our present; we cannot make a plaything or an artifact of our history, it is just as terrible and just as real as the other part. Because the words they used seem strange to us doesn't mean that they didn't feel. They *felt*. They suffered. Their intensity of feeling was as ordered and meaningful to them as ours to us. And they found structure in their possessions. I think we'd better go downstairs."

"Oh, Michael," she says, taking my arm and leaning against me in an ambiguity of gesture, "Michael, you're so intense. You take everything so seriously! Can't this just be a simple day of going out for us? Does everything have to be of such terrible consequence?"

"But I grew up where everything was serious," I say. "Everything was a crisis, everything was portentous. There was not a gesture, not a twitch, not a single convulsion of the corpus that was not analyzed and analyzed again. It lends a kind of high gloom to the proceedings."

"Someday you'll have to tell me about that."

"Yes, someday," I say and lead her from the room. Only when we have again set ourselves upon the stairs does it occur to me that we have left the bureau drawer unopened and the bed rumpled, but I right myself successfully against the idiot impulse to go back and straighten everything. In the long run, I remind myself, it makes no difference at all what we do or might have done—it is only the question of alternative which is interesting—and besides that, the guide will take the disarray for some incompetence of personnel and for that reason relish it to the degree that he feels it protects and renders more secure his own position. The living room is empty, indicating that the party has either reassembled and gone on or is still dispersed on its ways, but a murmur of voices from the rear indicates that we have indeed fallen behind the tour and I lead her straightaway into the kitchen where the tourists are standing once again in their solemn clump, confronting the guide who is standing behind the stove, showing them utensils and apparently talking about the cooking artifacts of that time. To my dismay, he stops talking when he sees us and then favors me with a long sweeping glance which completely forsakes Joanne in its assumed totality of knowledge. I can feel her shudder slightly against me and run a comforting hand over her back. The tourists also turn to regard us with distasteful expressions and the albino sticks out his tongue at us. I note that it is colored with a reddish substance indicating that he has apparently gotten his refreshments.

"Well, then," the guide says, "being so thoughtfully rejoined by certain errant members of our little troupe, I can now continue. I would think that there would be some consideration shown, you know; this tour is on a tight schedule and I can't be expected to work to the convenience of single tourists; also, you are supposed to be under surveillance at all times."

"I'm sorry," Joanne says. "We were just looking around the grounds."

"It doesn't matter," the guide says. "That's neither here nor there. To refresh you—I was speaking of the cooking habits of the Westfields and the way in which they dined. It is particularly illuminating material, although it may lack that sensationalism which certain of you seem to be seeking in this tour."

"Did they eat together all the time?" the thin father of the albino says. It is the first sustained line I have heard from him and is rather disquieting since his voice is quite resonant for a man otherwise so insignificant and seems to cause the crockery, in its place on the shelves, to shudder and bump in position.

"Oh, indeed they did," the guide says. "They always ate together except on Thursday nights when Mr. Westfield attended meetings of his local salesman's club and regaled himself not so much with liquor and companionship as a blessed feeling of isolation, undercut by the ironic realization that he could not conceive of himself as anything other than a displaced creature of his family. But otherwise they all ate at that large table you see in the adjoining room; Mr. Westfield would sit at the head, Mrs. Westfield at his side across from the daughter Katherine, and Michael opposite, facing his father at the foot. Of course 'head' and 'foot' are all relative terms, to the Westfields they were sitting this way but this was only in relation to the living room; someone coming from the bathroom or the spare bedroom in the rear would have found Mr. Westfield at the foot and Michael at the head. But these seating arrangements had some significance to the people of this time; it was considered a position of authority for the host or prime member of the family to sit at the 'head' of the table and, of course, the least significant—although not least loved—member would sit at the foot. There are some interesting documents available for private users indicating that the Westfields did indeed feel this way and that Mr. Westfield was most insistent upon what he considered his most important prerogative."

"Well, that shows again," the Ph.D. says, "that there was absolutely no question of homosexuality then with Mr. Westfield, not if he found important a simple stereotype which has long been thought of as a male prerogative."

"Indeed", said the guide, "but I think that your own orientation may be a bit off. There has never been, so far as I know, and I have been with this restoration for five and a half years, the slightest question raised anent Mr. Westfield's masculinity or pseudo-masculinity. It is thus irrelevant and redundant to introduce evidence in favor of his heterosexuality, although I am sure that this is a very praiseworthy thing and I am sure the curators would be delighted to know that you have been interested sufficiently in the project to want to write your dissertation on it."

"But that's not so!" the scholar says, his voice breaking slightly, almost toward an albino-register. "The trouble is that there's lots of talk, lots of scuttlebutt going around about the Westfields; every specialist is ready to smirk about Mr. Westfield and to say that there was something wrong with him. Something not quite right about him. Just because he married very late and liked ice-skating instead of church on Sundays and had a tendency toward temper tantrums and also seemed sufficiently uncomfortable in the presence of men as to never have one close masculine friend. We've got to get rid of that kind of thing at the source! I won't have it! It's a question of scholarship of normal rigorousness. If he were a homosexual, then I'd be all in favor of coming right out and saying it, but because he wasn't one might say that it's almost the holy obligation of the scholar to nip this kind of thing in the bud."

"This is very dull," Joanne whispers to me. "Why are they getting involved in this? It doesn't have anything to do with sightseeing."

"Well, I'm sure this is appreciated," the guide says. "Perhaps you'll be able to write something for our next edition of the brochure; I would think they'd be interested in having something like that. Of course it isn't my field. I was saying that the Westfields ate together every evening except Thursdays in the aforementioned positions and that their mealtimes were characterized by an air of unusual tension which the participants thought of as 'family life' but which we can now see in retrospect was something rather apart from that. Specifically, there was fear and mutual loathing between the siblings, and Mrs. Westfield's attempts to convert their sublimate giggles and threats into 'good normal conversation' were often provocative to the point of breaking up the meal entirely; one or the other of the younger Westfields would have to flee to his or her room to avoid 'making a scene,' and regurgitation, particularly on the part of the boy Michael, was frequent. Of course in later life the siblings got along much better and it is made clear from available documents that they eventually reached a true understanding, but the particular abrasiveness and hellishness of their relationship at this time cannot be dismissed and might well have served to permanently impair whatever relationship they later had. This is beyond the ken of the project of course, but you will note the table set as if for a typical dinner: the moderately priced china, the simple tumblers, the large serving plates into which the food was scooped from the stove to be brought and laid simply on the table, the silverware slightly baroque in its convolutions, the serving implements laid out ... It can be said that the Westfields lived a precise, orderly, regularized life. They never sat down to eat other than between 6:30 and 7:00 p.m. and were always finished by 7:30. Mr. Westfield did the dishes while Michael did the drying. Occasionally Katherine would help at the latter task but often she would not. Mrs. Westfield went into the living room and watched television. 'Television,' which I have not yet had a chance to talk about in detail, was one of the more popular activities in the Westfields' part of the world during the period discussed. Mr. Westfield did the dishes without protest nor did Mrs. Westfield protest her not doing them."

"Come now," the man with the umbrella says, except that sometime in the past half-hour he has discarded or hidden his umbrella and now appears so denuded without it that only his voice and manner give instant confirmation of who he is, "this is all a little bit too much for me to accept. That he would do the dishes certainly. But to not protest—"

"There was a grave matter-of-factness in the way these people lived. Things that were done were done because they were 'right' and the 'right' thing was, of course, unarguable. The Westfields saved their conflicts for things like politics or aggrandizement or tensions, but there was at no time any debate whatsoever over their life-style or the basic assumption which underlay it. That is why this restoration is so uniquely valuable; it is composed of the artifacts of people who never—at least in the case of the parental generation—undertook the slightest doubts about who they were and why they were doing what they did. For instance, Mr. Westfield got a new car every three years, not because he wanted one and not because he felt compelled to but because, as he said 'the car depreciates most between the third and fourth year.' Consider the regularities, the easy convolutions of an intellect which can sustain such a statement. This is something to think about, to reckon with! Incidentally, they often took Sunday drives and in the courtesy room are available maps of the routes which they took as well as moderately-priced miniatures of the cars they owned."

"Pardon me," Joanne says, "if I may."

"Yes?" the guide says with a kind of vague hostility. It is clear that he does not like Joanne but has already forgotten why this is so, and the need to amalgamate response and memory may well make his sleep this evening less peaceful than usual. It is strange the trivial basis upon which sleeplessness and terror can rest but then, with my unusual and growing precognition, I can understand this kind of thing as well as many other factors. "What do you want?"

"I wanted to ask a question about this basic assumption which underlay their lives. You said they never questioned it and you said it was one of the things that made this exhibit so valuable but you never said what it was."

"Ah," the guide says. "Aha. That is a good question, a truly important question and I am glad you have raised it. Once again, this is a query which in the normal course of events I would have answered in due time, when we came to the master bedroom, but there is no harm in answering it now and the fact that it is raised indicates that its answer would be apropos. Thank you, young lady." It is apparent that any source of discord between Joanne and the guide has now been abrogated so thoroughly that its original existence is disputable, and I feel myself torn between pride in her ingratiating manner and a kind of infuriation that these conflicts between people which I have always taken so seriously and which have caused me such pain are, in most circumstances, utterly frivolous, like the tugging of bears at one another in a zoo, and as easily forgotten. I make a note to myself to consider this further at some convenient time and with the rest of us lean forward to apprehend the guide's answer. He has some awareness of the suspense he has created because he takes several deep breaths before proceeding and then smiles.

"Well," he says, "well then, the fundamental assumption. Of course. The fundamental assumption behind the lives of the Westfields and so many others of their generation in similar circumstances is that what they did was right. That while they were neither the handsomest, the bravest, the brightest or the most fortunate of people, they had what very few others did and that was the assurance that they were 'nice,' that they were 'moral' and 'ethical' in the high degree and that at any time of metaphysical or personal crisis they could be expected to settle upon that procession of behavior which, in all moral and psychological terms, was 'correct.' This gave them quite an air of smugness, as you might expect, and they also would have been disconcerted to know that this entire heterogeneous wedge of people, of which they are a splendid microcosmic example, felt the same way; all of them. Nevertheless, these people must be given their due. They believed this. They believed that their acts came from decent motives for decent purposes and that they functioned in such a way that a disinterested observer would find them an exemplification of all that was 'right' and 'correct' in human conduct. In short, they believed—all of them believed this, I am not excepting the siblings here—that some fifty centuries of Western thought, struggle, suffering, achievement, injustice, brutality and pain had been superseded by their own code and indeed had reached fruition in their existence. That what all philosophers had toiled in the darkness to understand, what all writers had struggled in anguish to say, was subsumed by the Westfields themselves, who thus became the righteous capstone of all these lonely existences. These people were quite serious. You must give them that. And the demands they made on themselves were no less stringent than those they made on their contemporaries. These people cared. They always wanted to feel that what they did was 'right' and they concerned themselves deeply if it wasn't. They were not hypocritical. They were committed to this. It can be seen in every spoon on this table, every piece of hidden crockery in the kitchen."

"But that's impossible," the fat man says. "I find it impossible to believe that an entire life can be based upon a single assumption as banal as that. It's simply unrighteous and, besides that, it doesn't make any sense whatsoever. People aren't impelled by abstractions." He points a forearm at the floor for emphasis and then notes with some dismay that his umbrella has disappeared; this brings a deep flush to his face and he adds, as if he had heard remonstrance, "Of course it's all in the way you look at it."

"Indeed it is," the guide says, "but you are entirely wrong in saying that people are not driven by abstractions. You do not think that it was lust which drove the Westfield prick into the Westfield cunt, do you? Not that I have any wish to indulge in obscenity, of course, but a point is a point. No indeed, it is indicated by all available evidence as well as the documents available that for all but the first two years of their married life, Mr. Westfield possessed not the faintest twinge of desire for his spouse and could cheerfully have spent the time he used in copulation for reading or even for a spot of ice-skating which, as has been kindly noted by one of you, was a favorite Sunday activity of his. But did he? He most certainly did not. In fact, Mr. Westfield believed that copulation was a 'marital duty' of the 'highest responsibility' and despite mingled feelings of awe, revulsion, fear, guilt, horror and fatigue he performed the act of sex upon his wife an average of twice a week for some thirty years, a record of duration under stress which may never be equaled, according to the trustees. Of course physical evidences of his accomplishment are quite sparse, but you may rest assured that this has been verified by disinterested research opinion available and is not to be denied."

"But point out this, then," the doctoral candidate says. "Point out that these feelings you mention—awe, guilt, revulsion and whatever else you said—came not from any suspicion of homosexuality but only because, by any objective criterion, Mrs. Westfield was a singularly unattractive woman. In the sexual sense. I have made this the subject of a brief monograph which I did for the *North Dakota Studies In Historical Lore* which was published shortly before I took my orals, under the title 'The Role of Sexual Revulsion in the Westfield Marital Relationship As an Encouragement to View Licentiousness' and I think you might find it very illuminating."

"Indeed we might," the guide says, "and indeed all of this is very interesting but I am afraid we must now pass on. We have seen the 'kitchen' and the 'dining room' and I have described a typical 'evening dinner' with the Westfields and shown you some of the artifacts which they employed; we have not gone into the subject of breakfast or lunches to be sure, but that is really not necessary in this context. The fact is that both breakfasts and lunches were taken separately by all members of the family except on weekends, and those weekend lunches were of such a provocative nature that any reminiscence about them should be delayed until we get into the attic. Most of this you can posit anyway."

"I'm getting hungry again," the albino says. "Do you really mean there isn't any end to it? We just have to go on and on?"

"Hush," says his mother. "Now, we got you ice cream, we got you to the bathroom, we talked and listened to your prattle for fifteen minutes and now it's really time I think for you to show some manners. This thing wasn't gotten up for your convenience, you know."

"But yes," the guide says, as if he has not heard the mother's comment and, in any event, as if he found it irrelevant, "the young man has raised a very interesting and important point. I find myself happy to answer it. The answer is that indeed we must go on and on as he puts it, we must go on and on through this exhibit just as the Westfields went on and on through life. Did they glimpse cosmic purpose, did they think of the eventual destiny which they had to play in the working out of the heavens? Did any considerations of the second coming or the last temptation of Christ enter into the small calculations of their days? Did they base their plans for a weekend upon cosmology or the question of stars losing their radiance and exploding? They certainly did not. But despite this, it is to be noted—"

"But they could have," the Ph.D. says. "They certainly could have."

"Roger is right," his companion says, speaking for the first time. "They could not have gone on that way in any event. This is not to deny them." His voice sounds exactly like that of the scholar, but then, on the other hand what did I expect? Nevertheless, I cannot suppress the feeling of vague dismay which flicker through me at that moment. It is as if I get a complete and compressed foreshadowing of what is to come and in the enormity and placidity of its dimensions it terrifies me: it is a fate so consumptive and on the other hand so implacable that I understand that there will indeed be no answer whatsoever. I must tremble slightly because Joanne once again presses my hand and then kicks me affectionately in the shin. Our fucking has made her kittenish, an old phenomenon but one which I have never found more irritating than at this moment. "Stop this," I mumble to her and she pouts, then runs her tongue unevenly across her lips and blinks at me with the inconstancy and insight of a madonna plastered somewhere on a wall. "Oh, stop it yourself," she whispers.

"Of course he's right," the guide is saying enthusiastically; apparently I have again missed an important exchange. "But as I have said, this has no effect. The basic fact of the Westfields is that, profundity or none, they would have gone on. This project is the surest indication of their impermeability, their timelessness. Perhaps we can pass on now to the bathroom. There are some profound points of interest there before we get into the sitting room and then into the treasure trove of the three bedrooms, which I think will probably be the highlight of our tour. Except for the courtesy shop, of course. Incidentally, our tour will conclude at noon but the courtesy shop is open until 5 p.m."

"Not quite so fast," the scholar says. "I don't understand why you're trying to make this so easy for us. This is a national landmark, a first-rate museum which has become one of the most important cultural repositories of our generations, and yet you seem compelled to toss off its subtleties, conflicts and intricacies with clichéd simulations of thought. Nothing was quite that easy, you know. The Westfields lived on more than one level. If you have to package everything to make it palatable for tourists you lose the unspeakable terror and romance of history, isn't that right? I don't want to sound partisan but I happen to have put a lot of work into this material and I don't like to feel that it is being used merely as a way of selling goods from your factories."

"Now, wait a minute," the guide says. "You've got this all wrong. I'll have you know that I've been here for three and a half years and that all employees are put through a six-month indoctrination course which explores every aspect of the material and which enables them to see it in fullest dimension. Besides that, I have tenure. I'm not so easily spoken to, you know." It is obvious that the guide is nettled and I cannot say that I blame him; for the first time that day I have a streak of sympathy for the man who, after all, is only a civil servant—with all that that implies—and who is yet trying to perform with honor a very difficult job. The pain that the scholar's words have caused him is quite real and for an instant he pauses, then runs a hand across his forehead. "Listen here," he says. "They make us memorize the speeches for convenience, not because we don't care. And furthermore—"

"He's right, you know," I say to the scholar. "There is a great deal of passion and terror here and I would be the last one to deny this. I have done a little research into the Westfields myself. Nevertheless, the only way that material of any type can be made palatable and comprehensible to a heterogeneous audience such as this one is to label it and to attempt to give it an artificial structure and focus. The Westfields, let me remind you, would have struck you as ten times more banal than this guide, who is only, after all, trying to show not only their banality but their essential importance. I'll remind you then to keep a civil tongue in your head." And this final strange, twisted archaism—whose origin I do not understand and which leaves me rigid with embarrassment the moment I have said it— draws my speech into a croaking conclusion, where I let it reside for the instant. Joanne presses my hand and allows a breast to brush my elbow. "That's showing him," she said. "I'm proud of you. Look," and the rigidity of her nipple comes against my upper arm. I am moved and yet at the same time extremely discomfited; Joanne, for all her good qualities, is unquestionably something of a slut and at that moment I realize fully what I have been taking this enormous trip with her in denial: we will never marry. I cannot marry her. And never, up until this moment of decision, have I felt as close to her as I do now. I hold her tight against me and would kiss her with the pain and longing except that I know that this would not only create something of a spectacle but would cause me to possibly change my mind and I simply cannot bear it, not at this tenuous divide. "Thank you," I whisper and run my tongue inside the crevice of her ear, a motion which causes her to whimper.

"Well, sir, that is all I have to say to you," the scholar is saying. Apparently I have once again missed some important preliminary piece of dialogue, but it is too late; I nod politely and try to show him in my gesture that I appreciate what he has said and would not, for the world, consider arguing with him again. Actually, all my loathing for him has gone away in this moment of decision; not only the loathing for the scholar and my other companions but my very interest in the tour itself has suddenly eased to such a point that were the moment convenient I would devise excuses and leave. I have the feeling—wholly illusory as it might have turned out—that I have learned everything I need to know from the Westfields, that they have taught me everything which is important and that, my thirst for knowledge of them finally satiated, I could walk away from them forever ... if only the tour were over.

"And I would add," the guide says, "that I appreciate those remarks in my defense very much. It isn't an easy job, you know, and we take our responsibilities quite seriously. Nevertheless, you do have something there when you point out that we go in for easy answers too often. I plead guilty to this and I think my confreres would as well. The Westfields themselves went in for easy answers and it is difficult, if you take this job seriously, not to be absorbed, albeit unconsciously, by this kind of thing.

"Well," he says briskly in an apparent complete conversion of mood, a forced jauntiness which makes my heart, or what remains of it, go out to him, "I think that this completes the kitchen and the dining room then. I have, of course, ignored certain miscellaneous curiosa which I should go over briefly just in the interests of a more complete picture; they only confirm the basic impressions already given you, however. Under the table, quite often, reposed the bare feet of Michael Westfield, who had a lamentable habit of taking off his shoes at almost any given time and then not paying attention to his garb or the aspect of those shoes; this whipped Mr. Westfield into a virtual orgy of temper during which, for some ten years in Michael's life, he would curse him as irresponsible and beg him to wear bedroom slippers while putting restorative materials in the discarded shoes. But that never did any good, of course. It never did. Then too we might mention the fact that the television set was never on during dinner at the Westfields; Mrs. Westfield believed in a 'family occasion' at dinner time and permitted interruptions only to come from her own pattering between stove and table, her own chokings and gaspings when they ate 'boned but unboned fish', and certain motions performed with windows or fans during hot weather when the apartment seemed untenable. For these reasons dinner at the Westfields was often quite a quiet and uncomfortable occasion although none of the members, it can be safely said, recognized this."

"What do you mean, never recognized it?" I say "They certainly did recognize it! You cannot understand the pain, the suffering, the sheer terror of going through dinner with close relatives and knowing that you have absolutely nothing to say to them, will never have anything to say to them, the sounds of burping, chewing and light choking only augmenting this knowledge, the silence so oppressive that it seems to be the worst of all imaginable occupations until the conversations begin. 'Get the car waxed today?' and 'How were the kids?' and 'Thought I'd go out but the weather was so lousy that I didn't go out' and so on and so forth until the mind, I am talking about the actual *mind* seems to be draining, all intelligence, all possibility leaking out into the humid air as the gravies come from the stiff roast and you realize then that there is nothing you can do, nothing in the world, to change it and that it will always be the same. Oh, the pain, the terror! The loss, the horror, the irretrievable gloom! You misjudge, you misjudge terribly if you think that."

And then I stop, startled. It is apparent, even as I am speaking, that I have created something of a sensation, but on the other hand I found the words irresistible as they were coming and felt myself being driven on and on, like the motions of sex, toward a conclusion, but this conclusion, like orgasm, is simply not enough and I see that I have placed myself into deep trouble. It is possible, in fact, that I have unwittingly revealed my identity and the embarrassment of that, particularly in terms of Joanne's presence, would be untenable. "I was just talking," I say rather sullenly and try to move myself halfway behind the albino's father, an unfortunate decision since my bulk is at least three times his.

"Well," the guide says, "this is possible but how can we tell? Only the Westfields would know and they aren't available." At this attempt to save the situation his old features split into a dwarf's leer of confidentiality and my sympathy once again seems to extend right out toward him, embracing him, holding him; I would if I could then come to his side and with a single grip inform him of how I feel about the way in which he has tried to save the situation, but at the same time there is an undercurrent of dismay because I realize now that there is almost nothing that I can say in these rooms which will truly get through to the guide and, by proxy, to the restoration committee. There is something strange and very sad about distant people making property of your artifacts, manipulating them, trading them off, arranging them in patterns without any understanding of the passion which underlay these simple tools. Still, this is the sense of all historical study, I must remember that.

"Are you saying that the Westfields' lives were utterly terrible and without redeeming merit?" the fat man says to me rather portentously. His eyes wink and glitter and he seems to be measuring me for some kind of judgement, At the same time I feel Joanne's hand bite against mine again and a flicker of real distaste goes through me, something will have to be done about this dependency of hers very soon; even if I am leaving her she should still not be permitted to act in this fashion.

"No," I said, "I have no right to say that. I can only point out that there were aspects to their life which can be hinted at in no bare reassessment of their goods, and this reassessment seems to ignore what could be taken as a good quotient of suffering—"

"Ah," the fat man says. "That is truly interesting. Are you perhaps an expert on the Westfields? Are you claiming first-hand observation?" He gives me a slow leer, a slow rising comprehension spreading on the uneven pan of his face, and I would if I could lean back, gasp once and say, *Yes, yes, of course I do, I know everything about them; I tell you, you cannot let nostalgia or sentiment interfere with the memories here, nothing is that simple, everything is complex and terrible, utterly and ultimately terrible.* But I will say no such thing, of course, if I admit my identity the tour will become a fiasco and an embarrassment and in the bargain I may be forced to answer some very difficult questions before the trustees. It was part of the foundation agreement at the time the home was established as a shrine that no Westfield would ever visit the premises again or discuss it for the record; this was the only way in which the necessary funds could be secured. I learned all this third-hand in a letter from a distant relative who had hopefully addressed me care of general delivery in a distant city, and my impulse when I read the letter was once again to question the sanity of this insignificant relation because in no way could I conceive of myself, voluntarily or involuntarily, ever going home again. Nevertheless, a matter of years later, here I am. It is very odd and is part of the amnesiac mire which still coats my brains; I will have to work this out later and with some honesty. But of course that time is not now.

"No," I say, "I have no first-hand knowledge. I've done a lot of reading, of course, everybody who ever did any study in this area knows of the Westfields. But I can't say that I ever knew them or anyone who was associated with them."

"Ah, yes," the fat man says. "Oh, my yes. Then how come you seem to take all of this so personally? And why are you so quick with the countering detail? I wonder what your *real* situation is," he says and favors me with a slight smirk which passes over the others and then toward the guide where, surprisingly, it becomes somewhat apologetic. "Well, I was only asking," he says sullenly.

"Of course," the guide says. "I can understand this. You know I might favor you with a little detail off the record, an extra added bonus so to speak which does not go with the regular lecture but which you may find of some interest, and that detail is that this Westfield restoration seems to affect a large percentage of people in very strange ways. They were a very significant and symbolic family of course—this being their unique value—and the museum itself is so well-stocked and so carefully arranged that the exhibit can have a powerful effect upon visitors. Would you know that almost every week we find at least one person who comes out at the end of the tour and insists that he's really Michael Westfield, or she, as the case might be, is—Katherine? They begin to cry and create difficult scenes and maintain their identity and it's very hard to persuade them that they aren't these people at all. There's something about this that gets to people. Of course, there's no chance that anyone coming here could be Michael or Katherine Westfield. Under the terms of the grant for the project, the two siblings were denied entrance to the premises in perpetuity. Besides that, neither has been seen for years and years. They would be somewhere in their mid-thirties now and at last report were somewhere in the West or Midwest, possibly married and with families of their own, living under assumed names. They rather dropped out of circulation, you understand. Of course the marriages may merely be happenstance or rumor; I grant you that there is no indication in the restoration that either of these children would find the patience to get married or the ability to sustain any kind of relationship, but still, statistically, this is possible. Both of the senior Westfields passed away some time ago."

"Well," the fat man says. "That *is* interesting. Of course you'll hardly find me maintaining that I'm one of those people. I'm just passing through on a business trip—a damned lousy trip I might observe too, I haven't sold a thing—and since I happened to be in the general area, decided to take this thing in. It doesn't move me one way or the other, to tell you the truth. I don't understand why people get so excited about it."

"Well, they do," the guide says and stands. "I believe that we've now completed the kitchen and the dining room; the living room is behind us, of course, which leaves us only the bathroom at the rear to be finished with this floor. Upstairs are the three bedrooms and the 'sitting room,' which showing brings this tour to something of a well-timed climax, but it would be unwise not to pay close attention to the bathroom, which we will now make our way into; it has certain interesting secrets of its own to yield. Since it is quite a small enclosure the best way in which to handle the showing is to permit me to enter myself; you may then stand before the open door and I will point out the objects of interest. But for any of you to come in would only overcrowd the space as well as permit a certain infusion of scatology into the whole which we can presently do without."

He makes a hand motion and the group starts to follow him. Since the break there has been a change in the collective mood of my companions; now they seem not so much impatient or restless as possessed with a kind of grim thoroughness, a desire to see the job through so that they can go home in peace. I know this mood well, it must have passed into them from the very walls and eaves of this home because it is the one with which I lived for most of my early years and it can be reckoned on the scale of human values far above greed, if not necessarily being anywhere near wisdom. The point was to get on with what you were doing, subject to all kinds of external pressures, of course, and the end was very much as the beginning because the sheer circularity and predictability of this existence was subsumed and aphorized in every mannerism of conversation, every random object scattered. I detect, at this meandering, a certain infusion of sentimentality and, perhaps, self-indulgence and I push it away violently because this plays no part in my present life, has not played any such role for a long time and would be extremely dangerous if entertained in these tender cir-cumstances. Self-dramatization would be far easier and more accessible than the kind of mood I have devised for myself over the past years but it would also lead to the kind of situation in which I might well make an exhibition of myself with all the problems that that entailed. Fortunately, these ruminations are all interrupted by Joanne's rapid tugging on my coat sleeve. She presses herself against me and says, "I'm ready for a break again. Let's go outside, back into the garden. Let's get some air. They'll never miss us here anyway."

"But the bathroom—"

"Who wants the bathroom? Besides, you heard that business about scatology. I don't want to hear any dirty jokes and I don't want to know how Mr. Westfield took a shit. I'd rather get away for a moment. Please," she says and contrives a most attractive pout. "I only came because you wanted me to; I'm happy to go along with you but can't we take a break for a few moments? I can't stand these people. They're such strange types and they don't know what's going on anyway."

"Scatology?" I say. "You miss the point, Joanne, didn't you hear the guide say that he wanted to guard exactly *against* it? 'Infusion of scatology' I think he said and he was right. Why, there was absolutely *no* scatology in the home of the Westfields, not after Mrs. Westfield passed menopause anyway; there was the question of Katherine's first menstruation, of course, which was very tricky and difficult since Katherine thought she had been injured and Mrs. Westfield, who should have known better, thought that Katherine was injuring *her*, and there were family jokes about 'taking a good trip' and so on and so forth when really meaning to talk about defecation, but that was all harmless, harmless. No, if the question of meaningful sex or meaningful natural function had ever entered the lives of these people it would have been a far, far better thing, but the point to make is that it never did, and whatever was carried on of significance with these people occurred behind closed doors and was usually masturbatory. One can hardly see a jot of difference between Michael's masturbatory activities and those of Mr. Westfield while fornicating with his wife; both of them manipulating themselves in a tiny space, far removed from all but memory and regret, spinning out their small, awful necessities in a kind of perpetual gloom. This is something you must consider! There were no dirty jokes here, no revelation of private parts, none of the hearty, sweating, thumping lust of intercourse to filter out of the master bedroom and by proxy educate the children! No indeed! In fact and on the other hand—"

"I'm bored, Michael," Joanne says. "I'm bored. I know that you're a kind of expert on all this but I've never been very bright. Please let's walk away for a minute." A kind of real distress burrows its way to her surfaces, changing the color of her eyes, the shape of her face, and I am momentarily afraid that she is going to be ill, right on the

Westfield carpet, but then it passes away and I understand that she is only terribly bored. In different circumstances I would insist that she stay and see the exhibit through—I am very interested in the bathroom and know that after this lapse of many years it will bring back some stark and moving memories—but the knowledge that I will never marry her and will shortly leave her has made me tolerant, has made me almost generous, and so I only give an assenting shrug and, taking her by the concealed softnesses of her arm, lead us away from the pack and toward the open door.

"They're going away, Mama," the albino says behind us. "If they're going away, why can't we do that too?" And I think that I hear his mother rumble some kind of an answer, think that I even hear the guide beginning some kind of comment, but it is too late, we are through the hallway again and out the front door and even if I wanted to save the situation by going back, there would be no way of guarding against remarks. Besides, what difference does it make to anyone if we leave for a while? I remind myself that the guide has no legal power over me, that the tour is voluntary, the restoration not even a government institution (only government-supported) and that I retain the same license now near noon as I did at 7 a.m., only the circumstances have changed. Nevertheless I feel a kind of loathing overtaking me at the prospect of facing the tourists and guide again shortly and telling them precisely what I have had in mind. There is no easy answer.

We stand in the garden where we stood before and Joanne takes my hands, clasps them, raises them against her and lets me partake for an instant of the surfaces of her breasts, then brings them down to her waist. "I'm scared, Michael," she says. "That's all I wanted to say. I'm terribly, terribly frightened and I had to get out of there; I had to try and tell you that."

"Why? What's wrong? What's the matter?" I feel obliged to ask these questions although, actually, I am not very interested in the prospective answers. What I am truly interested in is the viewing of the bathroom but this is something which is obviously not to be.

"I don't know," she says. "It's just some kind of general anxiety, this thing that I have which comes over me now and then, and it's come over very strong now. Oh, why did we take this tour Michael! It's so depressing! These people lived so horribly. How could people live like this and not kill themselves?"

"They liked it. They thought that they were indeed living, and to the extent that their philosophy contained a question of alternative might only have conceded that their existence was a simulacrum of the real thing, but nevertheless to be respected for that alone. 'Some people live their way but this is our way,' Mrs. Westfield would say."

"But it's so terrible! You said so yourself. Didn't you say so yourself when they were talking in there about dinner time?"

"Yes, of course I did. It was just an outburst. Besides that, the dinners were very soothing. The Westfields all said that they looked forward to them."

"I don't know. It just depresses me terribly. And you're depressing me terribly too, Michael. You're so interested in everything there and it's really so dull! You wouldn't be Michael Westfield, now would you?" she asks.

I know that this last question has been framed only out of a kind of forced coquettishness, but nevertheless it is almost impossible for me to control the start-and-recoil with which I respond, a slow shuddering and contraction of the stomach which spills out to be consequential elsewhere. Fortunately, her eyes have drifted out to the street as she says this and she does not swing back to observe me until I put a slightly quivering hand on her shoulder and say, "Of course not. Don't be silly. The Westfields' whereabouts are unknown, you know that."

"Still, you have the same first name and you seem to know so much about everything that's going on here and you were the one who wanted to come on out—"

"The Ph.D. seems to know a lot more than I do," I say. "And be even more passionately interested. Maybe *he's* Michael Westfield."

"Oh, God, do you really think so? Yes, of course you could be right. Why that's too terrible to think about! That poor man, sneaking back to his old family home after all these years, seeing all his secrets made exhibits, seeing everything that he lived for converted to something to be gaped at by a load of silly tourists. Oh, it would be horrible for him! Why would he come back?"

"Maybe he couldn't bear to stay away. Maybe he had to see it one last time. Who knows?"

"What would they do to him if they found out that he was Michael Westfield?"

"Well, the terms of the restoration, I understand, are that no Westfield or relative may ever enter the premises. I suppose that they would expel him. They might even make a report. There isn't that much they can do actually. This isn't a government institution, you know. They wouldn't send him to jail."

"Oh," she says shrugging. "Oh, well, then. Then it doesn't make any difference at all what happens to him. It was just a thought. Listen, Michael, that isn't the real thing I wanted to come out here for. I wanted to come out for something else. I wanted to ask you—"

But I will never know, at least not for the duration of this tour, what she wanted to ask me because while we have been so intensely talking a dapper, well-dressed man wearing period garb has come out of the front door and has quietly come behind us, introducing himself with a series of throat-clearing noises. That is to say that I must make the inference that he has come from the door and up behind us, because the first reckoning I have of his presence is that series of chokes and slow rumbles with which he makes himself known. He is a tall man, immaculately dressed in the clothing of the Westfields' time and carrying under his arm a thin notebook with a glossy cover on which there seems to be some kind of decal. "Excuse me," he says.

"Yes?" Joanne says quietly, but I can feel the jumpingof her skin as I lay a restraining arm flatly on her shoulder. "Who are you? What do you want?"

"I'm one of the members of the committee," the man says. "One of the curators, we're always on duty. I presume that you're with the tour?"

"That's right," I say. "We just came out here to get some air."

"We wanted to talk," Joanne says. Never is she so protective of me, so confidential, so affectionate as when we are in the presence of strangers. I feel her fingers trickle up my inner arm and caress my armpit, feel an idiot surge of desire which I fear is immediately visible to the curator.

"Well," the curator says with an air of precision which in no way serves to conceal what I sense to be a certain sadness, "well, then, you see, guests aren't permitted on the grounds other than in the presence of a tour guide. Guests are not permitted to leave the tour other than on the dismissal of the guide and when they take their breaks under his supervision and so on. It's nothing we like to do," he says apologetically, "but we have to guard against trespass and despoiling of the property and people getting lost or taking objects or something like that. I'm sure you understand. I thought I saw the two of you outside before, but you had gone in by the time I came out. I'm sorry."

"We have to go back in there then?" Joanne says. "We simply can't stay and talk in the garden? What's wrong with that; we're not harming anyone."

The curator shifts his case and then, thinking better of it, takes it from under his arm and runs his hands over it absently. "Rules," he says. "Regulations. Civil service mandate. Of course, I'm not unaware of the irony of this: the Westfields themselves lived a very contained and ordered life and only did what were considered the 'proper' things to do while otherwise engaging in the most unspeakable fantasies. But the fantasies did them no good, of course. So in a sense we are only perpetuating this kind of misdirection with our very rigid rules and regulations. Nevertheless we have no choice. We didn't decide on this policy, our funding sources did. So if you will—"

"Well," Joanne says and unlinks her arm from mine, "well, if we must, we must. Would you do me a favor, though?" and at the same time she gives me an assuring nod. I know instantly that I am in for difficulty, for Joanne always precedes her most outrageous requests and behaviors with a girlish attempt to indicate that she means nothing by them.

"Within reason, certainly."

"Might I talk to you alone for a moment?"

"What? What's that? I don't understand."

Joanne squeezes my hand abruptly and releases it. "I just want to see you alone for a minute. My boy friend understands. I have a few questions I want to ask you. They aren't very important but I've always been curious. And Michael can rejoin the tour."

"Um," the curator says. "Um." A certain disorder seems to have come into his beautifully-arranged clothing and a bit of sweat sheens his forehead. "Well, I guess so. I mean, I don't know why not. Do you object, sir?"

Joanne gives me a sidewise glance with blackness deep toward the center and I say, "No. I have no objection at all. That's perfectly all right, she had told me she wanted to speak to one of the curators when we were on the way over." Since I will never marry her I need not be concerned with her behavior anymore and yet, strangely, as I say this I feel not rage so much as a kind of remorse. I do not understand this and know that I will want to investigate it later.

"Well then," the curator says, "shall we talk in my offices? Unless—"

"Your offices will be fine," Joanne says and turns briskly away from me, already heading back toward the home. "I'll see you in a few moments, Michael. Okay?"

"Now, let me remind you that you must rejoin the tour," the curator says over his shoulder. "I trust you to do this on your own recognizance but it's very important that you do so; we have limited guard facilities here and must trust in the honor of people. However—"

"Oh, I will, I will," I say and proceed to follow them slowly at a safe distance. Now, with yards between us, Joanne's face has softened, taken on the various colors of the foliage she passes, and seems to be illumined with a kind of vivacity as she leans toward the curator to say something and then impulsively takes his arm. They pass through the door and I am quite alone. I hear the door slam, Joanne probably having done this since the curator would not under any circumstances have encouraged me to stay out.

I am alone, then, completely alone for the first time in several weeks. The fact is that Joanne and I have not been out of one another's presence—barring simple trips to the bathroom and even then often in company—for at least two and a half months, and even my sleep has lost that fine, high isolation which I had thought was the most irrevocable part of it; now I seem to sleep not upon a cliff but in a low clearing surrounded by bears and other night-creatures, all of whom regard me with caution not unmixed with love. In sleep, awake, in the transition between the two I have felt overwhelmed, in the center of a constancy I can barely understand let alone come to terms with, and the truly numbing part of this is that it is a constancy created by only one person, and that a girl whom I did not even know a year ago. Once again I feel myself prowling through the amnesia, sifting through the rising scraps and convolutions of recollection, and I know that if I do much thinking on this situation, even for a question of moments, it will all come back to me and then I will be in enormous difficulty. For one thing, my decision to leave Joanne may not look so firm, so sane, so definite if I get into the question of antecedent. It is enough to know that I have known her with an intensity I have reserved for no other person and that that intensity seems to be finding its fruition this morning. Strangely, I am neither curious nor concerned about her decision to speak with the curator. I feel that this has absolutely nothing to do with me and that, in the long run, things will work out exactly as they are intended to, with or without regard to individual choice. I owe a certain amount of this fatalism to my parents, of course, but there are other forces mixed in: failure, loss, pain, a couple of small successes, all of them leading to a resignation that so vast and so metaphysical in all its implications that even the Westfields would not have comprehended it.

I remember though, I remember coming against her in the softness and shallowness of a random bed some time ago—was that bed mine or hers?—and revealing for myself one by one the gift of her breasts, so unassuming under clothing, so consumptive a reality without and bending myself over those breasts sucked and prowled myself toward an unseen consummation, and opening up all the way, all the way she let me work through her thighs and then into the cunt with a force which seemed ready to explode me through the other end and then I was whining and bucking in her arms charging with energy and with a kind of enthusiasm nervous and intermittent as a twitch and then came, came, came all the way into her while her mouth burrowed against my ear and she whispered curse words which someone had probably once told her he found exciting. The whole thing could not have lasted more a than forty seconds, although she told me afterward that it was fine, fine for her too; she hadn't come but then she wasn't expecting to and as far as she was concerned, the female orgasm was only a myth anyway; invented by men as a rationalization for their sense of guilt. But we fucked and fucked again and the same thing happened, although once I made her whimper, and toward the middle of our relationship she took to the assumption of animaline sound in the bed: dogs, chickens, cows, a whole menagerie of responses done for my titillation more than hers, and meanwhile all the time we were fucking, fucking: we were fucking here and there and almost everywhere until she decided— it was her idea—that since we were screwing almost indiscriminately anyway we might as well make it the real thing and take a long trip together, spreading, in a sense, my lust and her reception throughout the United States, and so we have done so for many months now. Or perhaps it is only weeks. There is some question of antecedent vaguely poking at me: surely I had a job, surely she had a job, but other than knowing that they had something to do with paperwork and depended, both of these jobs, utterly upon the invisibility of the people whom our jobs affected because to confront them would have made our tasks unbearable— other than this I do not know precisely what we have been doing nor at the moment do I want to know. I am sure that it will all come back to me. Everything in due course will become clear, the tour itself is proving that, for although I have been away from this house for fifteen years or more, for all the effect that it has upon me and for all apparent distance created, I could never have left it. "You can't run away from yourself," is the way my mother put it, and in certain senses, perhaps, she knew what she was talking about. On the other hand, if I had gone away to the Southwest in that, my seventeenth year, when she said that, things might have been different. If I had gone away alone (except for parental support) and sought the fortune which a distant relative had promised me in the oilfields and dark sands of the Southwest. Who knows? Who knows? Surely I would have come back here anyway. There is no place so far removed from it that home is not accessible. Perhaps this is a tragedy, I do not know.

I do not know; I do not know but I am beset suddenly with the urge to go back inside the house, and so I take the three familiar steps of the stoop in a leaping bound and pass through the door and am inside. The door is not locked, of course. There was no chance that it would be. The Westfields secured the door day and night against strangers. It should have but did not embrace the concept of their own son. I am in the living room once again but this time it is empty and although I am very anxious to rejoin the tour in the bathroom, find it irresistible to look around, which I do, and find my father's note behind the grand piano where doubtless he had left it thirty years ago for the committee to find, restore and replace, all chasms of time rendered obsolete by the permanence of this humble object.

THREE

I cannot restrain my desire to pick up the note and look at it. I should not feel this way: my father's notes are as familiar to me as the outlines of my own skin, and in my youth I have read at least a hundred of them; notes addressed to me, to the family at large, a few to himself, all of them written in a rhetoric which seemed to possess as little discrimination for object as it did tolerance for subject. I remember that once, when I was eight or nine years old, I fell into cryptograms through a puzzle book which had been given us by another of those vaguely distant relatives whose gradual attrition through the years seemed to be the only metaphor for impermanence which my parents would accept. The point of the cryptogram was to have friends write mysterious messages which only you, knowing the code, could decipher, and it struck me as well as the author as an enticing project; but since I had no friends, let alone the kind who would care enough to set up a secret language with me, I found the book more of an exercise in frustration than otherwise after I had exhausted my first curiosity. I begged my father, at last, to write me a note in code and leave it on my bed one morning before he left for work and, grumbling, he consented. He left the house in those days at dawn, long before any of us had arisen, and returned somewhat after dusk; but the interesting thing is that he was not a father by proxy and that all of us were quite aware of his presence during the missing hours, a presence carefully nurtured by my mother, who could make no sensible decisions of any kind— life-decisions as to whether we might borrow a quarter or go out alone somewhere—until my father was home. On this morning I awoke from a rather restless sleep convinced that my father had not done what I had asked him, but when I reached under the bed it was there, printed in his precise handwriting on a sheet of his blue office stationary and, in the bargain, Scotch-taped closed for security. I cannot make sufficiently dramatic the anticipation with which I tore open this note: for all that it might have been it could be the key to existence itself, some private message from my father which would render into perspective all of my suffering and explain not only its cure—which was minor business—but its cause. It was causes which I always sought, then and now.

Dear Michael: [the note said, being written in the simplest of all the suggested codes in the puzzle book, a simple substitution of the letter before the desired letter in the alphabet so that "dear" became "cdzq" and so on, but with what tantalizing joy did I break the code to find out what my father had said to me!]

> *This is your code. Be a good boy today. I am going to the office and will be home at about six thirty. Do not give your mother any trouble and try to do your homework as soon as you get back from school rather than wait until after dinner when you never do it. Remind mother that today is laundry day and that it should go out along with my shirts. Remind Katherine that she is to make her bed. Be a good boy again and I will see you when I get home. I look forward to seeing you. It should be a very interesting day although business is not good.*
>
> *Your Father*

Which note I actually saved until we left the premises many years later and got it lost in a series of tattered socks and torn underwear which my mother discarded. Otherwise it would doubtless be part of the restoration today and very valuable and provocative it would have been.

But that is of the past; I am considering the present now in the form of my father's note which I slowly unrumple and hold to read. There is a sudden wiggling burst of laughter from the bathroom, as if the guide had just told the punchline to a family dirty joke (the only dirty joke we ever had, having to do with a bird that only crapped once a year, but we will get to that somewhat later) and I feel nostalgia and pain wash over me again because I want so badly to be back with the tourists, trying to understand the significances of the bathroom, yet unwilling to give up this small treasure I have found and afraid to appropriate it. The note is a list headlined THINGS TO DO and appears to be dated although the dates have become quite smudged:

THINGS TO DO

Get out the garbage.
Get the laundry together (Katherine's underwear, Michael's socks).
Get sewing materials for pants.
Sew pants.
Shopping at either Bohack's and A & P. No meat in Bohack's.
Vegetables too in A & P.
Wash car.
Drive car (maybe?)
See what Josephine wants to do about
Look over
Get cold cuts.
Reading

It seems that there should be more of this, but there is not, and try as I may to understand the handwriting in the sentences whose last words drop off it is impossible. "See what Josephine wants to do about" ends with the muddled word "grozsles" which is obviously impossible (my father having never gone in for neologisms it can be understood as being illegible) and "look over" ends with the word "wu" which even interpreted as a deep pun on the word "woe" (my father never went in for puns) would still make no sense. So the note is as unsatisfying in the reading as it must have been in the writing—which under other circumstances might be given as a definition of serious art—and with a kind of disgust I prop it behind the piano again, wondering whether it will ever be seen by another to pass through here. I doubt it very much; it is in a well-concealed place (only a Westfield knew the secret of the piano-crevice as the hiding place for notes, pornography in later years and so on) and in any event, even if they were to find and begin reading the note they would probably be so untouched by it as to replace it without finishing; my father's rhetoric can never be described as falling within the range of things which might be considered "compelling." In so doing, of course, the guest would entirely miss the point of the note: its sly humor, its interesting inferences, its possession of levels of simultaneous meaning which are indistinguishable from the aspect of great art, its narrative drive, its unwavering sense of structure, its clear and present control of the pace which was always the key to any true apprehension of what my father was trying to do, which was, as he often said, only to "try and make a little sense out of all of this, get a little order." It is thus peculiarly to his shame, and by inheritance mine, that this note, possessing most of the qualities of serious vision, will undoubtedly be neglected, seen only as a piece of intermittent niggling curiosa revealing an obsessive-compulsive streak and little else. It is probable that the trustees themselves have misunderstood it in that way and I tangle for a moment with the impulse to take the note downstairs and try to explain it to them, but then decide that this would surely mark my identity even beyond the scholar's possibility, and along with thoughts of the note, put all of this out of my head.

The laughter from the bathroom is more intense now and is being succeeded by a series of barking shouts whose source I cannot quite detect. Although I am eager to remain in the living room and rummage through other objects—the one large chair is itself a treasure which I am sure would yield, if I went through it carefully enough, one of those demi-suicidal confessions of my sister to herself which for a long time passed as her own paradigm of feeling—I find the prospect of the bathroom, as I have often in other times, all too dangerously enticing and so I head in that direction, my mood one of total concentration. It is strange, but I am not thinking of Joanne at this time, nor of the question of her converse with the curator; I do not have about it even the faintest curiosity, and this may be the most dangerous sign of all because Joanne, if I know her well at all, had as one of the prime motives for her exit the desire to make me suffer. What she really wants me to think is that she might be fucking the curator in my parents' bedroom just as she was fucking me before, but the strange truth of the matter is that if she was I would regard not only the possibility but the act itself with complete indifference. Looking at their bodies huddled on the sheets, the slow swaddling drive of sex overtaking them, I would, as a matter of fact, lend them vocal encouragement. I would have done no less for my parents had I ever seen them thus, which I did not; I could do no less for my inamorata. Or is she my inamorata? And what is an inamorata? It is all too much for me; basically I come to terms once again with the realization that I am of simple stock with a basic talent for metaphor, a certain transitional skill in both relationships and reminiscence and little else. Still, it may be enough. My father had only his notes and his utter lack of conscious irony to sustain him and it certainly worked out for the best; as his son it is to be expected that I will make equal use of the very different gifts given me.

I go toward the bathroom. There is a furious argument going on between the scholar, his friend and the guide, interrupted by hoarse cries of laughter from the albino's father, and this is undoubtedly what I have already heard although it now appears—the argument that is, if not the sounds—to have reached some penultimate stage of termination. "Come now," the scholar is saying, "there is absolutely no question of anal fixation whatsoever. I find it crude, base and completely uninformed of you to make those suggestions. People of that generation had a far less restricted attitude toward the bathroom function than do you or I, that is all. They performed their needs simply."

The guide has the look of a man slightly at bay; he is standing to the right and slightly in front of the toilet, which has been flung open sometime during this discussion and now looks as if it might be on the point, that ill-shaped mouth, of seizing and devouring him. He is also sweating more than slightly and his eyes when they grasp me are those of a man who is in trouble perhaps more severe than even he can admit. "Ah," he says. "You again. And where have you been this time? Perhaps you don't find my services satisfactory; perhaps you find it necessary to do your own investigations. But why?"

"None of that," the scholar says. "None of that diversion. Let him alone; he doesn't matter anyway and he's hardly been with us all morning. We were talking to the point. Talk to my point."

"Coprophilia," the guide says. I have no idea of what he is talking about but apparently the scholar does. "You're crazy," he says defiantly. "Insane." The effort of saying this disjoints him somehow and his companion puts a steadying arm on his elbow, whispers something into the scholar's ear.

"Ha!" says the albino's father. "Ha, ha, ha!" It is the first enthusiasm the man has shown all morning and I wonder what turn events could have possibly taken to have put him in such a mood. "That's a good one! Coprophilia! That's a polite way of saying shit-eating," he says quietly to his wife and she stiffens, turns away from him, her features a mask of distress, while this time it is the albino who strangles with laughter and gives his father an approving pat on the trousers. They look at one another in a comity of understanding and it is evident indeed that they are father and son; the albino's father has dark hair and features but otherwise they are exactly the same. Perhaps this is the problem.

"Let's have some order," the guide is saying. "Let's show some manners, ladies and gentlemen, a little routine courtesy; the purposes of the restoration do not embrace this kind of spectacle, you know. I'm only taking you through the rooms and trying to give you some understanding of the way that life was lived in those antique days; I'm not interested in getting into controversy and there's nothing personal or scatological about any of this. I will remind you—I must remind you—that everything I say has been processed through the trustees, the curators and the foundation; exhaustive research has found it to be unarguable fact and it becomes then both premise and conclusion. There are many areas left dark, of course; many which we do not attempt to cover in this tour because they are controversial and still open for discussion and this is a popularization, not a methodology. I can only suggest to the specialists among you that if you find any of this so highly objectionable as to break courtesy, you take it up with the trustees themselves at their next annual meeting. I am only on a salary, I am only an employee and I am neither equipped nor willing to undertake this kind of thing." He stands silent for a moment with rather pleased expression; it has obviously been a good speech and he knows it, but he is still sweating and the two Edwardians are in deep conference now, the harsh sibilance of their whispers knifing through the general area. "Well, then," the guide says, "that pretty much covers the bathroom. I will finish by noting the fine assortment of objects in the medicine chest: toothbrushes, aspirin, oil of wintergreen, alcohol, Benzedrine compound and so on, but no prescription drugs since both Mr. and Mrs. Westfield had a horror of unprescribed medication and in the bargain lived in the constant fear that when antibiotics were in the house the children might be inclined to experiment with them and to do themselves unspeakable damage. Why the Westfields, who tried to live such an orderly existence involved with the denial of elementary human passions—why these Westfields, I am trying to say, would be quick to fasten upon the totally unreasonable but to them entirely credible fear that their children potentially were suicides—this is something, of course, that will have to be taken up in the further studies. It is sufficient to say that the medicine chest was always kept in perfect order, although the presence of severe toothpaste stains was a great concern to Mrs. Westfield, who found them there only minutes after performing the last cleaning; and their constant presence may have had something to do with the air of rather pernicious, snappish gloom into which she often fell. The question of her being the youngest child of a large, rather frenetic family also had something to do with this, however, and it would be unfair to look for a total or even partial explanation from the medicine chest. The toilet was always kept perfectly clean, the stall shower was a great pleasure to all of the Westfields, particularly young Michael, who used to sit down in it for hours, immersed in the slow falling stream of water and thinking such things as we will never know; and the bathroom indeed, in the presence of guests, won that hard-bought appellation of 'spotless' for which Mrs. Westfield worked so hard. One can say that although the Westfields did not spend the most important or pivotal moments of their lives in the bathroom, they never had reason to regret being there and often came out more knowledgeable than when they went in, an illusion of decor perhaps working along with the more natural biological processes, but all of it leading to perhaps the only philosophic experiences they had. If they had any they would have occurred in the bathroom. Mr. Westfield's joke, which has been well-recorded for the archives, is particularly illuminating in that regard, so I will finish off this particular lecture with a recounting of that joke, then take what questions you may have and then, after a very short break, we will go upstairs and finish off the tour.

"Mr. Westfield's joke. It is one of only three family jokes which have survived the passage of time, the obliteration of history, but its sources are indisputably authentic and it is quite clear that we are not dealing, as we do in so many other areas, with a question of apocrypha. Mr. Westfield's scatological joke went as follows." The guide rummages in his inner coat pocket, takes out a small bluish strip of paper and, affixing some glasses to his nose, begins to read.

For the first time the albino has come to a kind of attention, his eyes are fixed steadily and unwaveringly upon the guide, but that is not necessarily any observation, so are the eyes of all of us.

"You have heard of the bird called the whee bird," the guide says, reading. "Can any of you tell me why it's called the whee bird? Well then, I will tell you. The whee bird only defecates one day a year but when it does … *whee!*" The guide folds the paper and puts it back into his pocket, puts away his glasses. "There is an alternate version in which the name of the bird is the 'oh boy bird' which although probably funnier to the undiscriminating ear has never been verified, and this one probably *does* fall into the area of apocrypha."

"That wasn't very funny," the albino says. "I've heard better jokes than that. It wasn't very funny at all."

"Well," the guide says gently, "that is not an uninteresting point and I am happy to comment to it. The answer is that the joke is not funny but jokes, used as references of human behavior, do not have to be. It is revelatory, and that for the moment can be considered sufficient. If it were funny in the bargain it could be interpreted as a bonus."

"Coprophilia," the scholar says again. He seems to be in some kind of distress, tugging at his clothing while his companion chatters with dismay. "Coprophilia. But I won't have it, I tell you. The interpretation does not admit it. Nothing is that simple. There must be more to it than that. Sheer metaphor. Absolute simplicity. But crude, cruel. May I have your permission? To go outside and be excused for a moment? I feel quite nauseous if you will excuse me."

The guide looks discomfited but then bows his head, makes the tilting gesture once again with his palms. "If you must," he says. "I mean, this isn't a penitentiary, it's only a tour. There's so little compulsion involved that when we note it it looks like more than it is. Certainly go. There's a bathroom adjoining the courtesy shop for public use, if you will."

"Then, thank you very much," the scholar says and, assisted by his companion, staggers off. We hear their footsteps for a moment, clattering through the halls adjoining the living room, and then one of them finds a door and they are gone. The guide sighs and adjusts his clothing, pats a shirt pocket delicately, looks at his fingernails. "Immaturity," he says. "You find it from the strangest sources. Are there any questions now? I'd appreciate your keeping them brief and to the point; it's almost lunchtime and we haven't covered the upstairs yet, and the restoration closes at three so we really don't have that much time left."

"Well, yes," the albino's father says. "One question. How can I put this in the best fashion? You've just finished giving us an explanation of some of the scatology in the Westfield family as well as a dirty joke told by one of their members, but I remember you saying sometime earlier that these people lived in such a fashion as to believe that everything they did was 'right' and they were somehow moral exemplars if nothing else. How can you equate the two? Surely the Westfields did not think that this—"

"Oh, dear," the guide says, "you're missing the point. Entirely. In the first place, I am sure that it was made clear that Mrs. Westfield had absolutely no role to play in this bathroom scatology and had no taste for any of it; that her own use of the bathroom was confined completely to natural functions and she tried to make herself oblivious of her husband's small indulgences. In the second and more important place it should be noted that Mr. Westfield's joke was not declaimed but merely whispered, and even then under only two circumstances: when he had had his requisite one drink at a mixed gathering of adults or when he was trying to induce one of the children to enter or leave the bathroom to his convenience. And third and finally, any study of the period, any true apprehension of its history will certainly reveal that there is absolutely no conflict between the basic ruling assumption of the Westfields' life and the small taste for scatology involved; they were, in fact, only two sides of the same coin in that both embraced the concept of a certain conscious delimitation of existence. Didacticism is, after all, only the reverse face of the scatological and the two qualities, in the type of person exemplified by the Westfields, exist simultaneously and quite easily, so much so that the afflicted are even aware of this and ration themselves out a small portion of pornography in order to find relief from the more oppressive moral qualities. I must be a terribly inefficient guide today if I cause such a question to even be raised. Really, there is absolutely no question of complication here."

"What did they do in the bathroom?" the albino asks, giving his father a sidewise leer. It is apparent that he is out to make something of a sensation for his father's approval and this brings to me the most peculiar feeling of poignance; I have done the same thing in my youth and I know what it is like, but on the other hand, I could tell the albino that it makes no difference at all because the only ways in which his father could be reached (if he is at all like my father) are in ways which the boy would himself find noxious, and when he *did* reach his father, he would find what he discovered to be not at all interesting, a banality of thought and feeling which would make him only apologetic. All this passion for a wink! All this lingering and loss for an absent reminiscence! It is too much, even for a man of my own finely-attuned capacity for irony.

"You know what they did," the guide says. "I won't repeat myself."

"Did they like it?"

"Irrelevant," says the guide. "Totally irrelevant. I'm sorry but we simply have no time for frivolity. Unless there are a few brief sensible queries remaining, I think we'll now adjourn and go to the courtesy shop—"

"One question," I say. "Just one fast question and then we'll be on our way. Tell me, what is the purpose of this anyway?"

The guide gives me a look of such loathing that under other circumstances it would in itself be ripe for consideration, and says, "I don't understand you. And why did you go off before? Haven't you got any common respect?"

The fact that everyone has turned to look at our confrontation with an intensity of interest elicited by nothing that has been yet said this morning fills me with a flush of despair, but I persist. "We had to get away for a moment," I say. "No disrespect was intended. I just wanted to know what the point of all this was."

"Where did your girl friend go?"

"She went downstairs to talk to one of the curators. She had a few questions she wanted answered."

"Oh," the guide says. "Oh." I know exactly how he feels. The surest way in which to demolish a civil servant is to make reference to a superior, and yet at the same time I feel shame for his sake because, as is usually the case in civil service, he probably knows far more about the subject at hand than his superiors; should, in fact, be the man whom Joanne wanted to talk to. But his ill luck, the knowledge of which is scorching his features, is hardly to be changed by the likes of myself. He shrugs and says, "I don't think I understand your question. What do you mean?"

"I mean, the point of the Westfield restoration. Why have it? What does it mean?"

"By buying tickets to come you've answered the question, haven't you? You obviously find it of significance or you wouldn't be here."

"That may be true," I say. "But in general terms, what is the point of it? All this triviality, all this pain! Why try to subsume it in artifacts? Haven't we got enough of this ourselves? Do we have to go outside and search for it? In general terms, of course."

The guide tries to sneer but his training and his very evident enthusiasm for his job get the better of him and it does not quite come off. "That isn't a bad question," he says, "but, of course, I've tried to answer it by implication throughout the morning and will certainly continue to. The life of the Westfields was significant, important, a meaningful microcosm of the way in which people lived at this period in this place. By apprehending it, by trying to come to terms with it, we come into contact with our own history. Perhaps the Westfields are easier to understand because they are all gone and we can learn from their artifacts, which are far less confusing—and infinitely more precise—than actions, which are always discolored by conflicting motive. But by dissecting this life we can, in turn, dissect our own. I would think that this would be the purpose of any exhibition. I don't mind saying that I think this a valuable one."

"Yes," I say, "yes, yes, but they were such essentially trivial people, people so essentially involved only in themselves, not only unaware of great issues but, as you point out yourself, deliberately in flight from them. Wouldn't there be better people to try to understand?" In fact, I do not quite know why I am doing this; for all the good that the guide's answers will be doing me, I might just as well be addressing myself. Nevertheless I persist. "They weren't very important, you know."

"Sure, they were," the fat man says. "Certainly they were. How can you think that?"

"He's right," the guide says, for the first time engaging in what could be called a dialogue with us. "They were important, I don't think that this kind of thing can be disputed. By the very fact of their staidness, their stolidity, that accumulation of traits, mannerisms and cheap, mass-manufactured articles which spaced out their lives, they established some kind of a norm in the society they inhabited, a storm-center in the midst of the stillness where, at least, they had some certainty. It is well known that people go for objects, mannerisms and familiarity precisely because they can be dealt with in a way that the unknown cannot, and that by reshuffling these traits in a certain way, a true and proper metaphor for reality can be induced."

"But that's precisely the point!" I say loudly. "You see the point is that these people were surreal, these lives can be regarded as a flight-and-substitution and to understand them is to get further from reality, ever further, not closing in on any sense of it at all. By manipulating these objects and mannerisms they were trying to fool themselves into thinking that it was the same as reality, but we know better. Don't we? Don't we?" I say rather wildly, flicking my gaze frantically from side to side on those dull parched faces which now, right down to the albino, seem to regard me with a kind of tolerant amusement. *"Don't we?"*

The guide gives me a long, surveying stare in which all knowledge, all pity, all understanding seem to be encompassed, and says, "Son, if you don't understand the meaning of all of this, if you really mean it when you say you don't know why it's important, then I can't make you understand. There's simply no way. You'll have to be a little older, you'll have to know yourself a little better and then it should all fall into place. But I can't dispute this. I simply can't dispute this. This restoration, you see, is built upon an assumption as fundamental, as basic and as irredeemable as any of the Westfields', and that is that this is of importance and can be understood in its own terms. If you can't see that I can't make you. Everything here is vital and it is always with us, every part of it. Every artifact an admonition. Shall we take our break now and go downstairs to the courtesy shop? Or would you prefer to go straightway to the bedrooms? Myself, I could do with some rest; it's been a very difficult morning for all of us."

"The shop," the scholar says. In the interim he and his companion have unobtrusively rejoined us at the rear. His face, although somewhat ashen, appears to have retained its normal outlines and it is his friend actually, who seems to be more the sufferer, a certain twittering anxiety causing him to jump and twitch as the scholar moves against him.

"Are you feeling better now?" the guide asks.

"Yes. Yes, I'm sure so. It was all the talk of coprophilia that did it to me. We had a little fresh air outside and everything's fine now. But let's take a break; let's do if we can."

"Well, then," the guide says. "Certainly." By some trick of light he looks almost fatherly now although, of course, in a far subtler and thus less lasting fashion than did my own father. "We'll all go downstairs then and reassemble at the foot of the stairs in fifteen minutes. I shall lead the way of course," and he brushes by us with a certain gravity and grace of motion and leads us toward the stairs to the basement, a hint of beckoning in his upraised hand.

I am uncertain as to whether I wish to follow him or whether I want to stay and look around these rooms some more. On the one hand I am, of course, most interested in seeing the "courtesy shop" which should have many objects of interest mass-manufactured and thus rendered both nostalgic and significant; on the other hand I have not quite gotten the lure of the bathroom out of myself as perhaps I should have through the guide's abbreviated lecture. It is illegal, of course, to remain here without supervision, but none of them look back at me as they go and it is apparent that all of them are more concerned with factors downstairs than anything of me and that I have the place, in the most essential sense, once again to myself. Or, as my father put it when I was going through a particularly difficult and unfortuitous business of being bullied in public school around my twelfth year, "You just go right up and pass those boys; you don't even think about them. You don't really think you're so important, do you, that the whole world thinks about you and has you on its mind all the time? They don't even know you exist." Good advice, of course, but projected too deeply out of my father's persistent nihilism to have application to my difficult situation, and the first time I tried it—attempting to bypass a pair of cajolling bullies in the schoolyard—I got myself physically invited to join them and a good deal of punishment for what they took to be my newfound (and, as it turned out, extremely tenuous) arrogance. Nevertheless, in this situation, within the walls of the house in which he lived for some twenty-three years, my father's advice seems to have assumed the stolidity and permanence of an epitaph, and bowing to it I stay behind and walk eventually into the bathroom where, closing the door behind me, I sit down meditatively on the toilet and stay in a fixed posture for a long time.

It was on this toilet, of course, that I used to flagellate myself occasionally, but the majority of my adventures went on either on my own bed or, as I have said before, on that of my parents. Sitting on the hard, implacable weight of the closed toilet I feel myself once again overtaken by the pain, trembling and needful misery which always preceded my masturbatory exercises and, indeed, were it not for the fact that I have given up masturbation or a good part of it years ago and were it not for the fact that I have so recently and joyously possessed Joanne, I might beat off here once again, for nostalgia's sake if nothing else. But there is, to be sure, almost no impulse to do so below the basic urge of perversity, and in any event my semen would be a very frail tribute to this overhanging memory which sits in the fluorescence, darts through the cove of the shower, seems to perch on a windowsill. The fact is that I am very much at loose ends with myself.

It has been a difficult day, after all, a demanding day and one as well not without surprises, and it does not seem quite over even yet. Sitting across from the shower, looking at it, I remember a day in my eighteenth year, shortly before I entered college, when I had sat in exactly the same position, looking at that dull, shrouded glass, clusters of green floating toward the center, and had muttered to myself (I was stark-naked at the time, incidentally), "I am going to college and four years from today, having finished college, will be sitting on this toilet in exactly the same position, looking at this damned shower, and the only difference will be in my head, the only difference between the Michael of four years from now and the Michael of today will be a series of attitudes fixed in his head and *that* is why he is going one thousand miles away to a strange place with strange people, because he wants to make different connections in the head. Is it worth it? Isn't there an easier way to repair the network?" But of course there wasn't, and four years later, almost to the day, I sat once again opposite the shower, soaked in a summer sweat and debating whether or not I wanted to shower before I went out to the racetrack and decided, finally, not to. If there were different connections in my head I was unable to spot them, at least at that time. Later perhaps. On the other hand I have no doubt at *this* time that things *are* different and that there is all the necessary difference between this blank confrontation now and those two in history, but I am not so certain about even this, that if I were to hear my mother's pattering in the hallway and the sound of her fist urging me toward the completion of my business, I could know that everything would not go back to the way it had been and there it would be again. Everything as it was. Only the history unascertained. It is really too much for me to think about, even in this difficult mood, and I get up from the toilet quickly and go over to the medicine chest. Opening it I find that the guide has given an apt summary of its contents but has omitted, perhaps, its most important feature. Underneath a piece of towel paper, folded in quarters, is a note from my sister to herself, one of those notes which I have previously mentioned which, I am sure, the committee in its wisdom has gone over carefully and which it has selected to play its modest role, for veracity's sake, in the chest. It is unfortunate, of course, that no one will ever see it, but I am anyway, which is certainly sufficient, and turning to make sure that the door is still closed I open it unhastily and read it.

We wrote very few notes in the Westfield family to one another, but almost copiously to ourselves, and this letter from my sister is longer than it would seem to have any right to be in terms of its location. What it actually seems to be is a misplaced entry for her diary, and as I think of that long-discarded document, now reconstituted as someone's first edition of a paperback mystery or worse yet as the diary of another person, I feel a tinge of regret that this one, for whatever sake, was excluded; it is apparently a transitional chapter of no small significance and seen in context it might have made everything before or after it seem entirely clear. But then, having rarely seen my sister's diary and having almost never had a chance to inspect it closely, I cannot be entirely sure of this ... or of anything else:

August 13: We went over to Dorothy's house this evening. Dorothy lives just like we do only they put the dinner on the table when everyone wants it and not at any other time. Afterwards I went upstairs with Dorothy, with Joan M and with Helen and we talked about things. I learned a lot. Things are almost the same. Helen says that Burt K likes me but she doesn't know why and I told her that George T likes her too but also didn't tell her why. After that we played wrestling and it was very good and I almost lost. I wanted to stay but I knew they would only be coming out to look for me so I had to go home. After I came home I thought a lot about Burt but I don't know why he likes me because I've never done anything to make him like me and I've never had him over here because I am afraid to. Maybe I will understand this later. Dorothy isn't bad but she and the other girls on the block still feel there's something strange about us because of our religion and maybe there is. I don't know anything about my religion. I never studied it.

And resisting the impulse to put this one too among my effects, I replace the note back in the chest. The mention of religiosity sparks some long-hidden memories for me; I had never been aware until this moment of my sister's acuity toward the general issue or her ability to capsulize the problem in a sentence or two and irrationally, decades past the fact, I wish that I had made some attempt, when we were much younger, to talk to her. We talk to one another now, occasionally anyway, and I know enough about her life to understand that she is fulfilling the terms of the grant to the letter by expressing no intention of ever returning to the restoration as long as she is alive, but as to the exact quality of her existence, the scope of her ambitions, the meaning of her functioning, I am not quite sure. I have always taken it for granted that Katherine functions on a level somewhat different, by which I mean lower, than mine, but it occurs to me for the first time that this is not necessarily true—this day is full of insights—and that what I have taken for lower insight is merely a higher resignation, carried forth to this day with a certain stylishness and grace which is foreign to me. In any event it is very difficult and complex and I am consumed by the desperate urge to get out of the bathroom, an urge more desperate toward exit than any of my father's "hurry calls" to get in which caused such distress and dislocation for the one of us caught in there when the need did smite him. I leap toward the door, turn the knob and find it sliding in my hands, and for a crazed instant succumb to the feeling that I am trapped and will become an artifact myself, a piece of business to be included in the next edition of the tour guide ("Michael Westfield is on view in the bathroom in a characteristic posture of flight-and-immersion; of course you should not touch him under any circumstances as he fears touch") but the door spins open at last and I spin into the hallway gasping, surprised at the density of the air. It is incredible to feel that we were able to live so many years in such a humid atmosphere, but so we did and became unconscious of it; perhaps the very climate was the key to the way in which the Westfields functioned, a thought which in its delightful banality once again violently alters my perspective. I am about to dart for the stairs and the entrance to the courtesy shop when, to my surprise, Joanne comes out of the living room and puts her arms around me. Her face is bright, flushed, happy, her eyes almost twinkling; if she had been in search of something when last seen, it could be clearly understood that she had found it. "Hello," she says. "I was looking for you." The dismaying fact is that I had not missed her presence at all and might not have for the next several hours.

"Hello, yourself," I say. "They all went downstairs to the shop to take a break. They'll be going upstairs to the bedrooms soon." I am trying to present to her a normal demeanor but it is not easy and I wonder if it shows.

"That's nice. Was it a good lecture?"

"I just caught the end of the bathroom business. It was fairly interesting. But it's all starting to get a little bit dull."

"Oh. Too bad. Do you want to know what *I* was doing?"

I do not. "Of course," I say.

"You must have thought it very strange when I told that old man I wanted to talk to him alone. But you were very nice about it."

"He wasn't an old man."

"He acted the part. Do you want to know something? He propositioned me! Right in his office."

"Oh," I say. It is difficult to maintain the bright look of interest which I know is necessary because our posture is uncomfortable in this position and in the bargain I had been thinking of going to the courtesy shop. "Oh, for God's sake. Really. How about that?"

"We were just talking about one thing and the other thing and he leaned forward and put his hand on my knee and said, 'You're very beautiful. I've never seen a girl as beautiful as you in the way that you are. Couldn't we go to bed together? There are plenty of beds all over the restoration and we won't have any trouble at all finding privacy. Please say you will; it won't mean a thing to you but it will mean so much to me.' What do you think of that?"

"What were you talking about before he said this to you?"

"Oh," she says, "oh, just things. Nothing very much. I just had a few questions I wanted to ask about this museum and I thought I'd give you an opportunity to wander around on your own by getting him off your neck. You could say thank you! You've been dying to walk around by yourself all morning and when I give you the opportunity what do you do? You go right back to the tour."

"I looked around a little bit first."

"And get myself propositioned in the bargain!"

"I don't understand," I say and this much is true; I have no idea why government civil servants in the employ of a museum project would proposition female visitors to this project, no matter how desperate they are or how attractive the female visitors. The fact is that Joanne is not that terribly pretty; her figure, particularly with clothes off, is impressive and there is an unusual resilience to her skin, an almost masculine tautness, which I have always found extremely exciting, but her face is ordinary and she has, at the age of twenty-five, still no conception of the uses of makeup or any of its subtleties. She is, in short, acceptable but there is little in her to drive a curator to madness. It is another of those strangenesses of the restoration which I know I will have to, much later, come to terms with in order to proceed to anything else.

"Did you go to bed with him?" I ask perversely.

She gives me a look with a good quotient of pain in it. "I certainly did not," she says. "The man was insane. What do you think of me? Do you think that as insane as everybody else in this place seems to be?"

"I hope not," I say. "I hope not."

"I have an idea," she says, grasping my arm and leaning forward to me with real confidentiality. "While the rest of them are downstairs, let's go back to your parents' room and let's fuck!"

I look at her intensely. "We did that," I say. "We did that already about an hour and a half ago."

"Oh, really?" she says. "Oh, of course," but her eyes do not really register comprehension. "Of course we did. But what's wrong with doing it again? There's nothing to be done about it."

And it is only then that I feel the frozen, uncomprehending gloom of the massive double-take seizing with the ferocity and singleness of purpose of a fist. I stagger slightly in the hallway and am only successful in righting myself by reaching my arms toward her and balancing myself on the softnesses of her shoulders. "Wait a minute," I say. "You didn't say 'the Westfields' room.' You said 'your parents' room.' That's what you said."

"Oh?" she says and her eyes register a faint dismay which might be profound and which might on the other hand only be a polite reflection of my own expression. "Oh, did I say that? That was really silly, Michael, because I didn't want to hurt your feelings and I was happy to go along with you for your sake. But since it's out, it's out. Yes, surely, Michael, I know that these people were your parents. I know you're Michael Westfield. You've been acting so strangely all morning and you were always talking about this restoration when we were driving and I could just tell in hundreds of ways. But it doesn't matter to me. I feel the same way about you that I did. And I won't tell anyone. That old curator was starting to ask me all kinds of questions about you and who you were and what your name was and so on and I didn't tell him a thing. So you don't think that I'd ever tell a soul."

"Oh," I say, "oh, God," feeling the cave of the living room closing around me, the very clutter assuming that malevolent and personal proportion which disaster sites always seem to do. It is no coincidence that the closet drama is being played in the living room, which was, of course, in different guises, the crisis room and in which the few discussions of prior alleged seriousness were carried on at about the rate of one every two or three years. "Oh, God, I don't think I can stand it anymore." I stagger over the gate in an uneven ragged bound and sprawl on the couch. "It's just too much for me, all of it, all of it." I cannot explain why I am opening up so emotionally for Joanne but suspect—in fact I am certain or otherwise would not be able to do it—that it is all part of some highly contrived plan which my subconscious has already bought and is now essaying to sell to me.

"Oh, don't be so emotional, Michael," she says to me coolly, sitting next to me on the couch, working her thighs against mine and taking my hand to inspect it. "There's really no need for these kinds of dramatics; this was your idea in the first place you know, and how did you expect me not to suspect the way you've been carrying on about this and the way you've been acting here? Besides, plenty of us go back to the homes where we grew up; it's unfortunate that yours has turned out to be some kind of national shrine and that you're forbidden, but it's basically a healthy experience and it's good for you. I won't ever tell. But that dirty old bastard started to feel me under the table; he was squeezing my thighs and working against my knees and it was just too much. What kind of people are there working here anyway? I never knew of anything like this. Oh, come on, Michael, let's go upstairs and screw. If you feel strange about your parents' room we can do it in yours or your sister's but I'd really like to. It would be so nice."

"I don't think so," I say. "Can't you understand that all of this is too much for me?" And indeed it is, I lean forward on the couch in a posture of distress, cupping my head on the open left palm but the difficult thing about all of this is that I know exactly how it looks and the effect I am trying to bring around by doing it. This is all very similar to my mother's 'fainting fits' when she would pass out near the crockery or late on weekday evenings rather than face difficult choices, and also very much like my father's predilection for throwing tantrums precisely before some important economic issue was about to be discussed. We re-enact our history, re-enact our history, there is really no end to all of it. None, none. I feel the pressure of Joanne's fingers on my wrist and then she is guiding me, quite easily, to my feet; I am not resisting her at all of course. I feel her arm slip around my waist and her lips touch the panels of my cheek. "Come on," she says, "everything will be all right. You know that yourself. Let's go upstairs. Let's go upstairs and fuck. Then when the rest of them come up we'll join them and it will be like we know something that they don't know. I love you, Michael. Have I told you that today? I love you. I love you. Everything should be all right between us." Her breast, shielded, grazes into the sudden cup of my palm and I feel her warmth. I allow her to take me to the stairs, allow her to take me up the stairs and when it comes to the choice of rooms I allow her to take me where she will which, of course and inevitably, is once again the bedroom of the Westfields. Pater and mater. I do not think about this anymore, so urgent and rising is my need to fuck her.

FOUR

This time she draws the shades with a swift deftness which obviously is the extension of all kinds of planning, an ease and certainty about these things which has always evaded me, and then in the dark, toe to toe, foreheads touching, we unclothe like assassins and toss our clothing at a great distance from the bed, pile into the sheets together. It is almost as if we are now courting disaster, for should we hear the sound of the guide and his entourage coming up the stairs, even clattering at the door of the room, there would be absolutely no time to get out of bed and dress before we were intercepted. And so we would stand naked: stand naked before albino, his family, the two Edwardians, the fat man, the guide, only my swollen genitalia giving indication of the mortality contained in that nakedness, and there would be absolutely no way that the situation could be saved. In all likelihood we would be involved in the courts. Still, it does not occur to me to pick up the clothing and put it at a safe remove. I think the fact of the matter is that I want to get caught; that I want to bring down upon myself a disaster so large, so final, so damning in all of its implications and so irrevocable that it will be possible to subsume all difficulty in that disaster and thus abandon all responsibility. In one way or the other way it is possible that I have been looking for this all my life, have been looking for something to come along so enormous and damning that it will render the question of further struggles an irrelevance. It may be this more than anything else which causes my prick to speed toward Joanne with such enormous force, such great concentration; it may be the need to sink far below any sense of my purposes and never be seen again which gives voice to my groans, my mutterings, my shouts. I will have no way of knowing this, ever. There are no easy answers. There never will be.

My father too must have been looking for something of this sort, for no other reason could he have seen terror in an untied shoelace, all damnation and loss in an unshoetreed shoe; his instincts then were right (at least in terms of my own) but he was simply too limited a man to have the scope, the dramatic sense of history and the background that I do. For these reasons I am able to contrive large disasters which are of almost metaphorical sweep in their intensity and irrevocability, whereas he was only able to immerse himself in a constantly-reiterated banality. Of course it is all too late to care much about this or to change it in any way but I wish, unreasonably, that there were some way to travel my adult self back in time and confront my father with what I have since learned about really colorful ways in which to celebrate the death-urge. If I could get past his posturing, his remorse, his easy dismissals, I think that I might very well be able to do him a large favor and for it, perhaps, even win his favor. Of course I am not in the least interested in winning his favor, having lived my own life my way for quite a while now. And for no profit other than mine. My own. My life.

Witness Joanne. There is Joanne. For all this time, as this pure storm-and-welter of retrospection and indulgence tumbles through my mind, all this time I am atop her on my parents' bed in an orgy of concentration, brow furrowed, prick burrowing, trying to fuck her. She is tight now, surprisingly so, some miracle of psychic connection with the curator must have locked up her cunt because it is damnably hard, almost impossible, for me to penetrate her and I am only able to do so with great difficulty, forcing myself past levels of unchanging skin and arid glands in order to do so. I wish that I had some of my parents' Vaseline but that, of course, is quite impossible; it has not been in these quarters for ten years, I am sure, and if it was it would be unusable now by dint of age. Besides that, Vaseline in my home was used, to the best of my knowledge, only for thermometers and small, harmless burns. So I work my way into her slowly, frenzied in concentration, and at last it begins to work: suck of breast, flip of ass, rising nipple, deepening cunt and at last I am snugly all the way up to myself in her and our lips collide. "Fuck me," she whispers. "Oh, this is so exciting. I want you to fuck the hell out of me. Really do it now. Do it as if you were mad at me. Do it as if I had fucked that dirty old creep downstairs. Maybe I did. You'll never know."

"Bitch," I say, less out of conviction than necessity. "Bitch, bitch, bitch," and begin to flop upon her painfully; my cock is swollen and very hard and there is very little friction generated by the collision

of our genitals, but I close my eyes against all these concerns and try
to think only of spilling, spilling into her. "Oh, bitch," I moan, feeling
an ancient cry deep in the cells, a long lusting, a deep feeding."Oh,
cunt, oh, cunt," and she says, "You too, you too, you bastard, you can't
fuck me; you're not good enough for me," and, "Oh, you cunt," I say.
"You dirty wretched miserable bitch," and feel my orgasm yank me
out of myself, leaving me quite speechless as sperm pours and pours
into her. I raise my hands to cup her breasts and suck at them in-
dustriously and she inhales to place them in my mouth even more
deeply, and still dry, dry, she works out her last measures against me.
By any objective scale, I suppose it is possible to say that we have
had a satisfactory, if somewhat too complex fuck, but the look on
Joanne's face is unspeakable and leaves very little to the
imagination, being composed of distress, dismay and a kind of
smugness in equal parts, all of it quite horrifying, and set off against
the flop and roll of her large, meaty breasts, it has a rather Gothic
aspect. It is evident that she is unsatisfied and cannot decide
whether she is more anguished by this than she is pleased by the
fact that I have not moved her. Meanwhile I roll off to her side,
looking up once again at the ceiling, and for the first time then I see
it truly as my mother must have seen it, the greyness of its aspect,
the complete implacability of its color, the slow, subtle changing
shapes which optical illusion seemed to give it—yes, the ceiling was
the total metaphor for everything which sex meant to my mother,
and at this instant I can understand, if only for the first time, how
difficult it must have been for her to sustain herself in an
environment where sex was highly valued and often joked about
(but, I remind myself, where many of her friends must have had as
difficult a time as she). The thing was that my mother always
referred to sex as a "great joy" and a "beautiful fulfillment" and once,
in a moment of pique, confessed herself to me as being "wholly
satisfied with everything, which is why I don't want to see those
magazines and books of yours around," and how difficult indeed it
must have been for the poor woman, for the fact is (I can see this
now) that she *was* satisfied, that sex *was* a great joy and to the
degree that she understood this phenomenon of pain and relief
which is all that we may ever know of the heavens—to the degree
that she did indeed understand this, she was pleased with it. This
is a chilling line of speculation; it would be chilling for me to follow
even if I was in the humming safety of a motel room with Joanne and
some blankets huddled over me; here, in the truly dangerous

circumstances surrounding this room and this fuck it is entirely out of proportion. I shudder and jump on the bed and for no reason which I can understand find myself clinging to her.

"Why?" she says to me, taking me in with a slow sigh and allowing me to fasten my lips to her large nipple. "Why does it sometimes work out like this? It's like you're going away, that you're not going forward but retreating from me as fast as you can. I don't understand it."

"Why did you let him proposition you?"

"He propositioned me; I didn't *let* him."

"Then why did you go to talk to him? The poor bastard probably thought you were trying to pick him up."

"I had a few questions," she says unconvincingly and thrusts the breast deeper into my mouth so that I can suck more avidly. I am not quite sure exactly what profit I intend to take from this but remove my mouth and say, "There's got to be an end to this, you know."

"An end to what?"

"To us. To this thing."

"Well," she says, and her eyelids close over as she rolls against me, "we never expected anything different from the beginning, did we? We knew it would come to nothing eventually. No, don't move away. Suck on me. They're still ripe."

I immerse myself in her again and it is indeed very easy and very restful, it is something that I could do for a very, very long time without the necessity for any kind of thought, and I feel, in fact, that I am working myself toward the verge of a very real connection, some kind of genuine necessity at last answered, hot then, in the distance, we hear a dim clatter and the rumbling sound of footsteps. I can, of course, instantly place them from all my subsumed knowledge of this house; they have reassembled in the dining room and are about to take the steps to the bedroom.

"My God," I say and leap from her at full force, staggering back against the wall. "We've got about a minute to get dressed, even less. Hurry, for God's sake! You want to get caught?" I struggle with my pants, feel with gratitude my leg moving slickly into both sets, the touch of the shirt against my chest.

She leans back, her arms behind her head, breasts pointed to the ceiling and says, "Oh, come on, Michael. Don't be so nervous. It *is* your house," and giggles then, rather unreasonably.

"Don't you understand? They'll find us here and then—"

"And then what?"

"And then enough!" I say. She is being completely unreasonable; in fact she is being a little insane. The trouble is that I know exactly what she is thinking and how she is being driven in that direction. And I feel the same thing working within me as well, for of all the tastes of catastrophe, what could possibly please the disaster-gourmet more than the prospect of being caught *in flagrante delicto* by strangers in his own home, in his own parents' bed? The compulsion to lie down beside her and let what will evolve happen is almost irresistible, and to compensate for it I spring toward her, grab her wrist and pull her upright from the bed, twist it slightly then until she mumbles in pain and finally stands alongside me, sobbing. "Please," I say. "We can't have this, Joanne. Please don't do this to me."

"You bastard," she says. "You don't understand. You don't even know what's going on here." But she begins to dress quickly enough, simultaneously with the sound of steps working on the stairs. Her assumption of full dress coincides almost exactly with the sound of the guide's hand on the doorknob, but in an enormous, explosive leap full of energy I manage to get both of us over the gate to stand innocently against the wall just as he opens the door and all of them pile in. And—wonder of wonders!—he gives no sign of acknowledgement of our presence, possibly taking us for having been with him all along.

Then too, the guide seems very tired. There has once again been a change in my colleagues' aspect and demeanor since the last time seen; now where there was anticipation there is only a kind of sullenness and the guide's own dedicated civil servitude seems to have been replaced by an intricate kind of pallor which begins at his forehead, works down toward his neck and then doubtless into all of the invisible places. His eyes are very much like those of my father after a long day, slightly red at the rims, on the edge of tears or perhaps just past them, and his breath seems to snort unevenly, not quite catching his nostrils on the inhale. Only the albino seems slightly contented, he is working on the last leavings of an ice cream cone and sighing slightly as he puts the remainder into his mouth and—without chewing—swallows it. He seems to be at a kind of peace which is, of course, well beyond where I am at this moment.

If the guide notices the slight rumpling of the bedspread or the faint hint of semen he gives no clue. Indeed his visage at this moment seems hardly to be receiving much intelligence. He gives an indolent wave at the room as he climbs over the gate and then, with a weary groan, seems to assume the mantle of professionalism again. The scholar and his companion, I am pleased to note, look entirely restored in the physical sense although no less sullen than anyone else. Joanne, meanwhile, moves as far away from me as she can in the limited space and, folding her hands, looks downward and toward the wall. In other circumstances I would know exactly what this behavior forecasted in the way of remonstrations, arrangements, guilt and exercise later but now I do not care anymore. That is the thing that I sense within myself, and with almost a kind of joy I carefully explore this feeling, picking it up, looking at it from under the edges like a pancake. I truly do not care. I feel as if I will be able to leave the Westfield museum in due course and never think of it again. It is almost enough—but only *almost*—to redeem the day.

"Well, then," the guide says, "we are, of course, in the master bedroom, the bedroom where Mr. and Mrs. Westfield slept, copulated, read and watched television, although only the first of these activities was one which can be said to have been truly engaged in simultaneously by the Westfields. The television was kept between the beds and could only face one of them at a given time; the Westfields decided who, on a given night, would watch television and, since they never agreed on shows, who would read a book. The television was given preference. When they copulated, of course, twice a week, they would be in Mrs. Westfield's bed—this was the way in which things were done—but otherwise they would be quite apart and it is no mere error or failure of sentiment that has led the curators to designate these beds as shrines. They are the center of the mystery. They are as close, perhaps, as we can get in this entire tour to an apprehension of holy ground. For that reason we have taken you here first, the other two bedrooms to come are only a deliberately contrived anticlimax, supplemental to these.

"You will note," the guide says, sitting down on my mother's bed and rubbing his hand over the slightly disheveled linens, "you will note the presence of one semen stain right in the center here. This stain, which is a reconstitution of Mr. Westfield's own bodily juices, is a simulation of the actual stains which appeared, and if you will look through your brochures later you will note that it was given to us through special federal donation some seven years ago, thus completing the collection. I would ask you to consider it carefully, for there is no dearth of implication here.

"There is no dearth of implication because it indicates that Mr.

Westfield felt enough for his wife to render upon her that blending of his organic juices which he referred to as his 'gift' to her, and this illustration of capability, to say nothing of the implied enactment of Mrs. Westfield's response, should be sufficient, once and for all, to close the book upon those minor scholars who have insisted that there was something 'abnormal' in the basic marital relationship between the Westfields. There was not, of course. I am not talking about levels of implication or abstraction, obviously, when I say this."

"And not a moment too soon!" the scholar says in a high voice. Apparently his vomiting, or whatever he has done in the vicinity of the courtesy shop, has utterly reconstituted his spirits because he is facing the guide with more color and enthusiasm than I have yet seen him demonstrate today. Indeed, there seems to be a rather dangerous fluttering of the limbs as he continues speaking which causes his companion to put a concerned, restraining arm upon him and renders a certain supernatural glow to all of this. "Not a moment too soon indeed! Mr. Westfield lived a perfectly normal sexual life; it might have been distinguished by its high moderation, of course, but moderation can be a virtue as well as a penalty and in all basic matters this splendid gentleman functioned at a level of high morality. I despise those interests who say that his extrinsic behavior suggests some sexual abnormality! I despise the question of the ice-skating scholars! I wish to point out—"

"Enough," the heavy man says. His face is tense and strained in the odd light of the bedroom and he seems to be working himself into some kind of strange rage of his own. "I've heard quite enough of all of this, thank you. I am not interested in disputations concerning Mr. Westfield's heterosexuality, I am not interested in knowing whether or not he found Mrs. Westfield attractive; I do not care to know whether the semen stain we are witnessing is authentic or spurious. Irrelevant, irrelevant! I am bored! I am fed up with all of this! The basic question, which we have to resolve once and for all, is this: is it significant? Is it lasting? Does it mean anything? In terms of the long-range potentialities involved and the question of the accretion of scholarship on twentieth-century America, will it fit in?" He slams his fist toward the floor, apparently forgetting again that he has misplaced his umbrella. "These are the questions and I demand some answers right now!"

"Nonsense!" the scholar shouts, turning with a fury to equal that already spent. "Absolute nonsense! I have listened to this long enough this morning and I won't hear any more of this rot. No, get your hand off me; I feel perfectly all right and I'm capable of handling this myself. How can you ... how *can* you possibly make any final evaluation of these people until you have settled once and for all the question of heterosexuality? I tell you, it would be apostasaic and stupid to even make such attempts without backing off to this basic reasoning. Now, from my point of view, until and unless we can clear up this scuttlebutt, these vicious rumors, these small stories propounded by evil men—"

"God damn you!" the heavy man screams. "Goddamned nits like you are the ones who've fucked up the whole issue in the first place! How can anything be clear if the basic premises are all wrong, if the *assumptions* are foul? No, I want some answers to these questions now."

It occurs to me, of course, that somewhere during the course of the interval, my tour companions have gone completely insane. Certainly there is no other way in which to explain or understand the choler informing the heavy man's face with a series of dull, ill-matched red and white streaks, no way to understand otherwise the scholar's high-pitched bellow as he turns once again to confront the question. But the guide, to my surprise, appears to take this as a perfectly normal development; in fact—or is this merely an illusion?—he seems to favor me with a slow, diminishing wink, all knowledge, all precognition floating into his eye, and then he turns into the center of the argument and says, "Gentlemen. gentlemen. You both have points of great merit. And I am delighted to see at last that you are so involved in this tour. But if you will only hold your fire—or your questions, as you will—for a few moments I think that we can proceed to give you enough information to resolve the question and to show you that you *both* are right. There's nothing wrong with gentlemen of good will disagreeing, and it is these disagreements which contribute so much to the richnesses of the Westfield project, its unique contribution to Western culture; its controversiality is, in short, that life-force which simultaneously infuses and solidifies it toward a state of permanence. But calm, calm, and let me continue."

"You'd better answer my questions then," the heavy man says sullenly. "I won't put up with this anymore otherwise. You're evading the whole issue."

"No, I am not," the guide says. "I most certainly am not, and if you will only allow me to proceed I think that you will find that there has been a kind of fine, controlling superstructure to all of this and that in the last analysis nothing has been out of place, nothing has been random. Remember, we are now at the culminating exhibits: the two bedrooms, here are where all the pieces fall into place." His speech strikes me as being a shade frenetic, perhaps a shade forced on the last syllables, but then again it is impossible for me to envy the position into which he has been cast, and for the life of me, I would have no other way of handling the situation in his place. And would know far less than he. "Let me continue," the guide says.

"Yes," I say. "Let him continue. He's doing very well; he's done fine all day today. I think that we should hear him out; it isn't much longer now."

The guide nods curtly to me—torn obviously between gratitude for support and a kind of dull resentment at the interposition between himself and his duties, does this mean that he will lose a certain amount of promotion credit?—but the scholar and the other give me a look of loathing so intense that I find myself babbling, much as I did once to my father when caught in the act of subterranean necking with my sister when we were very pubertal, "Well, well, I have a right to do it, don't I? I mean I have a right to say it? I mean, it's something worth doing, isn't it?" I feel a rocking moment of confusion wrench me as I realize that I am not quite sure whether I am talking of the necking or the guide and decide to let it pass, let it pass, hope that this moment, as all the others, will be subsumed in the future moments, but not at all as confident as I was. I reach for Joanne's hand and to my relief I find it, squeeze it violently, feel no answering pressure but try again. I am waiting for her to whisper to me that everything is all right, that I have not disgraced myself and that my history, like my possibility, is as replaceable as any incident of human connection; but she says nothing at all and when I look down upon her (I am, I should have mentioned a good time ago, four and a half inches taller than she) her face is turned, the hard surface of one slightly flushed cheek jumping out its message to me in the smooth, cold, disordered twitching of a nerve. I clutch her hand toward my waist, afraid that somehow she will depart. "Anyway," I say. "Anyway, that's my position."

"All right," the guide says. "All right, if the three of you have calmed down sufficiently and can permit me to continue, I'd like to see what I can say now of value. You will note the large dresser to the rear of the beds and somewhat to the right; it contained Mr. Westfield's underwear, his socks, his various memorabilia and even for a while—until a cheap 'automatic valet' was purchased—his pants and unpressed suit jackets. In the bottom drawer, however, underneath a pile of his white and blue shirts, we see an object of the most particular interest which, to be sure, I would like to show you." The guide rummages through that aforesaid bottom drawer, having some not unexpected difficulty in pulling it out (I know exactly what he is going through) and after a while emerges with a small book bound in a blue jacket whose title is *Marriage Lore*. He shows it to us for a moment, then holds it over the gate so that we can gather around and look at it more closely. There is no need for me to do so, of course—I know the contents of this book somewhat better than I would even the sense of this narrative if recorded and reread at some date in the far future—but in order to stave off any suspicion I examine it as intensely as any of the others, rubbing my hand over the grainy surface of the jacket. It feels like human skin, like the buttocks of an aged female, an illusion which had overtaken me at the time of original contact some twenty years ago. I used the book often to masturbate to, and from the look which Joanne suddenly gives me—the first look of any kind I have had from her since the guide and tourists entered—I suspect that she knows so as well.

"This," says the guide, and there is a hint of pride in his voice and manner, almost a flourish as he retracts the book and sets it upon the dresser, "this was the sex manual of Mr. and Mrs. Westfield, purchased for the two of them by Mr. Westfield on the eve of his marriage and given to his bride for a companionate reading on their wedding night. You may think it strange that this couple, who had already copulated prior to their marriage, would either purchase or pay close attention to a work of this kind, but you must understand not only the personalities involved—Mr. Westfield felt that copulation was a pastime as earnest and meaningful and necessarily planned for as a laundry chore, for instance—but the period. In this quaint time, not so far removed from us as we would hope, sexuality was considered not to be a natural part of the question of human experience but rather an unnatural extension, something either delightful or terrible—depending upon who you were, what you wanted to be—and too often banal but in no case as easily related to the other areas of the physiological and psychological function as we, in these liberated times, do now believe. We have long since transcended any strain about sexuality—isn't that so, ladies and gentlemen? Why, I wouldn't hear a word of retort!—but the Westfields had not, and thus they felt they had to schematize the act and consider it in a way in which you or I might explore the roots of a dead plant or the viscera of an equally deceased chicken, and it is for these purposes that the book was procured. Of course it was put away on the third night of their honeymoon and never looked at by either of them again, they having felt that they had absorbed all that was necessary from it and were now qualified to put its admonitions into practice.

"Michael, however, the archives reveal, was aware of the location of this book, which the Westfields had negligently failed to either dispose of or better hide, and used it often in his early masturbatory activities, only going on to better things when he was able to secure an adult library card and consequent privileges from his local branch and found himself catapulted—and catapulted is the word—into a universe of far larger sensation. But most of Michael's early sexual awakening revolved around the pages of this very book, ladies and gentlemen, and it is, thus, a most remarkable document; if our sexual life is merely an enactment of those fantasies and desires implanted into us at the basic turning moment of puberty—if this is the fact, and it is the belief of the senior trustees and the research foundation that this is indeed a valid assumption—if this is so, then this very book is probably being enacted by the now mature Michael Westfield upon some unsuspecting—or perhaps all too suspecting—lady at this very moment. Consider that, the profundity of this recycling, the nightmare of history we are considering! If, of course, Michael Westfield is indeed alive and functioning still. There are many conflicting reports about him, as well as the sister Katherine, and there has yet emerged no definite body of opinion on their present whereabouts, if any. Perhaps if our contributions continue to increase as, happily, they have over the past decade, we will eventually be able to extend our research activities not only into a consideration of the extant documents but into an exploration of the present whereabouts and activities of the surviving members of the family as well as their relatives. This is a consummation which is devoutly, at least in scholarly terms, to be wished, although there is a considerable body of thought which holds that the location of Michael and Katherine Westfield would, in theoretical, research terms do little good and only serve to confuse the issue horribly. Also, as you know, they are prohibited by the terms of the grant from coming back to the restoration at any time."

The guide replaces the book almost reverently in the bottom drawer and closes it. "This is considered one of the high points of the entire exhibit," he says. "I myself find it very provocative, almost personally moving. Only an artifact, that book, but consider the effects, the consequences! The very implications! Incredible," the guide says and shakes his head ruminatively. "Incredible, incredible."

"The Michael Westfield question is an extremely interesting one," the scholar says meditatively. "I did a minor term paper as an undergraduate on him for extra credit. Of course the Michael Westfield area is so slight and so unimportant that no courses were offered in my undergraduate curriculum, but at the time that I did the paper I thought I might want to do my dissertation on him, finally deciding against it because the area of sexuality in the lives of the Westfield parents was so much more fruitful. Nevertheless, I don't think we need worry about him. Not at all," the scholar says somewhat mysteriously and shakes his head. His friend pats him on the shoulder twice and once again whispers something to him.

"Why not?" Joanne asks. "Why not?"

"Yes," the guide says. "I'd be most interested in hearing about any area of scholarship outside my purview. We aren't simply doing a job here, you know; we're entirely dedicated to our work. I applied for this position. What about Michael Westfield?"

"Oh never mind," the scholar says. "It isn't important. *He* isn't important."

"Why not?" Joanne asks again. I feel that somehow she is doing this for me and turn to look for her confidential smile, but she is staring straight at the scholar, her face set and determined. "If you say something, say it. Why not anyway?"

"Because it all comes to nothing anyway," the scholar says impatiently. "It absolutely comes to nothing and there's no sense involving further discussion of the purposeless. In the last analysis you have to look for origins, not consequences. The consequences merely enact the origins. Forget it."

"That isn't very promising," the guide says.

"I will say no more."

"That's the first time you've shut up all day," says the heavy man. "The very first time. To what quality of Michael Westfield do we owe this?"

Tension seems to come up again but the guide wearily, raising a hand, manages to simultaneously defer to it and pass it by. "All right," he says. "It's a long day, a taxing day and the peculiar communicability of the artifacts is indeed remarkable; it does the strangest things to people. Let us try to continue; there isn't very far to go at all. Let me summarize the objects of interest in this bedroom;

then once again I would like to hear sensible brief questions and then we will go to the rooms of the siblings and be done with this. The courtesy shop offers a particularly nutritious and inexpensive hot dinner, incidentally, and for those of you who care to dine substantially and early, I think you will find it a bargain. The waitress is garbed in the period fashions of the day, looking very much as Mrs. Westfield might as far as we can gauge from photographs, and the food is so authentic that it might have come from the Westfield kitchen. You have a choice of home-cooked meat loaf with mashed potatoes and peas or a tuna fish salad for a party of four, made of two seven-ounce cans of tuna fish with mayonnaise to taste and a quarter of a head of lettuce, butter and spinach side dish optional. Private parties can be accommodated on reservation, incidentally; should you ever happen to be in this vicinity on a weekend accommodations can be arranged. Let us consider the window shades and venetian blinds here; you will note that the venetian blinds are extremely snug against the invasion of light— Mrs. Westfield paid more than a little bit extra for these—and for this reason it was necessary to burn exceedingly bright lights during the days. The venetian blinds were never open, then, except during periods of extremely great humidity or when guests were in the house. The windows themselves are of a very fine glass, both protective and filtering of light; they had a tendency to stick under even the most pleasant weather conditions, leading to the tendency of the family to keep them closed almost all the time. This may have had something to do with the internal climate of the home which, as I have already noted I am sure, was almost unbearably warm during the spring, summer and fall. The bedroom, along with all of the other rooms on the second floor, was not coterminous to the bathroom, leading to a certain logistical problem for all of the Westfields, who, in the morning hours, would find themselves extremely uncomfortable and the traversion down the stairs to be exceedingly difficult. It is not impossible that a lot of the anal humor and urgency in the household was predicated upon the simple inaccessibility of the bathroom. I do not believe at this time that I have anything else to say about the bedroom so will once again invite questions and then we can go on, see the other two bedrooms briefly and finish off. Are there any questions?"

"Did they like to screw?" Joanne asks, rather abruptly.

"Oh," the guide says, "I thought that this was answered. I have gone into the most careful documenting of the sexual lives of these people and I don't understand why the question would come up now."

"But you're wrong, you see," Joanne says with a kind of menacing quiet which is also one of her moods—less familiar than most but still falling into the range of observed behavior—and which, if I could, I would warn the guide about with a wink and a sigh; she is nothing to be trifled with when she falls into this tone of query, but is indeed working herself into a certain series of postures which can be quite painful to those with whom she becomes involved. The fact is that like many girls of more or less casual sexual motive and behavior, Joanne has rapid inversions, convulsions of guilt and streaks of dread which afflict her, most often after she has fucked too audaciously and for her sake without too much purpose, and I feel a surge of pity and understanding for her, although there is very little in either of these emotions that I understand will do us any good. "Anyway I want to know," she finishes. I have apparently missed some interpolatory line of dialogue dealing with Joanne's belief in the importance of sex as the basis of human behavior, but I really feel as if I have missed nothing at all. We have been there before, you see.

"Well," the guide says, "I can only try to answer you along the lines already so clearly implied, which was that they neither liked nor disliked the act but, particularly in the case of Mr. Westfield, felt that its performance was integral to that picturalization of a 'normal life' which they felt they were leading and which, conversely, they desperately wanted to lead; and in line with that it was important for them not only to perform the sex act with a certain degree of regularity but to agree that they had shared 'mutual pleasure' from it, and so they insisted they did. As to whether or not they truly enjoyed it in the intense emotional physical sense, this is something which we can obviously not be sure of but which can only be surmised from the data. We think—"

"Mr. Westfield enjoyed it," the scholar says. "He enjoyed it a great deal. Studies—"

"I hate it!" the albino says in a high whining voice, and his mother once again cuffs him, a concealed blow on the side of the head almost hidden under her coat, but solid enough in its impact to make all of us stand a little taller and take some notice. The woman flushes and tries to work her head down into her collar and finally says over the thin cries of the albino, "Well, he was only making a nuisance. I was trying to keep him quiet." A certain fierceness overcomes her features and she says loudly, "It's not an easy thing to control, you know. It's terribly difficult. There's more to this than you can possibly imagine. The conflict, the possibilities—"

It is all too much for me. I feel for the first time that day in urgent need of the bathroom and this time, without even motioning to the guide, without giving any kind of indication to Joanne, I detach myself from the crowd and go outside, hit the steps at full tilt heading downward. It is possible that I hear the guide's voice raised in mild protest as I speed away, but this means nothing to me and I am in the interstices of the bathroom before I have even had time to give due consideration to the fact that when I took my hand away from Joanne's there was no pressure, no inquiry, not even a turning of the head, but only that blank disinterest which she has seemed to have since the very moment of my completion. Since I know that we will be parting I know that this should not distress me, but it nags, niggles, works into some corner of the being and disturbs me to such an extent that I am unable to properly start my stream when urinating, an old difficulty. Under emotional stress, it seems to be the urinary sphincter which first fails to function; only after that piece of business has presented itself does the mind seem to function.

Nevertheless I do begin to void thickly, jets of urine streaming from my organ, and a delusion overcomes me during this moment, the delusion that in any instant my mother will knock at the door and then come in unbidden to observe me, try to "straighten" certain things out on the shelves, try to "keep the place in order." This was an old family habit and may, indeed, have been one of the most workable and yet protective ways in which we could express our aggression; certainly my poor father was unable to take "a good crap" for a sustained period of time, and similarly my most irrepressible urinary urges would overcome me when my mother was in the shower. Of course the thick, mottled, uneven glass of the stall shower made it absolutely impermeable to disclosure and I can therefore offer in evidence the statement that I have never seen my mother nude, but the thought, in fact the principle, might have been there. It is all too complex for me and I flush the toilet vigorously. To my surprise, the restoration committee has done its job well and the toilet still functions, and I luxuriate for the instant in the sinuous hiss and piling of water, watching it recede from me violently and wondering as I did years ago where the water went when it was flushed. For a long time I believed that it went into the cellar—the place where the courtesy shop is now of course—and lay there thickly waiting for reconstitution in the form of further flushes later or in some of my mother's cooking, but now I do not believe that, of course. I know that the water goes out to the sea, adding its filaments, fragments and turgid piling of our history to the implacable water and that it is never seen again; tossed and aimless, thrown as far from us as the jets of liquid we exude during sexual intercourse. I do not believe any more in reconstitution, which may be one of the basic insights into that protective cynicism which has now nourished me for so many years.

I hear footsteps in the hallway as I am pondering all of this and decide not to emerge but instead to listen; this too being an old family habit, dating from the time in my early teens when I played "detective" by hiding behind doors to listen to my parents' conversations while allegedly doing my homework; this might have given me a feeling of power except that the conversations were so banal, the point of all of this so invisible that it reacted strongly against any megalomaniac feelings which might have developed. There is no exciting clandestine insight to be gained from the muttered requests of one parent to the other to exchange sections of the newspaper or consider tomorrow's dinner.

This, however, is a little different, the surest indication of my building theory that in the long range certain things do change, if only slightly and to no apparent purpose. As the flush fades I hear someone say, "I don't know about this. There's no real precedent."

"Of course not," another voice says. Apparently they are both men in their late forties, although I would hesitate to base further characterological assessments simply upon the sound of voices. "But how could there be? It's something entirely new."

"But not unexpected."

"Do you think we're right?"

"Well," the other voice says, and I hear them receding now; apparently they are going into the basement, "I don't think that it matters whether we're right or wrong. We're doing the necessary, which is the important thing."

"Yes. And then too, the whole thing is a cycle."

"Yes. The thing is a cycle."

"Cyclical."

"Exactly," the other says and I hear a door slam. Strangely, rather than wanting to draw inferences from the conversation (which I suppose had to do with some of the dry bureaucratic details of the museum and little else) I find myself only reminded through the use of the word "cycle" that this was, indeed, one of my father's favorite words, which was used almost more frequently in explanation or discourse than anything else with the exception of simple connectives like "the" or "cut it out" or "I can't stand it anymore." To buy a new car was to "go through the cycle" and the death of a relative was "a cycle" and the birth of another relative was "part of that cycle" and so on and so forth until I began to deduce my father's entire inference of the universe as being a simple curvature, somewhere along the Einsteinian plane, of course, but much starker, much simpler, much more geometrical in its precision. If everything indeed was a cycle (or was he indeed only punning on the word "circle" or worse yet, mispronouncing it?) then it was quite likely—or, at least, not entirely unlikely—that he and everything else would come back again. This was a thought to send me speeding out of the bathroom, all unheeding of possible interception, and I took the stairs two at a time in leaping bounds (I always did this anyway when we lived there although I was warned by my mother that I could "bring the house down") and rejoin the tour. In the interim they have once again moved and are, indeed, in Katherine's room when I come to their rear. Joanne is almost invisible now, pressed against the gate, hidden by the family of the albino and the shoulders of the heavy man who, by some trick of posturing and angle, seems to have his arm around her, his lips against her neck, his absorption total. "So much for Katherine," the guide is saying. "As I have said she is the least important member of this family, possessing many qualities and traits of her own, but unfortunately these qualities and traits tending to be merely extensions or variations of those of her parents. Also she was too young during the historical period to grasp some of the more important implications. She was bright enough and she felt enough but she lacked a metaphysic, a common problem among people of her age at this time, of course. It must be noted however that she possessed a kind of genuine sensitivity and her capacity to be pained by the events of the household went far beyond her ability to understand it; for this reason she may be a more interesting character than is commonly supposed, and indeed it has been the purpose of the restoration to inaugurate a detailed study of the lesser-known aspects of her life just as soon as sufficient funds can be secured. In all likelihood those funds will be available by government grant by the end of next year, and after a team of scholars go to work, I think we will find some very interesting material emerging in the years to come. The point is that the more we learn of Katherine, the more we can learn of Mr. and Mrs. Westfield, and this is no mean function. If the only way in which to comprehend parents is through the neuroses of their children, then this could be fruitful ground. On the other hand, nothing is entirely sure. Katherine slept with stuffed animals in her bed—you will note some of them—until well past her twenty-second birthday, converting a childish habit into a piece of contrived feminine whimsy, and who can blame her? She lived in the house as frequently as the brother Michael, although not as frequently as her parents. As to the exact quality of her inner thought, her inner relation, we could only surmise this, and but dimly. It is sufficient to say that at the present time we consider her a *ficelle*. In no pejorative sense at all, of course."

He motions toward the bed, which does indeed contain three of Katherine's familiar sleeping companions: a large yellow dog engraved with the crest and initials of my college which my father had bought for her on a weekend visit to the school: a large, rather misshapen pig which I recall as being named "Walter" and which Katherine claimed to have intricate dialogues with through her fifteenth year, not at all out of insanity but, as the guide had suggested, simply from a kind of apprenticeship in flirtation; and a large green dog with no name whatsoever which, although four feet high standing, stretched out to a more comfortable posture in the bed and might have performed for her a valuable surrogate function. I have no way of knowing. Did Katherine's desire in those long nights equal mine and were her occupations similar? According to all the texts I have read and the little I know of women, masturbation seems unlikely. I do not believe in a feminine sex drive at all comparable to or understandable by men. On the other hand, granted that she might have had—as I did—to do *something* as a means of discovering her identity in the darkness and somnolence of those twisted nights … what else could she have done? And does it matter? Will we ever know?

"And that is about that," the guide says. "I see no need in not being frank; there is very little to see here, and we are dealing with a marginal personality. Questions, of course. We are looking at a shelf of her schoolbooks, incidentally, and these happen to be an unusual acquisition; of all the objects in this house only these were actually excavated from the ruins whole and in no need of restoration before they could be shown. This may have something to do with the high quality of the bindings. Katherine insisted upon buying only the best and newest editions of her texts."

"No questions," the scholar says abruptly.

"Well," the guide says after a flat, slightly embarrassed pause, "well, that's all well and to the good, but there are other people here as well."

"She doesn't matter," the scholar says definitely, shaking his head. "Why waste our time? Any importance given to Katherine has been exaggerated."

"Nevertheless." the guide says, "we are trying to be thorough, and if all the pieces of this fit together as in the exquisiteness of an expensive puzzle, then Katherine too must be adjudged. The trouble is that we simply do not have the information at this time to do so."

"I want to see the boy's room," the albino says to his mother. "You promised me we would see the boy's room. Can we go in now?"

"Wait," the mother says. "We'll get there soon. This is very interesting." And indeed it is apparent that she has selected a new posture, her hands and lips folded in concentration, her head at an intense angle leaning forward. Somehow she has managed to convince herself, I gather, that the tour is "educational" and since it is almost over she can come to terms with knowledge.

"Well, then," the guide says, "so much for Katherine."

"Did she get along well with her parents?" the heavy man says. "What kind of relationship was it?"

"Much more equable than might be thought under the circumstances. Most of the obvious tensions were directed toward Michael and to the displaced idea of "other," somehow lower-class people who in some way menaced the Westfields' position, without ever menacing it to the degree that they were visible. Unfortunately, the level of ironic insight in this family was low and Mr. and Mrs. Westfield did not, perhaps, see that fine discrimination between the real enemy and the construction which we, in these more advantageous days, have been able to. In any event Katherine got along rather well and there does not appear, in any of the extant documents, to be any indication of dislocation, argumentation or neurosis. It is indicated that she might have withdrawn into herself to some degree, and it is similarly indicated, perhaps, that the girl was able to contrive an identity for herself as seen apart from the style of her life, and this might have been her salvation. I use the word 'salvation' loosely, of course, since we do not know where she is today or what she is doing. So be it. May we please now go into Michael's room? This way, please," and he leads us with a brisk wave of the hand in that direction, emerging through the gate and our huddle without visible discomfiture and moving at some high posture of attention through the hallway.

As we shuffle to follow him I try to intercept Joanne and say something to her, but apparently she does not see me, is seized in a kind of concentration of her own which sends her out in pursuit of the guide with an intensity and focus similar to that which she acquires during sexual intercourse. I was able to graze her elbow unsatisfactorily and whisper, "You okay?" but other than an absent shake of the head which manages to simultaneously conceal and reveal an extremity of feeling she says nothing at all; and feeling somehow useless and slightly shamed I sink to the bottom of my purposes, following the crowd at a good remove, and enter my room, seeing once again that familiar cubicle, so small that the guide must motion all of us to stand outside as once again he vaults the gate and confronts us. My room is even smaller than the bathroom, although, perhaps, the decor is more individual, the objects slightly more various. Still, it is only a bed, a chair, a small lamp table which could be contrived into a desk for writing (but which never was) and a couple of photographs of historical figures on the wall, these photographs having been given by a distant relative as a house present at some time and having been hung in my room because there was no place else to put them where they would be both on display and very much out of the way. It is these photographs to which the guide points first.

"These portraits of Abraham Lincoln, Aaron Burr, Jefferson Davis and Winston Churchill," he says, "are one of the most interesting aspects of this room. The prominence of their display and the obvious care with which they have been framed indicates that Michael Westfield was somewhat of a historical enthusiast who projected himself into the life and times of well-known political figures and who, by hanging their portraits on his wall for easy confrontation, probably obtained a good jolt of identification with them. Exactly why these portraits were selected is unknown, for aside from their prominence these men have little ideologically in common; but the suggestion has been advanced by several scholars that what they did all share was power and a certain sense of their consequentiality, and Michael Westfield was probably prone to power fantasies, which gives the clear link. At any rate. There is very little else to see here; the room is far more functional than the others, as you will note, and in fact is only functional; it contains a bed, a table supporting a lamp and a shelf full of books which upon inspection show an astonishing eclecticism and superficiality. It has been theorized that Michael Westfield had certain ambitions to be a writer, but if this is so we have been able to discover nothing that would support this thesis; certainly the room is not that of a writer, but only that of a person who tried to display the minimal contact possible with his surroundings, and it is indicated that a good deal of his waking time was spent away from his home. Perhaps his sleeping time as well, although no relationships have been verified.

"Michael is what the scholars have called 'the dark Westfield,' and although this is a rather dramatic way of putting what I take to be a rather dull issue, I think that this is understandable. 'Dark' not necessarily in terms of personality or configuration—although gloom would have been his natural posture as fully as that of any of the other members of his family—but 'dark' in the sense that so very little is known of him. It is apparent that he grew up in this house, interacted with it, lived through all of the great issues of the family, and yet the extent of his reactions is undetermined, the amount of direct written testimony to his experiences is almost nil. It has been suggested by one of the curators that Michael might have been a borderline schizophrenic operating toward the catatonic range, and that the reason so little is known of him is because there was so little which he evidenced; indeed these experiences, the life in the Westfield home might have had only a marginal effect upon him. It is interesting to speculate upon Michael in this fashion, as to whether what he went through in these corridors had any long-lasting, individual effect upon him or whether, by reasons of genesis or coincidence, he was of a certain personality fix which would have turned out the same way in any environment. If this latter would be the truth there is certainly irony here! Indeed there is irony because the life of the Westfields was so right, so provocative, so metaphoric and so indicative that it is strange to realize that it may have had no real effect upon their only son. Not because of lack of attempts, of course. Michael's present whereabouts, as well as those of Katherine, are unknown; it is suggested that he might be living and working somewhere in the Midwest. There has been no word from him, however, since the time of the restoration. No word from Katherine either. These siblings have certainly attempted to cut their roots and who—consider this carefully now before you make the easy answer—who can blame them?"

"Indeed," murmurs the scholar. He seems to be fascinated and for the first time that day uncontentious. "Indeed, indeed. Who can blame any of them?" His companion strokes his shoulder, mutters something.

"We have one interesting artifact however," the guide says, opening the drawer of the lamp table and producing a sheet of typewriter paper folded in quarters. "As I say, there are certain internal indications and evidences that Michael Westfield might have had aspirations to being a writer and we have here a piece of literary composition which, although still not officially accepted as by his own hand, is probably his. The curators have been unable to make a final decision and this piece is therefore considered to be contestable, but there are certain indications in the writing and in the plot of this piece which suggests the family life of the Westfields and which might well render it authentic. In any event, I will be happy to read it to you; it is quite short, probably written somewhere in the midteens of the boy, and you may find it of interest."

Indeed the typewriter paper—if it is what I think it is—is authentic, and if it would not bring all kinds of calumny and difficulty upon me, I would probably raise my hand and establish it as such for the guide, for indeed he seems to be taking more of a personal interest in this than in any of the other objects he has shown us all day. A small chuckle bloats his cheek, his glasses seem to gleam as he removes them from an inner coat pocket and sets them uneasily upon his head. "Aha," he says and opens the sheet, "here we are. You are all interested in hearing this, I presume? It is something of a highlight since, even unauthenticated as it is, it exists as one of the few possible pieces of writing actually emanating from the family."

"Yes," Joanne says and pats the guide on the wrist, a strangely offensive gesture, at least to me, but it seems to please the guide no end and his cheeks puff again. "Yes, let's hear it by all means."

"Ah," says the guide, "ah, yes," and reads to us:

THE DARKNESS AND THE TEMPER TORRENT

A novel by Michael M. Westfield

Chapter One: The Locus

Oh, lost! Oh, lost and by the sands wept, walking and walking in the eternal darkness! The unspeakable torment of the womb, the sun-greeting sunshine as it comes upon the infant's face. Ripped free and pent-tossed! Lost and not alone! Oh, spectre which may never come again! For who of us may ever know his father's touch, who can ever hear his mother's cry? Yet we struggle and struggle and in the end there is understanding. A madness. A cartharsis built upon a fine chain of tumult. Indeed, indeed.

The tall man turned and looked at the short one in the hallway. Both of their faces were strained but the short man's face was more strained than that of the tall man.

"It's a boy," he said.

"Really?"

"A boy. Seven pounds six ounces."

"Oh," the short man said. "A cigar?"

"Pleasure."

"It's my first son."

"Really now?"

"Yes. It is. Was it an easy birth?"

"It was a fine birth." The tall man's face wrinkled. He was a doctor. Around his neck hung the tools of his instrumentation, the instruments of his flight.

"A fine, fine birth."

"Everything is fine?"

"Yes, everything is fine."

"I will have to do something for the boy when he gets a little older. I am a father now and must do something for my son. Does this hospital seem very warm to you?"

"Yes, it does," the doctor said. "It seems to have a great deal of warmth. Of course it is July." They did not have air-conditioning then. It was about fifteen years ago.

"I will see you soon," the doctor said. "I must check on my patient."

"Yes, do that and tell me how she is. When may I see her? My wife."

"When she is cleaned up you may see her with the baby. I know how you feel," the doctor conceded. "I had a son too a year ago. I hope I can do right by him. Every father wants to do right by his son."

"Yes, he does."

"Yes, he does. I will see you then."

"Yes."

"Yes." The doctor walked away.

Oh, birth! Oh, pain! Oh, nightmare, oh, terror! But on the shifting sands of destruction still the life of the time must go on and trapped in every heart is a flow of circumstances which will reveal it.

A twig, a branch, a locked-up entrance. Oh, lost and by the thunder soothed, father, father, father, come back again!

The guide folds the paper and puts it back into the desk with a satisfied expression. "This appears to be the first chapter of a novel," he says, "apparently unfinished since, in any event, we are unable to locate further writings. It appears to be an autobiographical novel, and in the way in which it attacks the question of irretrievable loss and in certain evidences of the rhetoric, it seems to be derived from the talkings of Mr. Westfield and the writings of a minor American writer of the 1930s named Thomas Wolfe. The tensions are interesting and characteristic and, as I say, it is suggested that this material is indeed authentic. Well, that concludes Michael's room, ladies and gentlemen." The guide rubs his hands together with some high enthusiasm. "We will be going to the courtesy shop shortly. Any questions? We've covered these two rooms more quickly than I expected, so if you have anything to ask, go ahead."

"That's awful," the heavy man says. "I mean, the writing there sounds really dreadful."

"Indeed it does," the guide says, "but on the other hand the sources are clear. We are not interested in taking this as a piece of literary interest, but seek its merit in the sociological, and as such, although the document is questionable, it is extremely interesting."

"He must have had some difficulties with his father."

"Some difficulties!" the guide says loudly. "Indeed he did have some difficulties; if the net total effect of this tour has been to leave you in some doubt as to the nature of the problems which anyone would have in relation to Mr. Westfield, much less his son, then I have been a poor guide and this is no museum. Mr. Westfield combined great sensitivity and insularity with almost total inarticulacy on crucial emotional issues and virtually seethed with small resentments and old griefs—as all of us do—but was unable, as most people are, to find any metaphors for them, any question of extrinsic capitulation. He had, in short, no feeling of control over these problems since he was not able to externalize and hence manipulate them. The only activity which could be considered recreational was the ice-skating, and he did this only during the season once a week."

"I don't want to hear any more about that ice-skating, the scholar says.

"And neither do I," says the guide cheerfully. Now that he has at last reached the end of his assigned duties he seems to have relaxed, to have become, perhaps, the Guide That He Really Is, and it shows in the ease of his demeanor, an almost friendly smile with which he says, "I know there's a lot of controversy here. There are no easy explanations."

"The ice-skating was purely recreational!" the scholar says, and the albino's father says on the heels of this, quietly and with some malice, "But what if it wasn't? What if we read the obvious things into it?" and the scholar turns with a cry and raises a distinctly wavering fist.

"Oh, come, come, gentlemen," the guide says. "This is really ridiculous, to feel these passions and torment over such trivial issues. As I think any consideration of this exhibit will make clear, there are no easy answers either and no sense in this polarization. Let us relax; let us truly be with one another! You're one of the most consistently involved and discriminating group of people that I've ever had the pleasure of directing through these effects and I would like to feel that you can get along with one another. Any questions? Any more questions?"

"What did Michael Westfield look like?" Joanne says. "Do we know?"

"Now that," the guide says, "is an interesting point and I will answer it in a level, straightway fashion. We do not have photographs of either of the Westfield children. For some reason never clearly explained there were in the ruins absolutely no pictures of them. In fact, there were only two pictures available of the senior Westfields, quite muddied and both taken on their honeymoon, which would give no indication, of course, as to how they looked in later years. Both of the honeymoon pictures are blurred, revealing them on what seems to be a beach of some sort, probably on the East Coast. Because the faces are obscured and the outlines vague we have decided not to authenticate them. Instead, in the courtesy shop, you will find what we consider to be excellent simulated photographs and artistic impressions of what the Westfields might have looked like, posed by professional models selected for internal consistency or drawn by artists of high caliber, all of whom are employees of the project. We have aspired for a higher truth rather than a lesser veracity, in short, and we believe that these pictures give the sense of their subjects if not actually corresponding to them physically. Available in the courtesy shop are a fine variety of these drawings and photographs, ranging in sizes from 3 x 5 wallet-size inserts to full-scale 20 x 24 framed pictures suitable for display. The prices are quite moderate and the workmanship of the highest. Shall we adjourn there now? There is, incidentally, absolutely no compulsion for any of you to buy anything although I must remind you that the foundation is nonprofit and is always in need of funds to continue its fine work, and the courtesy shop is an important source of income. While we ask you to buy nothing, we do then hope that you will give the items on sale your highest consideration and will feel that you'll want to leave Westfield with a memento or two or three. Are we all ready then?"

"So, there really is no way of knowing what he looked like," Joanne says, and the albino's mother purses her lips in infuriation as the albino begins to squall with restlessness. For the instant I share her rage with Joanne, who is, after all, not being very reasonable now about many things.

"No," the guide says, "there is no way of knowing. We cannot be sure. He could even be among us for all we know. All we can do is suggest and infer. But one can imagine what he must have looked like in his mind's eye and that, for the moment, is enough. No more questions?"

There are no more questions. The guide comes from behind the gate, walks us to the door, points vaguely upward at the ceiling. "I mentioned the attic, of course," he said, "but we won't be visiting there today. There really isn't that much to see in there and the memorabilia are dusty and almost worthless, not having yet been covered by the restoration project. You will find excellent simulations of most of the objects in the courtesy shop. Let us go," and he retreats down the hall. With some eagerness my companions follow him, only Joanne lingering at the end. I wait for her and then take her hand.

"What was that meaning?" I say. "Why did you have to ask those questions?"

She shakes her head and continues walking quickly, so quickly that I can barely keep up with her, which is a very unusual thing indeed. "Never mind," she says. "I have a right to ask, don't I?"

"But why?"

"Look, Michael, you want it this way, then let it be this way," she says rather mysteriously and yanks her hand from my tentative grasp. "If you can't find any answers, why do you expect to find them here or from me? I just don't feel like talking now; I want to look through the shop and later on maybe we can go and settle this. But not now," and with a bound I find almost surreal she leaps through a doorway and patters down the steps leading toward the shop. I follow at some distance, musing. It is apparent that something of considerable dimension has occurred which I will need to think about in solitude later, as is my wont, but at the present time I simply have no taste for it, for as I go down the stairs at a quicker pace the sound and smells of the courtesy shop overwhelm me and I can barely restrain my eagerness. It is, after all, my first trip there. I almost stumble on the bottom step, then right myself and come into a large, airy, well-equipped souvenir shop with a series of counters, all of them attended by women in period dress who bear a vague resemblance to my mother. The place is so large that it instantly swallows up our small group and I succumb to a feeling of fine, high isolation, noticing vaguely that Joanne has gone over to the dress section while the guide has retired to busy himself in intense conversation with one of the counter girls in the postcard section. A huge portrait of a man who seems to look something like my father is on the opposite wall, and the walls are otherwise littered with photographs of the house, the grounds, the neighborhood, and a series of drawings which look like the scribbles that my sister brought home from public school up to her thirteenth year. "This is a chair," she would say, and, "This is a flower and a cow," and indeed they were all of that although her talent for illustration quickly withered, and it was obvious by mid-adolescence that she had only a small knack, no real creative predilection at all. I cannot think of it; I am going over to a counter which has a sign saying "MEMORABILIA" and look with fascination at the objects displayed, all of them that cheap mass-produced kind which I am so familiar with in other places but which looks quite strange in the present context. One thing I did believe in, until this moment, was my life's singularity and its unreproducability; this is apparently something which is going to have to be held up to further investigation.

Underneath me, in the front counter, are miniatures of the sex manual in my father's bottom drawer, the cardboard sign above them says "AS SEEN IN THE WESTFIELD RESTORATION, BOUND IN GENUINE IMITATION LEATHERETTE" and I pick one up curiously to find that it is indeed a one-tenth reproduction of the sex manual, bound in a peculiar, cheap gold-colored substance and containing not only all of the words and diagrams but a facsimile of the inscription from my father on the flyleaf: "To Josephine and to Our Marriage," which I find curiously affecting in this reproduction.

Next to it are imitation cigarette holders and cartons of cigarettes, probably in tribute to my own habit which I picked up somewhere during my eighteenth year and which has now been memorialized by the statement "AS SMOKED BY MICHAEL WESTFIELD." And then, burrowing down to the next container of objects, I see reproductions of my mother's kitchen calendar with its cover picture of a cheerful frying pan standing hands on hips with a balloon of dialogue stating "Things to do, things to remember." Inside are jottings in my mother's handwriting which are unquestionably authentic:

> Get the garbage ready.
> Check movies.
> See if dresses are there.
> Find out about PS 111.
> Gloria on Tuesday.
> Michael's doctor appointment.
> Katherine's teeth.

and so on, a banality which I find curiously moving since I had forgotten, until this moment, the woman's curious attempts to create precision where there was none; a certain grace, felicity and felicitousness of the spirit which was devoured constantly and almost whole by the events of the household, and which yet would strangely assert itself at odd moments and never be forgotten, even though a vagrant tantrum or disorder would cause it to vanish. Once, for instance, I found my mother up very early on a Sunday morning while my father had gone ice-skating and my sister to a sleep-in party somewhere and, showing her the book review section of a local newspaper containing an advertisement, told her that I wanted to join a book club. "Science-fiction book club," I said to her. "They'll send you three books for a dollar and the only obligation is to continue for four more at a dollar each. And if you don't like the first three you can return them right away."

"Yes," she said, actually leaning over to inspect the ad as she sipped her coffee, and for no clear reason she gave me an affectionate pat on the knee. "Yes, but I don't understand why you're so interested in science-fiction. Isn't it only an escape kind of literature? It really isn't anything I've ever been able to understand."

This was one of the rare times my mother had ever asked me the kind of question which could be given a sensible reply, and I said with delight, "But it isn't escape literature. Not necessarily. Not all of it. It is an attempt to make a serious statement in serious terms about a serious society." I was, at that time, very concerned with issues such as this, having read certain books of literary criticism. "It's satirical and symbolic."

"Yes, but does it say anything?"

"Some of it. Some of it is very good. I wouldn't mind writing some of it myself some day if I was ever able to do it."

"But then," she said, "who would pay for these books? Can you cover them from your allowance?"

"Yes. I just won't go to the movies on Saturday for a month and right there I'll have the dollar saved."

"Well," she said, finishing off her coffee, "well, then, if you feel that way about it, Michael, then you just do it," and it was a nice moment but then something fell from my pocket to the floor with a clatter— some change as a matter of fact—and she wanted to know how I could wear clothing that was in such obvious disrepair and didn't I take any pride and what was the meaning of it anyway and why didn't I take those pants off right this minute so she could do something about them, and the moment went away, passed into the noisome accumulation of incident which is mostly what I remember about my early adolescence, and it was many, many years before I discussed science-fiction with either of my parents again, and then only as an attempt to give an illustration of what I took to be the diminished nature of our reality. "We live as if we're in a spaceship!" I screamed in my sixteen-year-old metaphysic, "and the goddamned spaceship is full of machines and it isn't going anywhere!" But of course I was really not talking about science-fiction at all when I said this and I never got around to writing it. Not just quite.

The calendar then is a reminder of grace, and for that reason alone not to be taken without a certain amount of seriousness but, as is so often the case in relation to my family, I find myself diverted by articles in the next section; there are a collection of miniature ice skates also finished in black leatherette which are noted as being "as worn by Jonathan Westfield" and in an adjoining cubicle are good-sized miniatures of my sister's collection of animals. In all ways, it is apparent that the courtesy shop has provided well for the restoration.

"And let me remind you!" I hear the guide saying, as though seized again by a certain sense of propriety, a need to show that he is still doing his job. "Let me remind you that the shop is open until 5 p.m.

or even a little later, depending upon your convenience, and that this is not all there is to it; next door there is a fine restaurant serving many interesting specialties. So take your time, ladies and gentlemen; do take your time and let me now, on behalf of the restoration committee and the museum, bid you a good day and express my pleasure at having you come along with me; you're one of the most genuinely responsive and intelligent audiences I've ever had."

The guide, apparently determined to make some kind of an exiting speech, moves away from the counter and comes to the center of the room, but unfortunately there appears to be very little interest in what he is saying; the tourists are poking interestedly around the various counters and the albino, having found a replica of a watering can which was used in our garden during one fateful summer, is running around the open spaces of the shop, screaming in a rather shrill voice. Nevertheless, the guide persists. "The purposes of this project are educational," he is saying, "and have nothing to do with fantasy or the sensational; I hope that all of you will feel somewhat enlarged by what we have learned today and will carry the message forth to your friends and relatives. The restoration is open three seasons of the year for public viewing all days except Friday, and you may, in addition, give it a grant which is of course fully tax-deductible. Stamped, self-addressed envelopes to the foundation are available in most of the boxes next to the exit and your thoughtfulness will be most appreciated. So thank you again, thank you, thank you," but instead of ending on an enthusiastic finishing note, the guide's voice seems to waver uncertainly and it is more of a retreat than a procession as he moves from the center of the floor and back to the woman behind the counter. He appears to grasp her hand with a kind of dependency and leans toward her; she strokes his cheek and shoulder and his face relaxes somewhat. "Thank you again," he mumbles.

Seized by an impulse which I do not quite understand, I go over to the guide and tell him I want to pay my respects. The counter at which he is standing contains a number of photographs of common local scenes, as well as those simulations of my parents, and they are indeed distinguished by their workmanship if not their authenticity. The people in the photographs look like nothing in my family and I am particularly bemused by one beach shot which shows four attractive people posing in a rather ungainly posture near some blank seascape; there is a look of communion in their eyes which is most unusual and almost amusing, considering the circumstances. "It was very interesting," I say to the guide.

"Well, thank you," he says and shakes my hand. This is the first time I have been truly close to him and he is much older than I had taken him to be; apparently he is sixty years or more, his face blotted by wrinkles of retrospection and inner contemplation of the most disastrous sort, and a thin smell of liquor seems to be emanating from him as well. I am beginning to understand his willingness to cause constant breaks. The woman is plain, middle-aged, her figure not bad as far as I can tell from the covering of her uniform, which has THE WESTFIELDS! stencilled over it in plain blue pencil.

"It was very interesting," I say, "and it's difficult to make this kind of thing interesting, I know that."

"Well," the guide says, coughs and shrugs, "you know how it is. Originally I was supposed to be on the research staff but this vacancy opened up and I really had no choice. No choice at all if I wanted to move to a new rank. Actually I'm not entirely at my ease in public. But I try; I do the best that I can."

"I thought you made it very understandable."

"Really," the guide says and giggles rather disconcertingly. "Understandable? I'm not so sure that that's a compliment, you see, because I personally don't understand any of this at all. I mean, the notes of the lectures are pretty definite and I do the best I can, but I'm not sure that I really know what went on here or even that I care. On the other hand, it does give quite a portrait of the way in which these people might have lived."

"Indeed it does."

"The lives they led! Amazing," the guide says and rubs the woman's shoulder enthusiastically. "Too much to think about it."

"Yes, indeed," the woman says in a flat Midwestern monotone. "It was strange, mighty strange. Still, what are you going to do? There must be a reason why this has become national property."

"You have any particular interest in the Westfields?" the guide asks. Seen at his ease, in this informal posture, he is obviously trying to reciprocate with a personal approach of his own, but I am perceptive enough to know that he could not care less whether or not I was interested in the Westfields and, indeed, has been off duty since the moment we entered the shop and only wants a little solace now, a little respite. It is not an easy job.

"Not really," I say. "We were in the vicinity, my girl friend and I, and

I thought we'd just drop in, that's all." Saying "girl friend" I nod toward Joanne, who has been looking toward us, but as I smile, her eyes drop suddenly and she seems to become absorbed in some geometry of the floor. "My girl friend," I say.

"Very pretty."

"Thank you."

"Very nice."

"Yes. Thank you." There seems to be little more to say and feeling vaguely embarrassed, in the grip of some sort of grave unease, I wander away from the guide without any further comment, not quite sure of what exactly has happened to me. I find my eye caught by a series of masks which are dangling from fluorescence at a great height; apparently they are representational death-masks of my parents, colored in purple and a faint yellow and done with high style, but I find after staring at them for an instant that they depress me more than otherwise. As a matter of fact, I feel a kind of tangle of depression somewhere deep in the gut and intimate a sensation of falling into it; I am not quite sure why this is the case but know that for reasons I cannot locate I suddenly do not find the courtesy shop quite as rewarding and evocative as I had hoped. Instead I go over to Joanne, who is prowling through the book section, going through leatherette-bound editions of some of the works on my shelf, and, putting my arm around her, say, "You want to go now?"

She looks up at me with the bright, winsome distrust of a stranger. "What's that?"

"I said, do you want to go now? Have you seen enough of this?"

"Well, really, Michael," she says, disengaging herself slightly from me, "whose idea was it to come here in the first place? You must have been looking forward to being in this shop all day! Why do you want to leave?"

"I'm tired. I've had enough."

"Well, not yet. I want to stay. There are things here to look at. Why don't you kind of go off by yourself, Michael, and we can meet a little later."

It is true that I have known for some three hours that Joanne and I have no future and yet, even in those terms, it is impossible to stave off a feeling of terror which suddenly overtakes me. Perhaps it is truly that I cannot bear to be the disdained one and when this behavior is turned upon me I become hopeless, perhaps it is only that I care far more for Joanne than I would admit and than a few vigorous fucks here and there would indicate. Most complex and terrible, and yet, trying as always for that fine denial of feeling which has been the key to any of my moderate successes, I say, "Don't be silly, Joanne. Don't be unreasonable. We're going to go home together and—"

"Not necessarily," she says and shrugs. "Look at these paperweights. They're supposed to be the kind Mr. Westfield used in his offices. Aren't they interesting? They're quite strange."

"What do you mean we won't go home together?"

"I said I didn't know. Leave me alone, Michael." She turns toward me and confronts me fully, her face rising to a kind of tension which almost makes it transparent; I can sense the bones and blood moving within. "Haven't you had enough of this?" she says. "Isn't there a time to get off the cycle and live your own life? Leave me alone, Michael. Later, later."

"Cycle?"

"Yes, cycle, it's all a cycle but it's got to stop, Michael, and it's going to stop because I won't take it anymore. I screwed that dirty old bastard. He wanted me to and I let him and he loved it. We did it right in the cellar, they have beds there. I did it and I don't care. And then I told him everything. I told him who you were and what you were doing and why you were here and he was very interested. That's why I wanted to talk to him, Michael; that's why I went away from you. Because I had to tell him."

"You told him?" I say. I am dimly aware that our conversation has become so spirited that it has stopped the noises around us and that we have, in fact, an audience, but I cannot stop myself, not at this particular point; I am just like my father, worrying something far past its uses and into demolition. "You told him? For Christ's sake, why?"

"Why? Why? Why? Because it's got to stop, Michael; there's got to be an end to this nonsense, you've got to grow up sometime and come to terms with it, you can't go on living your whole life as if this was still going on, it isn't going on anymore and it never will again. And I won't be used, I won't be part of it, you just took me here because you wanted to do it all yourself and I tell you I won't stand it. Won't stand it!" she says and slaps me viciously across the face.

I recoil, blind for the instant, staring, gasping, and I see now that they are all looking at me: albino, parents, heavy man, the scholar, his friend, even the guide has taken an elbow off the counter, even his rustic companion has turned to me with eyes full of fright; a wideness to my vision seems to embrace even more than this and I hear the sound of my own voice, unreasonable, shouting, tinny in my ears. "Why did you do that?" I say and she slaps me again, even harder, and I feel the outlines of the room literally beginning to wave before me; it is all too much. Ah, God, it is all too, too much. "Bitch," I murmur, but there is no heat in it.

"Don't call me bitch!" she says and she is really screaming now, screaming and sobbing too, the two modes streaked together and adding a kind of resilience to her voice by a strange compounding which causes it to level as she goes on. "Don't call me bitch or I'll call you bastard; no, Michael, I tell you it's got to stop, it's got to stop now because there has to be an end to it. An end to all games, all gestures, all terror, all dreams—you've got to face the fact of what is and I won't have it any more. He went at my breasts and my neck and my cunt and it was good, Michael, it was good because I didn't owe him anything, not a goddamned thing. People don't owe you anything, Michael! Nothing at all," and she falls against me and rubs her head against my chest desperately, unreasonably. I lift my hands and touch her hair, wondering, wondering, and as I do so the enormous facsimile portrait of my father becomes dislodged, by some trick of gravity, from the wall and falls with a clatter to the floor, almost decapitating one of the clerks, who dodges from it with a terrified expression on her face. And indeed I can understand the terror, for from this closer aspect the face of my father is filled with hatred, the features bulging with a kind of knowledge which he is trying awfully to disseminate. And yet it is not quite like my father but some transmogrification of him which renders him, in the portrait, solid and terrible, all the things that he wanted to be and never was.

"That's Michael Westfield," the scholar is whispering. "My God, that's Michael Westfield," and as he says so they all begin to run toward me. Here they come now: the albino, his parents, the scholar, the heavy man, his friend, even the guide moving at great speed, their eyes wide and staring, and they are saying, "Michael Westfield, Michael Westfield! Michael Westfield?" and their hands are reaching to touch me as if I had some power, some corporeality which could be transferred. I feel myself sinking before them, still clutching Joanne, feeling the almost boneless glide of her body as it folds toward me, and I realize then and only for the first time that she is terribly frightened, frightened of things which I have never grasped or understood until this very moment and now I do see them and it is all too much, all too much for me. At the moment when they seem about ready to overtake me, literally climb me and rip my clothing away, the curator emerges from a side door like an actor from a special exit and points in my direction. He is carrying the heavy man's umbrella, apparently being the one originally responsible for its loss. His glasses glitter with spectral knowledge.

"All right now," he says. "All right, all of you, that's enough, that's quite enough, we've done what we had to do but now it's time to let the regular processes take over and let the law be satisfied; we will turn him over to the authorities and proffer the proper charges, now stop this, stop this," and for a moment they have indeed stopped but then some weakening tremor in his voice, some small tremor in his arm may tell them something which even he does not know and they come upon me, their rage now obvious along with their need and of the two it is only the need which I cannot understand because I know rage, have lived with rage all of my life, know nothing better nor ever will. But this knowledge is not enough; I cannot defend myself before them. There are too many of them. I clutch myself, the superfluity of Joanne already gone, feeling the rivers of waste moving under the surfaces of veins and at that moment they lunge all the way over and past me and I understand in the last instant before ascension that I have not been the object of their concern at all but only an interposition and that there is something beyond. I turn my head and see in the slowly opening door the figure of the Other and it is toward him that they plunge with their cries while meanwhile, suddenly exalted, I vault from the floor, past matting and superstructure and into the very matrix of the building and all is gone and I wake up then on the morning of my thirtieth birthday, coldness in my legs, coldness in the stomach, a taste of fire in the mouth and looking toward the sun coming through the window I find myself saying, "I can't stand this anymore; I don't think I can stand it," and my wife brings in coffee which I sip slowly, scrappling for a deadly cigarette, thinking about all the consequences and implications contained in this implacable but terrible structure which the ancients called chronology and which I will only know, as long as I live, as Time.

July 30, 1969
New York, New York

Afterword:
Behold Goliath

The autobiography inherent in fiction is the Devil's Pact; it is the first station on the nascent writer's subway to hell and for most it is the last stop, clever or luckless figures like Tom Wolfe push themselves or are pushed right there. Most hang on for one or three or fifty stops beyond, the fluorescence becoming ever dimmer, the detritus in the stations ever more forbidding to those tempted by delinquency but there is no doubt of it all being a one-way excursion and even in the most seemingly detached and precise work, even in the most seemingly transmuted, one can see the form and outline, the consistency which marks the pursuit. I went the usual route (the first fiction I remember attempting at age 7 was of a little boy unsuccessfully dodging a snowbank on the way to the second grade) tracking from received to imagined to long-feared to long-sought experience, adapting or adopting other personas, sometimes historical, sometimes at such apparent distance (a senile, incontinent ex-President of the USA in centers *The Last Transaction*) that I thought I had found an alternate subway—but no, none of it. In the mad odyssey of The Lone Wolf, in the first-person bleatings of Quir, the abducted alien of *In The Enclosure*, in the induced Jesus of *The Cross of Fire* I would always find the familiar form, the known landscape, the recollected convulsion of experience reproduced. Sometimes masked, sometimes parodied, sometimes set on Ganymede or in a Civil War platoon, the Beast in the Jungle would come forth. Who was I kidding? In the end, at the end, as I wrote of Robert Heinlein who tracked from "By His Bootstraps" to *Double Star* to sailing beyond the sunset, I would "Always confront my own screaming face." Heinlein made a decent living and a difficult career, I took the leavings which both are apt to leave behind.

That noted, that fully conceded, *In My Parents' Bedroom* falls both within and without the argument; it is a novel frankly addressed as autobiographical, a 30th birthday present to myself on the occasion of (I thought) getting at last out of the gate of youth and onto the mile and a quarter race which I imagined life to be. Horses are trained for sprints or routes or sometimes both, sometimes nothing at all, but I envisioned myself at 30 (the writerly equivalent of maybe five equine years) to have been already proven at low-grade allowances, now ready for some cheap stakes at Ak-Sar-Ben or the Fair Grounds. First though I had to pass the standard tests for stimulants, subtle defects in chemistry, hidden problems in a foreleg which might lead to breakdown and this novel was in effect the veterinarian's protocol. Could I manage an autobiographical work sufficient to prove that I would now be capable of transcendence. Or would I fall into what Delmore Schwartz called "The Wound of Consciousness" and be forever entrapped, a James Farrell replicating an imaginary daring youth or a Seymour Glass, a former wise child, now a guru and saint, long dead at 28 by his own hand? I did not exactly address the novel in that spirit but retrospection can impute authority.

I had already delivered eight or nine of the ten novels I published with the Olympia Press and it was quite evident in July 1969 to both Maurice Girodias and myself that we had no future; my adventure as his Leading Writer had ended as did all of his adventures with Leading Writers and whether I could even place this novel there was in doubt when, uncharacteristically, I started without a contract and then just went ahead and finished it in a few days. Some fiction is easier to write than to support logical argument why it should not be written and I finished this with even more than the usual speed, delivered it and waited for the rejection. I must have sustained myself through the work in the dim conviction that it was literary enough to be sold as a "literary novel." Girodias surprised me (he was full of surprises until he was not) by contracting for the work, paid me in agonizing spurts of $250 a week and then, looking upon what he had made, dithered and panicked. I don't think he would have allowed publication if he had been paying attention but like too many babies, this novel was born because no one was really paying attention.

Constructed in equal measures of fabulation and drear recollection, the novel has its moments and if nothing else persists as what Bill Pronzini deemed in an entirely different context "evidence," it is testimony constructed and real by equal parts, the narrator's first name is my father's, the apartment as described is pretty much as I remember the Flatbush abode on East 35th Street. It has more importance, perhaps, as another station on the train; my final novel for Olympia *Confessions of Westchester County* (reissued also by Stark House) is entirely apart from this but *In My Parents' Bedroom* had to be dislodged, the pebble in the shoe, so that I could continue the journey. It was originally going to be under the pseudonym "Arnold Gregory" and advance publicity deemed it such but then I gave voice to Laurence Janifer's favorite expression (and his philosophy of life), thought *what the hell* and let it lurch into the world. My parents never read it. My sister did (in their lifetime) and urged me not to inadvertently leave a copy behind on a return to the homestead. I did not and as is a generality with shakily transmuted work, that was a good thing. Everything was a good thing for a while until inexorably it wasn't. The human odyssey: autobiographical or otherwise.

August 2020: New Jersey

Barry N. Malzberg Bibliography

FICTION (as either Barry or Barry N. Malzberg)
Oracle of the Thousand Hands (1968)
Screen (1968)
Confessions of Westchester County (1970)
The Spread (1971)
In My Parents' Bedroom (1971)
The Falling Astronauts (1971)
The Masochist (1972, reprinted as Everything Happened
   to Susan, 1975)
Horizontal Woman (1972; reprinted as The Social Worker, 1973)
Beyond Apollo (1972)
Overlay (1972)
Revelations (1972)
Herovit's World (1973)
In the Enclosure (1973)
The Men Inside (1973)
Phase IV (1973; novelization based on a story
   & screenplay by Mayo Simon)
The Day of the Burning (1974)
The Tactics of Conquest (1974)
Underlay (1974)
The Destruction of the Temple (1974)
Guernica Night (1974)
On a Planet Alien (1974)
Out from Ganymede (1974; stories)
The Sodom and Gomorrah Business (1974)
The Best of Barry N. Malzberg (1975; stories)
The Many Worlds of Barry Malzberg (1975; stories)
Galaxies (1975)
The Gamesman (1975)
Down Here in the Dream Quarter (1976; stories)
Scop (1976)
The Last Transaction (1977)
Chorale (1978)
Malzberg at Large (1979; stories)
The Man Who Loved the Midnight Lady (1980; stories)
The Cross of Fire (1982)

The Remaking of Sigmund Freud (1985)
In the Stone House (2000; stories)
Shiva and Other Stories (2001; stories)
The Passage of the Light: The Recursive Science Fiction of Barry
  N. Malzberg (2004; ed. by Tony Lewis & Mike Resnick; stories)
The Very Best of Barry N. Malzberg (2013; stories)

With Bill Pronzini
The Running of the Beasts (1976)
Acts of Mercy (1977)
Prose Bowl (1980)
Night Screams (1981)
Problems Solved (2003; stories)
On Account of Darkness and Other SF Stories (2004; stories)

As Mike Barry
Lone Wolf series:
Night Raider (1973)
Bay Prowler (1973)
Boston Avenger (1973)
Desert Stalker (1974)
Havana Hit (1974)
Chicago Slaughter (1974)
Peruvian Nightmare (1974)
Los Angeles Holocaust (1974)
Miami Marauder (1974)
Harlem Showdown (1975)
Detroit Massacre (1975)
Phoenix Inferno (1975)
The Killing Run (1975)
Philadelphia Blow-Up (1975)

As Francine di Natale
The Circle (1969)

As Claudine Dumas
The Confessions of a Parisian Chambermaid (1969)

As Mel Johnson/M. L. Johnson
Love Doll (1967; with The Sex Pros by Orrie Hitt)
I, Lesbian (1968)

Just Ask (1968; with Playgirl by Lou Craig)
Instant Sex (1968)
Chained (1968; with Master of Women by March Hastings
   & Love Captive by Dallas Mayo)
Kiss and Run (1968)
Nympho Nurse (1969; with Young and Eager by Jim Conroy &
   Quickie by Gene Evans)
The Sadist (1969)
The Box (1969)
Do It To Me (1969)
Born to Give (1969; with Swap Club by Greg Hamilton & Wild in
   Bed by Dirk Malloy)
Campus Doll (1969; with High School Stud by Robert Hadley)
A Way With All Maidens (1969)

As Howard Lee
Kung Fu #1: The Way of the Tiger, the Sign of the Dragon

As Lee W. Mason
Lady of a Thousand Sorrows (1977)

As K. M. O'Donnell
Empty People (1969)
The Final War and Other Fantasies (1969; stories)
Dwellers of the Deep (1970)
Gather at the Hall of the Planets (1971)
In the Pocket and Other S-F Stories (1971; stories)
Universe Day (1971; stories)

As Elliot B. Reston
The Womanizer (1972)

As Gerrold Watkins
Southern Comfort (1969)
A Bed of Money (1970)
A Satyr's Romance (1970)
Giving It Away (1970)
Art of the Fugue (1970)

NON-FICTION/ESSAYS
The Engines of the Night: Science Fiction in the Eighties
  (1982; essays)
Breakfast in the Ruins (2007; essays: expansion of Engines of the
  Night)
The Business of Science Fiction: Two Insiders Discuss Writing
  and Publishing (2010; with Mike Resnick)
The Bend at the End of the Road (2018; essays)

EDITED ANTHOLOGIES
Final Stage (1974; with Edward L. Ferman)
Arena (1976; with Edward L. Ferman)
Graven Images (1977; with Edward L. Ferman)
Dark Sins, Dark Dreams (1978; with Bill Pronzini)
The End of Summer: SF in the Fifties (1979; with Bill Pronzini)
Shared Tomorrows: Science Fiction in Collaboration (1979; with
  Bill Pronzini)
Neglected Visions (1979; with Martin H. Greenberg & Joseph D.
  Olander)
Bug-Eyed Monsters (1980; with Bill Pronzini)
The Science Fiction of Mark Clifton (1980; with Martin H.
  Greenberg)
The Arbor House Treasury of Horror & the Supernatural (1981;
  with Bill Pronzini & Martin H. Greenberg)
The Science Fiction of Kris Neville (1984; with Martin H.
  Greenberg)
Uncollected Stars (1986; with Piers Anthony, Martin H.
  Greenberg & Charles G. Waugh)
The Best Time Travel Stories of All Time (2003)

www.ingramcontent.com/pod-product-compliance
Lightning Source LLC
Chambersburg PA
CBHW070921190726
48292CB00004B/1047